PRAISE FOR *HEART OF THE NIGHT* AND *NEW YORK TIMES* BESTSELLING AUTHOR BARBARA DELINSKY

"Delinsky writes about the emotional crises of everyday people and how those trials shape relationships."
—***Cincinnati Enquirer***

"Delinsky uses nuance and detail to draw realistic characters and ensure that emotion is genuine."
—***Providence Journal***

"[Delinsky is] a bestselling writer of top-notch books."
—***Booklist***

"Delinsky is one of those writers who know how to introduce characters to her readers in such a way that they become more like old friends than works of fiction."
—***Flint Journal*** **(MI)**

"Delinsky's prose is spare, controlled, and poignant."
—***Publishers Weekly***

"Soothing, sexy . . . The complexities of relationships and the angst of newfound love play a major role in this emotion-filled read."
—***RT Book Reviews***

"A timeless tale . . . as entertaining as ever. The author has created the ultimate fantasy man, one whose mere voice makes women go weak in the knees. HEART OF THE NIGHT is greatly engrossing."
—***BookLoons.com***

"Wonderful characters, warm, trustworthy, handsome, sexy—wow!! The book is sizzling and steamy hot . . . fresh and current . . . an excellent read."
—***RoadToRomance.ca***

O9-ABF-818

*Published by
HACHETTE BOOK GROUP

Barbara Delinsky

Heart of the Night

GRAND CENTRAL
PUBLISHING

NEW YORK   BOSTON

This book is a work of fiction. Names, characters, places, and incidents are the product of the author's imagination or are used fictitiously. Any resemblance to actual events, locales, or persons, living or dead, is coincidental.

Copyright © 1989 by Barbara Delinsky

All rights reserved. In accordance with the U.S. Copyright Act of 1976, the scanning, uploading, and electronic sharing of any part of this book without the permission of the publisher is unlawful piracy and theft of the author's intellectual property. If you would like to use material from the book (other than for review purposes), prior written permission must be obtained by contacting the publisher at permissions@hbgusa.com. Thank you for your support of the author's rights.

Grand Central Publishing
Hachette Book Group
237 Park Avenue
New York, NY 10017
www.HachetteBookGroup.com

Grand Central Publishing is a division of Hachette Book Group, Inc.
The Grand Central Publishing name and logo is a trademark of Hachette Book Group, Inc.

The Hachette Speakers Bureau provides a wide range of authors for speaking events. To find out more, go to www.hachettespeakersbureau.com or call (866) 376-6591.

The publisher is not responsible for websites (or their content) that are not owned by the publisher.

Printed in the United States of America

First mass market edition: October 1989
Reissued: August 1996, December 2003
First special-price edition: April 2009
Reissued: October 2012

10 9 8 7 6 5 4 3 2 1
OPM

ATTENTION CORPORATIONS AND ORGANIZATIONS:

Most Hachette Book Group books are available at quantity discounts with bulk purchase for educational, business, or sales promotional use. For information, please call or write:

Special Markets Department, Hachette Book Group
237 Park Avenue, New York, NY 10017
Telephone: 1-800-222-6747 Fax: 1-800-477-5925

To Steve and the boys,
with love.

And thanks to Greg Stoller,
WVBR-FM Ithaca,
for his time and patience.

Heart of the Night

Chapter 1

HIS VOICE WAS HEAVENLY. It flowed through her like a gentle wave, warming, and stroking her into serenity. When she was under its spell, she had a friend, a lover in the night.

She had no idea what he looked like. He was reputed to be a reclusive man, but she supposed that since he worked the graveyard shift, such seclusion was perhaps his survival. He had to sleep sometime.

But not now.

"It's twelve fifty-four," he told her in the deep, faintly husky drawl she had come to know so well, *"six minutes before one and a chilly twenty-eight degrees outside my door on the kind of night made for a hot fire, a snifter of brandy, and love. You're tuned to 95.3 FM, WCIC Providence, for a little country in the city. We're comin' up on a string of six, kickin' off with the latest from Alabama."* His voice grew more resonant, and much huskier. *"This is Jared Snow in the heart of the night. Stay with me. . . ."*

With a low half-moan, Savannah Smith closed her eyes. Propping her forehead on the eraser end of her pencil, she took a slow, measured breath. She liked Alabama's music, but Jared Snow was better. She could listen to his soft, tomcat drawl all night, and she wasn't the only one. She had heard enough wistful sighs in the ladies' room of the courthouse whenever his name was mentioned to know that most females within the sound of his voice were similarly entranced. Women of all ages were seduced by his voice, yet during the intermittent moments when he stopped talking, each felt she was the only woman on his earth.

Scowling, Savannah opened her eyes and lowered the pencil. Somehow his ability to so affect women seemed like a crime even though his victims were willing. No one forced them to listen to him night after night. Certainly no one was forcing her, yet listen she did. Night after night.

It was not the smartest thing to do, she realized as she looked at the blank sheet of paper on which her pencil lay. She had work to do. She should have prepared this pretrial motion that afternoon, but Paul had asked her to cover for him at the press conference on the Tabor murder, and when Paul asked, Savannah answered. Not only was Paul DeBarr the state's duly elected attorney general and her boss, but he was her friend. She knew the pressures he lived with. Whenever she could help him out, she did.

Unfortunately, by the time she'd returned to her office after the press conference, there had been a stack of telephone messages on her desk. She had farmed out some of them, but she had needed to answer most herself. When she finally pushed away the phone at six o'clock, she had developed a dreadful crick in her neck.

She was glad that the phone rarely rang at one in the morning. In fact, she realized, it had not rung once since she arrived home, which was something of a relief. Her sister, Susan, hadn't called. More importantly, her father hadn't called, which meant that Susan was, so far this night, behaving herself.

Of course, Savannah had no way of knowing if one of them had called earlier. After work she had gone to her aerobics class at the club for an hour, then returned to the office for a file she'd forgotten, and then she had been shanghaied by a contingent of the fourth estate to Payne's Pub for drinks. It was ten o'clock when she got home. Her father and Susan would both have been well into their respective evening plans by then. Life in Newport was never dull.

Pushing away the blank pad of paper, Savannah rose from her chair and wandered idly across the den to the window. Her hand skimmed the graceful arc of the swags, but her attention was trained on the night. Benefit Street was dark, lit but faintly by the gaslights that flanked its curbs. There was no traffic. There wasn't even a dog-walker in sight. Providence was asleep.

She should be, too, she told herself. But sleep did not come easily. Too many thoughts preoccupied her mind long after her body had wearied. She wondered if self-doubt came with age. She certainly had never lacked confidence before. From the time she had reached fifteen and realized that some women had careers, Savannah had known what she wanted to do. And she'd done it. She had attended college and law school, and then she had won an appointment to the attorney general's office. She had been there for the past five years.

She was not tired of the job. One couldn't possibly tire of a job where armed robberies, murders, and rapes were weekly cases. Savannah had her pick of the most challenging work. She couldn't complain.

Still, something about her life bothered her, she decided

as Alabama segued comfortably to Michael Martin Murphey.

Something about her life? Who was she kidding? She knew exactly what was wrong.

She was turning thirty-one in five days.

With a slight shiver, she left the window and returned to the desk. Her fingertips grazed its beveled edge, lightly brushing the smooth pine surface. It was a beautiful desk, an antique that had been stripped and restained in the light shade that so appealed to her. She found strength in the basic lines of the piece; it was a breath of antiquity made modern.

Taking the weight of her long, chestnut-colored hair into her hands, she held it off her neck for a minute. Then, twisting it forward over one shoulder, she slipped into the chair, took up her pencil and began to write on the legal pad.

Thirty-one.

She slanted the numbers into a top corner of the sheet and stared at them. On paper, they were innocuous. Not so in real life. Savannah hadn't been bothered by turning thirty; all the ballyhoo had prepared her for the worst, mitigating the reality. Thirty had been a novelty, a milestone to defy. Thirty-one was something else.

Then again, maybe her restlessness had nothing to do with her birthday. Periods of evaluation were common in life. When a person was as busy as she was, self-evaluation was inevitably put aside for sometimes long stretches of time. Just as inevitably, one had to periodically stop, take a breath, step out of oneself, and look back.

Professionally, Savannah liked what she saw. She was a good lawyer with a reputation for honesty and diligence. No one could fault her style. She had grown into her role well.

Personally, she was not sure she liked what she saw, but

then, she was uncertain as to what she ultimately wanted to achieve personally. She wasn't a wife or a mother. She was a daughter, a sister, and a friend many times over. Friendships meant a lot to her. She only wished they could fill the void that engulfed her in the dark of the night.

"You're cruisin' along in cool country," came the deep, lyrically raspy voice from the speakers that flanked the bookshelves to her left, *"on 95.3 FM, WCIC Providence. It's the top of the hour, one on the nose, and a quiet Monday night in Rhode Island,"* he drawled. *"Make yourself comfortable, put your feet up and your head back. I've got the Eagles comin' up, and Rosanne Cash, but first let's hear the latest on love from Gary Morris. Leave your dial where it is at 95.3 FM, WCIC Providence, kickin' up a little country in the city. I'm Jared Snow, stayin' with you in the heart of the night. . . ."*

It was not what he said that affected her so deeply. He rarely said much more than the time or the weather or the names of the artists whose music he was playing. Occasionally he injected a note of civic interest between songs, but he was not a political creature who used the airwaves as a forum for himself. He didn't take calls on the air. He didn't hold interviews. He simply identified the station and himself.

It was the way he spoke that touched her like a wet soul kiss. The deep husky tone of his voice was so quintessentially male and extraordinarily intimate that it would make even a traffic report sound erotic. The sound of Jared Snow's voice made Savannah's juices flow.

Acutely aware of the tripping of her pulse, she gathered every bit of self-discipline she possessed to grip her pencil and focus on her work. Experience told her that she would do enough work to avoid a calamity in court the next morning. Then she would set her briefcase aside and turn up the radio.

Jared Snow would be waiting for her. He was a saint, the most patient of men, her ideal. He was always there when she finished playing out her role as prosecutor, as daughter and sister and friend. He was there, talking softly, waiting until she took off her clothes, slipped into bed, and turned off the light.

Then he was her dream lover, the body that warmed her mind and soul. In the heart of the night he was the end to her loneliness.

"Kickin' in at one thirty-six, you're listening to cool country, 95.3 FM, WCIC Providence. The CIC forecast calls for clear skies till dawn, with low temps in the twenties. By morning, warmer air will be moving into the area, bringing clouds and a chance of rain." His voice grew more husky. *"Right now it's a frosty twenty-seven degrees outside our studios, but there's no frost in here with me, and there's certainly none on Kenny Rogers, who's heatin' the crowds with his latest tour. He's been one of the superstars of country music since '77 and 'Lucille,' singin' up a steady stream of hits. I've got 'I Prefer the Moonlight,' comin' up next on WCIC Providence, 95.3 FM, the home of a little country in the city."* He positively purred. *"Jared Snow here, in the heart of the night. Listen up. . . ."*

Susan Smith Gardner raised her glass in a toast to the man and his voice, then downed what remained of her scotch in a single swallow. It was a minute before the liquor settled, another before she breathed a slightly fiery, "I'm listening," yet another before she pushed herself up from the chintz lounge chair and headed for what had once been her husband's armoire. It was now her bar.

Dirk had been gone for a year, taking with him a colorful array of Polo jerseys, starched Armani shirts, and Perry Ellis sweaters, along with everything else he had personally brought into the marriage. Filling the closet hadn't been a problem; Susan had transferred all the clothes she'd previously stashed in the attic so that Dirk wouldn't know just how much she had. The armoire, though, was a monstrosity. Although she kept its doors closed, Susan had known what was behind them, and that nothingness had bothered her.

Using the piece to house liquor had been a brainstorm. Not only did it give her the convenience of a bar in the bedroom, where she needed it most, but it meant that the prying eyes that monitored the bar in the den saw little change in the liquor levels from one week to the next.

She told herself that she didn't have a real problem; she just enjoyed a drink now and again. She believed it was her right to get drunk once in a while. She was convinced that whoever meted out the good times in life had robbed her blind.

Slipping a lone ice cube into her glass, she added a finger of water and three of scotch. Satisfied after a sample swallow, she closed the armoire doors, then began to wander around the room. Kenny Rogers was singing about his woman, but it wasn't Kenny Rogers she wanted to hear, and she certainly didn't want to hear about his woman. It seemed to Susan that the whole world was paired off. She was the only one alone. She, and Jared Snow.

He was alone, sitting in that studio of his. She could close her eyes and picture him there in the heart of the night, talking to her. She loved listening to him, often waited through the music just to hear his voice again. Whether she was totally alert, or tired, dazed or groggy, if Jared Snow told her to climb the steeple of Trinity Church and jump, she'd do it in a minute. His voice was that seductive.

With one arm wrapped around her middle and the other propping the glass to her lips, Susan sluggishly stepped around the perimeter of the huge bed she had all to herself. Stopping at the nightstand where her sleekly housed radio stood, she lightly caressed the buttons on top.

Jared Snow exuded confidence. She had never met him; not many people had, it seemed, yet that split second's worth of silence that always followed the mention of his name said something to her. She was sure that Rhode Islanders stood a little in awe of him, because he was a mystery, a blank sheet of paper in an area where anyone who was anybody was a full dossier.

Rumor had it that he was from the West Coast, that he was wealthy, that he owned both this station and others. Susan couldn't understand why in the world, if he owned the station, he would be working the night shift. For that matter, she couldn't understand why he would be working at all. For *that* matter, she couldn't understand why, if he owned other stations, he'd chosen to work in Providence.

Not that she would have it any other way. She didn't know what she would do if he were no longer a voice in her night. She relied on his being there. On weekends, when he was off, she was depressed. When substitutes filled in for him, she felt let down.

She wasn't wild about his music. He played too many ballads about things that were too true, and the truth could be brutal at times. When he played songs about love, she felt jealous. When he played songs about love gone wrong, she despaired. But he was good, damn, he was good. So confident, so smooth, so able. She needed a man like that.

But what would a man like that, one who was rich and well known and totally together, want with a woman like her? Susan wondered. What was she, anyway?

With a disgusted grunt, she tipped the glass to her lips and let its potent contents sear a path to her stomach. Emboldened then and momentarily angry, she whirled to face the mirrored closet wall.

She was beautiful. If nothing else, she knew she was that. She was taller than Savannah, more shapely than Savannah, and the curls—which Savannah didn't have—of the huge, auburn mass that cascaded around her shoulders had taken more than one man's breath away. Even Savannah admitted that her sister was beautiful.

But beyond being beautiful, what was she?

Savannah was something. She was a career woman, a professional. She had made it in a man's world. As Paul De-Barr's golden girl, she'd become a visible presence on the Providence political scene. Her name was often in the morning papers connected with one or another of the most spectacular cases. She was known and respected. She was in an enviably prestigious position.

Although she was not beautiful the way Susan was, men looked, really looked at her. Susan had spent years trying to figure out her sister's appeal. For lack of any better explanation, she'd decided that Savannah had some kind of aura. Even when they had been kids, Savannah had been popular. She hadn't been the loudest or the most gregarious in their crowd, but friends flocked to her. Nothing had changed since then. Although Savannah didn't have much free time, the moments she had were filled. Savannah had everything. Even her name was better than Susan's. But then, Susan reasoned, Savannah had been born first. That said a lot.

"Tunin' in to the sound of cool country," came the grainy voice from the nightstand.

Turning toward it, Susan pressed the old-fashioned glass to her chest, heedless of its cold or the moisture that dampened the delicately embroidered bodice of her thin batiste gown. She held her breath, closed her eyes, and listened to the lazy drawl that stroked her from head to toe.

"This is Jared Snow, warmin' you in the heart of the night. WCIC time is one forty on a cold and quiet March Monday in Providence. Keep your blanket pulled up and your dial set at 95.3 FM, for a little country in the city. WCIC Providence, kickin' in now with K. T. Oslin and a cut from 80's Ladies . . ."

Perfectly timed, his voice faded as the singer began. Susan wondered how he did that. Wealthy or not, owner of the station or not, he knew what he was doing. He was competent, like Savannah. He had power, like Savannah. He was just what Susan wanted but couldn't have.

Taking a healthy swallow from the glass, she sank lifelessly onto the chaise and brooded.

Savannah could have Jared Snow; Susan would bet on that. Savannah could have just about any man she wanted, and none of them would be losers. During the past year she had dated the dean of admissions at Brown, the city editor of the newspaper, the evening anchor at WJAR-TV, and one of the more prominent professors at RISD. The fact that she didn't seem interested in getting involved brought them on, if anything, in droves. It wasn't fair. The less she cared, the more they persisted. And Susan, who *did* care about having a relationship, who would give anything for just one of those dashingly prominent men, was stuck on the same old carousel of Newport society.

Up and down, round and round.

Damn old wealth, she thought, and drained her glass. Then she lay back against the pillows and waited for the liquor to numb her, or sleep to take her, or for the song to end and Jared Snow to talk her through the night.

Megan Vandermeer sat in the center of the huge jacuzzi with her knees drawn to her chest. The long, fleecy robe that flared around her was the only thing that had flowed in the tub in weeks. Like the elaborate ice maker on the refrigerator door and the sophisticated burglar alarm system, the jacuzzi was broken. Repairing it would cost a bundle. Will didn't have a bundle.

Tightening her tremulous arms around her legs, Megan buried her face in the folds of the robe and rocked back and forth in gentle time to the slow ballad that hummed from the speaker on the wall. At least that still worked, she mused gratefully. How she'd loved lying in the jacuzzi late at night with the water swirling around her and Jared Snow's voice gentling her nerves. She couldn't use the jacuzzi now, but she could still listen to Jared Snow. He was so calm, so smooth, so reassuring. He suggested the kind of deep inner peace Megan had always searched for but never found.

Why was life so damned difficult, she asked herself despairingly. Why was life easier on some people and harder on others? Why did *she* have to struggle and struggle for the smallest reward?

Dropping her head back, she cast a pleading glance at the

stuccoed ceiling, but no answer was written there. All she saw was a spot where the toilet on the floor above had overflowed. The ceiling should be painted, she thought, then realized that the toilet had to be fixed first. But Will could not do even that until their finances improved. After all, no one knew that the toilet was broken, he had said, or that the jacuzzi, the alarm system, and the ice maker were broken. If one of the stately white columns at the front of the house were to fall, Megan suspected he would hawk his mother's heirloom china to fix it. Appearances were important. It was critical, he said, *critical* that people not suspect the Vandermeer fortune was gone.

Megan gritted her teeth and wondered whether there was a term for the Midas touch in reverse. Everything she touched fizzled.

"WCIC Providence," came the soft, deep voice from the wall. *"You're in cool country, 95.3 FM."*

She relaxed her jaw, closed her eyes, and listened.

"This is Jared Snow in the heart of the night, bringing you the best of Nashville at six minutes after two in the A.M. You've been listening to Foster and Lloyd, the Judds, and T.G. Sheppard. Stick with me at 95.3 FM, WCIC Providence, kickin' back now to an old favorite by John Denver. . . ."

She sighed, willing herself right into the speaker, through the wires and transmitters, and into Jared Snow's soul for a minute. He was so calm, so together. If only she could be that way. But her stomach was twisting, and her hands would have been shaking if they hadn't been clutching her legs so tightly.

And Will, bless him, was sound asleep in the bedroom.

She knew how he did it. He took pills. And maybe rest was what he needed more than anything. His world was crumbling around him. The pressure was extraordinary. The Vandermeers had been a viable force in Rhode Island circles practically since Roger Williams had established the state. Will had been born wealthy, he was used to being wealthy, and he couldn't conceive of life any other way.

Megan could. Her father had been a truck driver. He had died when she was two, after his truck went off a bridge in an ice storm. Her mother had gone to work, but there was not much money in unskilled labor, even less once the bills had been paid. By the time Megan turned fourteen, she was working to help out where she could, but theirs had been a losing battle. Any raise in pay that either of them received was promptly eaten up by a hike in the rent or in the cost of gas or clothing or food. Money slipped through their hands like water rather than accumulating and then working for them, as Megan's mother would have had it do. Money bred money, she told Megan, and she only had to point across the bay to Newport to illustrate her point. "Those people don't work," she had said. "They invest their money, reinvest the profits, and live off the interest. That's the way I want to live. That's the way I want you to live."

To that end, she had applied Megan to the prestigious Amsterdam Academy in Bristol. Judged bright and ambitious by the admissions department, Megan was accepted on full scholarship. Her mother had figured that three years among the East Coast elite would open doors for Megan. She had long since realized that her own salvation would come through Megan's.

While at the academy, Megan befriended the cream of Newport society and long after graduation, her friendship with the Smith girls endured. It was at a party on the Smiths' front lawn that Megan had been introduced to William Vandermeer III. Though he wasn't Newport, he came close. When Megan married him, both mother and daughter moved into the elegant Vandermeer mansion on the East Side of Providence.

We almost made it, Mama, Megan thought, and began rapid rocking back and forth.

"Takin' it slow and easy in the wee hours at 95.3 FM, WCIC Providence, where the country sounds are always cool. That was John Denver, and this is Lee Greenwood. Jared Snow here, in the heart of the night, I'm listenin' with ya. . . ."

Her rocking became less frenetic as she took a breath, let it out in a shaky sigh, then looked at the wall speaker as though it were the matching face to the voice she'd heard.

She wasn't in love with Jared Snow. She loved Will. But just then Jared was the one who gave her what she needed. He was an escape from the tension that constantly gnawed at her, a breath of stability in a shaky world.

With her eyes closed, she continued rocking. The music from the radio washed over her as the water from the jacuzzi should have done, and beyond the music was the memory of Jared Snow's voice. She let it take her from one song to the next, clearing her mind of everything but the dream it embodied. Comfort. Security. He seemed to offer so much, but as the minutes passed, the feeling faded as the rest of her dreams had already done, and she was bereft. Suddenly the porcelain beneath her felt cold. Pressing her lips to her robe, she caught a cry of fear before it could escape.

Her life was not supposed to be this way, she wailed silently. She was supposed to marry her prince and live happily ever after. But the castle walls were crumbling, and, alone, the prince was helpless. She had to do something.

"We're movin' along at two twenty-one with the smoothest of down-home sounds, cool country, 95.3 FM, WCIC Providence." He spoke gently, the words flowing with barely an effort, so soft, so laid-back. *"The temperature is twenty-five degrees and falling outside my door, so wrap up tight and stay warm while you're thinkin' country cool. This is Jared Snow in the heart of the night, kickin' around with you right up until six in the morning. . . ."*

Megan squeezed her eyes shut. She didn't have until six o'clock. Slowly, she released her knees from the cinch of her arms and folded her legs down against the bone-dry tub. Her eyes opened and fell to her lap, to the small, black gun that Will had given her when she had first become a Vandermeer. For her own protection, he had told her.

He'd been right, but not in the way he had envisioned.

Chapter 2

G OOD TIMING," Savannah's secretary called as Savannah rounded the corner and came into sight. Holding the telephone receiver high enough to be seen above the plants rimming her station, she wiggled it and mouthed, "The boss."

With a nod, Savannah increased her already rapid step. She was nearly flying, yet the only thing at all unsettled about her person was the long, loosely fitting blazer that flared out as she whisked past. Her hair was neatly anchored in a twist at the nape of her neck, her straight skirt shifted smoothly around her legs. The leather briefcase that hung from double straps looked professional enough, but it was her face that made the boldest statement. Her features were totally composed.

Janie Woo marveled at that, given the fact that Savannah had been in court since nine in the morning, arguing a series of motions that would have had many of the other lawyers in the office craning their necks against their ties. Savannah knew what she was doing, and her ability was evident as she surefootedly entered her office.

"Paul?" She snatched the button earring from her free ear and shifted the phone there in time to catch his response.

"Just get back?"

Her briefcase slid to the floor. Working around the phone cord, she shrugged out of her blazer. "Uh-huh."

"How'd it go?"

She stepped out of her heels. "We won on the motion to suppress, the bill of particulars, and the early trial date, but we lost on the grand jury transcripts."

"Three out of four. Not bad." Paul paused for the space of a breath, then went on in a suspiciously casual voice, "Can I see you up here for a minute?"

Savannah grew alert. She knew Paul DeBarr well, knew the meaning of each of the tones he used. She could accurately predict, simply from his voice, whether he'd been upset by an article in the *Journal*, whether he'd won a case or lost another to a lawyer on appeal, or whether his wife was sick again. The tone he used now, though, was odd.

"Trouble?" she asked.

His only response, still too casual, particularly in light of his words, was, "How soon can you be here?"

She hesitated for only a minute. Even if Paul hadn't been her boss, she would have been unable to resist. He sounded mysterious. Clearly he was not alone in the room, and she wanted to know what was happening. She'd been in the attorney general's office long enough to be conditioned to respond to unforeseen developments. The adrenaline was already flowing.

Stepping back into her shoes, she said, "I'm on my way." While one hand replaced the telephone receiver, the other reclipped her earring. Grabbing her blazer, she swept out of the office. As she passed Janie, she said softly, "You know where I'll be," then headed down the hall to the bank of elevators.

Three floors up, Paul DeBarr was perched on the edge of his desk looking far calmer than he felt. He, too, was conditioned to respond to extraordinary happenings. He shared the adrenaline flow and the sense of anticipation that made the heart beat faster. Moreover, he knew what this case was about, and if ever there were one with a potential for a political bonus, this was it.

Before him and to his left, elbows braced on the rib-high mahogany credenza, ankles crossed, was his first assistant, Anthony Alt. Before him and to his right, sitting tensely in a side chair, was William Vandermeer III.

Paul was looking at Will, who was staring blindly at the plush cranberry carpet. Anthony, whose eyes were aimed at the window, was drumming his fingers on the edge of the credenza and looking bored. An uneasy silence filled the room.

Paul's gaze shifted to the oddly shaped paper that lay on his desk. He studied it for a minute, then checked his watch. Very slowly, he straightened his legs, stood, and crossed to the door. He opened it just as Savannah traversed the reception area, and he closed it the instant she was in his office.

Her eyes met his, repeating the question she had asked on the phone. Then she noticed Anthony and Will. She had anticipated Anthony's presence; he was Paul's strategist and was always around at critical times. Will's presence, though, took her by surprise. She knew that he had contributed to Paul's reelection campaign and that he had even hosted a fund-raiser, though that had been three years before, when things had been going better for Megan and him. She knew that he and Paul were political friends, but she hadn't thought they were personally close.

Savannah knew Will mostly through other people. Fifteen years her senior, he partied more in her father's circles than her own. Though his marriage to Megan had created another link between them, she'd never gotten any closer to him. She had always found him aloof.

Now Will seemed heavily preoccupied. He was an attractive man—tall, slender and, though graying, of generally fair coloring. Today he looked positively ashen. Puzzled, she went to his side and touched his shoulder. "What's wrong, Will?"

Paul answered, lifting the piece of paper from his desk and handing it to her. "Take a look."

Savannah stared down at what looked to be a cutout from a brown paper grocery bag. An assortment of letters, cut from newspapers and magazines, had been neatly aligned and carefully glued across the creased surface: NICE WIFE. KICK IN A COOL THREE MILLION TO GET HER BACK. DO NOT CONTACT POLICE OR SHE DIES. WILL BE IN TOUCH.

Savannah's first thought was that the message was a joke. One look at Will's ravaged face suggested differently. Her gaze flew to Paul, but his expression was grim. Incredulous, she read the note again. By the time she'd finished, her own composure had slipped. "Kidnapped?" she whispered. Her heart tripped on the word.

"Looks like it," Paul answered quietly.

Weak-kneed, Savannah lowered herself to a second side chair. Perched on the edge of its leather seat, she quietly asked Will, "When?"

"This morning." He waved a jerky hand. "Sometime last night." He was a shadow of his former, assured self.

"How?"

"I don't know," he exclaimed in bewilderment.

"He was sleeping," Anthony offered, making only a

token effort to hide his disdain, then his skepticism, when he added in an undertone, "If you can believe that." His fingers drummed on.

Paul held up a cautionary hand to his assistant.

Savannah was less subtle. While she respected Anthony's political and administrative abilities, she had no faith whatsoever in his skill as a trial lawyer. He had no feel for cross-examination, and, in this case, he had a built-in prejudice toward the witness. Of all the questions there were to ask, Savannah suspected Anthony most wanted to know how William Vandermeer could possibly remember to neatly fold and insert a moss green handkerchief in the breast pocket of his natty navy blazer when his wife had just been kidnapped.

Though she didn't know him well, Savannah understood Will. She had been reared with dozens of Wills. She knew where he came from, understood what it was to habitually do something simply because it had been so ingrained that *not* doing it required true effort. But she had no intention of lecturing Anthony Alt on the subject just then. There were more immediate things to consider.

"At this point," she told Anthony, "I'd like to hear Will's story without editorial comment. According to the note, there's been a kidnapping. The victim has been a friend of mine for years." With a dismissing glance, she returned her attention to Will, who was looking more miserable by the minute.

"I sleep soundly," he said. "Megan doesn't. She has insomnia. You knew that, didn't you?"

"Yes."

"So she's often up in the middle of the night. She soaks in the jacuzzi, listens to the radio, reads."

"How do you know that," Anthony asked, "if you're sleeping?"

"Ease off," Paul warned levelly. Anthony was his right-hand man, invaluable as a political tactician as long as he stayed on the sidelines. When he stepped onto the field, he lost his perspective. As it was, Paul had had some doubts about including Anthony in this meeting, since Anthony and Savannah were like oil and water. In the end, it had been the gravity of the situation and its political potential that had led him to override his doubts.

Knees pressed together, Savannah propped her forearms on her thighs. The ransom letter dropped to the floor where she could see it. Freed of that burdensome weight, she locked her fingers tightly together and said quietly, "Go on, Will."

Will looked at Anthony and said in a burst of indignation, "I know what my wife does at night because I ask. Or Megan offers. We're very close." He shifted his gaze to Savannah. As his anger faded, he looked pained. "I'd guess that she was in the library when whoever it was broke in."

"How could you tell?"

"That's where the mess was."

"What mess?"

"Broken glass. Someone had bashed his way through the French doors."

Savannah swallowed hard. She knew just which doors he meant. She and Megan had passed many a Sunday evening in the library. It was a comfortable room, lined with bookshelves that were filled to overflowing with generations of Vandermeers' books. The French doors led to a patio that, in summer, was surrounded by waves of colorful flowers. In winter, the doors kept out the chill. They were heavy, solid.

"I thought they were wired," she said.

Will shifted one of his legs. "The alarm wasn't set."

"Why not?" Anthony asked.

Shooting him a tight look, Will said simply, "Because it wasn't."

Savannah straightened the fingers of one hand. "Forget the alarm. Let's go back and take things step by step." She was having trouble grasping what had happened, and couldn't begin to think of where Megan was and in what condition. The friend in her was stunned; the lawyer plodded on. "When did you first know that something was wrong?"

"When I woke up and Megan wasn't there. I went downstairs looking for her. That was when I saw the library."

"What time was this?"

He shifted the same leg again. "Eight, eight-thirty."

Anthony coughed. "You were just waking up on a Tuesday morning at eight-thirty?"

"Anthony," Paul growled, "for God's sake."

"There are some people," Savannah felt called upon to instruct him, "who don't work the same hours we do. Look, Anthony, I know you have little patience for those who have more money than you do, but I think some open-mindedness is called for here. It doesn't matter whether you're rich or poor, it hurts when you're mugged."

"Kidnapped," Anthony corrected. He'd made a fist and was lightly rapping his knuckles on the wood.

She refused to respond. Instead, she turned again to Will. "You said that you think Meg was in the library when the break-in occurred. Even if she had fallen asleep on the sofa, she would have woken up when the door shattered. Was there anything besides the broken glass? Any sign of a struggle? Meggie was a fighter. She wouldn't have calmly and quietly gone along."

"Not Megan," Will acknowledged, more appalled than proud. "Part of a row of books had been knocked from one of the shelves, like she might have tried to grab at something to hold on to. The cushions on the sofa were disturbed. The umbrella stand by the hall door was overturned. One of the walking sticks I kept there was broken."

Savannah's stomach was feeling hollow and it had nothing to do with hunger. Will was painting a picture in her mind of the scene of the crime, but she didn't know how vividly to color it. After a brief hesitation, she asked as quickly as she could, "Was there any blood?"

Will recoiled. "No. Thank God, no. So help me, if those bastards do anything—"

"Bastards—plural?" Anthony interrupted with a loud knock. "How do you know there were more than one?"

Will drew himself straighter in his chair, looking for a minute like his usual aristocratic self. "Because I'm not stupid, Mr. Alt. Kidnappers don't operate alone. Technically, it won't work. They need one person to stay with the hostage while the other drops notes or makes calls or picks up the money."

Savannah agreed. "At least if there wasn't any blood, we can hope they haven't hurt her." She was beginning to feel the reality of the situation. It brought a new urgency to her voice. "Was there anything else? Did you see anything else, find anything else that might tell us more about what happened?"

He shook his head and ran a shaky hand through his hair. That, in itself, was a telling gesture, Savannah mused. Will was always particular about appearances. His clothes were never wrinkled, his tie never crooked, his hair never mussed. He might have put the handkerchief in his pocket out of sheer habit that morning, but, right now, he was deeply upset.

Anthony didn't seem to notice. With several more loud raps of his knuckles, he asked, "What about a maid? You have one, don't you?"

"Not at the moment. We're between maids."

"So who cleans?"

"We have a service that comes in once a week."

Wearing a faint smirk, Anthony nodded.

Savannah, who hated cleaning as much as Megan did and saw nothing wrong with having a service if one could afford it, was faintly piqued. "Is there a purpose to this line of questioning?"

"Sure," Anthony replied. "Since Will seems to have slept through his wife's kidnapping, I was hoping to find someone who hadn't. A maid might have heard voices or cries. She might have looked outside and seen tall figures or short figures, a car or a van. I'm surprised you didn't ask the same question yourself."

"I didn't have to. I already knew there was no maid. Given that fact, the issue of who cleans is irrelevant for present purposes." Sending a brief look at Paul, who was perched on his desk again, Savannah went on. "Okay, Will. You found the note at eight-thirty this morning. Where was it?"

"On the desk."

"What did you do then?"

There was a moment's silence, then, "Nothing."

"Nothing?" Paul echoed.

"I didn't know what to do." His features were rigid, but

his tone became higher pitched. "I searched the house. Megan wasn't anywhere. Her car—both cars—were in the garage. Her keys were in the house, her purse, her wallet, her clothes. She'd been kidnapped, and the note said not to call the police, so I stood there for a long time without doing a thing, half hoping the phone would ring and it would be Meggie telling me the whole thing was a joke."

He was close to tears. Intent on giving him a minute to recompose himself, Savannah turned to talk softly to Paul. "They said they'd call. Shouldn't he be back at the house waiting?"

Paul nodded.

"But I couldn't meet with you there," Will cried. "I was afraid if they saw someone coming to the house, they'd think I called the police, and if they think that, they'll hurt Megan."

"Based on precedence," said Paul, "I'd say they'll be hesitant to hurt Megan if they want that money. And they won't expect you to sit in the house all alone. They'll assume relatives will be around, maybe close friends. Hell, you have to see other people, if for no other reason than to get the money together."

Anthony stopped his hand midrap. "I take it you do have the money," he said.

"Not on me at the moment," Will returned with a glare that Savannah lauded. But the glare fizzled when he turned to her. "I agonized all morning—do I see it through by myself, or do I go for help? The obvious thing is to sit at home, wait for that call, pay the money, and get Megan back. but can I trust that that's what will happen? Can I be sure that if I pay the money I'll get her back? And, damn it, whoever's done this should be caught." He stopped short, frowned at the rug, shook his head. "Forget catching them. I just want Megan back." He looked up. "I'm here because I considered you two to be friends," his eyes jumped from Paul to Savannah, "and because I figured you'd know what to do in a situation like this." His voice was rising again. "I don't want to make any mistakes. I want Megan back alive. What in the hell am I supposed to do?"

Sitting back in her chair, Savannah tried to still her nerves, all the while thinking that if Will thought she had a magical solution, he was mistaken. "First," she said, as much to herself as to him, "you'll have to calm down. Meggie needs you to stay cool. Second, you'll have to let us contact the FBI—"

"No!"

Paul rose from his perch on the edge of the desk. "Kidnapping is a federal offense. There's every legal reason for the FBI to be called in, not to mention the fact that those guys know exactly what to do. They're trained in this type of thing. They have equipment and resources that we don't have."

Will wasn't being persuaded. "I don't want the FBI. The note said no police, and that's the way it has to be."

"But you've already come to us," Savannah reasoned. "You've sought outside help, which is just what the kidnappers didn't want."

"They said no police. You aren't the police."

"We're a functional law enforcement agency," Anthony said, and neither Paul nor Savannah argued.

Will did. "You aren't the police. I can count on you to be discreet. I don't trust the police that way."

"Will," Savannah pleaded, "we're talking the FBI. We're

talking a few well-trained, carefully selected men who have had experience with this kind of thing."

But Will shook his head. "No FBI. I don't want them anywhere near the house."

She was about to argue further when something else occurred to her. "Speaking of the house, did you clean things up?"

He hesitated. "Should I have?"

In unison, three voices said, "No!"

He let out a breath. "I didn't. I didn't know where to begin. I haven't touched a thing, except to lock the door between the library and the hall. It was cold with the glass broken."

"That'll have to be fixed," Savannah said. "But first, we need to have someone comb through what's there to see if there's anything useful. Fingerprints, footprints, clothes or hair samples—"

"No police, Savannah."

"There are two fellows I work with all the time."

"No police."

"I'd trust these two with my life."

"It's not your life in danger, it's Megan's."

"I'd trust them with hers too. I *trust* them, Will. Sammy and Hank are on long-term assignment to the AG's office. They've handled dozens of sensitive cases for us. They're good. They're professionals. They'll go to your house looking like . . . like that cleaning service Megan uses. If our kidnappers are in the bushes watching, they'll assume you're just cleaning up the mess they made."

She paused to see whether Will would argue, but Paul wasn't giving him that chance. "Our men will sweep the place for anything that might be helpful in identifying the kidnappers," he said. "Something they find—even the smallest little nothing—could prove to be the key to finding out who they are. At the same time, we'll put a tap on the phone and sct up monitors in the basement. You won't even know Shanski and Craig are there, but they'll be listening and recording any calls that come in. There may be some background noise that will identify where the kidnappers are, and even if there isn't it'll be important to get their voices on tape. We're doing more and more with voiceprints. That could help with a conviction."

"If you catch them."

"Right. But if you don't let us do our thing, we won't have a prayer in hell of catching them. I don't know how to comb a room for prints or tap a phone. Neither does Savannah. Shanski and Craig do."

Savannah picked up the ransom note she had earlier dropped on the floor. "I think we'll need all the help we can get." She turned the brown paper over, then back. "This kind of bag has to be used in dozens of markets in Rhode Island alone. We could probably identify the papers and magazines these letters were cut from, but trying to locate one particular reader would be like looking for a needle in a haystack." She glanced at Will. "We need Sammy and Hank."

Will showed his first sign of wavering. "They don't look like they're the police?"

She would have grinned had the situation been less serious. "They don't wear uniforms, if that's what you mean. Sammy's hair reaches his shoulders. Hank has three earrings in his left ear. They could easily pass for workmen, or for thugs come to wipe you out while those French doors are out of commission. What do you say, Will? Let us do it. It's our only chance."

Will looked torn in two. "What if the kidnappers find out your men are with the police?"

"You didn't go to the police. You came to us."

"But those men you've mentioned are with the police."

"They're with us. The kidnappers will never know where they came from. They won't even know Sammy and Hank are at the house."

"Won't there be a car parked outside?"

"They'll be dropped off," Paul said. "Whatever equipment they need will be suitably disguised. Once they arrive at the house, they'll be there for the duration." He hesitated. "I take it no one's there now?"

"You're the first people I've told. I was afraid to call anyone. Word spreads too quickly. If this gets out to the papers, Megan will be in trouble. Everything has to be kept quiet."

"It will be," Paul assured him, and turned to Anthony. "Agreed?"

Anthony, who would have liked nothing more than to call a press conference there and then to announce that the attorney general's office was taking charge of the Vandermeer kidnapping case, agreed, in spite of himself, that immediate publicity would have to wait. There would be plenty of opportunity for grandstanding when the case was solved.

"Agreed," he said.

Paul reached for the phone. "Let me put in a call for Shanski and Craig. I want them over there ASAP."

Savannah stood, as did Will. He was looking bewildered again, as though he still didn't know what he was supposed to do. "You should have someone with you," she advised gently. "Is your sister around?"

He shook his head. "She's in Paris with husband number

three, but even if she weren't, she wouldn't come. She never liked Megan."

Not caring to belabor that point, Savannah moved on. "Is there someone else you'd feel comfortable having over?" She thought back to the people with whom the Vandermeers were most closely associated. "How about the Brogans? Or Carter and Julie West?"

But Will was shaking his head. Darting an uncomfortable glance at Anthony, who was fidgeting by Paul, he took several steps away. Savannah followed him toward the door, out of earshot of the other two. Still, he spoke under his breath, barely moving his mouth. His head was bowed. He remained visibly uncomfortable. "We haven't been seeing many people lately. Things have been difficult."

Savannah had guessed that, based on hints Megan had dropped the last time they'd seen each other, which had been two weeks before. "Financial things?" she asked.

He nodded and looked up to make sure neither Paul nor Anthony had heard. Then, tucking his chin low again, he said, "I've had some setbacks. Nothing that can't be remedied, but this couldn't have happened at a worse time."

Something that had been niggling at the back of her mind took that moment to come forward. "Answer me honestly, Will. Do you have three million?"

He took a shaky breath, raised his head, and looked her in the eye. "No, I do not have the money, but I can get it. I'm insured for this kind of thing." He tossed a pleading look skyward. "God, it's ironic. Megan thought I was crazy when I told her about the policy. She laughed. She said that she wasn't worth enough to be kidnapped. It was hard for her to believe what she was marrying into." He gave a bitter snort.

"And look what she got. Her husband isn't worth much more than a hill of beans, and she's been kidnapped."

He eyed Savannah in dead earnestness. "I don't give a damn about the three million. I honestly don't. I mean it when I say that if it were up to me, I'd sit home, make the payoff, and get Megan back. She didn't ask for this. She didn't have more than a couple of thousand dollars in the bank when she married me. It's because of who I am and where I come from that her life's in danger." His voice rose in emotion. "To hell with the kidnappers. I just want Megan back."

For a split second, Savannah was taken out of time and place and overwhelmed by a rush of envy. She had not often envied Megan over the years, but she did now. To be married to a man who felt so fiercely about his wife was truly something.

Regaining his composure, Will continued in the same low, private murmur. "But it's the insurance business. A condition of the policy is that an authorized person be involved. The insurance company is more than willing to hand over the money for the exchange, but they want to maximize their chances of getting it back. I figured that between you and Paul, I'd be able to satisfy them without antagonizing the kidnappers."

Grasping his arm, Savannah said, "You've done the right thing. Sammy and Hank are the best. Really." She paused. "Have you called the insurance people?"

"I told you, I haven't called anyone."

"I think you should. Get the ball rolling. In the meantime, you should have someone with you at the house."

"I don't need anyone."

Savannah thought guiltily that she was grateful Megan's

mother was dead. She wouldn't have wanted to break the news of a kidnapping to her. "A personal friend, maybe?"

"I don't need anyone."

"Not even for moral support?"

He gave a quick shake of his head.

"What if you're in the bathroom and don't hear the phone?"

"Oh."

"Isn't there anyone you want to call?"

He shook his head. "Megan's got no family. What's left of mine isn't worth notifying. I don't feel comfortable, well, I'd rather not call friends at this point."

The irony of the situation did not escape Savannah. Will could host a party the following Saturday night and there would be two hundred people in attendance. Yet when it came to calling a single friend to hold his hand through a rough spell, he came up short.

Anthony wouldn't have a drop of sympathy for William Vandermeer, but Savannah wasn't Anthony. She knew that Will played tennis three times a week as part of a regular foursome, that he and Megan had spent time during each of the past few winters in Saint Croix with two other couples, that they regularly went to the symphony with a completely different group. But the term *friend* was defined differently in social circles of the type to which both her family and the Vandermeers belonged. Things like pride, protocol, and petty rivalries prevented friendships from becoming close. Weakness was not something one showed willingly. Keeping a stiff upper lip was the order of the day.

So Will had no one to call. Savannah thought to contact one of Megan's friends, but she and Susan were the closest. And Will. In addition to being husband and wife, Will and

Megan were best friends. In spite of their age difference, they shared everything. Then again, perhaps it was because of their age difference that they were close; since Megan was too young for Will's friends and Will too old for hers, they turned to each other.

But Megan couldn't be with him just then, and he needed someone. "Will, let me call Susan," Savannah suggested. "She loves Megan like I do. She'd want to know what's happened. I'm sure she'll want to help out in any way she can."

"The less people involved, the better."

"Just one person. Just Susan. She cares about what happens to Megan, like you do."

"No one cares like I do."

"Okay," Savannah conceded, "but let me call Susan anyway."

"I'm sure she has better things to do than to baby-sit me."

"She has *nothing* better to do." That was a fact, and Savannah saw enough signs of weakening in Will not to want to argue further. "Listen, you go on home. Contact the insurance company. I'll call Susan from my office and clear myself up for the next few hours."

"You don't have to—"

"I want to be there to see you set up. I have a meeting at five that I can't miss, but Susan will be there by then. Sammy and Hank should be there even sooner. Once they've gone through the library with a fine-tooth comb, you can call in the glass people to fix the door. Meggie shouldn't have to see it broken when she gets home."

"Do I dare use the phone? What if the kidnappers try to call and get a busy signal?"

"They'll call again."

"Should I be ready with a suggestion for an exchange place?"

"They'll have their own place in mind."

"What if it's somewhere secluded?"

"It probably will be."

"They'll be able to take the money and run. They won't care about Megan."

"But you'll insist on seeing Meg first. You'll tell them that they can choose the place, but that the deal is the money for your wife, there and then."

"How can I demand that, when they're holding all the cards? How can I demand *anything*?"

"You can demand it, and you will," Savannah insisted, "because they're not holding all the cards. You're the one with the money. Don't forget, it's the money they want, not your wife. A little show of strength is in order, Will. If not for yourself, for Megan."

For a minute, Will didn't answer. When he did, he was looking puzzled. "Where do you get yours, Savannah?"

"My what?"

"Strength. How do you manage to stay so cool and rational?"

Savannah didn't answer, but gave him a wry look. A minute later, she nodded toward the door and said, "Go on home. I'll see you there in a little while."

A few minutes later, sitting behind her desk with the telephone receiver honking out a busy signal against her shoulder, Savannah thought about strength. Where did she get it? She wasn't sure. Strength was just something that came with her role, something that came with involving herself with details to avoid the overview.

Her strength was often a front. She could play the game

with the best of them, acting cool and rational when inside she was shaking like a leaf. It has been that way from the very start of her tenure at the AG's office. She had had to prove her worth, first, in a traditionally male world, and second, in a world of political favors. She had done it. She was a respected member of the team. She still needed to uphold that image of cool competence.

Perhaps that was why she understood why William Vandermeer did not want people to know he was hurting for money. He was trying to uphold an image, too. If she criticized him, she had to criticize herself.

Pressing the button on the phone, she dialed Susan's number, but it was still busy. She would keep trying. Sending Susan to sit with William was a good idea. Susan needed something to do and someone to think about besides herself. She wasn't a weakling, yet she allowed herself to act like one. Her low self-image needed correcting.

Everyone had a right to moments of weakness. Susan took too many, Savannah too few. There were times when Savannah wanted to relax, to lean on someone, perhaps cry on his shoulder. To some extent, though, she'd backed herself into a corner. She had come to expect competence from herself. Before she could ease up enough to relax, lean on someone, or cry on his shoulder, she had to find a man who could match her strength.

There was no one like that around the office. Nor had she found anyone like that among the men she had dated in the past few years. She was beginning to wonder if one existed.

Women got more picky with age. She had heard it said, seen it written, knew it to be true. At eighteen, she had been far more open to different men and relationships than she was at thirty-going-on-thirty-one. Of course, at eighteen she had been far less sophisticated than she was now. If she had married then, she would probably have divorced soon after. Instead she had been smart and spared herself some pain.

Unfortunately, there was pain in looking toward the future and seeing endlessly long, lonely nights. Perhaps she'd outsmarted herself.

Chapter 3

WHEN SAVANNAH ARRIVED at the Vandermeers shortly after two o'clock, she found Will sitting at the large captain's table in the kitchen, looking lost. Sam Craig and Hank Shanski were in the library, efficiently going about their work. They had already put a tap on the phone, but there had been no call, no contact at all from the kidnappers.

After taking one look at Will, who was staring blindly at the ransom note, Savannah went to the cabinet in search of coffee. There were three bags of beans. The mill was on the counter by the coffee maker. She made a pot of strong coffee and then sat down next to Will.

"Have you called the insurance company?" she asked softly.

He nodded. "They're sending someone over."

"How long will it take them to get you the money?"

He shot her a worried look. "They have to make sure this is a bona fide kidnapping. They said not to touch anything. Their man wants to do his own investigation before any cleanup is done."

"He may be satisfied with talking to Sammy and Hank. They're pretty thorough."

She was quiet for a minute. The coffee maker chugged and gurgled, reassuringly mundane.

Will glanced toward the hallway that led back to the rest of the house. "Have you taken a look in there?"

"Not yet. I don't want to risk contaminating anything." She reached into her briefcase and took out a legal pad. "There are other things you and I can cover in the meantime."

"If you're going to ask me who might have done this, don't," Will advised, sounding every bit as frustrated as he looked. "I've been sitting here, wondering where Megan is, wondering how she is, wondering who could have taken her. Since eight-thirty this morning I've wondered, and I've come up with nothing."

Savannah shared his anguish. Once again she wanted to beg him to bring in the FBI, but she knew what his answer would be.

"Can you think of anyone who had a grudge against you or your family, or even Megan?"

He shook his head.

"Anyone at the plant?" The Vandermeer money was in textiles. Though Will hid the extent of the damage, most people knew that the Vandermeer mills had seen better days. In the past five years, workers had been laid off and two of the five plants had been closed. "Maybe there was a manager who felt he should have been transferred rather than fired. Maybe there was a rabble-rouser who was fired to make room for a transfer."

Will denied both theories. "Whoever did this wanted money." He jerked a hand toward the note. "It's spelled out right there."

Savannah read the note again. It certainly demanded

money. But the wording was odd. *Kick in a cool three million.* Someone had spent extra effort cutting out more letters than was necessary. A simple *Pay three million* would have sufficed. *Kick in a cool three million.* She wrote the words, then studied them. The phrase bothered her.

"Mmm. The three million is pretty clear. Still, someone out for revenge could get it this way. The money would be a bonus." A different thought occurred to her. "It'd be particularly gratifying if the person knew about your present cash flow problems. How many people do?"

"Not many," Will said, then conceded, "I mean, the layoffs and plant closings are common knowledge. It's obvious that I'm tightening my belt, but not many people know why." He shook his head. "But I don't think it's revenge. I've never been an ogre. I'm just not a good money manager."

"Okay," Savannah said. "We'll guess that this was done purely for the money. Just in case, though, why don't you give me the names of your plant managers."

Will's eyes widened in alarm. "They're all good men!"

"I know," she soothed, "but I'd like to put them to work for us. They would know, or be able to find out, whether there's been any trouble—"

"They would have reported it to me."

She tried again. "Maybe trouble is the wrong word. What I'm looking for is different—strange behavior, something out of the ordinary, a change from the norm, like unexplained absences by a regular worker, a sudden grouping of two or three workers who hadn't been friends before, any recent complaints that seemed particularly strong or out of order."

Will remained skeptical. "I don't think it's anyone from

the plant. I told you, aside from the layoffs, my people are treated well. Maybe too well. If I were stingier, I wouldn't be losing money. My workers have a good deal."

Choosing her words with care, she said, "That may be so in your opinion and mine, but a worker may see things differently."

"Then he's crazy."

"Anyone involved in kidnapping usually is." With that, Savannah could see she'd made her point. "I have to consider every possibility, Will. Look at that note; we won't learn much from it. Sammy and Hank can dust this house from top to bottom, but if the kidnappers wore gloves, we won't get fingerprints. If they were careful about where they stood and moved, we may not learn anything from the lab reports. I may be groping around in the dark, but all I need to do is graze the light switch, and we're on."

Will looked deflated. "But I wanted this kept quiet."

"It will be. We'll be totally discreet in our inquiries."

"You'll be doing the asking?"

"No," Savannah said, then went on, taking the offensive quickly and confidently, if gently. "Time is of the essence. I can't do the asking myself and still coordinate things, and we need as much information as quickly as possible. Ideally, I'd take a dozen detectives and feather them through the state, but since I didn't think you'd go for that, I've called in two other people. Just two. They're like Sammy and Hank. They work full-time for us. They happen to be wonderful people, a married couple, very effective. No one ever knows they're law enforcement officers."

Will's frustration overwhelmed him. Slamming a fist on the oak tabletop, he cried, "Damn it, I didn't want this, Savannah! I didn't want the police brought in at all! You *knew* that!"

Savannah refused to be cowed. "We need information, Will. Ginny and Chris will be strictly in the field. They won't come anywhere near the house. They'll be asking questions, that's all."

"If they're asking questions, they'll be making everyone and his brother suspicious. People will wonder what's going on. Before long, rumors will be flying, and then we'll have no hope of keeping a lid on this thing." He drove a hand through his hair. "I shouldn't have gone to you people. Someone's going to blow it."

On the one hand, Savannah understood Will's position. In his social circle, questions sparked gossip, and on the tongues of the idle rich gossip was lethal. Yet she doubted Will's rich friends were going to be at the center of the investigation. They wouldn't need three million dollars. Nor would they risk a death sentence. There were easier ways to commit suicide—most of which the idle rich knew.

"No one is going to blow anything," she vowed. "As of this minute, there are seven people who know about this case—Paul, Anthony and me, Sam and Hank, Ginny and Chris. We're all professionals. Paul will be in touch with you and me; he'll do what we ask and only what we ask, and he'll keep Anthony at heel. If we get any information, we may hook into the pattern-crime computer program, but we'll be a code word, that's all. Sam and Hank will send their findings to the crime lab—which will know this case only by a number—then they'll sit here by the phones with us. They won't have contact with anyone on the outside, unless we ask them to."

"But these new people, Ginny and Chris—"

"Are right now cruising around talking with car dealers asking about recent purchases or rentals of vans. What we have to do," she explained in a soft but urgent voice, "is to think like the kidnappers. We have to psych them out. We have to reconstruct what they've already done and, from there, plot what they're going to do."

Realizing that she had Will's full attention, she continued. "A crime like kidnapping isn't committed on the spur of the moment. It's carefully planned. The kidnappers have probably been in this area for a while. They knew about you, knew that you had the means to deliver three million dollars. They probably staked the house out for a while before they chose their time of day and entry point.

"Given the distance from this house to the next and to the woods behind you, chances are slim your neighbors would be of help. So we'll focus on the commission of the crime. The kidnappers needed some form of transportation, preferably something without windows. A van would be perfect. They could have stolen one, but that would have been risky. We'll check it out anyway, but at the same time Ginny and Chris will concentrate on finding a dealership in Providence that sold a van within the past few days to anyone at all suspicious. I also have two people in the office making calls—" She held up a hand against the objection Will was about to make. "They don't know what case they're working on, simply that they're supposed to canvas the area beyond Providence about the recent rental or purchase of a van. They're collecting names, that's all, and they're parading as members of the consumer protection division. No one will ever suspect what we want the information for."

Will was temporarily mollified, if begrudgingly so, but Savannah was satisfied with that.

"When Ginny and Chris feel they've exhausted the dealerships," she went on, "they'll move on to local motels. The kidnappers have Megan stashed somewhere. If I were a kidnapper, I'd want a place near an airport for a quick getaway." She paused to look at him beseechfully. "Do you see what we're trying to do?"

Will nodded unhappily. "I just wish there were a safer way of doing it. The note says no police. I don't think I'll be able to live with myself if we find Megan dead."

"We won't find her dead," Savannah said with a force that was more personal than professional. Determinedly, she lowered her voice again. "Let's make sure we don't." She picked up her pen. "I'll need the names of your plant managers."

Will stared at her for a minute, then, in a tight voice, he gave her the names. On further questioning and only after significant prodding on her part, he also provided her with a list of workmen and service personnel who had been at the house in the last month. He gave her the names of the valets at the club, Megan's hairdresser, and the cab company Megan regularly used. When, slightly appalled, he asked whether Savannah was planning to contact all those people, she shook her head.

"Since you don't feel that anyone you've seen recently has behaved at all strangely, we won't do anything at this point but keep their names on a list. If it turns out that the valet at the club bought a van yesterday, Ginny and Chris will pay him a discreet visit."

Setting down her pen, she rose and poured two cups of coffee. After she'd given Will his, she put a gentle hand on his shoulder. "I think I'll wander around for a few minutes, I'll be back."

Heading out of the kitchen, she passed through the large foyer, continued on through the living room, and cautiously opened the library door. Sam Craig was on his knees on the carpet, gently pushing something Savannah couldn't see into a plastic bag. His partner, Hank Shanski, was carefully dusting the part of the bookshelf that had been disturbed. They wore their jackets to protect them from the cold air blowing from the broken glass door.

At her appearance, they both looked up. With a smile, Sam asked, "How's it going?"

She answered eloquently by raising her eyebrows. Clasping the coffee cup for the warmth it yielded, she looked around. The scene was much as Will had described. Had she not been prepared for the damage, she would have been far more upset. Right now her professionalism overrode any panic she felt within.

"How about here?" she asked. "Are you finding much?"

Hank answered first. Of medium build, he was the more easygoing of the two. Totally dedicated to his work, he wore a row of studs in his left ear as his token rebellion. "Lots of prints. *Lots* of prints. Of course, unless these books have been wiped down real good sometime in the last fifty years, we could be cataloguing prints of several generations of Vandermeers."

Savannah would have laughed if the situation hadn't been so frustrating. "That's swell. We can fingerprint Will for reference and probably get a makeup or perfume bottle with Megan's prints on it, but the Vandermeers of days past?" Pulling her blazer more tightly around her, she shook her head, then turned to Sam. "Anything over there?"

Sammy Craig was the true freethinker of the duo. One need not look at the patches in the knees of his jeans or the faded Snoopy that graced the front of his sweatshirt or the dark, wavy hair that fell to his shoulders to guess that. One look in his clear brown eyes and anyone could tell that he was daring. His most invaluable skill as a detective was his imagination. In some respects she felt it was a waste to have him searching for samples for the lab, rather than working in the field, but she trusted Sammy more than any other cop. She wanted him here with Will.

Sam looked at her and said, "I've picked up some bits of dirt—probably from the garden—and a couple of fragmented footprints. Whether they'll tell us anything, I don't know." He sat back on his haunches. "We're dealing with pros. Whoever did this didn't make any mistakes. I checked the patio, but there's nothing—no trampled shrubbery, no broken branches, no discarded gloves. They picked their day well. If there were any tracks over the lawn, the rain has obliterated them."

He glanced at the French doors. "I looked real close at those. The break was definitely from the outside, probably made with a large mallet of some sort." He smirked at Savannah. "Not your croquet variety. Whoever did this brought his own tools, then took them away with him when he was done."

Pensive, she nodded. "Have you been through the rest of the house?"

"Not yet. Did Vandermeer find anything disturbed anywhere else?"

"No."

Sam looked around the room. "My guess is that everything took place right here. The kidnappers knew that Megan would come downstairs at some point during the night. There's no covering on the French doors, so once she put on the light, she was in a goldfish bowl. They broke through the glass, opened the door, grabbed her, dropped the note on the desk, and walked out." He looked at Savannah with intently curious eyes. "What I can't figure out is how her husband slept through it."

Savannah wondered about that, too. The sound of a large object hitting glass would have made a racket. Besides, she assumed Megan would have screamed. "There are signs that she fought them. They must have silenced her somehow. Any traces of chloroform, or another kind of drug?"

Slowly and deliberately, Sam shook his head. "No obvious spills or drips. There was a dried ring of something on the desk, but it smells like coffee. It's probably been there several days. I've taken a sample. The lab will know for sure." He held Savannah's gaze. "No sign of any bodily fluids."

She swallowed hard. "Which means she wasn't cut."

"Or raped."

"Yes." She took a deep, slightly shaky breath and let it out in a shiver as she wrapped an arm around her middle. "God, it's cold in here."

Returning to his work, Sam said, "Give me a minute, and I'll warm you up."

She had to smile. "You've been threatening to do that for five years now." Turning to leave, she said over her shoulder, "One of these days I might take you up on it." The last of her words was cut short as she shut the door, but Sammy knew what she'd said. He knew, as she did, that she would never take him up on his offer, any more than he would want her to. They liked, trusted, and respected each other. They were both attractive, roughly the same age, and unattached.

But there never had been the slightest spark of physical attraction between them.

Returning to the kitchen, Savannah found Will in the same spot. His hair was disheveled and the knot of his necktie had been loosened. "No call," he told her, then murmured, "Stupid of me. You would have heard the phone if it had rung." He paused impatiently. "When are they going to call?"

She wished she knew. "It's early. They're probably giving you a chance to get your act together."

"Or sweat a little."

"Maybe. Have you had anything to eat?"

"I'm not hungry."

"Tired? When Susan gets here, you could try to get some rest."

"I got plenty last night," he said, making no attempt to hide his self-disdain.

She couldn't help but follow his lead. "What time did you go to bed?"

"Early. A little after ten."

"Was Megan with you then?"

"Yes."

"But she got up at some point. Do you have any idea when that was?"

"I didn't wake up, if that's what you mean. But from what Megan's told me before, she probably slept for a few hours, then got up at twelve-thirty or one."

"How long was she usually up?"

He shrugged. "A couple of hours. Then she'd go back to sleep."

"Did she last night?"

"How would I know that if I was sleeping?" he snapped.

She indulged his bad humor. "You might have woken, or been half asleep but aware of her beside you. I hate to have to ask these questions, Will, but I'm trying to narrow down the times during which she was taken. As things stand now, we guess it was somewhere between midnight and six. The kidnappers wouldn't have risked anything after dawn." She paused and studied his downcast expression. "You didn't hear a thing during the night?"

"No."

"No noise you might have thought was part of a dream?"

"Nothing."

She nodded, glanced around the room, then inhaled a deep breath. "I'd like to take a look around upstairs. Is that okay?"

He was suddenly cautious. "The kidnappers didn't go up there."

"How do you know?" she asked, but her brows were raised and a gentle smile touched her lips.

With his mouth compressed into a thin line of surrender, he sent her upstairs with a flick of his hand. Savannah wasn't sure what she was looking for, but there wasn't much more she could ask Will. He was wound tight, feeling frightened and bruised. It seemed best to leave him alone for a bit. Perhaps something would come to him.

Savannah had only been to the second floor of the house once before, when Megan had wanted to show her the diamond earrings and necklace that Will had bought her for their second wedding anniversary. Four years had passed since then. Megan hadn't bubbled about anything as exquisite as those jewels, and Savannah had never again climbed the stairs.

The change was subtle, but sad. The house had aged.

Trying to ignore that, Savannah wandered the length of the balcony railing. She peered into one guest bedroom, then another. Each appeared neat and stale. A third room was sadder, in its way. It was to have been the nursery. Megan had had it decorated soon after her marriage, at a time when she'd seemed sure children would be forthcoming, and indeed, soon after, she had become pregnant. In her fourth month, though, she had miscarried. To Savannah's knowledge, she hadn't conceived again.

Savannah came to a halt at the door of the master bedroom. It was truly a stunning room, with a four-poster bed, surrounded by brocade drawbacks that matched the drapes. The dressers were antique and the accessories—small oil paintings, delicate china figurines, brass lamps—were well chosen. She knew that Will had done extensive renovation and redecorating in the days immediately before his marriage. She suspected nothing had been done since then.

The bed was unmade, but otherwise the room was immaculate, which was surprising. As a schoolgirl, Megan had been a slob. Will was the neat one of the pair. Either he was doing the cleaning now, she mused, or Megan had turned over a new leaf.

Feeling like an intruder, she forced herself into the room. She noticed small things—the books on the nightstands, the gold earrings on Megan's, a pair of glasses on the mantel, cold ash in the fireplace. Stopping at the entrance to the master bath, she couldn't help but smile. She knew that Megan adored this room. It was huge, the by-product of an older, smaller bathroom and what had once been a gentleman's dressing room. The walls were lined with sinks and mirrors, the ceilings with recessed lights. Large plants were everywhere, and in the center of the room was a jacuzzi.

Savannah flicked the wall switch that turned the radio on. The sound of Reba McEntire's voice filled the room. Savannah listened for a minute, a small smile creasing her lips. The song drew to an end. Her pulse skipped a beat. She waited.

But the voice that followed was not the one her senses were conditioned to hear. It was louder, less intimate, more boisterous than gentle.

"You're listening to cool country, 95.3 FM, WCIC Providence. This is Joseph Allan Johnson taking you through the afternoon hours. It's three-oh-four now and warmer than it's been, thirty-seven degrees and drizzling outside our studio. I've been advised that there's been a three-car accident on I-95 southbound near the I-95 interchange, so if you're leaving the city early, you'll want to take an alternate route. We'll keep you informed of the progress on that one. 95.3 FM, WCIC Providence, for a little country in the city. At three-oh-four, we've got a five flush coming up without a commercial break, kicking off with the Nitty Gritty Dirt Band. . . ."

Feeling empty, Savannah turned the radio off and left the bathroom. She went to the hall, paused at the railing overlooking the foyer, glanced back at the bedroom, then down again. The master bedroom suite was almost directly above the library. If only Will had heard something. If only he had set the alarm. If only he would say yes to bringing in the FBI.

She paused at the top of the stairs, then went back to peek into the one room she hadn't inspected. It was smaller than the others. There was no more than a desk, several chairs, a file cabinet, and a lamp. The desk was strewn with official-looking papers. It seemed that Will did work at home. But why didn't he use the library downstairs, and why, fastidious man that he was, did he leave things in such a mess?

She went downstairs and for several minutes stood at the bottom of the staircase. If Megan had managed to escape her kidnappers and reach this spot, would Will have heard her?

"Did you find anything?"

Startled, she swung around to see Will at the head of the hallway that led to the kitchen. "Uh, no. Actually, there was nothing. No great inspiration." She paused, thought, frowned. "Will, why wasn't the alarm on?"

He shifted his weight from one foot to the other. "I suppose I could say that Meggie turns it off when she's up so she won't accidentally set it off, and that's probably what I will tell the insurance company." He hesitated, biting the inside of his cheek. "The fact is that it's broken. It hasn't worked for a couple of months. The repairs will require several thousand dollars' worth of rewiring. I figured I'd let it go until the business took an upswing." Savannah knew the admission caused him pain.

"Several thousand versus three million. Looks like you bet on the wrong horse." She tried to inject a lighthearted tone, but bitter shock shone through.

His laugh was the saddest she had ever heard. "That's nothing new. I've been doing it for years. If I had a knack for picking the winners, the business wouldn't be dying now."

"Why haven't you hired someone to help?"

"An outside consultant?" His anguished chuckle touched Savannah. "Because they're expensive."

Savannah had no response. It wasn't her place to lecture, nor was she in the mood. The emotional strain of Megan's kidnapping was beginning to get to her. She found it stressful to pretend otherwise.

"Well," she sighed, "that's neither here nor there right now." She glanced toward the library. "Let me see if Sammy and Hank are ready for a lab pickup." Just as she turned, Will started forward.

"Savannah?" He stopped short when she looked back at him. "I told you about the alarm system because I want you to know the truth. If anyone can help me get Meggie back, you can."

Savannah was not a genius or a miracle worker, and she resented his placing the bulk of the burden for Megan's return on her shoulders. But when she opened her mouth to argue, he rushed on.

"There are two other things you should know." He paused, looking faraway and very disturbed for a minute. When he spoke again, there was a faint tremor in his voice. "I know that I sometimes give the impression of being one-dimensional, but I'm not as dumb as people think. I don't know what to do to save my business, but I do know enough to worry about it." He paused again, then, as though realizing that the faster he did this the better, he continued. "I take sleeping pills. That's why I sleep soundly. It's a legitimate prescription given by my doctor. I can show you the bottle. You can check it out. But there's no point in your wondering why I didn't hear anything last night. I never hear anything at night. I'm totally out of it."

"Oh, Will," she murmured sympathetically, but he was intent on finishing what he had begun.

"The other thing is that Megan's gun is gone."

She felt herself pale. "Gun?"

"I've always been worried about her safety. For the same

reason that I took out insurance against kidnapping, I bought her a gun to keep in her nightstand. It's a small thing. I've looked all over for it, but it's not here. She must have taken it downstairs with her."

"Would she have heard the glass break and *then* gone downstairs?" Savannah shook her head, answering the question herself. "No. Meggie wouldn't be that dumb. She'd have woken you, or called the police."

"I figured that, too. I think she just took the gun with her when she went down to read. Maybe she's been doing it ever since the alarm system broke. Maybe she had a premonition." He ran a weary hand around the back of his neck. "Christ, I just don't know!"

Savannah was thinking of the reason why she had never wanted to carry a gun herself. God only knew, she had cause. She had sent some violent men to prison, and more than once, in a courtroom confrontation, she had been threatened. But she had always figured that a violent man would have the gun out of her hand and aimed at her before she could muster the wherewithal to pull the trigger.

She feared for Megan.

"I think," she said quietly, "that I'd like to share this with Sammy." Without another word, she went into the library, closing the door behind her and leaning back against the wood.

Hank spared her a quick glance. "We're almost ready to ship the first of this to the lab."

Sam looked at her for a minute, then stood and came to her side. "Are you okay?"

She nodded.

"You look pale."

"My blusher must be fading," she said softly, then,

"Sammy, there's a gun involved. Megan had a small pistol with her. She usually kept it in her nightstand, but Will says it's gone. I assume she brought it down here, and if so, she may have tried to use it when the kidnappers broke in. Have you found any evidence"—she sent a glance toward Hank, who had also straightened and was listening—"of a gun having been fired in this room?"

Sam, too, shot a glance at Hank, then looked back at Savannah. "Damn good thing I've got a change of clothes in my duffel. It could take a good long time to inch along every one of these bookshelves looking for a bullet hole. Why couldn't the damn walls have been covered with white plaster?"

Savannah looked at the ceiling, then shook her head, squeezed her eyes shut, and spoke through gritted teeth. "This case sucks shit."

Hank shushed her. "Ladies don't talk that way."

She opened her eyes. "Right now, I'm no lady. I'm a prosecutor investigating a case that I shouldn't be investigating in the first place, because I have a personal involvement in it." She held up her hand. "And as far as my language goes, whatever I know," her gaze took in both detectives, "I've learned from you." Swinging around, she left the room.

No sooner had she passed through the living room when the doorbell rang. She continued on into the vestibule and peered around the edge of the gathered sheer. The woman who stood on the front step, her head wrapped in auburn curls and her body in silver fox, was a welcome sight. Savannah quickly opened the door.

"I don't believe this," Susan said and hurried in past her sister. "I've been trying to grasp it since you called." Her voice was low and urgent. "Poor Meggie. Poor *Will*. Has anything happened? Anyone called?"

Closing the door, Savannah shook her head. "Will is waiting in the kitchen. He doesn't know what to do with himself, and there really isn't much he can do but wait." Belatedly, she wrapped an arm around her sister's shoulder and gave her a quick hug, then reached to relieve her of the large overnight bag she'd brought. "Thanks for coming. I can't handle this myself, and Will shouldn't be left alone."

Susan regarded her with a mixture of annoyance and nervousness. "I'm not sure I was the best one to call."

"I am," Savannah countered.

"I don't do well under pressure."

"You'll do fine."

"Will needs someone to give him strength."

"You can do that. You're Megan's friend."

"What does one have to do with the other?"

"Dedication," Savannah said. Dropping her voice, she urged Susan down onto the vestibule bench. "When was the last time you talked with Megan?"

"Last week."

"Did she say anything odd?"

"No," Susan said. She began unbuttoning the fur jacket. "But she didn't look great. I think she and Will are having problems."

"What made you think that?"

"We'd be talking, and suddenly she'd say things like, 'Why is life so hard?' or 'I'm tired of fighting.' I mean, as statements went, they were in context with the rest of the conversation, but somehow I knew she really meant it. You know Meggie; she spent most of her life struggling to break even. She thought that was over when she married Will. What happened?"

The question was almost rhetorical, but Savannah needed to talk as much as her sister needed to hear. Savannah, Megan, and Susan had been a tight trio for years. Though Savannah's career had distanced her somewhat, the emotional bond between the three remained. For that reason, Savannah had no qualms about betraying what would, in other circumstances, have been a confidence. Moreover, she had called Susan for a reason, and if she expected her to be of help, Susan had to know the score.

"Money," she said very quietly. "The business is failing."

Susan didn't seem at all surprised. "Then the talk is right."

"Talk?"

"Gossip. It's my specialty, Savvy. You know that. I may not be good for much else, but I do know the latest rumors."

"And the one about the Vandermeers—"

"—says that Will is slowly but surely running the business into the ground."

Savannah was silent for a minute before finally admitting, "Harshly put, but basically true. To use Will's own words, this kidnapping couldn't have come at a worse time." She looked up just as Will approached and raised her voice, "I was just filling Susan in on what's happening."

Susan stood and quickly went to brush her cheek to his. Lightly grasping his arms, she said, "How're you doing, Will?"

"I've been better."

"Meggie will be fine. You have to believe that. She'll be fine."

He said nothing.

Uncomfortable with the silence, Susan hurried to fill the void. "Savannah and her crew are the best. If anyone can foil this thing, they can."

"I wish they'd make their move," he said. "The waiting is unbearable."

Savannah rose to join her sister. "It could be a while longer," she warned. "They'll pick their own time."

Susan, who had assumed from what Savannah told her on the phone that she would be back in her own home by the next day, eyed her sister with caution. In a deceptively light tone, she asked, "How much time? What's the range for kidnappings?"

"It could be a day, a week, or more," Savannah said. She had answered honestly, but the immediate winces from both Will and Susan made her soften the blow. "Actually, in a state this size, it will probably be less than more."

"Why is that?" Susan asked with an indignance that covered up her growing fear. She sensed she had been snookered into something more extensive than she had originally thought.

"Because there's less room to hide."

"What if they leave the state?"

"I doubt they will. They'll want to stay close for the sake of phone calls and ransom pickups. In an area like this, which can be pretty well canvased, the longer they hold her, the better our chances of finding them. They'll want to get their money and run."

"We hope," Will murmured.

"Damn right, we do," Susan drawled. Catching a look from Savannah, she added a quick, "But I'll be here as long as you need me." Then she paused and said more drolly, "Of course, you may have second thoughts after a day. I'm a lousy cook." When Will didn't crack a smile, she said, "And I'm a worse housekeeper than Meggie." Still no smile. She looked at Savannah and muttered, "This isn't my day." Hoisting her overnight bag to her shoulder, she walked to the staircase, dropped the bag, and headed toward the dining room liquor cabinet.

Chapter 4

SUSE," SAVANNAH SAID softly as she came up from behind.

Susan didn't turn. Looking tense but elegant with her shoulders straight beneath the fox fur, she continued to pour her drink. "I need some backbone, Savannah. I'm not as used to situations like this as you are." Without capping the bottle, she tipped the glass to her lips.

"I'm not used to situations like this, either," Savannah said. "I've only worked on one other kidnapping, and the victim in that case was a total stranger. I'm emotionally involved here, which complicates things. But I still have to function, and I need a clear mind for that." She paused for a breath. "I need you to function with me."

Susan sighed in relief as the liquid hit her stomach. "There. Better."

"How can it be better, when it hasn't reached your bloodstream yet?"

"Just knowing it's getting there makes it better. Believe me." Susan took the offensive before Savannah could harp on her drinking. "What have you gotten me into? When you called on the phone, you told me everything was under control."

"I told you Megan had been kidnapped."

"And that Will had a note, that he was going to pay, that everything was going to be all right, but that he just needed someone with him in the house for a day. Now you tell me that no one's called, that Will doesn't have the money, that this could go on for a while." Her jaw was set. "I told you that I don't do well under pressure."

"You'll do fine if you set your mind to it. I need you. Will needs you. Megan needs you. All we're asking is that you stay here and be calm. You can do that, Susan."

With a brittle laugh, Susan took another swallow of her drink. "You never change. It's incredible. The eternal optimist. You were that when we were kids, and you're still that way. I'd have thought you'd be jaded by now. You see the darkest side of life day in, day out, and still you expect the best of people."

"What's my alternative?"

"Being realistic. Some people have limitations that you don't have."

"I have limitations. I fight them, that's all."

"Well, some of us can't fight them. Maybe if you'd accept that, the rest of us could relax."

Savannah was stung by that. "Are you saying that I make you feel tense?"

"Tense? No. Inadequate is more like it. You hoodwinked me into coming over here, and now I'm stuck feeling useless." She glanced toward the hall. Will had long since disappeared. Not knowing how far he had gone, she kept her voice low, but there was desperation in her tone. "What am I supposed to do here, Savvy? I love Megan, but I've always felt a little odd with Will. I can't sit and hold his hand. He wouldn't want that any more than I do."

"You can talk to him."

"Sure. Like I did out there? He wasn't listening to me then. What makes you think he'll listen another time?"

"He doesn't have to listen. That's the point, Suse. He needs someone with him. As time passes without word from Megan, he'll get more and more uptight."

"Swell."

"Talk to him. Reassure him that we're doing what we can, that the kidnappers want the money more than they want Megan, that she'll be back. Just talk. You're good at that."

"A cocktail party this isn't," Susan remarked and took another swallow of scotch.

"Could've fooled me," Savannah muttered.

"I heard that."

"You were meant to." She reached for the glass. "You don't need the drink, Susan."

But Susan wasn't letting go. "You're asking me to say sweet nothings at a time like this? Believe me, I need the drink."

Savannah didn't want to get into a full-fledged fight just then. "Okay," she said. "Have that one drink, but just one. Because I do need you clearheaded. I need you to try to learn more from Will about the situation here than he's told me. I need to know about anything odd that may have happened around here in the last few weeks. He couldn't think of anything when I asked, but something may occur to him with a little prodding."

Facing her sister, Susan remembered all the times over the years when Savannah had given out assignments. She was a natural at people management. "So I'm supposed to sit and prod?"

"Not all the time. Be diplomatic about it—talk a little, prod a little, keep quiet a little. Putter around in the kitchen. I don't think Will has eaten a thing all day, and the house is loaded with food."

"I was just kidding about that. Am I *really* supposed to be the cook?" She quickly took another shot of scotch. No sooner had she swallowed when she grumbled, "I should have told you I already had plans. It wouldn't have been far from the truth. Dusty and Joy had asked me to drive up to Boston with them, but the weather was lousy and—"

"Kidnapped, Susan," Savannah interrupted. "Megan has been kidnapped. We are not talking about her having her appendix taken out or getting lost at La Guardia. This is a little more important than a night on the town in Boston."

For a minute, Susan just stared at her. In a very quiet voice she said, "I know." Then her attention was caught by something behind Savannah, her eyes widened in fear, and she murmured quickly, "Uh-oh. Trouble. There's a guy behind you and he sure as hell doesn't belong here—"

Savannah whirled around. Sam was propped indolently against the arch between the dining room and the hall. She let out a small cry of relief and pressed a hand to her chest. "Sammy! Don't creep up on us like that!"

"You know him?" Susan whispered in disbelief. Her eyes took in the tall, rangy form with its worn jeans and sweatshirt, its distinct five o'clock shadow, its long, wavy hair. "What's he doing here, and why's he staring at me?"

Glancing back at her sister, Savannah whispered in return, "Maybe because you're staring at him." Continuing in the loud whisper that, if anything, mocked Susan, she said, "He's part of the detail assigned to the house. He'll be here as long as you will be."

"Detail?" Susan echoed. Not once had she taken her eyes from Sam, who heard everything that was said.

"Police," Savannah informed her sister. She took pleasure in Susan's shocked expression; her superior demeanor bothered Savannah.

"*He*'s with the police?"

Coming to life, Sam ambled forward. He extended his hand to Susan and said with a pronounced southern drawl, "Sam Craig, at your service, ma'am."

His hand remained empty and waiting for ten seconds, before Susan recovered her poise. As disreputable as he looked, the way he moved and talked bespoke sheer male power. Though Savannah appeared to be totally comfortable with him, Susan felt threatened.

Of course, she had no intention of showing it. That was the part of the game she could play well. Tipping her chin up a notch, she slipped her hand into his and returned a firm grasp. "On behalf of the Vandermeers, I'd like to thank you for being here, Officer."

"Lieutenant," he corrected in that same, slow drawl, then amended it to, "Sam."

Determined to hide her nervousness, Susan hurried on. "It's kind of you to give us your time. This is a new and frightening experience. I'm sure you've been through it before. We deeply appreciate your help." As smoothly as possible, she retrieved her hand.

He offered her the faintest tip of his head. "My pleasure." Then he turned to Savannah and without a trace of a drawl said, "This has to be your sister. Her pictures don't do her justice. She's stunning. Why have you been hiding her?"

Momentarily amused, Savannah argued, "I haven't been

hiding her. You saw her at the party I threw at my father's house last year."

He shook his head. "I would have remembered." He looked at Susan again. A faint smile touched his lips. "She really is a beauty."

"Uh-huh," Savannah said, still slightly amused.

Susan wasn't amused. With the disappearance of Sam Craig's drawl, she felt taken for a fool. She didn't like that at all.

Addressing herself to him, she said, "Did no one ever tell you that it's impolite to talk about someone as though she weren't there?"

"Is it?" Sam asked innocently. "Funny, you seemed to feel it was okay when you did it to me a minute ago."

"That was different. I didn't know who you were."

"Then it's okay in some situations but not others? If I'd have been a thug, like you first thought, it would have been all right?"

"When I first saw you, I was frightened. I was talking to my sister."

"About me, within easy earshot." His drawl returned. "You're a snob, Miss Susan."

"And you're out of line, Lieutenant. As a member of the police department, your job is to serve the taxpayers of this state. Given the hefty chunk the state takes from my income each year, I'd say a little respect is in order."

In a perfectly respectful tone, Sam asked, "And what do you do to earn that income?"

Impertinent question though it was, it held enough of a dare to goad Susan. "I allow various banks and foundations and corporations the use of my money. In that sense, I've been involved in urban renewal, cancer research, and higher education. I serve on the boards of two art museums, one historical society, and hospitals both in Rhode Island and New York. I also happen to know how to give a party, and considering that a single evening's event can raise several million dollars for one worthy cause or another, that's nothing to sneeze at." Drawing herself straighter, she said, "I'd think about that, if I were you, Lieutenant. I'd think about it the next time you put on that drawl and come at me with that sexy walk. We're not in the same league, you and I. Sorry to disappoint you, but it's true."

She started to walk past him, then, on impulse, stopped and reached up to lightly brush her fingers through the shorter layers of hair by his cheek. "Nice cut, though. Maybe you'd give me the name of your stylist. Lately I haven't been able to do a thing with my hair." With a haughty smile, she left the room.

Sam stared after her. For another minute, he remained silent. Then he muttered, "Jesus, she's tough."

Savannah shook her head. "It's a front. She's having a hard time finding direction in her life."

He snorted. "Could've fooled me. Sure sounded as though she knows exactly where she's at."

"She can be glib when she wants. It's a defense mechanism. She's really insecure."

He turned to stare thoughtfully in the direction in which Susan had disappeared. "She's so different from you."

"I have my insecurities, too."

"But you've never come on with a power play like that."

"I've never had to, at least, not with you. You don't threaten me. But you threaten Susan."

He looked perplexed. "Are you kidding?"

Savannah shook her head. "You're strong. You know where you are and why you're there."

He laughed in disbelief. "Your sister isn't threatened by me. Weren't you listening to her? She thinks I'm way below her."

"You didn't see her expression when you first came in."

"Sure I did. I was looking straight at her."

"But you didn't see her expression."

"She was terrified. She thought I was a thief."

"After that."

"She liked my sexy walk."

"It was more than that, Sammy."

He looked at her closely. "What are you saying?"

"I'm saying," Savannah explained slowly, "that you're very different from the men in her world. You exude a self-confidence that is truly powerful. That makes her nervous."

"Why should it?"

"Because you can see through her. You did. You put her down easily with that snobbery business. That's why she's threatened. That's why her defenses came up. That's why she came across as being tough. She had to. For her own sake, if nothing else."

Sam stood beside her, silently considering that for a moment. Finally he said, "So what can I expect? Will she be giving me the cold shoulder from here to eternity?"

"That depends."

"On what?"

"On how comfortable you can make her feel. If she's threatened, she'll lash out. If not . . ." Her voice trailed off and a small, suggestive smile curved her lips.

Sam studied that smile. "If I didn't know better, I'd think you were giving me a push."

"Me?" Savannah held up her hand. "I don't push you anywhere. You do your own thing. Besides, God only knows I have enough else to worry about."

It was an apt reminder for them both. Sobering, Sam said, "We're ready for the lab. Want to call a courier?"

She nodded and started off, then stopped. When she looked back up at Sam, she was less sure than usual. "Susan is nervous about all this. She's here because I asked her to come and because Megan's a friend, but given her druthers, she'd leave in a minute. If she stays, she'll be tense." She paused. "Go easy on her, Sammy. And keep an eye on her for me when I'm not here. She's not happy with her life right now. When I called her to come over, I was thinking that it would do her good to focus on someone else for a change. Will you let me know if you think I made a mistake?"

Sam gave her an understanding nod.

She smiled in gratitude before leaving to call the courier.

Soon after, Savannah returned to the office. She'd been able to reassign some of her work so that she could spend time at the Vandermeers, but there were some matters that couldn't be delegated. She was scheduled to go to trial the following week on an arson conspiracy case. There were witnesses to prepare, one of whom, an expert on insurance fraud, had flown in from Omaha and was waiting in her office when she returned. She spent two and a half hours with him, then met with the two police detectives who had been working on the case. She needed more information, including corroboration from one of her own witnesses. After that, she attended the weekly meeting of the criminal division. Technically, she was second in command in the division, but the first in command had been out of work for a month recovering from open-heart surgery, and it looked like it would be a while longer before he returned. Savannah had emerged quite naturally over the last year as the one others went to for advice, and she had easily assumed the responsibility of conducting division meetings.

By nine o'clock that evening, she was headed back to the Vandermeers. She felt guilty for not waiting with Will and Susan, but she had to keep up with her work unless she wanted a complete nervous breakdown. She couldn't spend the night at Will's as she had asked Susan to do, and she felt even more guilty about that. But she just couldn't. She knew herself. The tension was building inside. She needed a break.

Will was where she had left him, at his post by the kitchen phone. He had a blank piece of paper and a pencil within reach, ready to take down any information the kidnappers might transmit. He was alternately holding the pencil and setting it down, folding a corner of the paper and flattening it, turning to look at the clock and facing the paper again.

Wearing the same chic yellow jogging suit that she had arrived in, Susan was sitting in one of the eight captain's chairs that encircled the large round kitchen table. She was methodically sifting the old-fashioned glass in her hand by quarter turns on the wood surface. She looked up once when Savannah entered the room, then looked back at her glass. But that single brief glance had been defiant. Savannah knew not to mention the drink.

Sam and Hank were sitting at the table with drinks of their own. Rather than old-fashioned glasses filled with liquor, though, they held mugs of coffee. She guessed they were on their fourth or fifth cups. She was a coffee drinker herself, but not to excess. She recognized a caffeine shake when it was starting and knew when to stop. Sammy and Hank never stopped, but then, they never shook. They could drink coffee all night, while they took turns sleeping. And they would sleep soundly. The caffeine didn't faze them. She assumed it had something to do with the sturdiness of the male physique; strength was one of the few concessions she was prepared to make to the male of the species. It could make them exciting, or terrifying.

"What are they doing with her?" Will cried, his eyes tired now but no less alert. "Why haven't they called?"

Taking a seat between him and Hank, Savannah laced her hands tightly together. "They're waiting for the right time."

"Do you think she's okay?"

"I have to think that."

"Will they feed her? Make sure she's warm enough?"

"She'll eat when they eat and be as warm as they are. I'm sure they have no intention of either starving or freezing." She paused. "What happened with the insurance company?"

"One man came and looked around," Will answered.

Hank offered a little more. "We talked with him. He seemed satisfied."

"Is he getting the money together?"

Will grew agitated. "Sure he is, but he doesn't trust us to have it here. He wants to wait until we've gotten the call and arranged the payoff. Then he'll get the money over." He swore between his teeth. "You'd think we were trying to gyp him out of something. What in the hell have I been paying premiums for if not situations like this?"

"He has to be cautious," Savannah reasoned. "Three million dollars is a lot of money. It's his job to guard it well. We can't really blame him for that." She inhaled. "As long as he can get his hands on that money when we need it." Her gaze grew more concentrated. "Will, is anything else of Megan's missing? Any jewelry? Money from her wallet?"

It was a minute before he focused on what she'd asked, and even then he seemed confused. "I haven't looked through her jewelry. I assumed they were only interested in her."

"I saw a pair of earrings on her night table."

"She takes them off when she gets into bed."

"Where does she keep the rest of her things?"

"There's a safe in the library. It hasn't been opened. I checked."

"Was she wearing anything else—necklace, watch?"

He frowned, trying to concentrate. "I'm not sure."

"Think," she commanded gently. "If she was wearing something of value when they took her, they may have hawked it to pay for food or a motel room or plane tickets. We could possibly trace it."

Head bowed, Will thought for a minute. Finally he looked and said weakly, "I gave her a Piaget watch with diamonds around the face for her birthday last year. She used to take it off along with the earrings when she came to bed, but it's possible she put it back on when she got up and went downstairs."

Savannah did not remember having seen the watch with the earrings. She glanced at Hank who was already getting up to check. She turned back to Will. "How about money?"

He looked more frustrated than ever. "I don't know. I have no idea how much she had in her wallet. She cashes checks whenever she needs money. I don't keep tabs on her. I've never wanted her to feel restricted." More quietly, he added, "She balances the checkbook at the end of the month. I like it that way."

"Want to check her wallet?"

"But I told you, I don't know—"

"Check. For me?"

He glanced longingly, painfully at the phone.

"You'll hear it if it rings," Savannah assured him. "We'll be here listening, too. But I have to know about the wallet. Look to see if anything's been messed up, identification cards removed, money taken out quickly. I'd also like to know whether anything, even the smallest thing, is missing from any of the other rooms on the first floor. I doubt the kidnappers would have risked going far, but it'd have been easy for one of them to dash through and pick up a few little trinkets that could be sold for a few thousand dollars, which would be lovely spending money in Rio."

"They're not robbers," Will said. "They're kidnappers."

"Which is robbery once removed, isn't it?" she pointed out gently.

She had him there. Without further argument, he left the kitchen. She immediately turned to Sam. "I checked with the lab just before I drove over. The prints you picked up in the library are mostly Megan's and Will's. There's one set they can't identify. They're checking it through the crime computer. If we're lucky, it may match up with something."

"Where'd we lift it from?"

"The base of the desk lamp."

His mouth went flat. "That was the most obvious print we found—bright and clear, right there on the brass. I took it because it was looking me boldly in the face, but even then I doubted it belonged to the kidnappers. They wouldn't have been so dumb."

"Or careless. Not after being fastidious with everything else." Savannah sent Susan a dry look. "It was probably the cleaning men."

Susan snorted. "They're pathetic." She continued to turn the glass, quarter by quarter.

Sam looked puzzled. "What kind of cleaning man is going to leave a fingerprint on something that should be spotless and shiny?"

"Good question," Savannah said, "and I ask it every week when I write out a check. But good cleaning people are hard to come by. These guys are really good with the heavy stuff. They do a super job on bathrooms and floors and carpets and baseboards. They're not so good with the little things—"

"Like dust," Susan said.

"Or fingerprints," Sam guessed. He looked from one sister to the other. "You use the same cleaning service Megan does?"

"Savannah's been using them longest. Blame it on her."

Sam wasn't ready to blame anything on Savannah. "No one's making you use them."

"But Savvy's right," Susan argued. "You can't get good cleaning help anymore. The ones who can dust can't clean, and vice versa, so you take the lesser of the evils. I can't do heavy cleaning. These men can. And they bring their own equipment. The last thing I want to be thinking about is buying new vacuum bags."

"Might interfere with the party plans?" Sam said in a low, taunting voice.

No longer turning her glass but clutching it tightly on the table, Susan looked rigidly at Savannah. "This man is an idiot, do you know that? The gall of him to accuse me of being a snob, when he's a far worse one than I am. He's already taken digs at my coat, my rings, my clothes." She looked over what she was wearing. "Just because I buy a jogging outfit in a boutique rather than a department store doesn't mean I don't jog, and it certainly doesn't mean I'm any less of a person."

Savannah looked at Sam, who was the picture of innocence.

"She's too sensitive," he said. "She can't take a little kidding."

Susan turned on him. "Kidding! It's been nonstop criticism since I arrived."

"Not true. I told you dinner was great."

"Uh-huh, after you told me how surprised you were that I knew how to cook."

"I was. Am. You don't look like the domestic type. Let's face it, you were born with a silver spoon in your mouth. You didn't do badly when you married, either."

"Which goes to show what you know," Susan muttered in disgust.

"Dirk Gardner is loaded."

"And money can't make a marriage. Dirk and I were a disaster together. So, yes, I did do badly when I married."

The good-natured humor that Savannah had seen on Sam's face when he'd first begun sparring with Susan was replaced by something more sober. "I'm sorry."

"You should be. It's not easy for me being here, and you're not helping."

"I'm trying to. I'm giving you something else to think about besides Megan and that drink."

Furious, Susan stood. "Who in the hell are you to think you know what I need? If I want a diversion, I can promise it won't be with a jackass like you." Bumping the arm of her chair as she rushed past him, she stormed from the room.

Silence hung over her departure. Sam blew out a breath and eyed Savannah expectantly. "Your sister doesn't like me."

Sitting back in her chair, Savannah put her elbows on its arms, linked her fingers, and pursed her lips. "I think you may be right."

"I like her."

"Really."

"I do. But she doesn't take to my honesty. She's not used to honesty."

"Astute observation."

"Her friends are that shallow?"

"Not all of them. I'm her friend. So's Megan. I don't like to think either of us is shallow."

"But the others," Sam said, "the Newport crowd. Pretty shallow, huh?"

He was getting himself in deeper. She fought a smile. "My father is part of the Newport crowd. So are two aunts and uncles and numerous cousins."

"And you became a lawyer," he said without blinking. "Why, Savvy? Why not a society willow like Susan?"

Savannah sat in quiet admiration of the way he had turned the discussion to his advantage. Then she said softly, "I needed something more. That's all."

"And Susan?"

"She chose the world she knew."

"But she's not happy."

"She's almost thirty-one. Are you going to tell her to leave what she knows and try something new?"

"Someone should."

"You've seen what she does. She just leaves the room."

"She does that to you?"

"Sometimes. When I hit a raw spot."

"Like the booze?"

Savannah fell quiet again. When she spoke, it was in a softer voice that asked what the words themselves didn't. "She didn't seem drunk."

"She's not," Sam said. "Yet. You worry about that, don't you?"

Savannah looked at her hands. "Yes, I worry. She's my sister. I worry a lot."

"You look tired."

She glanced up. "I am. But it's not supposed to show."

"Why don't you go home?"

She wanted to. "Soon."

"Nothing's going to happen here until morning. I'll keep an eye on Susan for you."

Savannah gave a sad chuckle. "That could be tragic for both of you. At the rate you're going, I'll arrive here in the morning to find bits and pieces of you two strewn around the house—" She stopped short, all humor gone as she pictured the parody with far too much clarity. It reminded her of a murder case she had worked on, in which the victim had been mutilated. She'd gone through hell trying that case, and she still felt the bile rise in her throat each time she recalled the exhibit photos she had shown the jury. For a split second, she saw the fleeting image of Megan's face attached to that limbless torso. Then she closed her eyes and took a slow, shaky breath.

"Savvy?" Sam asked. He was rising from his seat just as she opened her eyes, but he continued around the table to where she sat. "Are you okay?"

"Fine." She forced a smile.

"You look green."

"Must've been something I ate."

"Maybe I should drive you home."

She shook her head and, as though to prove her point, stood up. "I'm fine. Really. You stay here and guard the fort. I'm counting on you."

Nodding, he took a step back to let her pass. She came face to face with Hank at the door.

"No watch," he told her. "Will just checked her jewelry box upstairs and it isn't there. She must have it."

Fighting the image of a detached wrist wearing that watch, Savannah swallowed hard. "I'll see that someone contacts the pawn shops first thing tomorrow."

"Are you okay?" he asked.

"Just tired," she said with a weak smile as she eased past him. She found Susan in the living room, sitting on the floor in front of one of the stereo speakers. Kneeling beside her, she said, "I'm taking off soon. I'm beat."

Susan gave her a sidelong glance. "You look it."

"You're the third person who's told me that in as many minutes."

"If Sam Craig was one of them, it may be the only thing he and I agree about."

"Sammy's a good guy."

"He rubs me the wrong way."

"Give him a chance. He has a good head on his shoulders. He may be a little too blunt sometimes, but his heart's in the right place."

"A little too blunt—that's putting it mildly. But maybe I'm being too harsh. Where we come from, social niceties are important. He obviously comes from somewhere else, and his roots show. He's a cop, not a diplomat."

Savannah sat for a minute, quietly listening to John Denver sing "Annie's Song" on the radio. She always found the song uplifting. It ended too soon. Without realizing it, she held her breath. But the voice that she heard was bright and bubbly rather than the one she longed to hear.

"Your dial is set at cool country, 95.3 FM, WCIC Providence. I'm Melissa Stuart, with you until midnight. Right now, it's ten twenty-three, thirty-nine degrees, and raining outside our studios. Look for showers to continue through the night with clouds beginning to break by dawn, maybe even a little sun by midday. Meanwhile, I've got three of the hottest coming up on 95.3 FM, WCIC, kicking off with the best of Shenandoah. . . ." The music began right on cue.

"Strange," Savannah whispered, "the words are practically the same, but the effect is so different."

Susan sounded bemused. "He's so much better."

"Was this already set at CIC?"

"Uh-huh. Megan listens all the time."

"Wonder if she was listening last night."

"Wonder if she's listening tonight."

Savannah shivered. "God, I hope she's okay."

"Me, too." Susan looked at her sister. "You really do look tired. Are you sure you're not sick?"

"Sick at heart, maybe. I wish there were more I could do."

"My God, Savvy, you've done so much already."

"But we haven't learned anything. The lab is coming up with zip. Chris and Ginny are coming up with zip. You can't believe how frustrated I feel."

Susan thought for a minute before saying, "I can believe

it. It's like I said before, you have the highest expectations of anyone I know. I watch you coordinate everything, but you think you're not doing enough. You can only do so much, Savvy. You're human. Just like the rest of us." That said, she raised her glass and took a sip.

Too tired to argue, Savannah sighed, then stood. "You won't have too much, will you, Suse?"

Susan shook her head. "I won't."

"Check on Will every so often?"

"Uh-huh."

"And call me if anything happens?"

Susan nodded.

Satisfied that things were under control with her sister, at least for the time being, Savannah went in search of Will. She found him in the dining room, glancing through the silver drawers. "Anything missing?" she asked.

Will looked as though he'd been through a wringer. Only his eyes moved, darting frantically from one tray to the next. "I don't know. How many knives are there supposed to be?"

The question echoed in Savannah's mind. How many knives? One dozen? Two dozen? Three dozen? Minus any that may have been snitched by the hired help over the years. Minus any that may have gone home to the wrong house in a casserole dish. Minus any that fell into the disposal.

His question accurately summed up the problem: They were grasping at straws.

"Forget the silver," Savannah said wearily. "They probably wouldn't have taken the time to open drawers. Anything missing on top?"

His eyes continued to dart through the flatware. "No."

Savannah slowly closed the drawer. Bracing her forearm

on the top of the cabinet, she looked into his face. "Why don't you try to rest, Will? It's been a long day."

"I won't rest until she's back."

"But there's nothing we can do now. Sam and Hank will take turns sitting by the phone. You'll be fresher in the morning if you try to sleep now."

He laughed feebly. "The only way I can sleep is by taking a pill, but if I do that and the call comes in, I won't be able to think straight."

"Then just lie down. Try to relax. It'll be better for Megan that way." Strung out herself, she wasn't about to argue further. "I'm going to run on home. I'll see you in the morning. Hang in there, okay?" Without awaiting an answer, she saw herself out.

The night was dark and wet. Despite the long wool coat that envéloped her, Savannah was chilled by the time she reached her car. She slid in and locked the door in a single, quick motion, then steadied her hand and put the key in the ignition.

The drive home was brief, thanks to the hour and the sparseness of traffic. She almost wished there were more cars, more noise, more life. The windshield wipers maintained a steady rhythm against the rain; the wet pavement mirrored the city lights. Still, the world seemed very dark, and she felt very much alone.

Parking in the garage behind her townhouse, she hurried across the small open space to her back door. Her hands trembled as she unlocked it and continued to tremble while she turned off the alarm to allow herself entry. With the door closed behind her, she took an unsteady breath and proceeded up the stairs to the first floor of the townhouse.

Hanging her coat in the closet, she carried her briefcase

directly into the den and set it on the desk. Then she sank into the old, leather wing chair, dropped her shoes to the floor, and drew her knees to her chest. Hugging them tightly, she took one shallow breath after another. All the while her body trembled.

She didn't cry. She never did when this happened. In place of tears, a fine sheen of sweat broke out on her forehead, her upper lip, the back of her neck. And the trembling went on.

She knew what was happening; it was no great mystery. In the course of a day, she went about her work in a very diligent, very capable and controlled manner. But some days the work she did deeply upset her. On those days, she held back her feelings until she felt she would burst, because the last thing she could do was show weakness at work. Only later, at home, sitting in her chair with the high back and wings to protect her, could she give vent to the emotions that cried for release.

It was a classic case of delayed reaction, and it didn't happen often. She could handle her job perfectly well nine-tenths of the time. The other tenth of the time, she suffered. It had been that way when she tried a case involving a pair of toddlers who had been sexually abused in a nursery school. It had been that way when she headed an investigation into the cult suicides of three teenagers at the local high school. It had been that way with the limbless torso case.

Megan Vandermeer's kidnapping wasn't blatantly grotesque or bloody. Optimally, it would end with the payment of a ransom and Megan's return, with little more physical harm done than a broken French door.

Optimally.

Unfortunately, Savannah knew too much. She knew how

the criminal mind worked. Despite the words of encouragement she gave Will, she had seen the results of irrational acts too often to believe that the optimal situation would come to pass. She did believe that Megan would return home alive; she had to believe that. What frightened her was the torment Megan might endure before then, and where that torment was concerned, Savannah's imagination was fertile.

Megan was her friend, and that made the pain she felt so much worse. She wanted to help. She was doing everything she could. But she was getting nowhere. And Megan suffered.

She kept taking soft, shallow breaths. Turning sideways in the chair, she pressed her damp brow to her knees and closed her eyes.

Gradually, the shaking began to ease. Gradually, her breathing deepened. With her eyes still closed, she rested her head back against the chair.

A few minutes later, she went into the bedroom to change her clothes. Despite the fact that she was physically drained, she had work to do. Work was her scourge and her salvation. Will took sleeping pills, Susan drank scotch, Savannah worked.

There were times when she wondered where it would end. But, hell, she had to do something until midnight.

Chapter 5

*I*T'S TWELVE-OH-FOUR, *and this is Jared Snow, comin' to you at the tail end of a cold and rainy Tuesday."*

Savannah had been waiting, focusing with only half a mind on the memorandum she was dictating. At the slow, husky sound of his voice, she turned off her minirecorder and pressed its narrow end to her lips.

"You're listening to cool country," he told her with a lazy smile, *"95.3 FM, WCIC Providence. I'll be playing nothing but the smoothest of country sounds till six. If you've just come home, find a comfortable place to dry off and warm up. If you've been home awhile, refill that mug with whatever feeds your senses, take a real slow breath, and relax. I've got Randy Travis, Juice Newton, and Exile comin' up on 95.3 FM, the home of a little country in the city, WCIC Providence, kickin' off a cool country streak with a new cut by T. Graham Brown. Jared Snow listenin' with you in the heart of the night. Enjoy. . . ."*

She did, oh, she did. The tension that lingered in her body seemed to ease with the sound of his voice. The images that plagued her with each break from her work disappeared. In a leisurely motion she set the recorder on the desk. Raising her arms, she linked her hands on her forehead, pushed up the dark bangs that normally lay there, and arched her back into a feline stretch.

Jared Snow. He had a sexy voice, and a suggestive way of using it. He was smooth and easy; it was hard to listen to him and not melt. He talked as though he were lying beside her in bed, as though they had just made heated love and were in a comfortable embrace, basking in the afterglow. When he identified his station, he could as well be saying she turned him on, and when he announced the song to come, he could be telling her he wanted her again.

Not for the first time, she wondered what he looked like. He had to look sexy. Not that looks mattered, certainly not when it came to Jared Snow. But she didn't want him to look sleazy. She saw enough of that during an average day in court. She wanted him to be a sight for sore eyes. She wanted the reality of him to be wonderful.

Maybe she wanted too much. Susan told her all the time that her expectations were too great. Maybe they were. Such had been her experience with Matt Briarwood. She had been twenty-one and in love, only to find that he merely wanted a few nights in bed. More recently she had entrusted a political corruption case to Bobby O'Neil and had learned a month after the case ended in an acquittal that Bobby had accepted a bribe to back off.

More than once Savannah wondered whether she was simply a poor judge of character. But she didn't want to believe that. She decided that there were times when she felt so strongly about things that she was blind to reality. In Matt's case, she'd been in love, which was enough to warp any young woman's judgment. In Bobby's case, she had seen a brilliant legal mind and had been so eager to put it to use that she had not been on the lookout for snags.

She supposed she was an eternal optimist. Her only alternative was to go through life expecting the worst. That was too depressing.

Dropping her arms, she leaned toward the briefcase that lay open on the desk and removed the pad of paper she used when she had talked with Will earlier. Chewing on her lower lip, she studied the words written there: KICK IN A COOL THREE MILLION.

Over and over she read the phrase. Closing her eyes, she pictured the original, recalling the message in its entirety. As a ransom note, it got its point across, but why those words:? *Kick in a cool three million. Kick in a cool three million.*

Kickin' off a cool country streak . . .

Kick in a cool three million.

Kickin' back to an oldie . . .

Kick in a cool three million.

Kickin' in at twelve twenty-two . . .

Lots of people listened to Jared Snow. He had been holding down the twelve-to-six shift at CIC for two years, during which time he had no doubt built a sizable following. Lots of people listened, people like her who either didn't want to sleep, didn't need to sleep, or couldn't sleep.

Kick in a cool three million.

Kickin' off a cool country streak . . .

The similarity had to be a coincidence.

Pushing the pad and pencil away, she retrieved the small recorder, rewound it to find her place, then resumed dictation. The music played softly in the background. If Savannah had felt it would carry onto the recorder, she would simply have lowered the volume. She wouldn't have turned it off. Jared Snow was too good to miss.

After finishing that memorandum, she dictated two letters for her secretary to type the next day. In the middle of the second one, Jared spoke to her again.

"That was Gary Morris, harmonizing with Crystal Gayle and I'm Jared Snow," he drawled, *"sittin' with you in the heart of the night. Don't touch that dial. It's set at 95.3 FM, WCIC Providence, all day, every day, your best bet for a little country in the city . . ."*

His voice faded as the music began, but she held its memory inside her far longer.

He was tall and dark, she decided. Rakish, rather than suave. He had the lazy smile she associated with his voice, and more often than not it was crooked. She imagined broad shoulders, a tapering torso, long legs. He wore form-fitting sweaters with nothing underneath, and jeans that fit like a glove, leaving no doubt as to his sex.

With a soft moan of dismay, Savannah snatched up the recorder, and inhaled, ready to speak. The breath silently seeped out. She had no idea where she had left off. Lips tight, she rewound the tape, listened for a minute, then finished the letter. She managed to quickly dictate another one before Jared returned.

"Ronnie Milsap. 'Where Do the Nights Go.' I spent some time with Ronnie not long ago. Nice guy. Nice song."

Savannah had been concentrating on her work, so she had not heard the song, but if Jared said it, it had to be so. Threading her fingers into her hair, she began to loosen the pins that had kept it in a neat twist since morning.

"I've got lots more coming up for you from the home of cool country sounds, 95.3 FM, WCIC Providence, starting

with one of the sweetest I've heard in a while, a new one from Dolly Parton. . . ."

Dolly started singing, and Savannah's hands went still in her hair. She disliked Dolly Parton. She wasn't sure why. Dolly sang nicely enough, beautifully, in fact. But she was too short, too blonde, too busty. Jared had called her song one of the sweetest he had heard in a while. Maybe that was what bothered Savannah. Maybe she was jealous.

"For God's sake," she muttered and removed the hairpins with a vengeance. When they were in a neat pile on the desk, she ran her fingers through her long brown hair to relieve the little kinks that had set in. Then, tossing the mane over her shoulder, she picked up the recorder again. But she was feeling restless, not at all like working. A hot bath and a cup of warm milk sounded nice.

Neither one hit the spot. No sooner had she sunk into the tub than she began to think about Megan. After no more than five minutes in the water, she climbed out, toweled herself dry and, drawing on a soft cotton nightgown, went for the milk. It left an unpleasant taste in her mouth.

So she climbed into bed, set the radio to play for an hour, drew the covers to her chin, and waited for Jared Snow to speak. She didn't have long to wait.

"It's one-twenty," he told her in the gently raspy tone that caressed her mind, *"twenty minutes after one in the Ocean State. The WCIC forecast calls for clearing by morning, but I can still hear the rain on my roof. Don't go out if you can help it, it's a raw thirty-nine degrees, a perfect night to curl up with a blanket, a glass of wine, a special someone. I'm Jared Snow. In the heart of the night you're tuned to WCIC, 95.3 FM. Still got more than four hours of the smoothest of*

country sounds. Stay with me while I kick in a cool cut from Conway Twitty. . . ."

With the start of the music, Savannah rolled to her side. WCIC. Kick. It was a natural. Jared Snow was not the only disc jockey to link the words. She had heard Joseph Allan Johnson do it. And Melissa Stuart. It was obviously part of the station's logo, like "cool country" and "a little country in the city."

Kick in a cool three million.

Kick in a cool cut . . .

Coincidence. That was all.

Still, she wondered. She thought about work, too, as she lay there. Had she properly prepared one of the witnesses for the arson trial? Would the upcoming fund-raiser for Paul be another small stepping stone toward the governor's office. She wondered about turning thirty-one on Saturday and whether she could have a baby at forty-one. Most of all, she thought about Megan.

She planned what she would do the next day, mentally shifting her schedule around to allow time with Will. She even climbed out of bed once to jot down a note of two appointments her secretary could postpone. Then she returned to bed, huddled beneath the covers listening to the rain, and waited for Jared Snow's voice.

The last thing she remembered was his telling her that it was coming up on two-thirty and he was kickin' off another string of six.

The taut and silent faces that met Savannah in the Vandermeer kitchen at eight the next morning told her that there was no news.

Sam joined her for a quiet meeting in the hall. "I just talked with Chris," he said, "and they haven't found a thing. No cash purchases of vans, no shady types checking into local hotels. If I didn't know better, I'd think Providence County had gone pure overnight."

"Not quite," she remarked dryly. "Did you give Chris the names of Will's managers?"

Sam nodded. "They'll split up, Ginny and him, so they can hit all three this morning." He glanced at his watch. "I'll give the lab a little longer, but I doubt they'll come up with anything useful. This was a clean job, Savvy."

"I hate clean jobs. They mean that our quarry is smart."

"Depressing, but true."

She nodded toward Will, who stood at the kitchen window. "Did he sleep?"

"For an hour or two. No more. He's pretty edgy."

"No wonder. How about you? Get much sleep?"

"Enough."

"Was Susan okay?"

"Not bad."

"What does that mean?"

"She decided to bake a cake at one this morning."

"That's nice."

"A rum cake," Sam said, then his eyes narrowed on Savannah. "Does she always drink, or is it the situation?"

"Both, I suppose."

"You suppose? She's your sister. Don't you know?"

"I'm not her keeper," Savannah said a bit sharply, then quickly gentled her tone. "I try to do more, but she denies there's a problem." She shrugged. "Maybe there isn't."

Sam said nothing.

"Is she still sleeping?"

"I guess so. She hasn't been down yet." His gaze shifted. "I take that back. Here she comes."

Savannah turned to find Susan approaching. She was wearing a pair of tight jeans with an oversized sweatshirt emblazoned with rhinestones that made her face look pale. Her hair had been hastily drawn into a loose, voluminous pony tail. She wore socks but no shoes. Savannah guessed she had just woken up.

"I heard the bell," she said in a groggy voice. Hesitantly, even a bit painfully, she looked from Savannah to Sam. "Anything new?"

He shook his head in silence. He was intently studying her face.

Uncomfortable with that, she turned to Savannah. "So we just wait?"

Savannah nodded.

"Will you stay here?"

"I'll be back and forth to the office. I've got a couple of appointments I can't change, and, anyway, there are a load of phone calls I can more easily make from there."

Susan accepted that. She looked too tired and worried to argue. Stuffing her hands in the pockets of her jeans, she said, "It's spooky here. Megan's everywhere. I kept waking up, thinking about her."

"So did I, and I was across town."

"Is it better or worse the longer they keep her?"

"I don't know," Savannah said. She looked questioningly at Sam, but he couldn't help her out.

"A kidnapping is a kidnapping," he said. "She's been gone for little over a day. We have to assume it'll be at least two or three before she's back. If the exchange hasn't been made by next week, ask me again."

Susan shot him a look of annoyance.

"What did I do?" he asked.

"You could have been a little more encouraging."

"You want me to lie?"

She faced him head-on. "At this hour, and with the night I just had, yes."

"You look pretty good."

"That's a bald-faced lie. I look like death warmed over."

"No," he insisted. "You look good. I like you without makeup." Barely pausing, he said, "How about some breakfast?"

She made a face. "How can you think of eating at a time like this?"

"I'm hungry. Dinner was a long time ago, and delicious as that rum cake was—"

"I thought I said to lie." She turned to Savannah and said in a prim voice, "The cake fell. I don't know what happened to it. I've never had that experience before in my life."

Savannah wasn't about to ask how many rum cakes Susan had made before. She suspected about as many as she had made herself, which was none. She could understand the attempt, though. Doing something would be better than doing nothing, and since the cupboards were full, why not? "Maybe something's wrong with the oven," she suggested.

Sam smirked.

Susan frowned.

Sensing she'd better quit while she was ahead, Savannah said, "I'm on my way to the office. I'll talk with you later."

The news at the office was no more encouraging. "Nothing from the lab," Savannah told Paul when he stopped by shortly after nine. "Nothing from Ginny and Chris. Nothing from the people we put on the phones. And as if that weren't bad enough, the Cat struck again."

"What does the Cat have to do with this case?"

"Not a thing. Just thought you'd like to know."

"What did he get this time?"

"Oh, roughly a hundred thousand in jewelry, silver, and art from the Monroe house in Cranston."

"Are they sure it was the Cat?"

"Who else helps himself and leaves without a trace?"

"Have they questioned Stavanovich?"

"Can't find him."

"Swell. This is getting embarrassing, Savvy."

"Mmmm." She inhaled an exaggerated breath. "Anyway, I've sent Hank out to cruise around. He's got one or two informants who will let him know if they've seen or heard anything about Megan. I even have someone in Corrections looking to see who of our dear friends has been released from prison lately. Beyond that, I don't know what to do."

Paul was totally composed, more so than any other person she had seen that day. But then, Paul was always composed. Part of it was the image he upheld, part was his experience, and part was the fact that, as attorney general, he was detached from the nitty-gritty details of things. He rarely bloodied his hands in the arena. He had assistants to do that, assistants like Savannah.

"There's nothing to do but wait," he said.

"It's hard."

"That's because you're a doer and doers don't usually wait. But we have no choice, Savannah. If we move too far, too fast, or too freely, we're apt to blow this case. Neither of us wants to do that."

She knew he was right, though she was uneasy with his pointed warning. Paul was, she knew, a political creature, while she was a humanitarian one. One of the reasons their relationship worked so well was that they tempered each other.

In this situation, however, Savannah didn't want to be tempered. Megan was her friend. The political ramifications of the case didn't concern her at all.

"I feel like I'm blowing it by sitting here doing nothing," she complained. "I wish Will would let us go to the FBI."

"I doubt they'd do more than you've already done."

"Maybe not," she mused. Still, the weight of responsibility was on her shoulders, and it was awesome.

Paul left. Savannah took several phone calls and made several others concerning her upcoming trial. She met with one of the lawyers to discuss preparation of a rebuttal to pretrial motions for an extortion case that was on the docket for a month later. She phoned the Vandermeer house, but nothing had happened.

Frustrated, she called information for the number of WCIC. She jotted it on her pad, stared at it for several minutes, picked up the phone call, then put the receiver down.

Coincidence. There couldn't be a connection. Or if there was, she had already taken care of it. That was why she had phoned the Department of Corrections earlier. The idea that one or more of Megan's abductors had spent time in Rhode Island correctional facilities, where they might have listened to and been inspired by WCIC, was a shot in the dark, but those shots seemed the only ones she could take.

Temporarily satisfied, she stashed several extra pads of paper into her briefcase and went to the law library. She could be reached there if anything happened, and in the meanwhile, she would be doing research.

By one in the afternoon, though, she was back in her office. Again she lifted the phone to call WCIC. Again she replaced the receiver without pushing a button. Then she took several incoming calls and an hour later she drove to the Vandermeer house. She already knew that nothing had happened, but she wanted to stop in, if only for a short time.

While she was there, Hank returned, but his informants had had nothing to say. "Either they really know nothing, or whoever is involved is so big that they're terrified."

Savannah chose to believe the first, since the second was truly frightening. "Who's big?" she asked. "Why would someone big get involved in a kidnapping?"

Neither Hank nor Sam had answers for her, and Sam had worse news to report. "We won't get any help from his managers. They haven't seen a thing."

"We're really striking out," Savannah murmured and turned toward Will. Exhausted, he had taken to sitting rigidly on the living room sofa with the phone by his side. "How're you doing?" she asked gently as she slipped down beside him.

He eyed her hollowly. "It's my fault. If I'd had the alarm system fixed, this wouldn't have happened."

"You don't know that."

"I do. It's my fault."

"Come on, Will, " she coaxed, "even if the alarm system had been working perfectly, any system can be disengaged if the kidnappers know what they're doing, and Megan's kidnappers knew what they were doing." She frowned.

Sam verbalized her thought. "But they didn't know the system was broken. They should have tried to disengage it."

He looked at Hank. "You check downstairs. I'll look outside.

They disappeared.

Susan, who had been standing on the far side of the room with her arms wrapped tightly around her middle, called, "Savannah? Can I talk with you for a minute?" As soon as Savannah had joined her, she murmured, "This isn't going to work. I'm not doing a bit of good here."

"Sure, you are."

"I cook. That's it."

"You soften things up just by being here. It's a woman's touch."

"I'm not helping Will. He's a zombie. The main thing I'm doing is arguing with Sam."

"Why does he bother you so?"

"I don't know, but he does."

"I've always liked him."

Susan frowned and dropped her gaze. Focusing on one glossy pink fingernail, she asked, "Are you interested in him?"

"Interested? Sure. Sammy and I have been through a lot together. I care about him."

"Do you date him?"

"No."

"Have you ever?"

"No."

"But you invited him to the party at the house last year."

"Him and about sixty of my other friends and colleagues."

Susan looked up. "You've never slept with him?"

"If I've never dated him, how could I have slept with him?"

Susan looked back down at her nail. "You said it your-self, you've been through a lot together. Sometimes things just . . . happen. You could be working on a case late at night, you're both tired and tense, you need an outlet."

"Sammy and I have never used each other that way."

"You're sure?"

Savannah gave a soft laugh. "Of course, I'm sure. Susan, what is this? I'd tell you if I had a thing for the man, but I don't. I think he's intelligent and sensitive and very attrac-tive, but he doesn't turn me on that way. And I don't turn him on that way. Neither of us is suffering. Believe me."

Susan was quiet for a minute. Then she said, "So you think he's attractive?"

"Yes."

"Even with that hair?"

Savannah nodded. "He's an individual. I respect that." She paused. Susan was looking sadly across the room. "What is it, Suse?"

But Susan didn't answer. She stared at that distant wall, then shook her head and shrugged. Before Savannah could pursue it, Sam and Hank returned. They said nothing until they reached her side.

"It hasn't been touched," Hank murmured. "Not from the inside or the outside."

Savannah shot a glance at Will, who had heard what Hank said and was looking more miserable than ever. He was right, after all. Since the kidnappers had been unaware of the alarm, if it had been on, the kidnapping might have been thwarted.

Unless they'd already known that the system was broken.

Sam, who was thinking the same thing, reached Will

first. "When the system went on the blink, did you report it?"

Will looked up blankly.

"It's important that we know," Savannah said, joining Sam. "If you reported it broken, someone with the alarm company had valuable information to pass on, particularly if that someone knew you hadn't fixed it."

Will rallied enough to say, "I called. But I got estimates on repairs from three different companies. No one of them had any reason to assume I didn't hire one of the others to fix the system."

Savannah, Sam, and Hank gave simultaneous grunts of frustration.

Susan wailed, "What are they *waiting* for?"

Sam went to her side and cocked his head toward the door. "Let's take a walk."

"It's cold out."

"Put on your fur. You'll stay warm."

"I'd rather stay here."

"I need fresh air. I could use some company."

"Take Hank."

"Hank's staying with Will."

"So should we."

"No," Sam said with a patient sigh, "we shouldn't. We should work off a little of the tension that's driving you nuts."

Susan stood straighter. "Nothing's driving me nuts. I'm just fine."

"Then, do it for me. Please, Susan?"

Savannah gave a weary sigh. "For God's sake, Susan, go!"

"Do you trust him not to rape me in the bushes?"

Taking a step forward, Sam took Susan's chin in his hand. "Lady," he growled, "the day I resort to rape in the bushes . . ." His voice trailed off. His thumb crept over the curve of her chin. Eyes holding hers, he dropped his hand and said softly, "Are you coming?"

Savannah didn't wait for Susan's reply. Giving Will's shoulder a squeeze, she walked past. "I'm going back to the office. See you soon."

"WCIC Providence, may I help you?"

Savannah started to talk, then cleared her throat to make the sound audible. "Yes. I'd like to speak with Jared Snow, please."

"I'm sorry, but Mr. Snow isn't here at the moment. May I ask who's calling?"

She twisted the telephone cord around her finger. "Is there another number where he can be reached?"

"That number is unlisted."

"I'm calling on official business," she declared. "It's imperative that I speak with Mr. Snow as soon as possible."

"If you leave a name and number, I'll see that he gets it."

With no promise that the call would be returned. "That's not good enough," she argued. "This is important."

"Your name, please."

Savannah held her breath. Closing her eyes, she realized that she must have sounded exactly like one of numerous other fans who no doubt phoned the radio station each week in search of Jared Snow. Her cheeks went pink. The hand that tightly gripped the telephone receiver very carefully replaced it in its cradle.

Mortified, she sat down behind her desk, bowed her head, and pressed a fingertip to her lips. It was a while before she regained enough composure to resume work.

"WCIC Providence, may I help you?"

The voice was different this time, as Savannah had hoped it would be. The first time she'd called at four in the afternoon. Now it was seven. She had counted on the daytime receptionist having been replaced by the evening one.

"Yes," she said with renewed confidence, "I'd like to speak with Jared Snow."

"I'm sorry, Mr. Snow isn't able to take the phone."

"Is he there?"

"May I ask who's calling?"

She wasn't sure what she'd expected. One part of her had known that it wouldn't be easy. The other part had dreamed. "I'm calling on an important matter," she said calmly. "If you would be so kind as to tell me when I might reach Mr. Snow, I'd be glad to call back."

"It would probably be better if you gave me your name and number. I'd be sure to see that he received them."

Determined to maintain her composure this time, Savannah said in the same cool and official-sounding voice, "I really do have to talk with him."

There was barely a pause on the other end. "I'm sure you do. If you'd give me your name and number—"

"The situation is urgent."

"Does Mr. Snow know you?"

"No, but he may have some information I need. This could well be a matter of life and death."

"Your name and number?"

She nearly gave it. No one at the station knew about the kidnapping. She wouldn't be endangering Megan by identifying herself. But something held her back. One part of her wasn't sure she should be calling at all. That part wasn't sure of her reasons for calling.

"Hello?" came the voice at the other end of the line.

Savannah quietly hung up the phone. Sinking lower in her chair, she propped her elbow on its arm and pressed her cheek to her fist. She actually looked at her door to make sure it was completely shut. She wouldn't have wanted anyone in the office to have witnessed that call. Or the earlier one. Timidity was not part of the image she tried to uphold. For that matter, even privately she didn't like to think of herself as being timid. But the lines were blurred here.

One part of her was unsure about calling. The rest of her desperately wanted to speak with Jared Snow.

She didn't try to phone again. Instead, she kept busy at the office, then stopped at the house to see how Will and the others were doing. No one there was happy with the silence, and as each hour passed, the tension rose.

Though Savannah had had the benefit of distractions through the day, she felt as anxious as everyone else. Despite all her attempts to find clues as to either the identity of the kidnappers or their whereabouts, she had come up empty-handed. She felt she had let Will down. She felt she had let Megan down. She felt she'd let Susan and Sam and Hank down.

Discouraged, she stayed with them as long as she could, then drove home. It was nearly eleven o'clock when she pulled into her garage, but rather than leave the car and go into the townhouse, she sat in the dark and thought.

She didn't want to go inside. It was too quiet and lonely there. She had work to do, but she felt too emotionally spent to do it.

Nor did she want to go back to Will's. Sam had a handle on things there. She felt useless.

Friends. She had lots of friends. But she could hardly be with them and not tell them about Megan.

For a minute she considered driving to Newport to see her father—but only for a minute. It wasn't a wise idea. For one thing, her dad would either be out for the evening or asleep, and he wasn't one to take kindly to a change in plans. For another, he had never particularly approved of her going to work, let alone her choice of profession. He would have little sympathy for the oppressive sense of responsibility she felt. And he was a terrible gossip. If she told him about the kidnapping, it would be all over Newport by morning.

She gripped the steering wheel tightly, backed the car out of the garage, and headed for the WCIC studios.

The address she had taken from her media file took her to a largely wooded, residential area on the outskirts of town where the houses were set widely apart, hidden from one another and the street by trees. Only the mailboxes stood as proof of habitation nearby.

Turning in by the mailbox whose luminescent number matched the one she had committed to memory, she drove down a short, unpaved path to a clearing. At the back of the clearing stood a large Victorian house. The night hid its details from her, but there were several cars parked around a pebbled curve and the first floor of the house was comfortably lit. She assumed she had reached the right place.

Turning off her own lights, she sat for a minute and took several slow breaths to calm the rushing beat of her heart. It seemed imperative that she look, sound, and act totally professional.

She felt, however, like a young girl excitedly awaiting a glimpse of her hero. Incredibly, the thing that frightened her most was not that he wouldn't be able to help Megan, but that he wouldn't live up to the image she had of him.

For a moment she toyed with the idea of starting the car and driving home. It still bothered her that she had been so cowardly with not one, but two phone calls. For her own pride, if nothing else, she intended to see this through.

Snatching her keys from the ignition, she buried them in her briefcase, laced the straps of the briefcase over her shoulder, and climbed from the car. The pebbles crunched beneath her heels, a sound so loud that she half expected floodlights to suddenly shoot out and spear her in the night. Pulling her cashmere topcoat more snugly around her neck, she hastened her step toward the front door.

The only indication that she had, indeed, found the right place was a small brass plate over the doorbell that bore the station's call letters. She rang the bell. Its sound came faintly through the door, a sweet long-winded chime. Looking down, she waited. Then she heard the muted sound of rapid footsteps. Her heartbeat accelerated accordingly.

The door was flung open, and a young woman started talking to her before she could fully see her. "It's about time! My God, we're starved!" she said. Savannah vaguely recognized her voice, although her rather plain features were not familiar. Her expectant expression quickly changed. "You're not the pizza house."

"No," Savannah said.

"Oh dear." The young woman looked to be in her mid-twenties. She was of average height, weight and build, and wore a jogging suit designed for exercise rather than the fashionable sort Susan wore. Savannah identified the voice.

"You're Melissa Stuart, aren't you?"

Melissa smiled. "You listen."

"When I can."

"And you're here for Jared. Quick, come on in. I'm supposed to be in the booth monitoring things."

Savannah stepped into the front hall. It was a large hexagonal room whose outstanding feature was a winding staircase that led to the second floor. Three doorways led to the center of the house. Melissa disappeared through one, leaving Savannah to wonder how she had known she was there to see Jared.

Her palms felt damp inside her gloves, so she removed them and held them in one hand. She felt trapped, and wished she could turn and run, but it was too late for that. She glanced helplessly around. A pair of lamps on a console table cast a gentle light in the hall. The floor was made of newly polished oak. The walls were clean, uncracked, and painted an almond shade. Savannah was surprised by the contemporary prints adorning the wall and the built-in speakers that played, at a just-audible volume, the station's country sound. In fact, the only concessions to the Victorian style were the delicately carved ballistrade and the patterned runner that climbed the stairs.

With another quick look around, Savannah realized that either the house had been thoroughly renovated within the last year or two, or it had been newly built not long before that. She was trying to decide whether that was relevant to anything when a man appeared at the door through which Melissa had gone.

He was exceedingly tall, exceedingly thin, exceedingly intense. The oxford-cloth shirt that hung on his upper body was tucked into a pair of chinos that fit better than the shirt, but in so doing only emphasized his thinness. She searched his face for the warmth she heard night after night, but his features were nearly as angular as his body.

Savannah wouldn't have called him handsome by any stretch of the imagination, and there was nothing remotely sexy about him. Her heart fell farther than she thought it could.

Then he said, "Hi," and her spirits bounced back up. His voice was deep but not as smooth or as breathtaking as the one she knew. "You're here to see Jared?"

She nodded.

"He wasn't expecting anyone."

"I know. But it's important that I see him."

"You look familiar."

She shrugged.

"Who are you?" he asked.

There was no way to get out of it this time. "Savannah Smith. I'm with the attorney general's office."

"What's he done?"

She gave a small smile. "Nothing. It's what he may be able to do that's brought me here."

"Mysterious," the man said. His tone was civil enough, but it had an edge. He made Savannah feel as though she were under investigation, which was a new and not terribly pleasing experience, particularly since she was, indeed, feeling guilty.

"Is Mr. Snow around?"

"He'd better be, since he's supposed to go on the air pretty soon."

"May I see him?"

"I'll have to—"

The doorbell rang.

For the first time the man's eyes came alive. "Here they are." He started toward her, or more accurately, since he seemed to have momentarily deemed her inconsequential, toward the door. "It's about time," he muttered. "We called in that order more than an hour ago." Pulling the door open, he reached into his pocket, drew out several bills, and plastered them into the hand of the delivery boy in exchange for two large pizza boxes. After elbowing the door shut, he made for the doorway through which he'd first come.

"Uh, excuse me?" Savannah called.

"Hold on," he said and disappeared.

She couldn't believe she was left alone. She wondered whether this was standard security procedure. If so, it was crazy. For all they knew, she could be a deranged killer, set to gun down the man who had driven her crazy night after night.

Of course, few deranged killers would be dressed as she was in imported leather heels, a full-length cashmere topcoat, and gloves of the finest kidskin. Then again, any number of interesting weapons could be concealed in her briefcase.

With no idea when the tall, skinny man would return, and too uneasy to stand still, she wandered across the hall toward the desk that stood by one of the doors. It was a receptionist's desk, tidied up for the night. Her eyes fell on the telephone with its panel of buttons, and, remembering the calls she'd made earlier that day, she felt a glimmer of color rise to her cheeks.

Averting her gaze, she looked into the room the desk guarded. It was the parlor, no doubt a waiting room in which visitors sat before being fetched. Savannah had heard enough of the daytime programming to know that the DJs frequently interviewed guests who were affiliated with the country music scene or, on occasion, with the state.

At night it was different. Jared Snow never interviewed anyone. He didn't need a diversion, nor did his listeners. His voice and his music were more than enough.

For a minute she listened to the music that was barely an echo in the background. Then, taking in a long, shaky breath, she walked into the room. She trailed a finger along the back of a Victorian settee, then along the edge of a modern marble piece. The combination was unusual. Looking around, she saw similar groupings. While the modern pieces were in sedate colors, the period pieces were made of distinctly modern fabrics. It was, she realized, a decorator's twist on "a little country in the city."

"Do you like it?" asked a voice from the door. It was deep, faintly raspy, as familiar to her as the cracks on the ceiling above her bed.

Aside from her pulse, which beat at a rapid tattoo, Savannah went still all over. Her back was to him. She didn't know if she wanted to turn. His voice was so warm, so rich and wonderful. If the rest of him was not as warm and rich and wonderful, she would be shattered.

So she prepared herself for the worst. In a split second's pause, she imagined that he was an inch shorter than she, twelve inches wider, bespectacled and balding.

Only then did she turn.

Chapter 6

HE STOOD AT THE DOOR with his right shoulder braced lightly against the frame. One of his hands was anchored in the front pocket of his jeans, the other hung loosely by his side. His legs were long and planted casually on the oak planks underfoot, but it was not the floor that commanded Savannah's attention. Nor was it his pale blue T-shirt, or the flannel shirt that lay open over it, or his soft, snug jeans. The entire man took her breath away—his sandy-colored hair, rough-hewn features, broad shoulders, trim waist, and lean hips.

Jared Snow in person was every bit as magnificent as the voice that seduced her each night.

Her relief was so great that tears actually came to her eyes. But she held herself erect and steadily met the gaze that sought hers.

"Do you like it?" he asked again.

Most definitely, she thought, although she knew he had been referring to the room. "It's interesting," she answered quietly. "I think it goes with the station."

"You listen?"

With a tentative smile, she nodded. When his gaze

dropped to that smile, her pulse tripped. She felt touched. The sensation was so vivid that it frightened her.

"Not many fans come around this late at night," he said slowly. "They figure I'll have dogs patrolling the grounds." His eyes rose to hers. "Melissa and Rick thought I'd made a date for the show."

She smiled again, wistfully this time. Much as she might have liked it, she wasn't his date. "Not quite."

His mouth twitched against a smile of his own. "I'd pretend, if you would."

She was melting. "I couldn't really. I'm here on business."

"At this hour?"

She nodded.

He looked her up and down once, then studied her face, feature by feature. "You do look businesslike," he admitted, "except for your face."

Unsure of what to make of his comment, she didn't say anything. For if he was interested in her features, she was positively intrigued by his. His straight hair was a heathery shade just slightly darker than blond. It slanted across his forehead, swept back to cover the tops of his ears, then curved down to his collar. Just a tad longer than the current style, it was unique without being extreme. She liked it.

She also liked his jaw, which was shadowed and firm, and his chin, which was gently squared with a hint of a groove at its center. She liked the straight, strong lines of his mouth and the chiseled cut of his nose. And she liked his pale blue eyes which were accented by his sandy coloring much like a clear sky over a beach. He was refreshing to look at.

"Your face," he went on in a husky tone, "isn't businesslike at all."

With a single hard swallow and a blink to combat the spell she felt herself under, she said, "That must be because I'm tired. It's been a long day."

"Then why are you here so late on business?"

"Because I wasn't sure when else to reach you. I knew you'd be doing your show at twelve. I was prepared to wait."

"Must be important business."

"It is," she said, though for the life of her she didn't feel any urgency at the moment. Jared Snow was a powerful presence. He excited her, separated her from all she had been. At the same time, he brought her an odd sense of peace.

"Rick says you're with the attorney general's office. Are you a lawyer?"

She nodded. "With the criminal division."

He arched a brow. "And you want to see me?"

Again, she nodded. She knew she should tell him about Megan and ask if he knew of any possible link to the radio station. But she wasn't ready to formally discuss business with him yet.

And Jared seemed content to wait. "Then you're a trial lawyer?"

"Uh-huh."

"Any specialty within the specialty?"

"I take whatever comes in. Since I've been at the AG's office—"

"How long is that?"

"Five years. Since I've been there, I've prosecuted everything from larceny to murder and rape."

He looked puzzled. When she returned his puzzled look, he explained, "You don't look like the type to try a murder case. You don't look hard enough."

A staunch feminist would have bristled at his remark. But Savannah wasn't a feminist. She did what she did, not to best the men of the world but because of a driving need to excel at whatever she tried.

But he was right. She wasn't tough enough emotionally despite her ability to function successfully in all outward appearances. She wondered exactly how revealing her face was just then.

"Let's just say," she said and drew herself up to compensate for whatever weaknesses her expression might betray, "that I rise to the occasion. Of the seven murder cases I've tried, I've won convictions in five."

"Not bad."

"Granted, part of that is making sure that the case is solid before we go ahead with it. There have been times when I've been pressured to go to trial with a very weak case."

"How do you handle that?"

"I plea-bargain."

His eyes held faint censure. "That's a lousy practice."

"It's better than nothing. If my case is shaky against a murderer and I go to trial and lose, he walks the streets. If I plea-bargain, he goes to prison—maybe not for as long as I'd like, but for a short time, at least, the public is safe."

Jared studied her quietly for a minute. "You've thought it out."

"I've had to."

"Have you been put on the hot seat?"

"On occasion."

"By the press?"

"The press, friends, family . . ."

He seemed surprised. "I'd have guessed you come from a long line of lawyers."

"Why?"

He was silent for a moment, then shrugged and moved on. "So you don't?"

Her mouth twitched at one corner. "Not quite."

"Hey, Jared?" came a call from every corner of the room. It was a second or two before Savannah realized that it came through the speakers. By then, Rick was saying, "Pizza's getting cold, and you're on soon."

Jared, who hadn't so much as blinked at the intrusion, said a quiet, "Be right there." His eyes held Savannah's, and for a minute he said nothing. Then, effortlessly leaving the door frame, he walked toward her. With each step, he seemed to grow taller and more real. When he stood before her, a solid six-foot-two to her five-foot-five, she felt a soft humming inside.

"Rick said your name was Susannah?"

"Savannah Smith."

"Savannah." He experimented with its sound in a voice that was low and gritty. "Savannah. Interesting name. Roots in the South?"

She nodded. "My mom was born there."

His eyes twinkled. Actually, she realized, one eye did most of the twinkling. The other had a slight cast to it, which, if anything, only enhanced his appeal as he asked, "Is she a southern belle?"

"She was. She's dead now."

"I'm sorry."

"It's okay. She died when we were twelve."

"We?"

"My sister and I."

"Twins?" he asked, grinning at that.

If his nearness had made her body hum, his grin turned that hum into deep vibrations. Her voice came a little higher. "Uh-huh. Fraternal. Very different."

"Jared?" It was Melissa this time, interrupting the music with her own singsong call. "We need you, Jared. If you're gonna take over at twelve, you gotta get in here."

The eyes that had been holding Savannah's didn't waver. "I have to go," he said quietly. "It's nearly showtime."

"What about your pizza?"

"I'll eat it between songs. What about your business?"

"My business?" Her expression changed. "Oh God, I need a minute of your time."

He smiled. "You've already had a couple."

"But you've been asking me questions. If you hadn't done that, I'd have gotten to my questions sooner."

"Mine were important. I wouldn't have answered any of yours without knowing a little about you."

"Why not? I'm here as an agent of the state."

"I don't know that for sure. I haven't seen any identification."

Opening the side compartment of her briefcase, she quickly took out her wallet, extracted her office ID, and handed it over.

He studied it for a minute, then said, "This is a lousy picture. How about a license?"

Without a word, she gave it to him.

He studied that for a longer minute. Then he passed both cards back. "I guess you're legitimate, but I do have to go." He said the last with a glance at his watch. It was a flat, black watch rimmed in gold, with a black leather strap that circled his wrist. Savannah found herself looking, not so much at the watch as at his wrist. It was sinewy, lean but strong, with a fine sprinkling of tawny hair. It was very different from her own.

· Too soon, the wrist moved away, along with the rest of the man. Savannah was horrified.

"Mr. Snow?" She started after him. "Jared?" His stride was longer than hers, and he had a head start. Quickening her step, she called, "I won't take long. It's still five before midnight."

He was halfway through the front hall. "I have to go over the program log. I should have done it already."

"Two minutes."

"And rack the carts."

"One minute."

He'd reached the doorway. Without either looking back or stopping, he shook his head. "No time," he murmured.

"But it's important!"

Her words hung in empty air. Jared had vanished through a door at the end of the hallway. She was left alone again, and in the same spot.

"Fool," she muttered in dismay as she whirled around and pressed her elbows tightly to her sides. She had come on business, and she'd blown it. She had wasted precious time drooling over Jared Snow, while Megan was being held for ransom. Thinking about her great expectations, she realized the gravity of her failure.

But then, she reasoned in a moment of pique, Jared had to share some of the blame. She had told him that she was there on business. More so than she, he had known how much time he had and when he would be needed. If he were a gentleman, he would have let her speak instead of distracting her with his sexy eyes. If he were a responsible citizen, he would have put her official business before his. She would have thought he'd do better than to waste her time.

"Hey."

She looked up, but the sound hadn't come from a speaker, so she glanced over her shoulder. Jared stood in the middle of the hallway. His weight was shifted to one hip, his arms hung loosely by his sides. Though the stance was as casual as ever, a small frown marred his brow. He looked a little annoyed, a little impatient. But when he gestured her forward with a flick of his wrist, she went.

Well before she reached him, he turned and started down the hall. She followed. "If you wait until I get myself straightened out with the show," he tossed back, "I'll answer your questions."

"Okay. That's fine," she said, trying to sound as cool as he, although she felt suddenly light-headed.

At the end of the hall he turned to the right, into a room that held two desks, a row of file cabinets and, on one wall, floor to ceiling shelves lined with tapes. The desks were covered with papers, pizza, and Rick. The file cabinets were littered with colored labels, the spines of the tape cases with identifying data written in black.

But Savannah looked past all that to the glassed-in room beyond. She had been in radio stations before, doing her share of programs as a spokesperson for the AG's office, so she knew she was looking at the sound booth. Melissa was there, sitting at a bank of controls with her headphones in place. She had one hand on the mike button, the other on a vertical slide as her voice came through the speakers.

". . . glad you could join us. We'll be tapping into the news at the top of the hour, then Jared Snow will be here for your pleasure. I'll see y'again tomorrow evening at six. Melissa Stuart for 95.3 FM, WCIC Providence, kickin' in for the night with Holly Dunn . . . ."

With the release of the mike button and a shift of the slide, her voice gave way to music. After flicking another switch, she removed the headphones, grabbed a pile of notes she had nearby, and headed for the door.

Jared was already moving to take her place, carrying an armload of carts he'd scooped from a shelf. "Thanks, hon," he said, holding the door for her and then passing through it himself. It swung shut behind him. Making straight for the cart rack, he began removing tapes, tossing them into a pile, replacing them with those he'd brought in.

"Want some pizza?" Melissa asked Savannah. "There's plenty of it. It may be getting cold, but it's good."

Taking her eyes away from Jared, Savannah smiled her thanks, but shook her head.

"Then at least take your coat off. You're staying, aren't you?"

Savannah shot another glance at Jared, who seemed oblivious to her presence, and sighed. "For a little while, I guess." Tucking her gloves in her pocket, she shrugged out of the coat and laid it on the desk chair nearby. She set her briefcase on top of the coat, but it promptly slid off. So she knelt to retrieve it, settled it more securely, then straightened to find Jared staring at her. Actually, he was staring at her legs, then her thighs, then her breasts. By the time his gaze reached her eyes, she was trembling inside, but before she could decide whether he was pleased with what he saw, he went back to his work.

Tucking her hands in the pockets of her hip-length knit blazer, which matched her navy knit dress, she waited.

Melissa, who had been stowing papers in a file cabinet, turned to Rick. "I'm set, babe. Want to go?"

Rick answered by drawing his lanky frame from the desktop on which he had been lounging, reaching for two bulky parkas that had been stashed in a large wire basket on the floor, and tossing Melissa hers. She pulled it on, then went to the glass and knocked. When Jared looked up, she waved. He acknowledged her departure with a nod and returned to his work.

Passing Savannah, she said, "Remind him to eat. He forgets sometimes." Then, with Rick close behind, she left.

Savannah felt something protective curl through her, and she looked more closely at Jared. He was lean, not thin. She could see the fine muscle tone in his thighs as he knelt before the cart rack. He was solidly built. He had substance.

Taking a deep breath, she looked up at the ceiling. From there, she looked at the walls, on which were tacked an assortment of posters, photographs, calendars, and notes. Then she looked at the telephone and thought of calls that came into the station. In the next breath she thought of Megan.

A small shudder of frustration and fear shook her. She told herself that Megan was a survivor, that she would be all right. But she had been gone for two days. Savannah didn't want to guess at how she was being treated, but in idle moments like these, she couldn't help but wonder.

Sensing the beginnings of a quaking inside, she turned anxiously back to Jared. The sight of him helped. He was calm and confident. Looking at him, she felt the same comfort that came with the sound of his voice on the radio.

But another voice spoke now. It was the news.

Jared met her gaze. Taking in her troubled expression, he went to the door. "Want to come in?"

She wanted that more than anything just then. Nodding, she joined him before he could change his mind. When the door to the booth was securely closed behind her, he took a seat at the control board, put the hcadphones around his neck, and faced her.

"We have three minutes before I'm on," he warned, but he didn't seem annoyed that she was there. Rather, he looked curious, even a little concerned.

She started talking. "Yesterday morning, the wife of a prominent Providence businessman was kidnapped. A ransom note was left, but there's been no follow-up and we've been over a good part of the county, looking." She wrapped her arms around her middle. "Right about now, we're stymied. So we're stretching our imagination."

"Do you want to sit down?" he asked.

She guessed that she looked pale. But she shook her head. "I'm okay."

"What can I do to help?"

His gentle tone was a help in itself, but she had more to ask. "The ransom note was strangely worded. It said, 'Kick in a cool three million.' I couldn't help but think of WCIC. The sound is the same."

"It's our thing. Country in the city. CIC. Kickin' in this, kickin' up that, kickin' back to something else."

"I know," she said, then stopped short.

"All my DJs use it, and I can personally vouch for each and every one. None of them would even remotely be involved in a kidnapping."

Though she said nothing, she looked awkward.

"But you were wondering whether we've gotten calls from any weirdos lately?"

She released a soft breath. She hadn't mentioned a word

about the station to Paul or Sammy or Hank for fear they would think she was nuts to check it out. But Jared's face held no ridicule.

"I keep telling myself," she confessed, "that the similarity of the wording is coincidence, but since we haven't found anything else, I'm desperate. *Have* you gotten any calls from weirdos lately?"

"We get them all the time."

"Oh."

"All stations do. You'd be amazed at the calls that come in. Some people are bored, so they call. Others are lonely or depressed. Then there are those who are either ornery or just plain crazy. Those are the ugly calls."

"Like . . . ?"

"Like the guy who calls Melissa and threatens rape in all kinds of explicit terms. Or the one who calls Joe with the same threat. Or the one who tells you he's got his girlfriend wired and he'll blow her to pieces if you play a certain song one more time. Some of the calls are more of a nuisance than anything else—like the lady who calls each day at eleven-thirty in morning to complain about something or other she just bought at the supermarket that was spoiled."

"Your DJs don't take those calls do they?"

"Sometimes. None of us takes calls on the air, but the daytime DJs push our phone number for the sake of requests, and if the music's on, they're not averse to speaking with a caller. It's great PR, and sometimes it's fun. The ladies who answer the main phone and switch calls in here are pretty good about sifting out the legits from the crazies." He shrugged. "Sometimes they miss." Holding up a finger, he swiveled to face the control panel and put the headphones on. Simultaneously sliding a vertical fader up and flipping the mike button, he began to speak.

"Welcome to cool country," he drawled in a voice that was low and husky, "95.3 FM, WCIC Providence. I'm Jared Snow, keepin' the home fires warm with you all the way to six in the morning. I'll be playing the best of contemporary country, kickin' off the overnight with a string of six from superstars like Randy Travis, Rosanne Cash, and Alabama.

"If you're worried about the weather," he glanced at a monitor to his left, "don't be. The CIC forecast calls for clearing skies by morning, with temps climbin' into the forties. It's a chilly thirty-five degrees outside our studios at twelve-oh-four in the A.M.," he punched a button on the console, "but we'll warm you up till dawn."

With each hand on a slide, he went on. "So keep it right here at 95.3 FM"—his eye was on a small clock counting the seconds as the introductory beat of the music began— "WCIC Providence, for a little country in the city. This is Jared Snow in the heart of the night, listen in. . . ."

With the shift of the slides, the sound rose to catch the first of Lee Greenwood's lyrics. Jared switched off the mike, slid the headphones to his neck, and turned to Savannah.

"That's incredible," she remarked. "You do it so easily."

He shrugged. "I've been doing it awhile."

"Two years here. Where before that?"

"Midwest. Northwest. I started in college." He snorted. "I really have been doing it awhile."

Savannah estimated that he was in his late thirties, which would give him eighteen or nineteen years' experience. "Do you own the station?"

For a minute he said nothing. Then he shrugged, which was as good as a yes.

"And others?"

His brow lowered. "Does the AG's office keep files?"

She smiled. "No. It's just gossip. Back home in Newport, gossip is big business." She pictured Newport, her father, then Susan, then Megan. Her smile faded, and she said quietly, almost apologetically, "That's all pretty petty, I guess."

Her tone seemed to soothe him. "I don't mind your questions. But they don't relate much to your case."

She inhaled a loud breath. "Right." Leaning back, she propped her hip on the edge of a slanted panel. Almost immediately, she jumped back up and, placing a hand on her chest in alarm, looked at the array of switches and buttons she feared she had disturbed.

"It's okay," Jared said, smiling. "You won't hurt anything there."

Curling her fingers into a fist against her chest, she lowered herself to the panel again.

"We were talking about the phones," he prompted in a gentle voice.

"There isn't anyone answering calls for you now."

"An answering service takes over at nine."

"What if there's an emergency and you have to be reached?"

"There's a private line." He gestured toward the telephone that was built into the wall within easy reach to the right of the control panel. "The light flashes. The people who have that private number know to let it ring until I've put the music on and can pick up and talk."

She nodded. "So you don't get any of the weird calls yourself."

"Not directly. The answering service takes note of them, though."

"Keeps a record?"

He nodded.

"Is that true of calls that come in during the day?"

"Yes and no. Requests go into the request book. We keep score of those. We get lots of hang-ups—people calling, asking for one DJ or another, then hanging up when he can't take the phone. We don't record those."

Savannah thought of the two calls she'd made herself and worked to keep her expression neutral. "But the others—the ugly ones?"

He nodded. "We've got them."

She felt in inkling of hope. "Can I see them?"

"There's not much to see. The phone isn't tapped, so its not like we have a transcript of tapes. All we've got is the notes of the person who answered the phone when the call came in. And that, only for the daytime. The records from the answering service are at their office. We don't have cause to collect them regularly. If there's anything unusual or particularly deadly, they tell us, but I haven't heard anything lately. I can guarantee you that we didn't get any calls about a kidnapping. I would have been notified."

She pushed her hands so deeply into her pockets that her arms went rigidly straight. "There has to be something."

"You can take a look, but I don't think you'll find a thing." His voice had an edge. "I'm sensitive to any irregularities. Believe me."

She did. Yet she felt more helpless than ever. "I need a lead," she cried softly, more to herself than to him. More loudly and with a hint of despair, she said, "It would be natural for someone who is in some way associated with the station to use wording like that."

"Thank you," Jared said, "but I don't have criminals associated with my station." He swiveled away, but it was only to punch another button on the console. With one hand on each of two slides, he waited for just the right moment to fade Lee Greenwood out and Randy Travis in. Only then did he swivel back.

Savannah picked up where he'd left off. "Kidnappers aren't necessarily hardened criminals."

"You said it was a clean job. You think just anyone off the street could have pulled it off?"

"No, but someone bright could have, someone who had thought everything out and could probably vanish into thin air faster than someone with a record. Has anybody here quit lately?"

He shook his head.

"Anyone been under really tight financial pressure?"

Again, he shook his head.

More meekly, she asked, "Anyone been asking for the names of good hotels in Iran?"

He didn't bother to respond to that one. Instead, he eyed her more closely. "This means a lot to you, doesn't it?"

"Of course, it does. Kidnapping is a serious crime."

"From what you say, you deal with lots of serious crimes. Do you go at them all this intently?"

She sensed subtle criticism in his tone. "I take my job seriously."

"Is that why you're out working in the middle of the night?"

She frowned. "When else was I supposed to reach you?"

"You might have called during the day. If you'd identified yourself, I'd have returned your call."

"Would you have?" she asked, then hurried on. Jared Snow was fast falling from his pedestal. "Excuse me for being skeptical, but I've been in this business long enough to know that if I want answers, I don't wait for a call back."

"And you want answers on this one."

"Yes, I do. A woman's life is in danger."

"Is that it? Is that what's got you so worried?"

She didn't understand. "Wouldn't you be worried if a woman's life was in your hands?"

"Come on, now," he chided. "You're not God. You're an assistant attorney general. This is your job. You do your best, and you feel bad if your best isn't enough, but you're satisfied to know that you tried."

"It's not enough just to try!"

"Why not? You can't run the world." He paused long enough to take in her appalled expression. "Is that it? Is that what you want? Is this case some kind of stepping stone for you?"

"No."

"Maybe you're aiming for a promotion. If you show your grit on a big one, the AG will move you up."

She shook her head in an attempt to negate what he said as well as express her disbelief that he was saying it at all. Jared Snow was supposed to be compassionate, trusting, understanding. He was not supposed to be cynical.

"Maybe you're aiming to be AG yourself. Or is it the governor you're trying to impress?" he asked.

Hurt, Savannah rose from the cabinet. She put a hand to her churning stomach. "You don't know what you're talking about."

He leaned back on one elbow. His pose was lazy, his eyes anything but. "Enlighten me."

She did just that. "I have no political aspirations, none at all, and as far as climbing higher in the AG's office, I've already climbed as high as I want to go." She paused for a breath. "But you're right. There's a good reason why I'm desperate when it comes to this case." She was trembling inside, doing her best not to let it show, not quite making it.

"The woman who was kidnapped happens to be a dear friend of mine. I want her back, and I want her back well."

The echo of her words blended into the background music as they sank into Jared's consciousness. His expression lost its smug challenge and grew sober. Rising, he went to her.

The first time he touched her she pulled back. He opened both hands wide, held them near her arms, then touched her again. This time she didn't flinch.

"I'm sorry," he said. "I had to know." The warmth of his hands penetrated two layers of navy knit. "I have a thing about politics. And about ruthlessly ambitious women. I'm sorry."

Savannah struggled to regain her composure, but Jared's nearness seemed to coax out more words. "She's been a friend of mine since high school. On some level, I've always felt responsible for her. Maybe because she never had much and I had so much. Maybe because she met her husband through my family and if she hadn't been his wife, she wouldn't have had a ransom worth demanding." As she looked up into his face, her throat grew tight. "I haven't seen Meggie as much as I should have lately, but I do love her."

Lifting a hand, Jared touched her cheek. His fingers were large but gentle, his expression curious. She wanted to cry.

Taking a tremulous breath, she glanced at the ceiling. Then she stepped back, away from his touch. "I'm really stronger than this." Averting her gaze, she looked through the glass wall to the outer room. "It must be the hour."

"You look tired."

She gave a short, high-pitched laugh. "Why is everyone always telling me that?"

"Maybe because it's true. And they care."

She looked at him. "You don't care. Not in that way. You don't know me." But as he looked back at her, she wondered. While his features remained strong, there was a look in his eyes that was so intimate and touching that either he knew her as well as anyone, or everything about him was a lie.

Not up to deciding which was true at that moment, she sighed. "Anyway. You're right. I am tired." With her arms stretched straight in her pockets again, she took another step toward the door. But Jared was turning away, this time to fade Randy Travis out and Rosanne Cash in. As soon as he came back to her, she said, "Could I take a look at the records of those calls?"

"Now?"

"Tomorrow."

"It'll take me a few hours to get them together."

"That's okay. If you let me know when they're ready, I'll come by." She looked at the door, then at the two large speakers, then at the control panel, and asked hesitantly, "Can I leave?"

Crossing the sound booth, he pushed the door open. She passed him, went to her briefcase, and removed a business card from inside.

"My number," she said, handing him her card.

He studied it, ran his forefinger along its top, pursed his lips.

She turned away for her coat. "There may be nothing in your records worth pursuing—"

"In the ideal situation, what would you like to find?"

"A call that makes some reference to crime or money or the station's logo."

"But what good will that do you? You'll have no idea who made the call."

Lifting the collar of the coat, she turned to him. "True, but then we can put a tap on your phone. If a kidnapper called once, he's apt to call again."

"It's a long shot."

"I know." Looking at him, she suddenly wanted to stay. But she had work to do in the morning. "Jared? What I've told you—it's strictly confidential. If word leaks out about the kidnapping and the press picks it up—"

His raised hand interrupted her. "What you've told me stops here."

"Thanks," she said softly. Again, she had an overwhelming urge to stay. There was something about Jared's strength, the gentleness of the hands that had touched her, the understanding in his expression. Going out into the cold night and back to a dark and empty apartment didn't appeal to her in the least. But it had to be done.

And, besides, he hadn't invited her to stay.

"I hope I haven't put you out in any way."

He tossed a glance at the control panel. "My 'string of six' still has a few to go. Maybe I'll interrupt it just to remind people I'm here, but I sometimes think they do just fine without me."

"No, no. They tune in because of you."

"Because of my voice. They like it, so they fantasize. But they're not tuning in because of me. Any guy with a deep voice and a lazy drawl would do."

Savannah didn't argue further, because to some extent

she wanted to believe he was right. Let any guy with a deep voice and a lazy drawl take over for him. Then she'd have him all to herself, without half the female population of Rhode Island as competition.

Then again, she was being foolish. If she had Jared Snow all to herself, she wouldn't know what to do with him. She was constantly busy and the only time she missed a man was during the late-night hours, and she couldn't ask a man to wait around for just those few moments. Besides, that was when Jared worked.

"Go on in," she said, tossing her chin toward the sound booth. "I've kept you long enough." She put the straps of her briefcase in place.

"I'll call you tomorrow."

The thought warmed her. "Thanks." She glanced at the pizza, which had to be stone cold. "Don't, uh, forget to eat."

Following her gaze, he grunted. "I'll heat it in the microwave when I play a reel-to-reel. That will buy me ten minutes."

Nodding, she headed for the door. "Bye," she said softly.

He dipped his head in a short salute, then turned into the sound booth. Returning through the hall, then the front foyer, Savannah let herself out.

As soon as she started the car, she turned the radio on.

"WCIC Providence, 95.3 on your FM dial, this is Jared Snow keepin' you company in the heart of the night. That last song was a former chart-topper by Rosanne Cash. She's gettin' some competition from Kathy Mattea, who'll be singin' live at the Severance Coffee House next Monday night. Catch Conway Twitty this Saturday at the civic center, or catch him right now at 95.3 FM, WCIC Providence. Listen good on the long drive home. . . ."

The drive home wasn't really long, but Savannah listened anyway. By the time she pulled into her garage and went upstairs, Jared had spoken twice. Each time, her pulse raced. And she let it. Thinking about Jared was better than thinking about Megan, and Jared Snow was a distraction of the sweetest kind. He said it himself—people fantasized about his voice. Now Savannah could fantasize about more. Nothing would ever really happen between Jared and her. She knew that. And that was why fantasizing was fun. It was convenient, comfortable, and safe.

She climbed into bed, pulled the covers up high, and listened in the dark to his voice.

". . . so get tucked in and enjoy. I'll be right here, listenin' with you in cool country, 95.3 FM, WCIC Providence. Jared Snow in the heart of the night." His voice became deeper, more intimate. *"And now, I've got 'Georgia on My Mind'. . . ."*

It was a long time before Savannah's heart slowed down enough to allow her to sleep, but when it did, she slept more soundly than usual, which was a good thing. Shortly after seven the next morning, Sam called to say that the kidnappers had phoned. The switch was scheduled for that night.

It was going to be a long, tense day.

Chapter 7

AT EIGHT O'CLOCK THURSDAY morning, Savannah was in the Vandermeers' basement, listening to a playback of the call. It was short and concise, cooly professional.

"Hello?" Will had said.

The voice that answered him was just muffled enough to complicate voiceprint analysis without obliterating the words. Its sound was unearthly, chilling Savannah to the bone.

"Do you have the money?" it demanded.

"Yes."

"Small denominations. In a brown grocery bag."

"I want to talk to my wife."

"Tonight. Just you. Eight o'clock." The voice rattled off an address that meant nothing to Savannah. "There's a dumpster at the corner. Put the money in and leave. Try anything funny with the cops and you won't see the lady again."

"Will she be there—my wife, will she be there?"

"Once the money is safe, she'll be dropped at a phone booth."

"She has to be there when I drop the money. She has to be there. I have to know she's all right—"

The line went dead.

Trembling inside, Savannah swallowed hard. "No Megan," she whispered and swore softly. They had been counting on some reassurance that Megan was well, but the kidnappers had denied them that, and there wasn't a thing they could do about it.

Struggling to accept the setback calmly, she looked up at Sam. "Can we get a number?"

"It's on the way. Don't hold your breath, though. The call was probably made from a phone booth miles from where they're holding her."

"Did you hear any background noise?"

"I didn't. The lab might. We'll get them working on it."

"Do you know the drop spot?"

"Sure do. It's a construction site in the West End. There's a dumpster there, plus a lot of dark alleys. He could come and go in any one of a dozen different directions. The site is like a maze. The only chance we stand of catching him would be to cordon off a five-block area, but we can't do that without being seen."

"You can't do anything until he frees Megan," Susan argued. She was stone sober and very tense. She half wished she was hung-over enough to blunt her awareness of what was happening. But Sam Craig hadn't let her drink enough for that. She had long since decided he was the devil in disguise.

"We could follow him," Sam said. "If we could get a tail on him, we could bide our time until he contacts an accomplice or gets Megan himself. But in that location, the risk of his seeing us is pretty high."

Savannah was trying to think of viable alternatives. "What about putting a homing device in with the money?"

"I'm not sure we can risk that either," Sam replied. "The guy's pretty smart. He's going to check the money pretty quick. Chances are he'll dump it out of the bag into a sack of his own. If he finds anything suspicious, he'd take it out on Megan."

"How do we know he hasn't already?" Susan cried. "He wouldn't let Will talk with her."

"He was probably calling from a pay phone. Even if Megan had been stashed nearby, he wouldn't have risked dragging her out in the open."

Susan didn't like what Sam said or the factual way he said it. He was too sure of himself, while she was a nervous wreck. "But we don't have any proof she's still alive! How can Will hand over the money without knowing?"

"How can he not?" Sam returned.

Slowly and inevitably, the truth of his words sank in. Not even Savannah attempted to deny it.

Hands knotted at her waist, Susan picked at her nail polish. "I can't stand this. We're totally powerless. Some criminal is calling the shots, and we're doing just what he says."

"For now," Savannah said. "For now."

"But it's disgusting. The Vandermeer name is *worth* something."

"No," Sam corrected. "The Vandermeer *money* is worth something. Our guy doesn't give a damn about the name."

"Is there a difference? Name, money, power—it's all tied together. The Vandermeers have been a force in this state for a good, long time. They don't deserve this."

Savannah put a hand on her arm. "Careful, Suse."

"Of what?" Susan asked haughtily.

"Of me," Sam said tightly. "You're talking nonsense. What makes you think the Vandermeers should be exempt from crime just because they have money or power? You think that the poor schnook who works his butt off in a factory sixty hours a week and still can't make ends meet— you think he deserves to be victimized any more than the Vandermeers? No one deserves it, but it happens."

"The Vandermeers contribute more than their share in taxes *and* to charity."

Sam laughed at that.

"There must be something that can be done!" she cried.

"Someone to call?" he taunted. "Someone to pull a string here or there? Someone to fix things so no one's inconvenienced and the whole thing just goes away? Sorry, sweetheart, but life doesn't always work that way."

"It isn't fair," Susan told him. When she saw no sympathy forthcoming, she turned to Savannah. "It isn't fair."

"No."

"Doesn't it infuriate you?"

"All the time."

"Still, you do it. Day in, day out you play the game. It's like cops and robbers, with only one side following the rules. The robbers come and go as they please. They do whatever they want." She made a choking sound. "And to think I envied you your job. If this is the kind of excitement you thrive on—"

"I don't thrive on it," Savannah bit back. "I'm as worried as you are."

"You don't look it."

"It's my *job* not to look it."

"She's worried," Sam assured Susan. "She's got sunken eyes, just like you." He was looking from one sister's face to the other's. "So there's a resemblance after all. Sunken eyes."

"Those are shadows," Savannah informed him dryly. "Tension shadows."

Susan glared at him. "That was just what I needed. Thanks."

Savannah gave her arm a squeeze, then turned to Hank, who, after nearly two days with Susan and Sam, had learned to stand out of the line of fire. "Will's taking care of things with the insurance company, I gather."

Hank nodded. "In the kitchen."

She looked back at Sam. "Do we let him go alone tonight?"

Sam shrugged. "We could scatter a few winos around to relay info, but the guy's apt to smell a rat. The construction site is usually deserted after five. We can post a few unmarked cars at random spots on the chance he'll pass them. It'd be nice to get a make on his vehicle and there won't be much traffic, but that can work against us, too. If our guy catches wind of a tail, Megan could be in trouble. So we'll have to be careful. Our first priority is to get her back in one piece. Once we've done that, her kidnappers are fair game."

Susan snorted. "It'll be too late then."

"No. Megan may be able to help us."

"Oh? If I were a kidnapper planning something as neatly as this one did, I'd make sure the victim didn't see or hear a thing."

Savannah responded. "They'll make a mistake, Suse. Somewhere along the line, they'll make a mistake."

"Vintage Savvy," Susan said, rolling her eyes. "Optimistic to the end."

But Savannah was shaking her head. "This is just the beginning. Once Meggie's back, we'll have manpower on our side. Local police, state police, FBI—they'll all be involved. I don't care how professional those kidnappers are, somewhere they'll slip up, and when they do, we'll be waiting." She paused. "If only Will would let us call in help now." Then she shivered, looked around at the somber, concrete walls, and muttered beneath her breath, "I've had enough of this basement." Rubbing her upper arms with her hands, she headed for the stairs.

An hour later, she sat behind her desk looking over the list of convicts who had been released from prison during the last six months. She found it depressing.

Some of her favorites had hit the streets—a bank robber, a drug pusher, a pimp, the mastermind of a stolen-car ring. None of those on the list had ever tried his hand at kidnapping, but she was sure that there were half a dozen who would have been willing to give it a shot if the jackpot were high enough. As a precaution, and because she felt she could safely do so without risk to Megan, she called a friend in the parole office. He agreed to check on the whereabouts of several of the more dubious parolees.

That done, she sat back for a minute and studied the list again. She was notified each time someone she had seen convicted got out, but she usually stashed the notices in a corner or under piles of papers. They made her nervous.

She'd had her share of threats. It was common for defendants to shout things at prosecutors, particularly when a prosecutor had been either unusually powerful, dramatic, or effective in the pit. When the prosecutor was a woman, things were worse.

Paul had always told her to ignore the threats, and she had. She was the optimist, the good guy who wore a white hat, rode a white horse, and had the law on her side. To date, she had never had a problem aside from the periodic fear that hit her. She could ignore the notices that were sent to her. She could stash them safely out of sight. They registered nevertheless in the corner of her mind.

"Got a minute, Savannah?" came a voice from the door.

Savannah looked up. After a disoriented second, she focused on Arnie Watts and took a steadying breath. "Sure, Arnie. Come on in."

But he hesitated. "Everything okay?"

Pushing the list aside, she forced out a smile. "Sure." She motioned him in with a small wave, then dropped her gaze to the folders he carried. "The exhibits for the arson case?"

Arnie crossed the floor and put them on her desk. "Yup. I want to make sure they're right. We don't need any surprises."

Savannah looked over the material, but everything was in order in each folder. "How about the jury pool?"

"I was told I'd see the list later today."

"Bring it here when you get it. I want to take a look." The phone rang. Pushing a button, she took up the receiver. "Yes, Janie?"

"Detective Monroe is calling about the house-break business in Wakefield. Do you want to take it?"

"Tell him to hang on. I'll be right there." She held the receiver to her shoulder while she finished up with Arnie. "Jury selection will probably take most of Monday. On the chance it goes faster, I'm spending Sunday here working on my opening argument. I'd like to see Brady again before we put him on he stand. He's the fire inspector. His testimony is crucial, but he comes across wishy-washy. I think we should prepare him a little more. He may be okay on direct, but he's apt to fall apart on cross-examination. Can you do it?"

"No sweat," Arnie said and turned to leave. "And I'm free all weekend. If you think of anything else, just call."

Smiling her thanks, Savannah punched the button on her telephone panel and switched gears to deal with Detective Monroe. By the time she was done with him, Paul was on the line, calling from his car en route to the airport and a regional attorneys general conference, wanting to know the latest on the kidnapping. By the time she was done with him, her father was waiting on the other line.

"Hi, Dad," she called lightly into the phone.

The voice at the other end was not as light. "You are one very difficult lady to reach, Savannah. I've been trying you for two days now, but you come home late and leave early. Where is Susan?"

Savannah grimaced. "Didn't she call you?" She had specifically asked Susan to do that.

"She left a message with Mrs. Fritz that she'd be gone overnight. That was on Tuesday afternoon, and I haven't heard from her since. I'd say that's damned inconsiderate of her."

"She's a big girl, Dad."

"But I worry. She hasn't been behaving well lately. For all I know she's off somewhere getting drunk, and if that's so, I'll tell you right now that I have no intention of going after her. I've had to fetch her from parties once too often. It's embarrassing."

"She's going through a rough time."

"Is that your excuse for it?" He made a gruff sound. "I shouldn't be surprised. You always did make excuses for her. Why do you do it, Savannah? There you are, straight as an arrow, with a job and lots of friends, and she's doing nothing. *Nothing*."

Savannah touched a tender spot on her forehead. "Last time we talked, you weren't thinking too highly of either my job or my friends."

"You know I don't approve of your working, and I certainly wouldn't choose your friends for my own, but still you have them." His tone turned imperious. "Why doesn't Susan?"

"She has friends."

"She's losing them right and left. Give her too much to drink, and she gets bold. I won't repeat what she told Bobo Dietz last week. I wasn't even there, but word filtered back. It was downright offensive. You can be sure that she won't get any more invitations from the Dietzs' and, to be perfectly honest, I don't blame Bobo in the least."

"Bobo Dietz happens to be one of the most obnoxious women in Newport. If Susan told her so, good for Susan."

Oliver Smith wasn't thrilled with his daughter's stand. "Bobo Dietz happens to be one of the wealthiest women in Newport—"

"Which isn't saying much. The only people in Newport who aren't wealthy are the people who service the wealthy, and most of those can't afford to live in Newport. Come on, Dad, Bobo Dietz isn't worth arguing over."

"And that, young lady, is why you had to run away to Providence."

"I didn't run—"

"You never could learn what was important and what wasn't. You never understood that there were certain rules to be followed in certain circles. Susan understood it. Why couldn't you?"

"Because I'm not Susan."

"Obviously. Susan has the makings to succeed here. It would have been better if she hadn't split with Dirk, but she can still pull it off. She has the looks and the charm, and she does even better in Palm Beach. She was only down there for a month this winter. I don't know why she didn't stay longer. But that doesn't matter now. Most everyone is back or coming soon. And Susan will do fine, as long as she stays sober." He barely paused before yelling, "Where the hell is she?"

It was Savannah who took the breath. "She's at Megan's."

"Ah. Megan. Megan. The only redeemable quality in *that* child is her husband. The Vandermeer name is solid."

Savannah didn't know whether to laugh or scream. In lieu of either, she pressed her fingers harder to her forehead and prayed for strength. "Megan happens to be a good friend. We go back a long way together. She's been very loyal, which is more than I can say about some of the others I grew up with."

"That's your problem, Savannah. You took off to become a lawyer, and suddenly you didn't have time for those friends. What did you expect them to do—wait with bated breath until you deigned to give them a call?"

"I didn't—"

"You've distanced yourself. So don't blame it on them. You've distance yourself from all of us. What does that say about *your* sense of loyalty?"

"I'm loyal—"

"I call to take you to lunch and you're busy. Alex Porter calls to take you to a party in Manhattan and you're busy.

Muffy Adams calls to invite you for a weekend in Westport and you're busy."

"I *am* busy—"

"Working. Always working. You're a very boring person."

"Dad, please—"

"I'm serious. Your work always comes first."

"This isn't the time—"

"There's never a time. That's the problem."

She didn't attempt to say another word, but sat with the phone to her ear and her fingertips to her forehead, and waited. Her father would eventually quiet down. Until then, nothing she tried to say would register.

"Actually," he ranted on, "the problem is that I never had a son. I wanted someone to pass the business on to, so what did I get? Two daughters. The odds were that one of you would be a boy. But no, I got two daughters. Not much to found a dynasty on." He paused, listened, demanded, "Are you there, Savannah?"

"I'm here."

"Well, listen good. I want to know what your sister's doing. Are you going to call her, or should I?"

"I'll do it, by all means."

"I'd appreciate that," he said, somewhat mollified. "You can tell her to call me by three. I'm playing tennis at four, and after that I'll be leaving for Stowe. Jack's boy is flying us up for the weekend. The skiing is just fine, they say. So, you'll keep an eye on Susan while I'm gone?"

"We're spending Saturday together." She held her breath, wondering whether he'd remember what Saturday was, but the significance of the day eluded him.

"Good," he said. "Well then, I'll talk with you when I get back."

"Fine."

"Bye, Savannah."

She nodded. He had already hung up.

Quietly, she replaced the receiver, then bowed her head and lightly massaged her temples. She always looked forward to her father's calls, and she was always disappointed afterward. She knew he could be a charmer. What she didn't know was why he never charmed his daughters. He reserved a sharp tongue and a critical eye for them, and lately, whether because of age or sheer orneriness, he had been worse than ever.

She could take it. She had her own life and her own rewards. But she worried for Susan.

Sensing a presence nearby, she raised her head and immediately caught her breath. Jared Snow stood at the door, exuding quiet confidence and staunch maleness. The confidence was like a welcome balm; the maleness sparked a sweet curling in her belly.

He tossed his head back toward the spot where her secretary normally sat, and said in a deep, sandy voice, "She must be on coffee break. Am I interrupting anything?"

Savannah managed a wispy laugh. "Yes. A mammoth headache. Come in. Please. And close the door. If any of the ladies out there hear you speak, they're apt to start a stampede."

He cleared the threshold and closed the door. His eyes held hers with warm probing. "What's the headache from?"

Normally, she would have shrugged and left her personal problems behind. But when it came to Jared Snow, nothing she felt was quite normal. He could penetrate her professional veneer with one look. "My dad. He's a difficult man."

"Does he live around here?"

"In Newport."

Jared acknowledged the significance of that with a quirk of his brow. "Close enough to make his presence felt."

"Actually, I don't see him often."

"But he calls."

She sighed. "Oh, yes." She wondered if Jared had a similar situation with one of his parents. He looked sympathetic.

"How old is he?"

"Sixty-eight."

"Does he live alone?"

"He has a housekeeper and frequent houseguests, so he's not lonely."

"Is he ill?"

"Thank goodness, no. Health has never been a problem. He leads as active a life as ever." She paused.

"But?"

Still, she paused. Then, with an added look of encouragement from Jared which destroyed any reticence she might have had, she said, "But he's extremely demanding in his way. He expects that we should do just what he does, which is not much of anything—by my standards, at least."

She stopped for an instant, feeling as disloyal as her father had accused her of being. But she desperately needed to talk. "He takes pride in being one of the idle rich. I had to be something else. I don't think he'll ever forgive me for that. Susan has tried to be Newport, but it's not working for her. On the one hand, I want to stand up and cheer, but she doesn't have an alternative like I do, so she's floundering."

"Is she married?"

"Divorced, with no kids."

"So she lacks direction."

"In a nutshell," Savannah conceded, then considered what she had said. She was usually tight-lipped about her personal life, and family certainly fell into that category. But Jared Snow wasn't like the people who usually passed through her life. He was different and somehow separate. If she let her fancy run free, she could imagine him an angel sent to ease the weight from her shoulders. In his presence she certainly did feel lighter, both of head and of heart.

It was all she could do not to sigh with pleasure. She could look at him forever, she decided, particularly when he did things like tilt his head just as he was doing now.

"You two must be very close," he said. "I've often wondered what it would be like to have a twin."

It was easy to smile, less easy to concentrate on what he was saying. But she did it. "I have, too," she confessed in a quiet voice. At his bemused look, she explained. "Susan and I are fraternal twins. We're sisters who just happened to have been born on the same day. I've often wondered what it would have been like if we'd been identical, if we'd been able to do things like switch places at school or on dates. Susan and I can't even switch clothes. We are different sizes."

"She must be bigger than you."

"How did you guess," Savannah said dryly. Though she had never thought of herself as petite, others often did. She supposed it had something to do with her slimness. While her sister was slim, too, she was more curvaceous. "Susan is about five-eight. She has a fantastic figure. And great eyes.

And *super* hair. She has dad's height and mom's looks. She should have been a model."

"Why wasn't she one?"

"Because someone told her that modeling was hard work, and where we grew up, hard work wasn't highly prized."

"You do it."

"I'm the odd one. The black sheep."

"And your dad isn't proud of what you've become?"

"Not quite."

He gnawed on the inside of his cheek for a minute, then asked, "How about Susan? Is she proud of what you do?"

Savannah didn't answer as quickly. For one thing, the answer wasn't cut-and-dried. For another, she was distracted by Jared's mouth. His lips were as lean as the rest of him, as uncompromisingly male, and when they slanted into a grin, or gentled, they were all the more enticing.

With an effort, she answered. "I suppose she's proud. One part of her, at least. Another part, I think, is a little resentful."

"Resentful?"

"Of my success. By contrast, it makes her feel more lost, and Dad," she threw a glance skyward, "bless his soul, compares us constantly. I don't measure up to Susan, Susan doesn't measure up to me, neither of us measures up to him, or to what our mother was—it goes on and on." Abruptly she stopped talking, then bit her lower lip, then said in chagrin, "I think I'm the one who's going on and on."

"I don't mind," Jared said.

But Savannah was embarrassed. He had come on business and she didn't normally waste time. But he distracted her. Something about the way he looked at her invited confession. He looked at her as though he was intrigued, as though there was nothing on earth that could have interested him more than what she was saying, as though he truly needed to hear her words. There was an intensity to him despite his relaxed attitude.

In recent years she had dated plenty of men, but not many more than once or twice, and for good reason. Strong, interesting men, men who were leaders in their fields appealed to her. Unfortunately, most had also turned out to be eminently interested in themselves, which was fine for a date or two, but boring for longer than that.

Jared Snow seemed every bit as strong and interesting, every bit as skilled in his field. Yet he was more interested in hearing about her than talking about himself. The risk, she realized, was in eventually boring him as she had always eventually been bored. So, sitting straighter in her chair, she put both hands on her desk and eyed him with an expectant, down-to-business kind of look.

But the effort was lost on him. He was glancing around her office. "This is cozy."

She hesitated, then yielded. A minute's more distraction wouldn't hurt. "Yes. It's cozy." She usually called it small. "It serves the purpose, though."

"It must be convenient being in the courthouse."

"Very."

He looked past her to a tall bookcase filled with thick, official-looking tomes. "Are those all yours?"

She glanced at the books. "Most of them. A few belong to the law library."

He looked at the etchings on the wall, a series of five courtroom scenes that she'd picked up in Paris two summers before. "And those?"

"They're mine."

"They look authentic."

She grinned. "Authentic, as in dog-eared. But that's okay. They were a find. I ran across them in a little bookstall on the left bank of the Seine. They were done in England at the turn of the century."

"They must be valuable," he remarked, but his attention had returned to her.

"They give me pleasure," she said with a short smile. "That's value enough."

He stood silently then, simply looking at her, and surprisingly, Savannah didn't feel awkward. For one thing, he was a delight to look back at. He wore jeans, just as he had at the studio, but the sneakers had been replaced by boots, the T-shirt and flannel shirt by a black turtleneck sweater that was a perfect foil for his tawniness, and over the sweater, a bomber jacket of butter-soft leather accentuated his broad shoulders. He had showered and shaved, and looked totally refreshed, which was remarkable for two reasons—first, because he'd managed to improve on something that was outstanding to begin with, and second, because he couldn't have slept more than two or three hours.

For the first time she noticed the two large manila envelopes he carried under his arm. Neither was particularly thick.

"The records of the calls," she breathed and might have been chagrined at not having noted them sooner if Jared had not looked as though he'd momentarily forgotten them himself.

"Uh, I just picked them up. Thought I'd deliver them right away."

She eyed him cautiously. "Do you think we'll find something?"

"I don't know. One batch is from the station, one from the answering service." He held them out. "Want to take a look?"

Rising from her chair, Savannah rounded the desk and took the envelopes. She opened one and fanned out the papers on the desktop.

They contained notes made by the station's receptionists and were dated by week with the most recent on top. Straddling the papers with stiffened arms, she leaned forward and began to read. Each entry noted the date and the time, plus either a quote, a paraphrase, or a simple description of the offensive call.

She read silently for several minutes, then turned to the second sheet and perused that. Straightening, she raised a hand to her shoulder. It was a protective gesture; she felt chilled. "I had an answering machine once," she said quietly. "It seemed to make sense. I was on call so much of the time, and it was nice to think that I could come home and know exactly who had tried to reach me and when. But the heavy breathers felt the machine was fair game. They got to me pretty quickly. So I gave the machine to one of the guys at the office."

She looked up to find Jared within arm's reach, and again, she was struck by his height. He was tall, sturdy, and strong. He could overpower her in a minute, yet that was not what she feared. What frightened her was the force of his pull. She felt it as something magnetic, drawing on every one of her senses until she was all but leaning his way.

She forced her eyes back down to the papers and said, "Thanks for bringing these. I shouldn't keep you longer."

"I don't mind."

"You must have other things to do."

"Nothing that can't wait."

He wasn't going to leave until he was ready. And she could no more have kicked him out than she could have stripped and paraded naked on the desktop.

She felt naked anyway. In Jared's presence, she felt stripped of defenses that had stood her in good stead for years. She wondered if he knew. She wondered lots of things about him, and it struck her that it was time she did a little probing herself.

"What—" She cleared her throat and started again. "What do you usually do during the day?"

His raspy voice was accompanied by a lazy smile. "A little of this, a little of that."

The smile would have distracted her again, had not her phone buzzed. Moving only her upper body, she reached for it. The call was from a lawyer in the office who wanted to know which judge to request for an upcoming bribery trial. "Cramer," she told him. "He can't stand bribery. He's cautious enough to avoid grounds for a mistrial, but he'll give you every benefit of the doubt." She answered one other minor question, then replaced the receiver and looked up at Jared.

His eyes riveted her. The slight cast to the one was intriguing, but that was only the beginning. Strewn amid their pale blue rings were flecks of gray that darkened or lightened with his mood. She wondered why she hadn't noticed that before, particularly in light of their power. Then she realized that the power was the key, and it came from within. Fighting its lure, she cleared her throat again and asked, "'A little of this, a little of that.' What do you mean?"

He seemed unperturbed by her challenge. "I do a lot of reading."

"What do you read?"

"Fiction, nonfiction, you name it. I also have to keep up on what's happening in the field. Country musicians tend to be around longer than, say, pop-rock stars, but that doesn't mean their lives are static. So I keep current with trade materials. And I listen to new stuff that comes in."

"Do you decide what to play on the air?"

"No. My music director does that. It's his job to keep tabs on what Rhode Islanders want to hear. A song that may make it big in Tulsa could bomb here. It's like the logo says, a little country in the city. Too much country and the city tunes out."

She could believe it. "What else do you do, besides read?"

He studied her for a minute, than ran a finger along the side of his nose. "I dabble in real estate."

"Beyond radio stations?"

"Yes. I have interests in various properties."

"In Providence?"

"No. They're kind of scattered."

"Then you have to travel."

"No. I have people to do the traveling. I keep in touch with them by phone."

"It sounds like you do a little more than dabble."

His answer was a negligible shrug.

She took that in. On the one hand, he had such a rugged, woodsy look that it was hard to imagine him as a real-estate mogul. On the other hand, he exuded power, and in that sense, she believed he could rival Donald Trump.

"When do you sleep?" she asked.

"When I'm tired."

"Aren't you now? You couldn't have slept much after work."

"I don't need more than a few hours at a time. I'll sleep later." He nodded toward the papers he had brought. "Want me to go through one envelope while you do the other? It would save you some time."

Savannah felt a rush of pleasure. With Jared wading through half the records, she would be done in half the time. More importantly, if he helped, he would stay with her a bit longer. She wasn't sure of the long-range wisdom of that, but in the short run, it was appealing. He was a stimulating companion. Everything about him, from his sandy hair to the solid breadth of his chest, from the way his jeans fit in the vicinity of his hips to the faint scent of leather that clung to him—everything about him absorbed her. She knew it was an absurd time to be excited by a man, but the excitement was an antidote to all else she was feeling. He was her talisman, warding off headaches and chills, and in that sense, he was helping far more than he knew.

The phone rang again. This time it was Janie saying that Susan was on the line. Savannah immediately took the call.

"Susan?"

"I think you should come back here. Will is on the verge of breaking. He's convinced, absolutely convinced, that Megan's been mistreated. He's talking about taking a gun when he goes to drop off the money tonight."

"But he won't be seeing anyone. He'll be dropping the money and leaving."

"He says he's going to stay."

"He can't do that. He'll either get himself killed or blow the whole thing."

"I've told him that, Sam has told him that, Hank has told

him that, but he doesn't believe us. I think you should get over here, and bring Paul."

"Paul's out of state. But I'll be over. Keep Will calm until I get there."

Heart pounding, she hung up the phone. She was so lost in thoughts of Will and Megan that Jared's deep voice startled her.

"You heard from the kidnappers, I take it."

Her head came up fast. "This morning." It never once occurred to her not to tell him. "The exchange is set for tonight, but Will's having a rough time of it. He's sure that Megan's been hurt. Susan thinks I should go over, and I will, but I'm not sure what good I can do. I can't assure him Megan hasn't been hurt. All any of us can do is to pray she's all right." She looked down at the papers Jared had brought. "I'll have to go through these later."

"I'll go through them."

"You don't have to do that."

"I know I don't have to, but I'd like to. It's my radio station that may have something to do with your kidnapping."

"It's such a long shot "

"But it's worth looking into. Come on, Savannah. I don't have anything pressing to do until early evening. This'd be a change of pace for me."

It was minute before she recovered from the sound of her name on his tongue. It was low and intimate. It stroked her senses and would have brought on a purr if the circumstances had been different. Instead of purring, she eyed him askance. "What's happening early this evening?"

"I have a conference call set for six o'clock with a group of investors from California."

That was not only impressive but far better than if he'd

had a date. Turning away in relief, she gathered the papers together and slipped them into their envelope. Then she handed both envelopes back to him.

"Thank you," she whispered, and for a minute she drank in his features as if they were an extra dose of courage. She feared things were going to get worse before they got better at the Vandermeer house.

Then, turning away before she positively threw herself at him, she snatched up the phone. "Janie, would you call me a cab?"

Jared took the phone from her hand and, in a voice that was deeper and huskier than ever, said, "Cancel that cab. Janie. Thanks anyway." Then he hung up.

Savannah was shaking her hand in a slow, chiding way. "I can't let you drive me there."

"You haven't got much choice," he said. "I just canceled your cab."

"I'll order another."

"I don't think so."

"Why not?" she asked, sounding nearly as haughty as Susan had sounded earlier that day with Sam.

Jared's eyes were darker, his voice a near growl. "When a woman looks at me the way you just did, she's not running off in a cab when I have a perfectly good car sitting at the curb."

Savannah opened her mouth to protest that she hadn't looked at him any special way, then shut it without uttering a word.

"Thank you," he drawled. Glancing over his shoulder, he spotted her coat hanging on a hook on the back of the door. Seconds later, he was holding it for her. She slipped her arms in, closing her eyes for a brief moment when she felt his hands still on her shoulders. Seconds afterward he opened the office door.

"I'll be at the Vandermeers," she murmured to Janie Woo as she started past. She stopped in her tracks when she saw how Janie was staring at Jared. "He's helping me out with something, but as far as anyone's concerned, he wasn't here. Right, Janie?"

Janie, who knew that the security of her job relied heavily on discretion, nodded.

Satisfied, Savannah started off again. She didn't have to look around to know that Jared was close on her heels. She felt his heat, felt the vibrancy of his body. It occurred to her while he stood, straight and tall, waiting beside her for the elevator, that on another day at another time, she would have let him drive her anywhere his heart desired.

Chapter 8

JARED HAD DONE HIS SHARE of living. In his thirty-nine years, he had had many friends, and of those, many had been women. He had been through numerous relationships, two live-in loves, and one wife. But no woman had ever looked at him with quite the need he had seen in Savannah's eyes. From the moment at the studio when she had turned around and looked at him, he had seen the need. And the admiration. There had also been admiration in his eyes.

He was used to admiration. Women took to his looks, just as they did to his voice, and he played on the latter. His voice was a marketable commodity. It was largely responsible for the appeal of his show. He intentionally enhanced it with his choice of words and his tone.

But he did nothing to enhance his looks and deliberately kept as low a profile as possible. He enjoyed the anonymity he'd found in Rhode Island; he enjoyed being able to walk the streets unknown. When a PR event took place, he sent one of the other DJs. When the request was specifically for Jared Snow, he turned it down with a firm excuse. He treasured his newfound privacy. It was critical to him at this time in his life, when he was feeling his way along, waiting for the ultimate inspiration to hit.

Then along came Savannah's need. He had been skeptical at first, wondering if she was after something as simple as sex. As they talked, though, he'd begun to wonder. She didn't make a play for him. She didn't do anything remotely seductive—at least, not intentionally. There had been that moment when he'd been in the sound booth and had looked out at her through the glass. She'd just taken off her coat. He suspected he would have stared even if she hadn't bent over to retrieve her briefcase.

She was not striking. Nor was she gorgeous. But in an understated way, she was sexy as hell. Her features were smooth and appealing, her skin soft and fair. Her hair was a glossy brown mass gathered into a sedate knot, begging, just begging, for release. In fact, that was what was so sexy about her—her neatness was a challenge. She was the consummate professional, yet she held hints of sweetness that tried a man's soul. She didn't hide the slender length of her legs or the slight turn of her hips or the gentle swell of her breasts, yet none were boldly broadcast. There was a mystery to her. She was alluring.

She turned him on.

"I won't hold it against you, y'know," he teased in a voice that was just loud enough to rise above the noise of the idling engine.

Safely strapped into the passenger seat of his Pathfinder, Savannah focused on the pedestrians passing by.

He tried again. "You can look at me any way you want. I don't mind."

She turned her head away, but not before he caught a hint of color on her cheeks.

"You're under a lot of pressure," he said. "I'm glad to help."

The traffic light turned. He accelerated smoothly, and for several minutes the noise of the engine was the only sound in the car. Then, speaking quietly, she said, "I would have pegged you for a Porsche."

He kept his eyes on the road. "Me? Nah. I need something more practical."

"For what?"

"Hauling equipment."

Her voice remained wary, but he sensed her eyes were turned toward him, which was a step in the right direction. "Don't you have gofers to do that, or is that only with TV?"

"TV, mostly. We don't have the need. But I wasn't talking about the station. I was talking about my boat."

She was silent for a minute. "What kind of boat is it?"

"A forty-six-foot Morgan." He kept his voice low and slow. "She's in dry dock right now, but I'll be putting her in the water in another month. From April through November, she's my home."

"You live on a boat?" she asked, unable to conceal her enthusiasm.

He nodded.

"What's it like?"

He thought for a minute. "Peaceful. You've been on the ocean, haven't you?"

She nodded.

"Sensed that freedom?"

"Uh-huh."

"Well, it's kind of like that. It doesn't matter how tightly you're moored or how calm the tide, you still feel that lulling. And the sense of freedom is always there. You know that whenever things get tense, you can cast off. Even if you don't often do it, knowing you can gives you a psychological edge."

He stopped at another red light. Savannah was staring out the window again. "There are times," she said in a distant voice, "when I'd give anything to be able to cast off, when I want to get away from everything, to run away." Returning to the present, she sent him an awkward half-smile. "Irresponsible, hmm?"

"If I say yes, I condemn myself. Everyone feels that at times."

She wasn't so sure. There were people in the world without worries or responsibilities. Looking away again, she said, "When I was little, I was always zipping around. My energy level was incredible. Sometimes I'd lose control and run smack into whatever was in my path. But that was okay. I just had to stand up and brush myself off.

"Then I got my driver's license, and I imagined the same thing would happen, that I'd get going too fast and lose control, only if I started colliding with things, I'd be in real trou ble."

She focused unseeingly on the scenery that, with the turn of the traffic light, was passing once more. "There are times when I feel that I've lost control of my life, that I'm on the verge of a huge collision. It's like I'm on a slide; I'm steadily gaining momentum, and I want to get off, but I can't."

"Sure you can."

"No. There are commitments, responsibilities. I'm an adult. An adult can't quit when the going gets rough."

"I take it," Jared said softly, "this is one of the rough

times." He glanced at her in time to catch her nod. "What happens during the easy times?"

She gave a high-pitched laugh. "I'm usually bored." With a quick breath, she looked over at him. "Between the rough times and the easy times are the times I love. They're the times when the challenge is there without the trauma. Thank God, they come most often."

"You're lucky. Some people can't say that."

"I know." Her voice lowered. "Take your next right."

They drove along in silence for several minutes, but Savannah didn't mind that. Jared was still a comfort, a solid presence. He was someone separate from her career, separate from her past. He was an eye in the storm of her life.

Too soon, she directed him to the Vandermeers' circular drive. At the front door, he shifted into neutral and asked, "Will you stay long?"

"That depends on how Will is. If he's running around the house waving a gun, it might take a little longer to calm him down than if he's just sitting in a chair tossing off threats."

"Can I wait?"

She shook her head. "You shouldn't be here at all. We've tried to involve as few people as possible. As it is, I'll have some explaining to do when I get inside. I'm sure they've seen us."

Jared would have been glad to come in and help with the explaining. Instinctively, he knew that she would not allow it. For all her talk of escape, she wasn't a coward. She was a professional, through and through.

But she wasn't racing to get out of the car.

So he asked gently, "When is Megan due back?"

"The money is to be delivered at eight. Sometime after that, Will should get a call telling him where she is, and sometime after that we'll pick her up." She looked worried. "God only knows what will happen then."

He reached over and touched her cheek lightly with one finger. It was a gesture of encouragement that came, left its mark, and vanished. "You'll be working late."

She nodded.

"You were with me last night, then at the office today. Tonight you'll be here, or wherever. When do *you* sleep?"

"I'm like you, I guess. I don't need much. And when I need more than I get, I make up for it on weekends."

"But weekends should be for regenerating."

"Sleep is regenerative."

"I was thinking about taking in shows and concerts and museums, skiing, shopping, sunbathing on the lawn."

"Sunbathing on the lawn." She smiled. "Mmmm, that sounds nice."

Her smile was so soft and alluring that Jared wanted to take back what he had just said. He could spend the weekend in bed with her, and it would probably be the most regenerative thing he would ever do.

Watching the gray flecks in his eyes darken, Savannah felt an answering awareness deep inside. "I have to run," she whispered and reached for her briefcase. When she had its straps firmly on her shoulder, she gripped the door handle. Although she knew she should resist, she looked back at Jared for a final eyeful of his strength.

He swore softly. Nearly as softly, and very hoarsely, he said, "I may have the patience of a saint, but I'm not made of stone. So help me, Savannah, the next time you look at me that way, I'm going to kiss you."

Her heart beat wildly. "I have to run."

"Did you hear what I said?"

Opening the door, she said, "Thanks for driving me here. It was a break." She slid out.

He leaned across the seat. "Savannah?"

She swung the door closed, but he quickly rolled down the window. As though she'd intended to all along, she leaned in. "Will you let me know if you find anything in those reports?"

"You know I will," he said gruffly. Tugging open the glove compartment, he pulled out a small pad of paper and a pen. He jotted down several phone numbers, tore off the sheet of paper, and held it out. "You can reach me at any time."

Savannah grasped the paper but he didn't immediately release it. Uncompromisingly, his eyes held hers.

"I have to go," she whispered in a pleading tone.

Still he bound her, reinforcing the bond between them with each second that passed. Finally, when his own heart was thudding under the pressure, he released the paper.

Savannah quickly pocketed it. "Thanks. Thanks for everything, Jared."

"Savannah—"

"I'll talk with you later." With a wave she was away from the car, an elegant figure trotting up the front steps. The door opened as soon as she reached it. Without a backward glance, she was gone.

William Vandermeer wasn't running around the house waving a gun, mainly because the gun had vanished with Megan, but he was far from the numb creature he had been through much of the wait. There was a wildness in his eyes, a combination of desperation and sheer terror that was chilling in its own right.

Surrounded by Susan, Sam, and Hank, Savannah sat with him and talked. She ran through one argument after another, trying to convince him to stay cool, and when she'd gone through them all, Sam thought up more. Between them, they seemed to calm him.

With the insurance company set to deliver the money at four that afternoon and nothing to do until then, Savannah managed to convince him to rest for a while. Soon after he went upstairs, she and Susan went into the living room to talk.

"Are you okay?" she asked quietly. She sat sideways facing Susan, who wasn't drinking but looked as though she badly wanted to.

Susan leaned back against the sofa's brocade cushions and closed her eyes. "Ask me that in a week when I'm back home with all this forgotten."

"I'm really grateful to you. You know that, don't you? I couldn't be here and at work at the same time, and Will needed one of us."

Resting her head against the sofa, Susan opened one eye toward Savannah. "It's sad, Will needing us. The Vandermeers were always such a well-known family. He should have dozens of people rallying 'round."

"This is a kidnapping, not a party. He wanted to keep things quiet."

"What he wanted," Susan corrected, "was to keep the shortage of money quiet. You should see this place. It's looking pretty dumpy."

"Not dumpy. Just tired. And only at spots."

"What *happened*? What did Will do to the business?"

Savannah shrugged. "By his own admission, he's a lousy money manager."

"But he could have hired people to manage the money for him. When you come right down to it, how many people in his position do you know of who don't have armies of financial advisers and accountants?"

"The Vandermeers were always different that way. They were self-contained. Will's father and uncle built the business from scratch. Each had a strength. Apparently, Will's uncle was the whiz with figures, not Will's dad, and certainly not Will."

"I still can't believe he's blown it all. Meggie deserves better."

"She does, but only because things were so tough for her growing up. Will adores her. Maybe that compensates for whatever financial problems they have."

Susan wasn't buying that. "I can't imagine a love that strong. I mean, if you're talking a decrease of income from eighty thousand a year to sixty-five, that may be true. There's no abrupt change of lifestyle then. But from a million down to three hundred thousand, with most of that being poured back into the business—when a woman assumes she's marrying onto easy street and suddenly finds that she has to budget money for a weekend away, that love would have to be phenomenal." She shook her head. "No love's that strong." Stretched out in her yellow sweat suit, with her ankles crossed over leg warmers and aerobic sneakers, she looked and sounded surprisingly authoritative.

"Sad to feel that way," Savannah mused.

"Realistic."

"But sad. Don't you ever dream that you'll love a man that way? Or that a man will love you that way?"

"No."

"Never?"

"Never. Do you?"

Savannah hesitated before saying tentatively, "I have."

"Because you're a romantic. You dream through rose-colored glasses."

"Isn't a dream, by definition, something rosy?"

"Not necessarily. A dream can be practical. It doesn't have to be so overblown as to be unattainable. That's your problem. You shoot too high."

"There's nothing unrealistic about hoping for love."

"Not when it's a realistic kind of love."

"How would you define a 'realistic' kind of love?"

"One where two people take pleasure from a relationship. That pleasure can be financial or social. It doesn't always have to be interpersonal, and it *certainly* isn't the kind of all-powerful thing you have in mind. Your expectations for love are as high as your expectations for everything else in your life. But you're only setting yourself up for a fall. Don't you see that?"

Savannah didn't want to. "The way I look at it," she said, "if my expectations are high, I stand more of a chance of getting what I want than if I'd aimed lower to start with."

She grew quiet when Sam wandered into the room. She smiled at him when he moved on into the library. The French door had been fixed. Propping a forearm high against its frame, he looked out over the patio.

Susan resumed the conversation in a voice that was low and private but carried conviction. "The thing that matters most in a relationship is respect. Respect comes from power, and power comes from money. Statistics show that financial pressures are behind most divorces."

"What do statistics know? If the marriage is strong, the couple can handle the financial pressures."

"But money matters." Her eyes strayed to Sam's lanky frame. "It's a sign of power. When a man has money, he has a name for himself. People seek him out. They listen to him. He has clout. I respect a man who can make things happen." Her mouth slanted into a catlike grin. "I love him if he can make them happen for me."

"Did Dirk do that?"

The grin vanished. "No." Her eyes stayed on Sam.

"But you loved him."

"I thought I did." She paused. "Dirk was great in bed. He made things happen for me there, all right."

"But not elsewhere? I don't understand. You had a great house, a Jaguar, clothes, and jewelry, and—"

"I had to fight for everything. Dirk was one of the tightest men I've ever met. Not a romantic bone in his body." She lowered her voice to a whisper. "Now, if sex was all I wanted, I'd go after Sam. He has a kind of raw, male appeal, don't you think?"

Savannah knew other women felt it, though she'd never personally been drawn. "He doesn't have much money," she whispered back as a reminder to Susan, to whom money meant so much.

"Maybe not," Susan breathed, "but, Lord, he fills his jeans well."

Savannah debated that, finally conceding, "He has a nice butt, I suppose."

"Wait till he turns around and shows off the front."

"You sound as though he's purposely flaunting something."

"I've been wondering about that."

"Well, don't. Sam Craig isn't an exhibitionist. It's not his fault you're fixated on his fly."

Susan shrugged.

Savannah grunted. "This conversation is totally inappropriate."

"Not really. Let me tell you, there have been times in the past two days that I've wanted nothing more than for that man to throw me over his shoulder, take me up to bed, and make me forget everything that's happening here." She pursed her lips, then sent Savannah a sidelong glance. "Are you shocked?"

Savannah wasn't shocked for one very good reason. In essence, there wasn't much difference between Susan's thoughts about Sam and hers about Jared. She had made love to Jared in her mind countless times when she had been alone at night with only his voice for company, or when she'd needed an escape from the worries of her life.

Shocked? If Susan thought Sam well endowed, she should see Jared.

"You are shocked," Susan said. "You're blushing."

"I'm not shocked." She took a breath, then blurted out in a whisper, "Would you do it?"

"Do what?" Susan whispered back.

"Go to bed with him?"

"If he asked me nicely."

"Come on, Susan—"

"I don't know, Savannah. How can I possibly answer that? I'll be going home later, so if the opportunity was ever really here, it's gone. There will be absolutely no cause for me to see him again."

"Unless he calls."

"Why would he do that?"

"Maybe he likes you."

"He hates me."

"What if he did call—would you see him?"

"Probably not," Susan said, but she knew it was a lie. Sam Craig got to her. He annoyed her, frustrated her, excited her more than any man had in years. If he called her, she'd probably give him a hard time, but she'd probably see him, if only to find out whether the bulge in his jeans lived up to its promise. Then she'd dump him. He was, after all, just as unsuitable for her as she was for him.

"Hi, Savannah." Jared's deep voice sizzled over the line.

A breathless Savannah returned the greeting. "Hi there."

"You sound like you just got in."

She struggled to hold the phone, remove her coat, catch her breath, and talk at the same time. "I did. I was just coming down the hall when Janie signaled your call."

"Want me to call back?"

"No, no. Give me a second." Setting the phone on the desk, she hurried out of her coat and tossed it aside, unclipped her earring, put a hand to her chest, closed her eyes, and took a deep, measured breath. Then she picked up the phone again. "That's better," she said, knowing full well that the racing of her heart had nothing to do with the dash she'd made down the hall.

"How did it go?"

"Okay. He calmed down."

"Have you been there all this time?" It was nearly four in the afternoon. He had dropped her off before noon.

"No. I had a meeting in Pawtucket. But I stayed at Will's

for a couple of hours. I wanted to spend a little time with Susan, too. This has taken something out of her."

"Were you able to help her?"

"I don't know. I hope so."

"Did she help you?"

Savannah didn't answer at first. Then, a slow, wry smile formed on her lips. "Was I looking that bad?"

"Not bad. Never bad. You just looked like you could use someone to talk to, and who better than a twin."

"A sister," she corrected. "We're very different."

"Okay, a sister. Did she help?"

Again Savannah paused. No, Susan had not helped, at least, not when it came to Jared. Susan's mind was on all-out lovemaking, while Savannah was still debating a kiss.

A kiss was a milestone. It was a turning point. If Jared kissed her, their relationship would take a new path. If he kissed her, a barrier would be breached. All kinds of things were possible then, and that made her nervous, because she had expectations. She expected that she and Jared would be dynamite together in bed. Jared would be a spectacular lover; she'd be one in return. But what if he wasn't? What if *she* wasn't? One part of her, the cowardly part, thought it better never to try, than to try it and fail. Then she could still have her dreams.

She sighed. "No, Susan wasn't much help, not this time." She cleared her throat. "Did you find anything in those records?"

Yielding to her change of subject only because he acknowledged the pressing issue behind her question, Jared said, "I learned that some crazy has a thing about red licorice. For the past three months he's been bugging my receptionists about whether they like it. We're talking one or two calls per receptionist, per week, not enough to warrant an official complaint, just enough to be annoying as hell. But that's all, Savannah. I've pored through these papers three times, and there isn't anything that could even remotely be suggestive of a kidnapping or the kind of ransom note you have. Maybe you should go over them yourself. Something may strike you that didn't—"

"No. There's nothing." She sighed again, this time more wearily. "You were looking. If there'd been anything, you'd have seen it." Instinctively, she trusted him. "Besides, the kidnappers have been so careful in every other aspect of this crime, I don't know why I thought they'd leave tracks with you. It wouldn't fit with the way they've worked."

"It was worth a look."

She wasn't sure about that, but then from the first she'd had doubts about her reasons for seeking Jared out.

"Anyway, we're so near the exchange that it probably doesn't matter. Once Megan's back, we'll call in the FBI." She went suddenly quiet, then said in a lower voice, "I wish I could call them in now. I keep thinking and rethinking what I've done on this case, and it never seems to be enough. What do I know about kidnappings?"

"What does anyone know about them?"

"The FBI knows lots."

"Do you honestly think they'd have done more than you have? Think about it, Savannah. Even if you'd brought them in, given the threat in that ransom note, they'd have been hamstrung just like you. There aren't any miracle answers to a kidnapping. The first order of business is to get the hostage back, and that's what you've been working to do."

Again, Savannah was quiet, this time for a longer stretch. "Savannah?"

"I'm here," she said in a small voice.

"What is it?"

Still she was silent.

"Savannah?"

She felt the words bubbling up. They were out before she could stop them. "I'm frightened, Jared. What if something goes wrong?"

"Nothing's going to go wrong. Does your friend have the money?"

"He will. But I'm worried. I've been in charge of this case, and I've done my best, still things could blow up in my face."

"What things?"

"I don't know—Will could go bonkers halfway to the drop site, the kidnapper could decide the money isn't right—something bizarre that would make mockery of all the care we've taken. And more than anyone, I feel responsible."

"You've done everything you could."

"It may not be enough."

"It's as much as anyone else could have done. The kidnappers wouldn't allow more."

She twisted the phone cord back and forth. "Maybe I shouldn't have listened to them."

"You had to listen to Megan's husband. It's his wife, his money."

"But he came to us for help."

"Us. You and your boss. What's *he* done through all this?"

She paused, then admitted, "Not much."

"So? He put the weight of responsibility on your shoulders, and you've done your best. If he didn't feel that was enough, he could have stepped in at any time."

"I suppose." Her thoughts took a slight turn. "I didn't tell you about Paul."

"You didn't have to. One attorney general is like another. They're political creatures. Your boss knows that when a case of this kind hits the light, the media will scrutinize every step that was taken. What you do—or don't do—reflects on your boss. He's not going to let you jeopardize his career." He took a quick breath. "Am I right?"

She was quiet for a minute before murmuring, "You're right."

"He wouldn't do things any differently from what you've done."

"I suppose not."

"Whatever happens now is out of your hands. But you've tried your best. You have, Savannah. You have to keep telling yourself that."

She sighed. "I know."

For a minute, there was total silence on the line. Jared broke it by saying, "Are you okay?"

"Mmm. I'm okay." She actually felt a little better for having aired her concerns.

"Can I come over?"

"No. You're not supposed to know about this. You're not supposed to know about any of this, and here I am, blabbering about every little worry. Don't you get sick of it?"

"Sick of what?"

"Women pouring their hearts out to you."

Jared frowned. "They don't do that."

"They must. There's something about you that invites it."

"If there is, they don't see it. I lead a very private life, Savannah. I go my own way, do my own thing."

"But half of Rhode Island is in love with you."

"Half of Rhode Island may be in love with my voice," he said firmly, "but that's the extent of it. Most of Rhode Island doesn't know who I am or what I look like, and that's just the way I want it."

Savannah was startled by his vehemence. "I just assumed—"

"You assumed I had a steady string of women waltzing in and out of here, each one pouring out her heart and soul? Not quite. Even if I had the time, I wouldn't be interested. I work by night and sleep by day. I don't date a hell of a lot, because no one has interested me a hell of a lot." His voice went low. "Until now."

Savannah was without a comeback. Men as gorgeous as Jared didn't go through life alone. "I don't understand," she murmured. "There are dozens and dozens of women who'd be on your doorstep in a minute."

"I don't want women cluttering my doorstep. I'm not desperate. I don't need a woman to survive."

"I know that, but still I'd have thought—"

"That I'd be unable to resist what was offered? I'm thirty-nine years old, Savannah, not some rutting teenager. I like to think I've become a little discriminating with age."

"You don't date much?"

"I've already told you that, and why. Besides, when do I have time?"

"Weekends." She let her imagination wander to sweet places. "Evenings before work." And even sweeter places. "Early mornings after work."

Early mornings after work. Following her to those imaginary spots, Jared felt himself begin to swell. "Savannah . . ."

"What?"

He cleared his throat, which did a little to cancel the thickness of his voice. "You have it all figured out."

"I was just answering your question."

He swore under his breath, then said gruffly, "I must be nuts, chasing after a lady lawyer. My ex-wife was one. I thought I'd learned my lesson."

Savannah wasn't sure which statement to react to first—the fact that he was chasing after her, or that he had an ex-wife. A previous marriage meant that he valued the concept of monogamy enough to give it a shot. Of course, something had gone wrong. His wife was an ex.

She closed her eyes. "You're being very unfair."

Jared was still trying to cool his arousal. "Look who's talking."

"How was *I* being unfair?"

"Early mornings—do you have any idea what it does to a man to hear a woman talk about early mornings in that soft, very feminine tone of voice?"

"You're a fine one to talk about tones of voice," she accused. "Yours are nearly pornographic."

"Does my voice turn you on?"

"Damn right, it does."

"Then maybe we're even," he mumbled. A second later, he raised his voice. "How was *I* being unfair?"

"By dropping that little bomb about your ex-wife when I don't have time to follow it up. I'm supposed to be back at Will's by five."

The thought was sobering. "What will you do there for three hours?"

"Go a little crazy," she said in a grim tone. "I want to be sure everything's set for the drop, then make sure Will stays sane. If it weren't for Megan, I'd work here until later. But I'm having trouble concentrating, so I wouldn't accomplish much anyway. We'll probably waste a little time ordering in dinner—waste, because I doubt any of us will be hungry. Except Sammy and Hank. They always eat."

"Can I drive you over there?"

"No."

"Can I deliver dinner?"

"No—uh, maybe—no, you'd better not."

"Why not?"

"I don't think it would be smart."

"I'll take Melissa's Volkswagen, and it'll be dark, anyway. Just call that number I gave you—the private one—when you decide what you want. I'll call in the order, pick it up, and deliver it."

"What a pain in the neck for you."

Jared didn't respond with words. She felt his answer in an uncanny sense of awareness that came over the line. He wanted to see her again. She couldn't fight that.

"You have that conference call to make at six," she said softly.

"I'll make it at five."

"Can you do that?"

"I'm the one with the most money. I can do it. I'll be free by six."

"Are you sure you don't mind?" she asked very softly.

"I'll be waiting for your call. Talk with you soon." He hung up before she could say another word.

* * *

At six-thirty, Jared showed up at the Vandermeers' back door carrying an assortment of Big Macs, Chicken Mc-Nuggets, salads, fries, and drinks. Savannah met him, led him into the kitchen only far enough to put the bags on the table, then hurried him back to the door. Once there, she tried to press a twenty-dollar bill into his hand. He promptly slid it into the vee of her pale gray wool blouse. His fingers lingered for a split second on her skin, then left. His eyes lingered longer.

"Let me know what's happening?" he asked in a husky murmur.

"I don't know where I'll be or when I'll get home." She was gently pushing him toward the door.

"Try. Okay?" Taking her hand from his arm, he enclosed it in his. "Why are you trying to get rid of me? Do I embarrass you?"

She tugged her hand free and resumed her pushing.

"You're supposed to be a messenger, and a messenger wouldn't stay this long. Besides, I don't want you to see my sister. One look at her and you'll think I'm a dud."

His eyes strayed past her. "Is that her? The one with the gorgeous red hair, the sexy bod, and the bottle of Chivas?"

Savannah bit her lip, which was precisely where Jared looked next. The cast of his eye became more pronounced, the gray flecks darker, creating a smoky look that made her burn. Her teeth relaxed their hold; her lips parted.

"It's you I want," he whispered. "Call me later?"

She gave a jerky nod, which was all her hammering heart would allow.

"Promise?"

She nodded again, then gripped the door as he left. It seemed the only static thing in sight. She closed it, locked it, took the twenty-dollar bill from between her breasts, and buried it in her pocket. Then she turned.

Susan, who'd been watching her, put down the bottle of scotch and began to unload the first of the bags. "A messenger, you say? He sure didn't look like a messenger, not the way he was dressed. That jacket didn't come from Kmart. How well do you know him?"

"Not well."

"Did you see the way he was looking at you?"

"He was delivering our dinner."

"He looked like he wanted to eat you for his."

"For God's sake!" Scowling, Savannah glanced nervously toward the hall.

"He was big for a delivery boy. Looked more like a bodyguard. You should have invited him in. He could prove helpful later."

Savannah set one drink after another on the table. With each she regained a bit more control. "He won't be needed. Everything is going to be just fine, Susan. Just fine."

At first, it looked that way. Will was nervous, which was understandable, but he seemed to know exactly what he was supposed to do, and he hadn't lapsed into wildness again. So Savannah, Susan, and Hank were optimistic as he and Sam left.

The plan was for Sam to follow him most of the way, wait until Will made the drop, then trail him home. Both cars were equipped with two-way radios. If Will panicked at any point, Sam could help.

Will didn't panic. As though taken by a drugged calm, he

put the paper bag filled with money into the dumpster as directed, then sat quietly in his car.

When he didn't signal that he was leaving, Sam began to get nervous. "Will? Can you hear me, Will?"

"I'm waiting," Will informed him.

"For what?"

"That guy."

"No, you're not. Get out of there, Will."

"I'm waiting. That man hung up on me before I could speak with Megan. I want him to know that if he dares harm her—"

"Buddy, he'll do more than harm her if you don't get your tail out of there."

"I'm waiting."

"You do that and you'll blow the whole thing."

"I'm waiting."

Sam touched the gun holstered under his arm. "Fine. You wait, and I'm coming in with my lights flashing and my badge on display. You want that?"

"I'll report you."

"I don't give a shit. We've played by certain rules this far, and we're gonna go all the way. Now, do you come out, or do I come in?"

There was a lengthy silence. Sam was reaching to start his car when Will said, "Fuck you."

"What does that mean? Are you coming or not?"

"I'm coming. But I'll report you."

"Fine. Just get the hell out of there, and do it now."

Two minutes later, Will's car bombed past. He was suddenly in a big rush to get home, so much so that he ran two red lights. Shoving a portable flasher to the top of his car,

Sam followed him right through and stuck close behind until he'd pulled up at the house.

Savannah was on her way out, working into her coat as she ran. She stopped first at Sam's window. "The call just came in." She gave him the address of a phone booth on the street corner in Warwick. "The Warwick police are on their way. They'll be there before we will. Did you see anything?"

"I didn't, but my plants did. A battered blue Camaro, a gray Plymouth, and a dusty LeMans. We've got plates for the last two. I've already called them in."

"Megan will have to tell us more. The state police are on alert. They're setting up ID checks at the local points of departure and will question anyone who looks suspicious. They're ready to move on whatever Megan gives us."

Susan was climbing into the car. "You go with Will," she told Savannah. "You're better with him than I am."

Hank had already pushed Will over to the passenger's side. Savannah ran to the rear door and climbed in. Her door was barely shut when they were off.

The drive seemed endless. If Savannah had been able to tell Will that Megan had been the one on the phone, things would have been better. But Megan hadn't called. The voice had been the same as the one that morning, this time offering nothing more than an address. Megan's condition was still unknown. And given that, every doubt, every fear of the past two days surfaced.

Hank followed Sam, who was given detailed directions by radio. Will sat stiffly in the passenger's seat, staring at the road. Savannah was grateful to be alone in the back.

When they crossed into Warwick, they were met by a local cruiser. Given the day and hour, lights and sirens were unnecessary. But the escort was a help, showing them the fastest way to the commercial district, then the telephone booth that stood at the designated spot.

A ring of police cars were already there. Sam and Hank pulled up quickly. Will was out of the car and running almost before they'd stopped. The others were close behind.

At first Savannah saw nothing but police officers. Several stood clustered around the phone booth, several knelt by its door. They parted for Will, who came to an abrupt halt. Two steps behind him, Savannah did the same, then caught her breath.

Megan was huddled in a corner of the phone booth floor, looking as though she had seen the far side of hell.

Chapter 9

SAVANNAH REMEMBERED the first time she had seen Megan as though it had been fifteen hours, rather than fifteen years earlier. They'd been starting their sophomore year in high school. She and Susan had arrived at the academy old hands at knowing what to do and what not to do, and, along with their friends, had taken pleasure watching the new girls arrive. As veterans, they felt cocky; the initial fear of leaving home, looking right, fitting in was a thing of the past. They smirked at the girl who arrived in a stretch limo trying to impress someone, smiled warmly at the one whose gorgeous older brother was helping her move in, laughed at the one who came laden with every electrical appliance imaginable since there were only two outlets per room.

Megan had been one of the last to arrive, and she had been different from the rest in every regard. Her clothes were not chic, her nails were not painted, her hair was not carelessly arranged, and if those things hadn't given her away, her mother would have. The woman drove an old Ford and was as unadorned as the headmistress' secretary.

Megan was clearly on scholarship, which wasn't unusual at the academy. What was unusual about Megan was her sense of dignity. Her eyes held fear of the unknown, yet she went about the business of unpacking and settling in as though she intended to do as fine a job at that as she would at everything else. For a girl, who had come from modest means at best, her poise was remarkable.

Her mother was equally remarkable. Though plain, she was incredibly warm. Savannah and Susan, who had lost their own mother three years before, gravitated toward her.

And they adored Megan. She liked the music they liked, hated the teachers they hated, and was always ready to try something new with them. She was the third Musketeer. The fact that she looked like Savannah, far more than Susan did, was a constant source of amusement, but she complemented them in other ways, too. When they were impractical, she was down to earth. When they acted spoiled, she was sparing. When they opened her eyes to certain pleasures in life, she reflected those pleasures back with fresh insight.

Savannah had always known that, of the three of them, Megan was the brightest. Her grades were consistently the highest. She was imaginative, hard-working, and street-smart in ways that Savannah and Susan, for all their travels, never were. And she always had a smile, which made her a joy to be with.

Savannah saw nothing remotely joyous about the woman huddled on the floor of that phone booth. When Will called her name in a broken voice and reached for her, she shrank into the corner. Her eyes were forbidding as she looked up at him. Without a sound uttered, everything about her screamed, "Don't come near!" The Megan who had always been eminently approachable didn't want to be touched.

"It's me, Meggie," Will cried brokenly. "It's over. Thank God, it's over." He tried to touch her arm, and she flinched, crowding into her little corner with her legs drawn in ever tighter. "No one's going to hurt you. I've come to take you home." Again he reached out. She made a faint sound, gave a short, harsh shake of her head.

Frantic, Will looked up at Savannah. "What's wrong with her? Jesus, what have they done?"

Savannah didn't know. Megan's eyes were hollow, her face ashen, but there were no bruises to suggest she'd been beaten. She looked dirty—her face, her hair, her hands— though her robe was as fresh and clean as ever.

"Meggie?" Savannah said in a voice that was soft and far steadier than her insides were just then. She crouched beside Will. "We want to take you home, Meggie. It's cold here. Your robe isn't heavy enough, and your feet are bare. Can we take you home?"

The same hollow eyes that had stared at Will turned on her.

Savannah tried to soothe her. "Everything's going to be okay. You're safe. It's all over." She extended a hand. "Let's get you out of here. They're gone now. They can't do anything more to you."

Lowering her head, Megan pressed her eyes to her knees.

Savannah reached back for Sam, who was quickly beside her. Her fingers dug into his arm. "We need a doctor," she whispered. "Something's very wrong."

Will was trying again, sounding more frightened by the minute. "Talk to me, Meggie. You know who I am. I've been waiting so long for you to come home. Look at me, Meggie. Talk to me."

Easing Savannah aside, Sam hunkered down in her place. He held up a hand to quiet Will, inched closer to Megan, whose face was still buried, and said in a low, very gentle voice, "My name is Sam Craig, Megan. We've never met, but I've been wanting you home, too. I know that this is overwhelming—all the police cars and lights and strange men standing around. We can take you away from this as soon as you want. It's up to you to say the word."

He touched her hair. When she didn't object, he began to lightly stroke it.

"You've been through so much," he continued on in that same soothing voice. "You need a rest. A warm bed. Something hot to drink. I can get you all that. Come with me, Megan?"

She didn't answer. Nor did she pull away from the hand that was gently, gently stroking her hair.

"I'm going to come a little closer," he said, matching the act to the words. "I'm going to pick you up and take you back to my car." As he carefully lifted her, he said, "Will and Savannah will be with us. Susan, too. We've all been very worried." She buried her face against his chest as he started toward the car.

His eyes gave commands to the others as he walked, and all the while he talked softly into Megan's ear. "You feel chilled. You'll be warmer in the car. Everything's going to be fine, Megan, just fine. When was the last time you ate? Are you hungry?" He slid her in past the steering wheel of his car and slid in right after her. Savannah took up her other side, Will and Susan climbed into the back. Putting an arm around her shoulders, Sam said, "Lean against me, Megan. You must be exhausted. Sleep if you want. I'm going to take you to see the doctor. Then I'll take you home. Everything's going to be fine now. Everything's going to be just fine."

His words were highly optimistic. Megan remained silent during the drive to the hospital. Looking frightened and frail, she didn't move, not even to take back her hand when Savannah held it gently. It was as though she despaired of something which none of them quite understood.

The hours that followed were long and tense. Megan was examined by doctors and counselors trained to handle crisis situations. The verdict was that she had been abused for nearly three days. Megan wasn't offering any details herself, though. She nodded or shook her head, even occasionally murmured a word or two in response to questions, but she had to be carefully led to each answer and she didn't volunteer a thing.

Over Will's objections, but at the doctors' insistence, she was admitted to the hospital. It was nearly two in the morning before the physical and mental prodding was done, nearly three before she was taken to a private room, nearly four before she'd been bathed and made comfortable, nearly five before she fell asleep, and then only under sedation.

When Will finally left to go home for several hours, Savannah stayed to talk with Sam, Hank, and the other law enforcement people they had finally been able to bring into the case. It was after six when she punched out the number that was written on the slip of paper she'd pushed into the pocket of her coat.

The voice that came through the receiver was as good as a lifeline. "Yes?"

"Jared?"

There was a moment's silence, then a deep and relieved, "I've been worried. Is everything all right?"

Eyes closed, she concentrated on the low, sandy sound that soothed her so. It was the sanest thing she'd heard all night.

"Savannah?"

"I'm at the hospital," she said quietly.

"Is Megan back?"

"Uh-huh."

"Is she okay?"

"I don't know." She took an unsteady breath. "I'm so tired. I want to go home, but I don't have my car."

"I'll be right there."

"You don't mind?"

"I'll be right there."

Within ten minutes he was at the hospital entrance. Savannah left the step she'd been sitting on and by the time she reached the Pathfinder, he'd leaned across the seat and opened the door. Climbing up, she pulled the door shut, put her head back against the seat, and closed her eyes.

"Get me away from here," she whispered. "Please."

Jared didn't have to do more than glance at her face to see how upset she was. Her skin was pale, her features tinged with an anguish that was muted only by fatigue.

Without a word, he left the hospital and headed for the center of town. Worried, he looked at her often. She didn't move, didn't open her eyes, didn't speak. He was beginning to wonder if she'd fallen asleep when, just as he pulled up at her townhouse, she raised her head.

He didn't ask whether he could come in. By the time she found her keys in her briefcase, he was helping her out of the car. Taking the keys from her hand, he unlocked her front door and pushed it open, then stood back while she disengaged the burglar alarm. When she closed the door, he was inside.

Dropping her briefcase on the floor of the foyer, she looked up at him, but he had no idea what she saw. Her eyes were distant. "I'm—I think I'll take a bath," she murmured.

Without another word, she turned and started up the front stairs.

Jared looked after her until she'd rounded the railing on top and disappeared into what he assumed was her bedroom. For a split second he considered following. She seemed so out of it. He would gladly have run her bath, helped her in, brought her a glass of wine, bathed her—with no sexual thoughts in mind.

But she hadn't asked him to follow. Much as he craved her need for him, she was still an independent woman. She hadn't invited him up; he couldn't go.

Ten minutes later, he thought differently. The house was too quiet. He hadn't heard a sound—not footsteps or the creak of the wood floors, not the open or close of a drawer or a closet, not the faintest trickle of running water.

He wouldn't have been surprised if she had passed out. She'd been going for nearly twenty-four hours under intense stress. He was worried.

Knowing that he couldn't just sit and wait, he went quietly up the stairs. There were three doors at the top, two open and one partially closed. The open ones led to a bathroom and a bedroom. Both rooms were empty. He went to the third and knocked lightly.

"Savannah?" He pushed the door open. The room was dim, with only the pale light of dawn filtering through the window. It was enough to light her slim frame. She was curled sideways in a large wing chair. Her cheek was pressed to the leather, her arms wrapped tightly around her middle. She was shaking all over. The sight wrenched his insides.

Crossing the carpet, he knelt down by the chair and whispered. "Savannah?" He touched her face with the backs of his fingers. "What is it?"

She shook her head and held up a hand to tell him she'd be fine in a minute, but he closed his large hand around hers and took it to his neck. The warmth of his skin contrasted so sharply with the chill of her own that she greedily opened her hand. She needed more of that warmth.

Her eyes opened and told him so. He didn't need to be told twice. Drawing her down to where he knelt, he settled her between his legs and wrapped her in his arms. The same cheek that had pressed to leather was now pressed to his chest.

Still she trembled.

"It's okay," he whispered, tightening his arms around her. "It's okay. Just try to relax. It's okay." He rubbed his chin against her hair, massaged her back with his hand. All the while his heart beat rapidly. He worried about her, but mixed with the worry was a kind of pleasure. She was such a strong woman, yet she still had her moments of weakness. And in this one she needed him.

He looked down at her face, brushed his lips to her brow. It was damp, clammy. He held her head flush to his chest, wishing he could do more, knowing instinctively that nothing more would help. She just needed to be held.

So he held her while she trembled, murmured soft words of encouragement from time to time, rubbed her back, stroked her hair, absorbed her shivers until gradually they lessened. She took longer breaths, then deeper breaths. At last, flattening a hand on his chest, she eased herself back.

Reluctantly he let her go. As she stood, she nudged her knit skirt down to where it belonged just above her knees.

Her head was bowed, her eyes on the floor, her voice paper-thin.

"I'd like that bath now."

"Can I wait here?"

She nodded. Then, in her stockinged feet, since her shoes lay where she'd kicked them by the side of the chair, she padded out of the den.

This time, Jared heard sounds. He could monitor her activity by listening—to the whine of the closet door, the rattle of hangers, the slide of a drawer. She was not deliberately broadcasting what she was doing, but his ears were well trained in the art of detection.

There had been many nights in that elegant home in Seattle when he had listened to the prominent woman who was his wife dress for one political affair after another. He had listened to her undress later. He had even listened to her work, to the sound of her pencil rasping across the paper as she plotted her latest brilliant trial tactic. He hadn't listened hard enough or long enough, or he'd have known when she'd called her lover.

He had been trusting. He had been a fool.

Of course, he had known that Elise was a scrambler. He had known that she had ambitions in life. All of Seattle had known that. And it wasn't as though he was an innocent entering the marriage. He had ambitions of his own, into which Elise fit nicely. When she cheated on him, those ambitions became tainted.

The sound of running water snapped him from the wave of memory, and he smiled. Savannah was taking her bath.

He trusted Savannah. He didn't wonder how or why, he just did. Perhaps it was arrogance on his part, but he didn't think she could look him in the eye and lie. If anything, the reverse was true. When she looked him in the eye, she opened up—reluctantly and unintentionally, perhaps, but he wasn't complaining.

Shifting on his heels, he looked around the room. It was den, library, and office combined, and was small, cozy, and charming, none of which he had noticed when he'd first entered the room. He had only seen Savannah trembling then.

She was quiet now. The occasional ripple of water told him just where she was. He pictured her, but this time he didn't smile. She wasn't happy. Whatever had happened to Megan had spread its ugliness to Savannah, too.

Rising from the floor, he went to the window and stood looking out over the awakening city until he heard the water begin to drain from the tub. Seconds later, Savannah rose from the water.

The water continued to drain. Then all was silent.

He waited, unsure of where she was or what she expected of him. Unable to wait longer, when images of her slim body trembling filled his mind's eye, he went out, through the hall to her bedroom. She wasn't there, but the adjoining bathroom door was ajar. Knocking softly, he called her name. When she didn't answer, he cautiously opened the door.

She was sitting on the rim of the tub, her hands clasping its porcelain lip on either side of her hips. She wore a soft, white, knee-length nightgown with a scooped neck and long sleeves. Her bangs were damp and brushed to the side, while the rest of her hair fell over one shoulder, not quite reaching her breasts.

Jared felt as though he'd been punched in the gut. He swallowed hard, then swallowed again when she looked up at him. Her eyes were glazed, and when she spoke, her voice trembled.

"We found her crumpled up in a phone booth. She wouldn't respond to Will or to me. It was like she refused to make the connection between what she used to be and what she'd become. Sammy was a stranger. He managed to get through to her enough so we could get her into the car and to the hospital."

She paused, swallowed, looked unseeingly at the tiles on the floor while her knuckles went white. "I held her hand in the car. It was so cold and lifeless. We hadn't seen any marks on her at first, but there in the car I could see marks around her wrists, rope burns." Her voice grew weaker. "And she was filthy—her hair, her face, her hands and feet—but her robe was immaculate." Her voice fell to a whisper. "No wonder. She hadn't worn the robe for three days. The entire time they'd kept her naked—tied to the bed—her hands over her head—" she faltered and flinched, "her legs spread."

Pressing her own together, she closed her eyes and tucked her chin to her chest. Her arms began to shake at the elbows.

Lowering himself beside her, Jared drew her against him. Her fingers closed convulsively on handfuls of his sweater, and if they took several chest hairs with them, he didn't care. The tweaking was a welcome pain.

"They raped her, Jared," she told him in a tormented voice that was only slightly muffled by his throat. "They raped her over and over again. Two men. Taking turns. She was raw and bleeding inside, but that must have turned them on more. They kept her tied to that bed."

Swallowing a moan, Jared held her tighter.

"The doctor said she was bruised all over. Black and blue marks, teeth marks on her breasts and her stomach. They untied her long enough to turn her over, then they abused her that way until they turned her again." She gasped for air and wailed, "What kinds of men are we dealing with? What kinds of animals could do something like that?"

"Animals don't," Jared said angrily. "That's the interesting part. Animals don't hurt others of their species that way. Only men do. They even take pleasure in the pain they inflict."

"But why? Why Megan? What did she ever do to deserve that kind of pain? All she ever wanted in life was a small measure of financial security. She didn't ask for the world. She certainly didn't ask for wealth. She married Will because she was in love. What did she do so wrong?"

"I don't know," he said, working to get a handle on his anger. It wouldn't help Savannah any. She needed soothing. Rubbing his jaw against her hair, he inhaled her sweet, clean smell and said gently, "Some things happen without any reason at all."

"They got the money. They knew they'd get the money. Why did they have to put their filthy hands on Megan?"

He didn't answer. There were no answers to give, and he knew Savannah knew that. The best he could do was to hold her tightly and let her vent the anger and pain and frustration that festered inside.

"I should have done more," she murmured. "If I'd known what they were doing to her, I'd have brought in every law enforcement agency in the state."

"They brutally raped her. That has to tell you what they're capable of. If you'd openly brought in the law after they'd warned against it, they'd have killed her."

"I've been telling myself that, but I'm not sure there's much difference between rape like that and murder. You didn't see Megan's face, Jared. It was awful—not a bruise in sight, but it was totally changed. Like she'd been hollowed from the inside out. Like something inside her had died."

"She's not dead, Savannah. You have to remember that. She's not dead. She'll heal. There are counselors who'll help, psychiatrists."

"She was practically catatonic."

"She can be treated."

"It was awful. She looked at Will as though it hurt to see him. She looked at me the same way. Do you know how that felt?" She gave an anguished cry. "Talk about setting off a guilt trip!"

Taking her face in one hand, Jared turned it up to his. "Not guilt. There's no reason at all for that. You did your best. You made decisions based on the information you had. It's easy enough in hindsight to say what you should have done, but given the same situation again, you'd have to do the same thing. There's nothing you could have done differently. The risk would have been too great."

"If I'd known—"

"No. Nothing differently." His voice was at the same time firm, but gentle and pleading like his eyes. "Savannah, you tried. You had people working with you and none of them told you to do anything but what you did. It wasn't like you were going against orders, or even advice." He paused. "Have you spoken with your boss?"

She gave a single nod against his hand. "He's not thrilled. He was hoping we'd rescue both Megan and the money."

"How did he hope you'd do that?"

"He didn't say."

Jared swore. "Politicians are assholes. So concerned

about the next election that they lose sight of what they're elected to do. So what was he doing while this rescue was taking place? He was probably in some woman's bed, screwing her wild."

"He's at a conference."

"Same difference. You know that guy's reputation, don't you?"

"Paul's wife is a cripple. She's been unable to respond to him for years. Still he's been wonderful to her, faithful in every respect but that." Closing her eyes, she took in a long, tired breath, then let it out in a quiet, "Oh, God."

Jared knew it had nothing to do with Paul DeBarr, and he felt suddenly contrite. Pressing her head close again, he massaged her scalp. For a strong woman, she felt fragile in his arms. "Want to get some sleep?"

"Each time I close my eyes, I see Megan."

"She'll recover, Savannah," he said by her ear. "The bruises will fade. Each day she'll feel stronger."

"But emotionally—"

"That's what I'm talking about. She'll recover. She'll have people around her who love her. She'll mend."

Savannah sighed and rested more of her weight against him. "I'd like to believe that."

"Meanwhile, the cops will do their thing. Was she able to give them any clues?"

Savannah shook her head. With the outpouring of the tale, she was feeling purged, and very tired. "Two men, that's all," she said softly.

"No descriptions?"

Again she shook her head.

"No names? Nicknames? Locations?"

Another headshake.

"Savannah?"

"Mmm?"

"Want to sit someplace else?" he whispered. "This tub's killing my butt."

She would have smiled if she hadn't felt so drawn. "I'm going to bed," she said. Mustering the sum total of strength she had left, which wasn't much but did the trick, she levered herself off him and stood up.

He followed her into the bedroom, watched her pull back the comforter and slide between the sheets. He caught fleeting glimpses of nice things like manicured toenails, delicate feet, and slender legs before they disappeared. But those things weren't of prime importance just then. The focus of his attention was her face. It lacked color. She was exhausted.

Crossing to the window, he adjusted the blinds to blot out the rising sun. then he returned to squat by the side of the bed. "I take it you're not going to work."

"Not this morning," she murmured. She lay on her side looking at him, but her eyes were leaden. "I'll call in at nine."

"You'll be asleep then."

"I'll wake up."

"You have to sleep."

"I can sleep later."

She dragged in an uneven breath. "I'd better call, myself. I'll have to tell Janie what to postpone to when." She closed her eyes.

"Should I set the alarm to wake you?" Jared whispered.

Her eyelids didn't flutter. They were too heavy for that. "No," she whispered back.

He said nothing more, satisfied to study her features in silence. They were delicate, sculpted by a fine genetic tool. Unable to resist, he lightly brushed the pad of his thumb over the shadowed crease between her eyes.

She didn't blink, didn't seem to notice what he'd done. Her breathing was soft and slow. Assuming she'd fallen asleep, he was surprised when she whispered his name.

"Jared?"

"Right here."

"Talk to me."

"Talk to you."

"Say something, anything. I like listening to you when I fall asleep."

"Do you now?" he asked, inordinately pleased by that.

"Mmm."

He bobbed lightly on the balls of his feet, then braced his forearms on his thighs and let his hands fall between. He didn't know what to say. She was used to listening to him at work, but he couldn't very well break into a lazy monologue as though he were on the air. He wasn't self-centered enough to talk about himself, and the things he wanted to say about Savannah were too whimsical to air. Nor could he talk about Megan.

So he took a deep breath and said in a voice that was low and lyrical, "Once upon a time, there was a princess. She had pretty brown eyes, chestnut-colored hair, and a sprinkling of freckles across her nose. She lived in a huge castle."

"Where?" Savannah murmured.

"Hmm?"

"Where was the castle?"

He hesitated for a mere second. "In Frewschnort."

"Frewschnort?"

He rather liked the sound, thought it worth repeating.

"Frewschnort. She lived there with her father, the king, and her sister, princess number two."

"How did you know I was born first?"

"I didn't. Who says this story's about you?"

"Is it?"

"I don't know yet. Give me a minute and we'll both find out." He took her silence as permission to continue. "As kingdoms went, Frewschnort was on the small side; but what it lacked in size it made up for in beauty. There were rolling hills and meadows, forests and streams. The temperature hovered between sixty and seventy-five, and smog was a thing of the future. In fact, Frewschnort would have been an idyllic place if it hadn't been for the Grumpslaw. . . ."

His voice trailed off. He waited for Savannah to prod him on, but she didn't. Nor did she respond when he whispered her name. Slowing rising to his full height, he stood watching her for several minutes. Then, very quietly, he left the room.

Sam Craig hammered on Susan's front door with his fist, making enough noise to wake the dead— though it wasn't the dead he wanted to wake, just Susan. She hadn't responded to the doorbell. She wasn't responding to his banging. He was worried.

He'd been worried since she left the hospital by cab at four that morning. She had been in rough shape and he would bet she headed straight for a bottle. While a drink or two might have helped her relax, he doubted she would stop there.

Leaving the steps, he started around the house, scrutinizing overhanging trees, latticework, and windows as he went.

He finally settled on a tree whose limbs came comfortably close to a small balcony. Within minutes, he was on the balcony and easily jimmying the lock on the door.

He found himself in a small guest bedroom. From there, he made his way down the hall. He stuck his head into each room he passed and shouted Susan's name with increasing regularity. She wasn't expecting anyone to be in the house with her. His intent wasn't to scare her to death, but to make sure she was all right.

At the end of the hall was the master bedroom. It was the one room that looked at all lived in. Clothes were scattered on the unmade bed. Shoes trailed from the closet. A large armoire stood open to reveal a hefty supply of liquor, a collection of glasses, and an ice bucket.

There was no sign of Susan in the room.

For safekeeping, he checked the adjoining bathroom. Towels lay strewn on the sink and the edge of the tub. He closed his hand around one; it was damp to the touch. Returning to the hall, he trotted downstairs.

She wasn't in the living room or the dining room. He found her in the den at the end of the hall, sitting on the floor beside an elegant cherrywood bar. Her back and head were against the wall. Her feet were flat on the floor and bare, her knees bent. The folds of her long wraparound robe fell between her legs. Half buried in the material was the glass that dangled from her hand.

Through eyes filled with misery, she watched him approach. His step slowed as he neared. He stopped several feet away.

"Are you all right?" he asked. He had fully expected to find her stone drunk, but, looking at her, he wasn't sure. More than anything, she seemed tired and unhappy. When she didn't answer, he said, "I tried to call. Didn't the phone ring?"

She tipped her head a fraction and gave a single nod.

"Why didn't you answer?"

With her head at the same slightly tipped angle against the wall, she lifted a shoulder in a weak shrug. It struck Sam then that she did look weak. He could understand it, after the few days she'd been through. He still didn't know if she was drunk.

"Have you gotten any sleep?"

Her eyes didn't move from his, as though she didn't have the power to direct them. But, very slowly, she moved her head from one side to the other.

"Don't you think you should? It's been more than twenty-four hours."

She spoke then. Her speech wasn't exactly slurred, though she barely moved her mouth, and the sound that came through was meek. "How did you get in?"

"I climbed a tree and snuck in through one of the bedrooms."

"That's breaking and entering."

"No. It's trying to be a Good Samaritan. You might have made things a little easier by answering either your telephone or the door. I've been worried."

Susan straightened her head against the wall. That was the only change she made. Her mouth moved as little as it had before, her voice was as meek. "Savannah sent you."

"I haven't spoken with Savannah."

"She sent you."

He shook his head. "I haven't spoken with her."

"You wouldn't have come otherwise."

He frowned. "Why would you think that?"

"Because you respect Savannah. You'd do anything she asked."

"I work with Savannah. I'd do what she asked if it made sense. But I'm not here on business. This is personal."

Susan raised the glass to her mouth and tipped it, but only to take in an ice cube. When the glass was back dangling between her thighs, she closed her eyes. "You're not making sense."

Coming closer, Sam squatted before her. "I was worried about you, Susan. You've been through a lot this week, and last night wasn't a picnic to top it off. I've been through things like this before. You haven't. I wanted to help."

Her eyes were open again, but vague. "Why?"

"I like you."

She inched her head from side to side. "You think I'm spoiled and stuck-up. You like my looks, but you don't like me."

"Half right. I do like your looks. But I like you, too. I'm just trying to decide how much."

She looked mildly confused as she considered that. Then she turned sullen. "Don't bother. It's not worth the effort."

"Why not?"

"Because what you see is what you get. There's not much inside the shell."

"That's a lousy way to talk about yourself."

She gave a minuscule shrug.

"Do you really have that low an opinion of yourself?"

"There's not much evidence to the contrary, as my sister the lawyer would say."

"Savannah never said that about you."

"Maybe not, but I'm sure she's thought it often enough."

"I don't think so."

"Well, I do. She's made something of her life. What does she see when she looks at me? A big zero."

"She sure didn't see that this week. You were there when she called. You stayed with Will when she couldn't be there."

"I was a body. That's all. And don't tell me that I cooked, because you did as much of that as I did."

"I like to cook."

"Great. Good. Be my guest."

"Are you drunk?" he came right out and asked.

Her look was venomous. "No, I am not drunk, and that's the real bitch of this whole thing. I can't even do that right!" She took a shallow breath. "I've tried, God, I've tried. I've had glass after glass of the stuff, and I keep waiting to feel numb." The venom in her eyes had faded, giving way to a slow rise of fear. "But it's not coming. I don't know if I'm not drinking enough fast enough or what, but I'm not feeling better. I think of Megan and it hurts. God, it hurts."

Her eyes had filled with tears. She raised both hands to her face, unaware of dropping the glass in her lap. Sam grabbed for it quickly and set it aside. Then he curled his fingers around her wrists.

"Come upstairs, Susan. You'll feel better after you've had some sleep."

The heels of her hands were firmly anchored against her eyes. "I won't feel better again."

"Sure, you will," he coaxed. He rubbed his thumbs lightly over the insides of her wrists. "You need sleep and a little distance from all this. Drinking hasn't helped—"

"I need more." She took her hands from her eyes, took Sam's hands right down with them. "One more," she said, hopeful through her tears. "That's the one that will work."

He held tight to her wrists. "It won't. Trust me. It'll only hurt more."

She shook her head, vigorously this time. "No."

"Yes."

Her face crumbled. "It can't. Nothing can hurt more than what I feel right now." She let her head loll against the wall. But she was breathing quickly, shallowly, and her throat was working in a convulsive kind of way.

Sam knew what was coming before she did. He drew her quickly to her feet, and by that time she had shaky fingers pressed to her mouth. She ran out to the hall, tore open the powder-room door, and reached the toilet in time to be violently sick.

He was right there to support her. He stood behind her, legs set wide, one arm around her middle as she bent over, the other holding her head.

The spasms continued until her stomach was empty, and even then the dry heaves went on for a bit. When he was sure that she had nothing more to throw up, he put the toilet seat down, propped her on it, and began to bathe her face.

She tried to pull away, but he wouldn't have that, so she closed her eyes and whispered, "I'm sorry. Oh, hell. This is disgusting."

"Shh." He wiped around her mouth.

When he dropped the cloth in the sink and wet another, she cried softly, "How can you stand being in here?"

"I'll live."

"I may not. I feel dizzy, Sammy. I want to lie down."

"Soon." He mopped her forehead and eyes, then he did what he could with her hair. All the while he bent over her, he kept her propped against his hip.

"Do you know," she breathed weakly, "that the cloth you're using was hand-monogrammed in Milan?"

"You don't say," he said, and couldn't have cared less. He eyed the front of her robe. It needed a washing, too. "I have to hand it to you," he sighed gently, "when you do things, you do them big." Slipping an arm around her back, he helped her stand. "We're going upstairs now. Stomach steady?"

Susan nodded. She felt as limp as her hand-monogrammed towel and had to lean heavily against his side. He wasn't much taller than she, perhaps three or four inches, but he was far stronger. Just then, she was grateful.

Once upstairs, he led her through the bedroom to the bathroom and immediately turned on the shower.

"I want to lie down," she protested weakly.

"Once you're clean."

"I can't stand up in there."

"I'll hold you."

"You'll get wet."

"I could use a shower." Steam was rising in the stall; he adjusted the heat of the water so that neither of them would get burned. "It's been a long night for me, too."

"You can't come in my shower."

"Are you gonna stop me?" he asked. Setting her against the glass shower door with a knee between her legs, he whipped his sweatshirt over his head. He stepped away from her only long enough to kick off first his sneakers, then his jeans.

She made a strangled sound. "Sammy?"

"I'll leave my briefs on, okay?"

"Just let me go to bed."

"Is that an invitation?"

"No!" She closed her eyes and murmured, "No-o-o—"

But he was already untying her robe and letting it fall to the floor. She was wearing a pair of panties that were briefer than his. Swearing softly, he stripped them off. Then, without allowing himself the luxury of looking at her, he helped her into the shower.

Susan had never been so humiliated in her life. It wasn't that she was ashamed of her body, but having Sam Craig see it like this was not quite the way her fantasy went. If she had the strength, she would never be letting him do this to her, but she didn't have the strength. Her limbs felt like rubber, her eyes wouldn't focus, and her head hurt, all of which conspired to keep her leaning on him for support.

He concentrated on washing her face, her hands and her hair, and assumed that the run-off would take care of the rest. When he was satisfied, he turned off the water, ushered her out, and wrapped first her, then himself in towels that he grabbed from the floor. Sitting her on the commode, he scrubbed the moisture from her hair with a third towel. Then, rather proud of his self-discipline, he stood back and rubbed his hands together. "A fresh nightgown. Where would I find one?"

"I have to lie down, Sam."

"Nightgown?"

"In the closet. The drawers on the far right."

He was in the midst of looking when she stumbled her way from the bathroom and collapsed into bed. He figured the nightgown would wait. By the time he reached her, she'd curled into a ball on her side and buried her face in the pillow.

"Better now?" he asked, covering her up.

She grunted.

"Can I get you anything?"

She didn't answer.

He worked one damp auburn curl, then another, back from her cheek. "You'll feel better when you wake up."

Her voice came from a distance. "I'll have a splitting headache."

"So you'll take aspirin. You'll be able to hold it down by then. But don't take another drink, Susan. That'll only make things worse." He glanced toward the armoire. "That's quite an arsenal you've got."

"Don't tell Savannah. Please?"

"Why would I tell Savannah? She doesn't know I'm here, and even if she did, I'm not her spy."

"What are you to her?"

"A friend, co-worker."

"And to me?"

"I'm trying to figure that out."

"Why are you here?"

"Because I like you."

"I'm not your type."

"How do you know what my type is? Christ, you're amazing. You're half-zonked and still you think you know it all."

"I don't know it all. I don't know much of anything."

He sighed. "Why don't you go to sleep now?"

"What are you going to do?"

"I'm going to get dressed and go home."

She was quiet for a minute. Then she murmured, "Better do your hair first. There's a blow dryer in the bathroom."

Had it not been for her weary tone, he'd have had a comeback. But she was exhausted. She needed sleep far more than she needed his barbs. So he said, "I'll give you a call later to see how you feel."

"The way I feel now, I may be dead by then."

"I doubt that." He looked around the room and considered that if he were truly a Good Samaritan, he'd clean up. He guessed he wasn't that good. Leaving the bedside, he took the towel from his hips and worked it over his hair. He was nearly at the bathroom door when Susan called his name.

"Sam?"

He turned back. "Mmm?"

Her face was still buried, her voice muffled, but he heard every word. "Right now I'm not feeling real great—"

"I know."

"But some other time, when I'm feeling better, will you show me what's in your briefs?"

Sam was no novice with women. He had had come-ons from respectable ladies and come-ons from hookers. But it was the first time that he had reacted to a come-on quite the way he did to Susan Gardner's. In seconds, he was rock hard.

"Name the day," he vowed. "Name the day, honey, and it's yours." Not trusting himself further, he went into the bathroom to retrieve his clothes.

Chapter 10

SAVANNAH CLOSED THE DOOR to Paul DeBarr's office. "Sorry I'm late. That was the *Journal* on the phone. Before that, it was the *Call*, and before that, the *Globe*. Word's out."

Paul rocked back in his chair. "We've had calls up here, too. It was inevitable."

Perched against the credenza, Anthony Alt tapped his foot and stared at Savannah. "The issue is how we handle it. We could deny the whole thing, but there are too many people involved. It'll come out, and then we'll look worse than we already do. We could try to palm the press off on someone else, but the police department has already palmed it back on us." His eyes hardened. "I can understand why. This case is a mess. The wife of a prominent citizen was kidnapped, three million in ransom was paid, the woman was returned brutalized, and we haven't the foggiest notion about who did it or where the money is." He shot a glance at Paul. "Not much to campaign on."

Paul had the good grace to ignore the comment and, instead, ask Savannah, "How's Megan?"

"I just came from the hospital. She's resting."

"Will she be all right?"

"Physically, yes."

"And emotionally?"

She shrugged. "Time will tell. She's not saying much of anything to anyone."

"Translated, that means she's not cooperating," Anthony said.

"No," Savannah corrected slowly and clearly, as though she were talking with a child. "It means she's focusing inward, trying to come to terms with what's happened before she can share it with us."

"Doesn't she know time is important? The longer she waits to tell us what she knows, the farther away her kidnappers get and the dimmer their tracks."

"It's possible that she doesn't have much to tell."

Anthony wasn't buying that. "She heard, she smelled, she saw—unless she was blindfolded the whole time." He tapped a forefinger on the credenza. "Was she?"

"They stuffed her in a large laundry bag coming and going. She wasn't blindfolded while she was in the room where they kept her, but she said it was dark."

"The human eye adjusts to the dark. She had to see something."

"If she did, she's either blocking it out because it's so reprehensible to her that she can't cope with it, or she's frightened. It's not uncommon for victims of rape to want to distance themselves from their rapists. They don't want to think about them or talk about them. They're terrified that if they breathe a word, they'll be sought out and attacked again as a punishment."

"That's ridiculous," Anthony scoffed. "Megan Vandermeer is safe now. Her husband will probably hire a bodyguard. She doesn't have anything to fear by telling the police what she knows. And what about anger? Rape victims are often so angry that they'd do most anything to have their assailants apprehended and punished."

"The anger will come."

Looking at Paul, Anthony tossed his head Savannah's way. "She's in the wrong field. Sounds more like a therapist than a lawyer."

"I'm a woman," Savannah said with surprising vehemence. Her gender wasn't an argument she usually used, but she refused to back down. "I can imagine what I'd be feeling if I were in Megan's place. Right about now, I'd probably want to climb into a cocoon, curl up in a ball, and stay there for a good, long time. She's been traumatized, Anthony. I know that's hard for you to understand, but, believe me, she's feeling pain."

"She could try to help," he argued, drumming his fingers. "It would make our jobs a hell of a lot easier."

"I doubt she's thinking about our jobs right now."

"Well, I am. We have to come up with a strategy for dealing with the press that's going to get us out of this one, if not smelling like a rose, then at least smelling sweeter than a rat."

"Why would we smell like a rat?" Savannah shot back. "We haven't done anything wrong."

"We haven't done anything right, either. That's the point. We haven't done much of anything at all."

Savannah felt her temper rise. She worked to keep it in check. "In the first place," she said with care, "we got Megan back alive, and if that doesn't count as something right in your book, you've got your priorities messed up. And in the second place," she went on, staring at him hard, "there are those of us who have spent the past few days suffering along with this case. You wouldn't know about that. You weren't sitting with Will or worrying about Megan or trying to coordinate an underground investigation."

"So, what did it turn up?" he goaded. His fingers beat out an annoying tattoo on the credenza.

Unwilling to stoop to his level, Savannah gripped the doorknob behind her, took a measured breath, and gave her answer to Paul. "We are dealing with two very shrewd men. They've covered their tracks from the start. Even with the manpower that's now on this case, nothing's turned up. Very honestly, I don't know what to tell the press."

Paul folded his hands across his middle. "We'll tell them we're working on it. We can stress the strength of the resources we've brought in and simply say that we're hoping for a break." He arched a brow toward Anthony, who promptly took the plan a step further.

"Secrecy. Play on the need for secrecy. Say that the investigation is in full swing but that to comment on the details would put the whole thing in jeopardy. Whatever you do, imply confidence. And Paul's right—talk about the different agencies involved, praise them, set them up to share the blame if things go wrong." He began doing drum rolls with the eraser end of a pencil. "And stress that Megan's fine. It doesn't matter whether it's true or not, say it."

Savannah had plenty of experience evading pointed questions from the press. She just wasn't sure whether this time around she could do it with her usual aplomb. It was going to be a challenge.

"Tell them," Anthony went on, "that we've been monitoring the case from the start but that, to some extent, we've had to honor the kidnappers' demand that the police not be brought in. You can even go so far as to say that you have a tape recording of the voice of one of the men."

Savannah shook her head. "The tape is practically worthless."

"So? At least it will sound like we have something."

"But we don't. The voice was distorted, and the lab hasn't come up with a thing by way of identifying background noise."

"Who has to know? Come on, Savannah. You know how the game is played. We're not lying. We do have a tape. So we let people draw their own conclusions about its usefulness, and if their conclusions are wrong, that's their problem, not ours."

Savannah was uneasy with that. "Supposing, just supposing one or both of the kidnappers is still in the area and follows coverage of what we say. How would they react to news that there's a tape? Would they get nervous and run? Or would they get angry?"

"What difference does it make?" Anthony asked. "If they run, at least they'll be smoked out. And if they're angry, so what? They wouldn't dare try anything more."

She wasn't sure she believed that, but then, she suspected she had imagined Megan's fear so well that it had become her own. She couldn't seem to control the flashing images of a naked Megan tied spread-eagle to a bed, being raped again and again. More than once, she had seen her own face there instead of Megan's. It was foolish, she knew, but it did unsettle her.

Paul studied her face. "Why don't we call a press conference for two o'clock? At this point, I think speculation may be getting out of hand. That has to stop. If we make our own statement, we'll have some control over what hits the news." His look became gentle. "Want me to handle it?"

Paul rarely offered to do something that was not in his best political interest. She appreciated the considerate gesture, as a sign that he had an understanding of the emotional strain she was under. She also knew he was paying her back for the loyalty she had shown him over the years.

With a sad smile, she said, "Thanks, Paul, but I'll do it. My relations with the press are as good now as they've ever been. Yours aren't."

Paul chuckled dryly.

Anthony went further with a snort. "Hammerschmidt is waiting to screw us on page one of the *Journal*. You can bet he'll be watching this case with a magnifying glass."

"I can handle Hammerschmidt," Savannah said. "I haven't spent a Tuesday night a month for the past five months buying him beers for nothing."

Anthony smirked. "Was that the extent of it?"

"Excuse me?"

"Did you stop at beer?" His snare drum roll picked up tempo. "Or did you throw in a little something extra to sweeten the pot?"

Savannah bristled. "I'll forget you said that."

"Don't. It's worth considering. You've got something that Paul and I don't. Maybe if you tried using it once in a while—"

"That's enough," Paul said and rose from his chair.

But Savannah held up a hand to him as she faced Anthony. "One of the reasons I have the credibility I do is that I don't sell myself that way. Sure, I have drinks with the guys. I consider it good PR to make myself accessible, informally, to the press once in a while. I laugh at their jokes, listen to their complaints. I pass on little tidbits of news that they'd have picked up by themselves if they'd been on the ball. They like me because I spend that time with them, and because I do that, they're more likely to do me a favor when I call. Not *once* though, not *once* have I done anything improper."

Anthony's grin was snide. "Did I hit a raw nerve?"

"You hit them all the time."

"Just wanted to see if you're on your toes. You were looking a little subdued there for a while."

"Not subdued. Tired. I had three hours of sleep last night—this morning—and your incessant drumming doesn't help."

"Are you sure you're up for a press conference?" Paul asked.

She drew herself very straight. "I'm up for it. This is my case, Paul. I intend to see it through. When we find out who did this to Megan, I want to be the one who prosecutes."

Anthony had his arms crossed over his chest and was seesawing the pencil against his sleeve. "I wouldn't want to be in those guys' shoes."

"How could you be?" Savannah asked. "As far as I'm concerned, there's only one appropriate punishment for men who do to a woman what those two did to Megan." She dropped a pointed gaze to his fly. "But you haven't got 'em to start with." Ignoring the sudden snap of the pencil, she looked at Paul. "Two o'clock. I'll be there." Then she turned and left the office.

Megan Vandermeer lay in a sedated haze, content to neither move nor think. When she did move, she hurt all over, which was strange. She hadn't hurt so much before. The doctors said that the healing process was taking over, that nerve ends were screeching their way back to life, and she accepted the explanation mainly because she didn't have the will to argue.

Besides, she didn't mind the pain. She deserved it.

But she didn't want to think about that. She didn't want to think, period. Thinking was more painful than moving. All she wanted to do was lie in her bed and tune out reality.

Unfortunately, the world wouldn't let her do that. Since she'd woken up, there had been a steady stream of people passing through her room—doctors, nurses, counselors, detectives, agents—all with questions that she didn't want to answer.

Why didn't they leave her alone? she wondered. Couldn't they see that she didn't feel well? Couldn't they see that she didn't want to talk?

All their questions blurred together in her mind. *What do you remember? Does it hurt here? Can you give us a description? Were you taken in a car? Where did they hold you? How about a nice, soft-boiled egg? Were there any sounds in the room? Did they call each other by name? Would you like another bath?*

With a soft moan, she turned her head on the pillow in an attempt to blot out the noise.

"Meggie?"

Frightened by the voice that was so much more real, so much nearer than the others, she quickly opened her eyes and saw Will. He was sitting close by the side of the bed and was the only person in the room.

"You were moaning," he said. "Is the pain worse? Should I call a nurse?"

Oh yes, the pain was worse. Each time she looked at him it intensified. Her heart ached. She loved Will. But he looked awful. He had been home for a little while, she knew, and had come back showered, shaved, and wearing fresh clothes. But the shave had only accentuated the pallor of his skin, and in contrast to the fresh clothes, he looked more tired than ever. He was forty-nine years old. In the six years they had been married, she had prided herself on keeping him young. Now, though, he looked every bit his age. He looked worn—and it was all her fault.

What had she done to him?

She had fallen in love and married him, which was just fine for her, but not for him. He could have done better. If he'd married someone from his own social station, he would have had the support he needed. If he'd married a wealthy woman, none of this would have happened.

She was a liability.

"Meggie?" His voice wavered. Very lightly, tentatively, he took her hand, and she let him, not because she was doing him a favor, or because she deserved the comfort, but because she needed his touch.

Selfish. She was selfish. And dirty. The bruises on her body were stains that would never go away.

"What can I get you, sweetheart?"

Closing her eyes, she shook her head, then turned it away on the pillow. Will continued to hold her hand, but he didn't speak, and she was glad. What could he say? What could she say back? She needed time to figure out what to do.

Savannah hadn't talked much, either. She had been in to visit earlier, standing by the bed for several minutes. She had softly called her name, but Megan hadn't opened her eyes or answered. She was a coward. After all Savannah had done, not only in the past three days but over the years, Megan had betrayed her. How could she look her in the eye?

She didn't deserve Will or Savannah—or Susan, either. Susan had waited at the house with Will during the entire three days. Although it had must have been an ordeal for her, she had done it. And what had Megan done in return?

She should have stayed on the wrong side of the tracks. That was where she belonged.

With another moan, she turned onto her side. In the process, her hand came free of Will's, but she barely noticed. Her sole focus was on finding that blank spot in her mind where she could hide, forget, vanish.

Savannah strode boldly back from the conference room. The press conference had been over for several hours, but she had been waylaid by reporters who had lingered in hopes of learning something more than what she had said publicly. When she'd finally freed herself, she'd gone straight into a meeting with lawyers who hoped to plea-bargain their clients' way out of the trial on Monday. Her case was strong, which was why the defense was getting nervous. In good conscience, though, she could not deal—at least, not to the tune the defense wanted. She had little sympathy for intelligent men who used arson as a means to collect insurance money on buildings that were heavily overinsured, particularly when those fires resulted in adding scores of people to the ranks of the homeless.

Arnie Watts was with her during the meetings, as was Katherine Trask. Both would be assisting her during the trial. Both agreed that the defense was asking for gifts the prosecution simply could not grant.

So the meeting had ended in a stalemate, with the trial still set for Monday. Wondering how she was going to get herself together for that, when she was still so shaky about Megan, she left for her office. Just beyond the conference-room door, though, she was ambushed by another local reporter.

"A minute, counselor?"

Her step didn't falter. "If you can keep up with me, you've got it." The reporter was young, new to the newspaper, and female. Particularly in light of the last, Savannah was willing to cooperate. She steeled herself for more questions on the kidnapping, but instead, the reporter asked. "Can you tell me about the Cat?"

Savannah turned a corner. "The Cat?" She hesitated. "What do you want to know?"

"I hear he struck again."

"Where did you hear that?"

The reporter shrugged. "Is it true?"

"I don't know. Most everything you do with the Cat is speculation."

"But there was a break-in Tuesday night in Cranston, and the MO was the same."

"There are break-ins every night of the week."

"Not on that large a scale. I understand that your office has been questioning Matty Stavanovich for years. Is that true?"

Savannah didn't see any point denying it, since the number of times the man had been brought in was a matter of record. "It's true."

"Have you taken any special measures to apprehend him?"

Savannah sent her a wry half-smile. "Now, if I told you that, I'd be tipping my hand to the Cat, wouldn't I?"

"Then you are?"

"I won't say one way or the other. I will say that this office is working in conjunction with police all over the state to solve house-breaks of the type that happened last Tuesday."

"But are you zeroing in on Stavanovich?"

"We're zeroing in on whoever the evidence points to."

"Who does the evidence point to?"

Lips pursed, Savannah sent her a chiding look. She passed Janie, closing her hand around a pile of pink slips as though they were a baton in a relay race, and went on to her office door. There she stopped. "What's your name?"

"Beth Tocci."

"Well, Beth Tocci, there's something you have to understand. In our system of justice, a man is innocent until proven guilty. It would be unethical of me to earmark the Cat, or any other thief, for that Cranston break-in, before an arrest is made—unethical, and unwise. You'd go back to your paper and print what I said, and that would throw a wrench into the investigation, not to mention make it impossible to gather an unbiased jury if the case ever came to trial. This is one of those instances where your job is to report the news, not alter it."

"Is it true that Matty Stavanovich is a legitimate businessman?"

"That's a matter of public record."

"Is it true that the IRS audits him every year and can't find anything wrong?"

"You'd have to check with the IRS on that."

"What about the allegation that Matty Stavanovich is the

alias for a man named Joseph Stevens, who served time in a California prison and was released and given a new identity after he testified to crimes he heard about while he was there?"

"You'd have to check with the FBI on that."

"I have. They say they've never heard of either man."

Savannah shrugged, then held up an apologetic hand and said softly, "I have to run. Sorry." She went into her office, smoothly but firmly closed the door, then felt her pulse trip and her heart lift.

Jared was there. He was standing by the window wearing a navy sweater, taupe slacks, and loafers. Though his hair still fell rakishly over his brow, he was newly shaved and showered. A tweed topcoat was looped over his arm, held there by the hand resting in his pocket. He looked different than he had in jeans, more formal but not a bit less gorgeous.

It was a minute before she caught her breath, a minute after that before she inhaled and spoke. "Janie must be wondering who you really are."

"I told her."

"Your whole name?"

He nodded.

"Did she recognize it?"

"Her eyes went wide for a minute. But she didn't fall over in a faint. She's a nice girl. Let me in without a word."

Savannah could understand that. Jared Snow had a way of making women forget to breathe, let alone speak. He was doing it to her right then, with nothing more than the light in those blue eyes of his.

Jared was no less entranced. He was acutely aware of the fact that the last time he had seen Savannah, she had been wearing a nightgown in bed. Now she was wearing a calf-length skirt with a silk overblouse belted at the hip, and a long blazer over that. Her hair was pulled back into its knot, and her skin was lightly made up. She looked very together, very professional. Still, she looked sexy.

"How are you?" he asked, his voice a bit softer and more husky.

She took a shallow breath. "Okay."

"Did you sleep?"

She wrinkled her nose. "A little. I had lots on my mind."

"How's Megan?"

"I saw her for a minute late this morning. I'm not sure if she was sleeping, but she didn't respond when I spoke. She still looks awful. I haven't had a chance to get back to the hospital. Things have been a little hairy here."

Jared could imagine. "Are you pleased with the way the press conference went?"

The *Evening Bulletin* would have hit the stands by then and she assumed he'd seen it. Eying him warily, she asked, "How did they portray us?"

"I don't know about the paper. I overheard talk downstairs."

"Good or bad?"

"Nonjudgmental. It centered more on the kidnapping itself than on the efforts to solve it. I think you're off the hook for a while."

"Not for long. People get impatient when arrests aren't forthcoming, and in this case, arrests are about as far from forthcoming as in any case I've ever had."

There was a knock on the door. "Yes?" Savannah called.

Janie Woo stuck her head in. "I'm ready to leave. Is there anything you want before I go?" Her gaze wandered to Jared with a nonchalance Savannah found to be sweet.

"I'm all set, Janie. Have a good weekend."

"You too," Janie said. With a final glance at Jared, she closed the door.

Savannah looked at the floor, then at Jared. "You do know that she'd normally buzz me to say she's leaving."

The image of innocence, he shrugged. Then he asked, "Who's the Cat?"

For the second time in less than an hour, the Cat took her by surprise—until she realized that Jared had overheard the last part of her conversation with Beth Tocci. She sighed resignedly and crossed the room. "The Cat is Matty Stavanovich." She deposited both the handful of pink slips and her briefcase on the desk. "He's the kind of character who gives law enforcement officials ulcers. If I didn't know better, I'd say he owned blocks of Maalox stock."

"Does he?"

"No. Then again, he might, but under an alias we've never heard."

"So he does use them?"

"Oh, yes."

"Is he that man from the California prison?"

"No, but he inspires plenty of stories like that. Years ago, he spent a brief period of time in a California prison. Unfortunately, he's never been a protected witness. If he had been, we'd have a little more control over his comings and goings."

"Why is he called the Cat?"

"He's a cat burglar."

Intrigued, Jared gave a curious grin. "A real cat burglar? Smart and silent and quick-fingered—scaling the walls of buildings, falling great distances, and landing on his feet?"

Savannah had to admit that there was a certain romance

to it, which was why she indulged Jared his interest. "Yes, a real cat burglar. He's done time for heists in Oklahoma and Kansas, too. Now he's here, having learned from his mistakes and perfected the art. We've had a rash of robberies that have his pawprints all over them—that is, there are no clues at all. He gets in and gets out, snaps his fingers, and bingo, he and the stolen goods disappear. When he resurfaces, he always has an airtight alibi. Beyond that, he never even tries to put together a defense, because he knows that we don't have enough evidence to indict him."

"How many robberies has he committed?"

She looked at the ceiling and put her tongue in her cheek. "Oh, in the five years he's been in the state, he's probably pulled off eight or nine big ones."

Jared whistled. "And you can't nab him?"

She shook her head. "As far as we can figure it, he carries out the heist on his own. But he has to have help disposing of the goods, so we've been concentrating on that. Six months ago, we found some of the stolen artwork in a Manhattan gallery, and for a while we thought we were this close"—she put her thumb and forefinger a fraction of an inch apart—"to catching the fence."

"What happened?"

She dropped her head. "He vanished into thin air. Just like the Cat does."

"When was the last robbery?"

"Tuesday night."

"And you can't find Stavanovich?"

"Nope. But he'll be back in a day or two, whistling his way to work, as carefree as you please."

"Is his business legitimate?"

"Oh, yes. He has an automotive repair shop." Her lips

twitched. "He services luxury imports—Jaguars, BMWs, and Mercedes. Have you ever heard anything so obvious? He comes into contact with the wealthiest people in Rhode Island. He has their keys in his possession long enough to make as many copies as he wants. He knows just when they're going north for the summer, just when they're staying right here. And you know what?"

Jared arched both brows in question.

Savannah slapped a hand against the desk. "He has never once robbed a customer of his. He takes the expected and does the opposite. It's like he's standing there thumbing his nose at us, because we'd like nothing more than to be able to say, 'See, that's how he knew that so-and-so was out of town and that's how he got into the house.' It is," she said slowly, "the most exasperating thing in the world."

Jared was trying not to grin.

She was about to chide him when another knock came at the door. This time, she didn't have a chance to speak before the door opened and in walked Anthony Alt.

"You did okay," he told her, rapping his fingers against the doorjamb. "The coverage wasn't as bad as it could have been." He gave Jared a once-over. "The early TV reports are stressing the fact that the AG's office is coordinating a wide-scale investigation." He looked back at her. "We sound in control. That's good. As soon as you solve the case, it'll be even better."

"I'm not the one who'll solve it. We have detectives to do things like that."

"But you'll direct them."

"Unless you'd like to," she offered. "If you have your heart set on it—"

"I don't have the time." He shot another, more curious glance at Jared. "Have we met?"

Jared complacently shook his head. "I don't think so." He made no move to volunteer anything else. Nor did Savannah.

Anthony stuck out his hand. "Anthony Alt. I'm Paul De-Barr's first assistant."

Jared's hand met his in a grip that was firm, authoritative in its way. He nodded. But he didn't say a word.

Nor did Savannah.

Anthony tried staring harder, as though the force of his gaze could cow the man before him. It might have worked on others, but it didn't touch Jared. At last, with his forefinger beating against his trousers, he said, "You are . . ."

"A friend," Jared said.

"Of hers," he cocked his head toward Savannah, "or the state?"

"Is there a difference?"

"My God," Savannah muttered, "you make this sound like a dictatorship. Don't worry about my being distracted, Anthony. I've worked hard enough long enough to prove my dedication. Paul gets his money's worth out of me."

Anthony looked her up and down. "Ah, an admission, at last. I've always had my suspicions."

The insult was too blatant to miss, too absurd to acknowledge. So Savannah smiled. "You're a sweetheart to come down and tell me about the press reports." She went to the door and opened it. "I'll be working on Sunday. If you hear anything else, give me a call."

Anthony apparently decided to quit while he was ahead. Without so much as a backward glance at Jared, he gave Savannah a salute and left the office. No sooner had she closed the door when Jared said, "You shouldn't let him get away with comments like that."

"It's okay. I zinged him one earlier, so we're even."

"He's a creep."

"I won't argue with you there." She watched his face, could almost see him debating whether there was, or ever had been, something between Paul and her. To his credit, he didn't ask.

"Is he uptight about all your work, or only the big stuff?"

"He's uptight, period. Never stands still. But he's worse when I'm around. We get on each other's nerves. Not that this case helps." She grew thoughtful for a minute and whispered a laugh. "It makes the Cat seem like child's play. I mean, Stavanovich is taking *things*, not people. And no one is harmed. Aside from a few hefty insurance claims, life goes on."

"Still, the law is being broken," Jared maintained in an attempt to justify her investment in seeing the Cat caught.

"True. More, though, Matty Stavanovich is an embarrassment. Talk about political liabilities, he's a prime one. Elected officials around here rely on a relatively small, but wealthy group of contributors. Those are precisely the people who wonder if they're slated to be the Cat's next target. The longer they wonder, the more nervous they get, and the more angry. And when they're angry, they don't open their wallets as freely.

"At least," she qualified herself, "that's Paul's dilemma. Mine is a little more mundane. I just want Stavanovich caught. He's become an obsession among law enforcement officials and a cult figure among their secretaries. The guy is brilliant. He hits where and when we least expect it. There are a number of us who would love to trip him up, if only to prove to ourselves that we're smarter than he is."

"He keeps you on your toes."

"I'll say. Not that I need it right now. I've got plenty else to keep me on my toes."

Jared straightened. "That's why I'm here. I want you to have dinner with me."

Her heart beat faster. She wasn't sure whether it was because he suddenly stood taller or because he had invited her to dinner. Either way she was impressed. And excited. And frightened.

"Uh . . ." She sent a glance toward the pink slips on her desk, then the papers beyond. "I don't know, Jared. I didn't get in until noon. I've got a bundle of work to do."

"You have to eat sometime."

"I was planning to grab something on the run later."

"That's not real healthy."

She shrugged. "It's better than nothing."

"I'm offering you an alternative that's better than both. One hour. A decent meal. A little relaxation."

A little relaxation was precisely what he had already brought her. His presence in her office took the edge off her anxiety. The thought of having dinner with him was tempting.

But she had so much to do. "I have phone calls to answer."

"Go ahead. I'll be back whenever you say to pick you up."

"I wanted to stop in and see how Megan's doing."

"I'll take you to the hospital before or after."

"I wanted to do some aerobics. I haven't made it to the club since Tuesday. I feel it."

Jared thought about aerobics, thought about Savannah exercising to music wearing shorts or a leotard or whatever aerobics fanatics wore. Shifting his stance, he linked his fingers before him, letting his coat shield the front of his trousers.

"Sounds like fun," he said in a throaty way.

"It's therapeutic. It works against tension." She knew something else that would work against tension, and she knew that Jared knew it. The gray flecks in his eyes had gone darker than normal, pulling her in.

"I'll drop you at the club after you've seen Megan."

"But I didn't want to do either of those things until I'd done some of this work."

"Do the work tomorrow."

"I can't. I'm spending the day with Susan." Her eyes widened and she whispered, "Oh, hell." Reaching for the phone, she turned it and punched out Susan's number, then worriedly counted the rings. She was about to hang up after the sixth when Susan answered.

"Hello?" Her voice sounded vaguely belligerent.

"How do you feel?"

There was a pause, then a less belligerent, "Better than I did when you called before."

"You got some sleep?"

"A little." Susan's pause this time was wary, as was her voice when she spoke. "Have you seen Megan?"

"Just for a minute. I'll drop by again later."

"Did she talk with you?"

"No."

"Was she sleeping?"

"I'm not sure."

Susan sighed. "Same thing with me. I think she knew I

was there but didn't want to talk. It's like she's ashamed of what happened, like she thinks we'll think less of her." She gave a harsh laugh. "It's really pretty funny, when you think of it. Here she is, kidnapped and raped, none of which is her own doing, and she's ashamed. Here I am, supposedly of sound mind and body, and I get disgustingly sick in front of your friend."

"What friend?"

"Sam."

"When was this?"

"This morning. Didn't he report back to you?"

"I haven't seen him all day."

Susan was surprised at that. Sam had said that Savannah hadn't known he was there, but she hadn't believed him. Now, she was doubly embarrassed. "Then forget what I said."

"Were you sick?"

"Forget it. I'm fine now."

"Are you sure?"

"Of course. As a matter of fact, I'm getting ready to go out. There's a dinner party at the Brannigans'. Skatch Sherman's going to be there. It'll be a great diversion."

Skatch Sherman was the life of every party. Savannah found him to be totally offensive. "Some diversion."

"Don't knock it. It beats what you'll be doing. One of these days, you're going to work yourself to death."

"Maybe," Savannah conceded. "We're still on for tomorrow, aren't we?" They'd planned to spend the day in Boston.

"Sure."

"What time should I come by?"

"Noon."

"Make that ten."

"I can't. How about eleven-thirty."

"Too late. Ten-thirty."

"Eleven. That's the absolute earliest."

"I'll be by for you at ten forty-five," Savannah said and added a stern, "Be ready," before hanging up the phone.

"Is everything okay?"

She spun around. "Uh, yes. I guess. She likes to sleep later than I do. That's all." It wasn't really all. What worried Savannah was that Susan would have too much to drink at the party and wake up hungover. Or sick. Apparently, she'd been sick in front of Sammy that morning. She found it interesting that he'd been there.

Then again, Savannah shouldn't have been surprised. Sam Craig was no coward. Susan interested him. He would keep after her.

Sam wasn't the only persistent male around. "One last chance," Jared said. "Dinner?"

She wanted to. Lord, she did. But somewhere in the back of her mind she feared that if she gave in to temptation, she would be lost. Or let down. Or humiliated. Jared wanted a woman who could drop what she was doing and have dinner with him. She had never been that kind of woman.

She wished she were.

Flipping his topcoat to his shoulder, he headed for the door. "Maybe another time," he said quietly.

The instant he disappeared from sight, the office felt empty. Then Savannah realized that she was the one who felt empty. It was such a familiar feeling, such a dreadful feeling. Suddenly she didn't want it at all.

Without further thought, she ran into the hall. "Jared?" He was nearly at the bend. "Jared!" She started after him.

Calmly he stopped, turned, waited for her to catch up.

After she'd covered half the distance, her step slowed. But she continued on until she stood before him. Then she said softly, "I'm not used to putting work off. It's always been very important to me."

He studied her features, searching for the meaning behind her explanation. "If it's that important, you should do it."

"I'd rather be with you."

Perhaps because she couldn't have chosen words he wanted to hear more, he didn't quite believe she had said them at first. Then he broke into a slow smile.

Savannah felt the dangerous lure of that smile. But she had made her decision. "One hour," she whispered.

"That's fine."

"Would you take me to the hospital afterward?"

"I said I would. How about aerobics?"

"I'll have to do it with Jane Fonda later tonight, at home."

Jared could think of a form of exercise that she could do with him later that night, but he knew enough not to voice it. He had just won a concession. He wasn't about to endanger the victory by pushing too fast. Better to let the time they spent together do that on its own.

And it would. Because when they were together, whether it was in her office, in his studio, in the car or the Vandermeers' back hall or even on the phone, there was a powerful attraction between them. That attraction had nowhere to go but to bed. He doubted it would need much of a push. Even now, Savannah was looking a little wide-eyed, a little wild-eyed.

It was all he could do not to swoop down and capture her mouth.

But he would wait. If it killed him he would wait. "Do you need some time?" he asked.

"For what?"

"Those phone calls."

"Phone calls?" She frowned, then forced herself to focus in. "Phone calls. Lord, yes." She headed back toward her office, stopping at Janie's desk to turn and look at Jared. "How long can I have?"

"How long do you need?"

"Thirty minutes?"

"Done. I'll go find a phone and do some work of my own."

"You can use one of ours. Most everyone's left." She went to the office next to hers, peered inside, then pointed. "It's all yours."

Dipping his head in thanks, Jared went inside.

Chapter 11

⁓

THEY HAD AGREED on an hour, but things didn't work out quite the way they planned. No sooner had they walked into the restaurant, an artsy place on Wickenden Street, when an acquaintance of Jared's spotted him. Without an invitation, the fellow pulled up a chair and spent fifteen minutes discussing the management of the marina at which both men had slips.

No sooner had he left when his seat was taken over by a lawyer with whom Savannah had given a seminar on victims' rights the year before. He had been lobbying heavily for the cause and wanted to share his latest news. Short of being rude, Savannah couldn't send him away. She and Jared were nearly done with their main course by the time he finally left.

Jared set down his fork. "How's your food?"

"Fine," she said hesitantly. His expression was dark. "How about yours?"

"I've barely tasted it. That has to be the most inconsiderate thing a person can do. Would you walk over to someone and impose your presence when he's having dinner with someone else?"

"No. I'm sorry, Jared. I kept trying to think of a way to get rid of him."

"Didn't it occur to him that we might want to be alone?"

"He left his wife by herself all that time. I'm sorry."

Jared grunted. "Don't apologize. It wasn't your fault. And my friend was no better." Glancing at his watch, he raised two fingers for the waitress. "Let's get out of here. We can get coffee at the hospital."

Once at the hospital, though, Savannah was besieged by a slew of Will's friends. They weren't really there to visit, since Megan wasn't seeing people. They simply wanted to show that they had made the effort. Savannah suspected that several had come out of curiosity alone. But whatever their reasons, Will's friends were also her father's friends, so she had to be cordial.

Jared tried to understand. He knew that regardless of whom Savannah was talking with at any given moment, she was aware of him. He could see it in the frequent glances she sent his way, and he could feel it in the incline of her body toward his.

Still, he felt cheated. He had been given a gift when she had agreed to have dinner, then someone had sat on it and crushed it to bits. All he had left were fragments of what might have been.

As a kid, he had experienced that more than once. His older brother, Mac, had been a bully, and Jared had been his favorite target. For his seventh birthday, Jared had received a remote-control car, but by the end of the day it only went in reverse. The watch he'd gotten for his tenth Christmas sported a crack in its crystal from New Year's on. The shiny racing bike he'd bought when he was fourteen soon after had key scratches down each narrow fender.

But Mac was the firstborn, the favored son. If the senior Walker Snows had been asked, they'd have confirmed that the sun rose and fell with Walker, Jr. Early on, Jared had learned to make his own life and, above all else, avoid his brother.

He'd come a long way since those days, yet, apparently, some things never changed. He felt the same burning frustration now that he had felt then. He was regressing, he knew, and he was ashamed of it, but there was nothing he could do to stop the feeling. He couldn't remember craving anyone or anything the way he craved time with Savannah.

All too soon, he was walking her to the door. Silent through most of the drive, she turned to him then.

"Thanks, Jared. I appreciate all you've done."

He gave a single nod.

"Don't be angry," she whispered.

"I'm not angry," he said. "Just frustrated. Is your life always this infested with people?"

She had to smile at his choice of words. "Providence is small. It's hard not to go places and see people you know."

"There are some people who thrive on seeing and being seen."

"Not me. I'd have been just as happy if we'd seen no one tonight. This has been one of the longest short workdays I've ever put in."

"You'll be able to sleep in tomorrow."

"Knowing me," she said wryly, "I'll be up at seven." She took her keys from her briefcase. "It's always the days when you *can* sleep in that you can't."

He took the keys from her hand. "Want to run that one by me again?"

Smiling, she shook her head. "Not worth the repetition. Are you on the air tonight?"

"Sure."

"I'll listen."

His features softened. "I'd like that." He pushed open the door.

She entered the townhouse and disengaged the alarm, then turned back to him. One hand was tight on the strap of her briefcase, the other tight around the key he'd pressed into her palm. "Thanks," she whispered.

For a long lingering minute they faced each other in silence. Then, with a visible effort, Jared tore his eyes from hers and returned to his car.

Feeling an incredible sense of loss, Savannah stood in the doorway until the car was gone from sight. She had been hoping that he would kiss her. It looked as though he'd wanted to. She could have sworn she had seen desire in his eyes. She'd certainly felt it herself.

In theory, there was nothing wrong with that. She was a normal, healthy woman and Jared was a man like few others. In some respects, though, it was odd.

For one thing, of the men who had passed through her life in the past few years, none had stirred her this way.

For another, she barely knew Jared.

And for a third, she was afraid of getting in over her head, still she wanted him. Worse, the wanting seemed to grow each time she saw him. Even now it was simmering low in her belly, a knot of expectant nerve ends and unfulfilled need that wasn't going away. All she had to do was to conjure him up in her mind, hear his voice, remember the touch of his hand, and she was off.

Tired as she was, she suspected she was going to have a devil of a time falling asleep.

His voice was low and gritty. *"Hi, there. I'm Jared Snow, and you're tuned to 95.3 FM, WCIC Providence. It's twelve-oh-four in cool country, that's four minutes after twelve on a TGIF kind of night. I've got good news if you're takin' off for the weekend. Skies will be clear through Sunday, with day-time temperatures climbing into the mid-fifties."* His voice grew deeper. *"They say that warm days and cool nights make for perfect maple syrup, and they must be right, 'cause the sap's sure flowing."* After a suggestive second's pause, he said, *"Here at the hot spot for a little country in the city, 95.3 FM, WCIC Providence, we're flowin' into a fearsome foursome from the Judds, Willie Nelson, and Sawyer Brown, kicking' off with Billy Mata and 'Macon Georgia Love.'"* His purr was low and deep. *"Jared Snow here in the heart of the night. Stay close."*

Savannah's sleep was fitful, growing deeper only as morning approached. She was groggy when she opened an eye and looked at her clock, then sank back to her pillow resentfully. Seven o'clock. She'd guessed it.

Then the doorbell rang, and she realized she hadn't woken on her own. Opening her eye wider, she tried to think of who would be at her door at seven o'clock on Saturday morning, particularly *this* Saturday morning. She had wanted to sleep until ten and have time only to shower and dress before picking up Susan. She had wanted as little time as possible to think.

The bell ran again. Climbing from bed, she drew on her robe and hurried downstairs. Whoever was there was going to have some explaining to do.

Drawing back a corner of the shade that covered the side-light, she felt tiny flares of excitement. Jared was standing on her doorstep looking as she had never seen him look. He was wearing shorts and a damp sweatshirt. His hair lay in wet spikes on his forehead. His cheeks were ruddy. His legs were long and leanly muscular.

He had been running. Dropping the shade, she quickly opened the door. Her voice, which hadn't had time to wake up, was deeper than usual. "What are you doing here at this hour?"

Grinning, he brought a bunch of bright tulips from behind his back. "Happy birthday."

Savannah's jaw dropped. Then she closed her mouth, clamping her lips together as she looked from the flowers to Jared's face and back. She didn't have to think long to realize how he'd known; he'd seen her driver's license. But the fact that after working all night, he was personally running flowers to her was more touching than she could believe. It had been years since she had woken up to a birthday wish.

He nudged the flowers closer. She closed both hands around the cellophane stem and brought them to her heart. "My mom made a big thing about birthdays. All that stopped when she died. I could never figure out whether my dad did it on purpose so he wouldn't have to remember her, whether he didn't feel he could match what she did so he didn't try, or whether he just didn't care. Susan and I always try to do something together, but I think it's more my need than hers." She looked down at the flowers again. When her eyes returned to Jared's, they were moist. "Thank you," she whispered. On impulse, she threw her arms around his neck and hugged him hard.

Threading his fingers through her hair, Jared turned her face up. Her expression said that the excitement wasn't his alone. He didn't need to hear more. Lowering his head, he captured her mouth in a kiss that was as uncompromising as the desire they shared.

Savannah had never been touched by a more powerful fire. As though she were kindling, dried and seasoned by months of lying in wait, she burst into flame. When Jared stroked her mouth, she caressed his back. When he sucked on her lip, she scraped his lightly with her teeth. When he explored the inside of her mouth with his tongue, hers sidled against it. He was fierce in his hunger, but gentle. If she'd made the slightest sound of protest, he would have stopped.

But she didn't want him to stop. For too long she had dreamed of being loved this way. So many nights she'd lain awake, alone and lonely in the heart of the night, lost in fantasy. She half thought she was fantasizing now, because what she felt was so good. The insecurity that had plagued her was forgotten, crowded out by the wealth of sensation he created with only the movement of his mouth.

The gentleness of his hands as they held her head, the strength of his body as he bent to her, excited her. The brush of a night's growth of beard, the chill of the morning's air on his cheek and the scent of heated male skin beneath his clothes intrigued her. She remembered the rasp of his voice in the night and the darkening of gray flecks in his blue eyes, and she felt his arousal pressing against her.

She strained closer. The movement brought a low groan from deep in Jared's chest. Within seconds, he'd drawn back and was dazedly searching her face. Then he was kissing her eyes, her nose, her cheekbones, her chin, until, with a searing hiss, his lips bonded to hers once more.

Somehow he'd known it would be this way, known that once he kissed Savannah there would be no holding back. He might have been frightened by the strength of what he felt if he'd been capable of thought, but sensation overrode thought. There was nothing but the heat of the moment, burning from one touchpoint to the next.

Then something contradicted that heat, a fine trembling in Savannah's body, a reminder of where they were, what they wore, and the early morning chill that surrounded them.

"Let me in?" he asked against her mouth.

Taking his arm, she drew him into the house. The instant the door was closed, their lips met again. They were both breathing heavily, pausing to gasp before returning for another kiss, another touch. The flowers Jared had brought had become an extension of Savannah's hand, held tightly against his back but forgotten amid the flames.

When he drew back this time, he pressed his temple to hers and dropped his gaze. His large hands stroked her neck, then slid inward, parting her robe to reveal the prim white nightshirt beneath. He went at the buttons one by one, his fingers unsteady in the effort to take care. His breath came in uneven sighs that echoed Savannah's own.

When he had released three buttons, he spread the material to the side and bared her breasts. For several seconds, he didn't move. His hands seemed intimidated by the tender ivory flesh he had uncovered. Then, with a tentative, reverent touch, he slid his fingers around her soft outer curves.

She was beautiful, he thought, not voluptuous, but firmly rounded like a delicately sculpted figurine—only she was alive, swelling at his touch.

His hands grew bolder, caressing her flesh. He traced the intricacies of her shape, running a thumb over each rosy nipple until it hardened. He heard the quickening of her breath; heard her gasp. The sound was as great a turn-on as her free hand desperately clutching his sweatshirt near his waist.

The fire spread. Hastily, he pushed aside her robe and freed the last of the nightshirt's buttons. When he looked at her then she was a breathtaking expanse of soft flesh with only a wisp of lace at her hips.

He breathed her name in a rough whisper, and while he took her mouth, his hands slid down her body. He felt the texture of lace, but beneath the lace was the heat he sought. He palmed it, stroked it, sent his fingers around and through it.

Savannah cried out. She was trembling again, but this time not from a chill. Her body was begging him for release.

Slipping one arm beneath her knees and another around her back, Jared lifted her and started up the stairs. His kiss was as fluid as his step. It flexed with the movement, yet maintained a near-steady contact until he reached her bedroom.

Very gently, he set her down on the bed. Her robe and nightgown fell open. He made no attempt to take her arms from their sleeves; instead he simply stripped her of the lace panties. Within seconds he had whipped his sweatshirt over his head and kicked off his sneakers and shorts. Naked, he came down to her.

The first touch of their bare bodies was electric. In the sizzling wake of that touch, he found his place between her open thighs and thrust upward. Savannah arched off the sheet with a choked cry, but when he would have withdrawn, she clamped her legs around his hips and held him tight where he was.

She squeezed her eyes shut. The focus of her being was the part of her that felt so full. Sensations of newness became sensations of excitement that, in turn, became full-blown desire. Her legs relaxed their grip to allow him movement.

His first strokes were slow and deliberate, a searing withdrawal and reentrance that made her hunger for more. Driven by a hunger of his own, he moved ever faster, ever deeper until he heard her catch in a sudden breath and go utterly still, then release that breath in a spate of ragged pants. The sound was all it took—that and a final intense thrust, to send him into a climax that shook his large frame from head to toe.

The spasms seemed endless. When he was totally spent, he lowered himself to her side, taking her over with him.

For several minutes, as he lay in the afterglow with his eyes closed, Savannah watched him. Her body still tingled, still felt his possession, but the mind-block that had seized her in the heat of passion had cleared. The old fears took shape.

Finally, he opened his eyes. When he saw the way she was looking at him, he brought gentle fingers to her face. "What is it?" He caressed the tiny crease between her eyes with his thumb.

"Was it okay?" she whispered.

Astonished, he waited a minute before he asked, "Are you kidding?"

She shook her head on the pillow.

He shaped the curve of her ear. "It was incredible. Couldn't you feel it?"

"I knew you'd come, but—"

He put a long finger to her lips, then replaced that finger with his mouth and drank a deep kiss from her lips. "How about for you?"

"Special," she whispered, dazed from his kiss. "Powerful. A little frightening."

"I've wanted that since Wednesday night."

"I've wanted it longer than that." At his curious look, she said, "You've been seducing me with your voice for the past two years. How could I help but fantasize about what it would be like with you?"

"Was that why you did it—just to see?"

"You know it wasn't," she chided, and as he thought about it, he realized she was right. The attraction between them was an irresistible force. She hadn't been in control of what had happened any more than he had.

"It's been a while for you."

She colored. "Was it obvious?"

For the second time in minutes, Jared sensed she was unsure of herself when it came to sex. He smoothed a long strand of hair from her cheek. "Not in technique." He kissed the tip of her nose. "Any more perfect and I'd have gone up in smoke. But I was worried I had hurt you at first."

Her cheeks were pink. "Not hurt. I'm not sure I can describe the sensation."

"You could try *wonderful*," he said, and it occurred to Savannah that maybe, just maybe, he had some insecurities of his own.

"Wonderful, incredible, deep, hot, new—" She arched a brow. "How am I doing?"

"Just fine," he said and hugged her close for a minute. Then the minute stretched into several, because the feel of her body against his was so remarkably right that he had to savor it longer. But the more he enjoyed it, the more curious he became, and before long he was exploring all the little curves that made her so special, and that led to a resurgence of passion.

He was slower this time, touching her body more leisurely. He wanted to see her response when he drew the backs of his fingers over her breasts, when he dipped his pinkie into her navel, when his thumb disappeared in the nest of chestnut curls between her legs. He wanted to watch the slow rise of heat, wanted to see her when she came. But his own desire took over before then, and all he was aware of was clasping her bottom and directing her hips before he exploded again.

He wasn't the only sweaty one this time. Savannah's skin was dewy. Jared loved it. Once he'd begun to breathe normally again, he propped himself on an elbow and looked down at her. Her hair was a wild tangle on the pillow, her nightshirt and robe were rumpled beneath her, her eyes were closed, and her face glowed.

"You look," he said, still slightly short of breath but thick of voice, "absolutely beautiful."

Though Savannah didn't believe him for a minute, she was feeling too satisfied to argue. She opened an eye. "You're supposed to be sleeping."

"And miss this?"

"Men sleep after sex."

"Not me. I've got adrenaline picking up where testosterone left off."

She couldn't help but laugh as she grabbed a fistful of his hair and held on. "But you haven't slept all night."

"I slept yesterday afternoon." He touched her neck, explored the hollow formed by her upraised arm, climbed to trace the delicate line of her jaw.

Covering his hand, she held it still against her throat. She had both eyes open and couldn't look at him enough, couldn't quite believe that he was real, rather than a fantasy. "Do you run every day?"

He nodded. "It's therapeutic—like aerobics."

She gave a small, puzzled smile. "You seem so totally laid-back and at ease. What's the therapy for?"

He shrugged. "Midlife thoughts. The usual."

She couldn't imagine that he was having to make career choices, which meant that his midlife thoughts were more personal. "How long have you been divorced?"

"Four years."

"Tell me about her."

Sitting up, he tugged the pillow from under Savannah's head, turned it vertically and layered it with a second pillow against the headboard. Then he leaned back and drew Savannah under his arm, against his chest. "There," he said, satisfied with the position.

She ran a hand over the contours of his chest. His muscles were solid without being bunchy. His skin had a tawny hue that made the sprinkling of hair look almost golden. He was beautifully male, and she felt suddenly and strangely possessive. "Jared?"

"Yes?"

"Tell me."

"You don't have to have Elise in your bed."

She tipped her head back against his arm and looked up at him. "I don't have to have you either, but I want you, and she's part of who you are."

"She's part of my past."

"And your past is what makes you you. I'm curious."

Put as innocently as that, he wasn't sure he could argue. Savannah had just given of herself with an honesty he had never run across before. He owed her.

"Elise was a driven woman, a typical type-A personality."

"Like me."

"No. Elise was *driven*. She came from a family of lawyers. Her father was one, two uncles, three brothers. She was determined to be the lawyer to outdo all of them."

"Was she?"

"She was a fine lawyer, but I think she's still working on the outdoing part. She picked litigation to be different—the others do corporate work—and she had enough style and determination and sheer nerve to develop an extraordinary practice. She had her eye on Congress. Last thing I heard, she had her organization in place and was about to announce."

"Sounds like she was a busy lady. Where did she find the time for marriage?"

"She didn't."

Savannah studied the glittering lights in his eyes. "But she married you."

"I married her. It was a mutual mistake, which is why we're no longer married."

She considered that for a minute. "You don't sound upset."

He shrugged with his face. "It's over."

"Were you upset at the time?"

"At the time I was relieved. Elise is exhausting to be with."

"Didn't you know that when you married her?"

"Yes. But it worked two ways. At the time, I saw myself as an up-and-coming real-estate tycoon. Elise was a stunning woman; she was as good for my image as I was for hers. But over five years of marriage, that was pretty much all we were to each other—images—and by the time it ended, I'd realized that I didn't want to be a tycoon at all."

"What did you want?"

"Quieter things. More private things. I wanted to have kids. Elise couldn't bear the thought. She actually became pregnant, but she had an abortion."

"Without consulting you?"

"There was no need. I wasn't the father."

His words ended in an abrupt silence. Searching his face for remnants of anger or pain, Savannah found none. But the beat of his heart had quickened beneath her hand, telling her that despite his outward complacence over the demise of his marriage, Jared had been hurt by his wife's betrayal.

"I'd have your baby," she said.

He gave her a crooked grin. "You may just do that. I didn't exactly run over here with a rubber in my sock. Unless—"

"I'm not."

"How's our timing?"

She tilted her head from side to side in a could-be-better, could-be-worse gesture.

"You don't look worried," he said.

She didn't feel worried, either. "I wouldn't mind a baby."

"A career lady like you?"

She shrugged.

Jared felt a sudden tightness in his throat. He coughed to relieve it. "DeBarr would love that."

"Paul wouldn't have a say in it."

"He's your boss."

"What I do with my body," she said with surprising force, "is none of his business."

Looking down at her, Jared felt a swell of gentleness. She was a fighter. He rather liked her cause at that moment. Recalling Anthony Alt's snide innuendo, he said, "You've never been with Paul."

"No. I work with him. It would be dumb to confuse the issues."

"If he turned you on, it wouldn't seem so dumb."

"Maybe not. But he doesn't."

"Do other guys in the office?" When she gave him a what-is-this look, he said, "It's intimidating for me to think of you there in an office full of men."

"I don't date them, and I certainly don't sleep with them. I thought we'd established the fact that I've been chaste for some time."

"That doesn't mean you haven't been tempted. AIDS has wreaked havoc with temptation."

"I haven't been tempted. Trust me. Besides," she sighed and returned her cheek to his chest, "I've been too busy to get involved."

"If that's so, how could you manage a baby?"

"I'd do things differently if I had a baby."

"How?"

"I'd go into private practice and work part-time. I'd move into a bigger place, hire an au pair, and have her stay with the baby while I was gone."

"You've mapped it out."

She was silent for a time before admitting softly, "I've dreamed."

Jared thought the dream was just fine, except that it was missing one major element. "What about the baby's father?"

"I don't know."

"Wouldn't you like a husband along with your baby?"

"Not for the baby's sake alone. If the father and I were in love, we'd marry anyway. But I don't need marriage. I'm loaded."

"What's money got to do with it?"

"If an unmarried woman becomes pregnant, she might look to marriage for financial security. I wouldn't have to do that."

"What about emotional security? Raising kids is hard work. Wouldn't you want someone to share the load?"

"If that someone and I didn't get along, the child would be worse off than being raised by a single parent."

"I don't want my child raised by a single parent."

"I doubt I'm pregnant."

With no warning at all, Jared shifted her on the bed and loomed over her. Though his hold was gentle, his expression brooked no argument. "I want to know. If you are, we're getting married. No child of mine is going to be raised by one parent when he can have two."

She swallowed. "I doubt I'm pregnant."

"Well, if you are, you know how I feel."

"Yes."

He was staring at her, but increasingly the stare was more indulgent. "Why do I get the feeling that I lost that one?"

"Because I doubt I'm pregnant, and I feel foolish carrying on this conversation. We only met three days ago. Besides," she winced, "I think I'm lying on my birthday flowers."

He rolled away and retrieved the flowers. Taking them,

she slipped from the bed and went off in search of a vase and water.

Jared watched her leave, watched the swirl of her robe behind her. Then he sat up and looked around the room. The last time he'd seen it, he'd been preoccupied with Savannah to the exclusion of all else. Now he wanted to see what clues the room gave.

It wasn't a large room, though the high ceilings gave that impression. Savannah had furnished it simply in white wicker with a dresser and dressing table, an easy chair, a low table with several magazines on top, and a pair of nightstands flanking the double bed. The accessories were pale blue, and between the swirls of the wicker and that blue, the effect was feminine in an airy sort of way. It reflected her personality, he decided. As professional an appearance as she made, she was refreshingly feminine inside.

On impulse, he reached for the radio that stood on the nightstand. The music came through softly, a ballad that was high on the country charts. Grinning smugly, he flipped off the switch, climbed from the bed and went to the window to see what it was Savannah saw when she awoke each morning. Propping an elbow high on the jamb, he gazed out over the chest-high, gathered sheers.

That was how Savannah found him. Her steps faltered just inside the door, and she stared, awed by the magnificence of his shape. He was a sculptor's dream, a masterpiece of long limbs and handsomely carved muscle. Her view was mostly of his back, a broad expanse of smooth skin made dynamic by the slant of his arms. His shoulders were corded, his back tapered to a narrow middle and waist, his buttocks tight. His legs were those of a runner, long, lean, and solid.

Just looking at him made her insides melt.

Catching sight of her, he dropped his arm and straightened. "I was getting lonesome," he said in a deep, very Jared Snow voice. He started toward her.

Head-on, he was even more impressive than from behind. Without his clothes he seemed larger, more firmly developed. He wasn't hairy; there was a spray of tawny down on his upper chest, but it quickly descended into a narrow line that disappeared into his navel. Below that, the hair was darker, thicker, and below that, he was amply endowed.

Savannah's mouth had gone completely dry.

Taking the vase of flowers from her hands, he set it on the nightstand. Then he returned to her, framed her face with his hands, and kissed her very lightly, very gently. When he had satisfied himself with one angle, he tipped his head and tried another, and after he'd explored that with the same lazy curiosity, he tried a third.

By the time he raised his head and looked down at her, the gray flecks in his eyes had gone noticeably darker. He lowered his hands to her shoulders, whispering hoarsely, "I want you as naked as me," and slid off her robe and nightshirt with the single sweep of each hand.

Taking a step back, he looked at her. She tried to cover her breasts, but he easily captured her wrists and held them away.

"You're beautiful."

She shook he head. "My sister's the beautiful one. I'm the smart one."

"You're beautiful and smart." Drawing her closer, he flattened her hands on his chest, moved them in slow circles over his nipples, then guided them lower. When they reached his groin, he closed her fingers around his erection.

He saw her eyes widen, knew what she was thinking. "That's how much I want you," he said in a low rasp. "You've already taken all of me inside. I won't hurt you."

Savannah dropped her gaze to her hands. She moved them in a gentle caress, loosened them to touch the velvet head, then trace the length of the ridge underneath. The more gently she explored him, the harder he grew, and the harder he grew, the more she wanted him.

Trembling inside, she came closer. Her view was obstructed when Jared began to touch her nipples. Already tight, they grew painfully so, mirroring the knot that had gathered low in her belly. She let out a low moan, dropped her head back, and closed her eyes.

Nudging her around, Jared sat her on the edge of the bed, perched sideways next to her and covered her open mouth with his. His kiss was deep and wet, and while she was in the throes of it, he spread her legs and slid one finger, then a second, inside her.

She cried his name, but it was muffled in his mouth. He wasn't ending the kiss any more than he was removing his fingers, and then he started doing such wonderful things with both that the only sounds she made were ones of pure pleasure. She was unaware of spreading her legs wider, even raising her knees, unaware that she was clutching his shoulders for dear life. The pleasure he gave her was so intense that she knew nothing until he quickly brought her over to straddle his lap and thrust into her, when she shattered into a million fragments of joy.

When she returned to earth, her face was buried in his hair, her arms were coiled tightly around his neck, every meeting place of their bodies was wet with sweat, and he was breathing as roughly as she.

"Jesus," he croaked.

She sputtered out a laugh. "My thought exactly."

After another minute of slowly diminishing gasps, he said, "What do you do to me?"

"Me? You were the one who started it." She imitated his deep drawl. "I want you as naked as me."

"It seemed only fair."

"Fair? I'll probably be bowlegged for a week. I'm not conditioned to this."

"Thank God." He fell backward and rolled over, came up on his knees, and hoisted Savannah higher on the bed. Grabbing the sheet that had been kicked into a bunch long before, he came down beside her, settled her comfortably in his arms, and drew the sheet high. "I think," he said slowly, "that I'd like to sleep now."

Savannah brushed her nose against his chest. "Fine for you to say. You're not picking up your sister at ten forty-five. If I fall asleep now, I may not wake up."

"You'll wake up."

She hummed out a sound that quite perfectly captured his own sense of pleasant exhaustion.

"You should have set it for twelve," he murmured against her hair.

"Mmm."

"Call her and change it."

"She'll be furious if I wake her up to tell her she can sleep later."

"You sound like you're afraid of her."

"No."

"Are you?"

"No. It's just that she wouldn't understand why I wanted more time to sleep."

"You mean to tell me," he asked slowly, "that she's never been zonked by early morning love?"

"I don't know, but that's not the point. The point is that she doesn't expect it of me."

"Because you're the smart one, not the beautiful one?" He gave a sleepy chuckle. "Clue her in."

But Savannah couldn't do that. Susan prided herself on being the stronger of the two when it came to sex appeal. As smug as Savannah felt at that moment, she didn't want to rob Susan of that edge. Her sister felt confident about so little else.

Jared's breathing lengthened. He was soon asleep. Lulled by the rise and fall of his chest, Savannah followed. When she awoke, it was nearly ten.

"Oh, no," she murmured, scrambling away from Jared and off the bed. She made straight for the bathroom, within seconds was under the shower, within minutes was out and drying herself as quickly as she could. It was ten-thirty when she picked up the bedroom phone and punched out Susan's number.

The line was busy.

Jared was sleeping soundly, sprawled on his stomach with one arm over the spot where she should have been.

She tried Susan again. The line was still busy.

Coming down on the edge of the bed, she watched him sleep. He looked totally comfortable and very masculine against the feminine decor. She couldn't quite believe that he was there, but he didn't go away when she blinked.

She tried Susan again. This time she got through. "Hey, just wanted to tell you I'm on my way."

There was a pause, then a mercifully sober, "You're late."

"Not by much, but I didn't want you to worry. I'll be

there soon." She hung up before her sister could say anything else. Then she looked at Jared. He was still sleeping.

Unable to resist, she leaned over and put a light kiss on his cheek. He didn't stir. For a final minute, she enjoyed the sight of him. Then she rose from the bed, crossed to the dresser to pick up the purse and heels she'd set there a short time before, and, with a last, longing glance at Jared, she left the room.

Chapter 12

SUSAN WASN'T ALONE when Savannah arrived. Dianne Walker, Susan's former sister-in-law, was there to open the door, swathed in fur and Obsession.

"Happy birthday, darling," she said, offering first one cheek, then the other to Savannah. "We missed you last night. The party was divine, wasn't it, love?" she said to Susan, who had come up from behind. Without awaiting an answer, she addressed Savannah again. "You're such a stranger. Always working. I'm glad you're taking Susan off for the day, though. It's been a dreadful week." She was studying Savannah closely. "But you're looking wonderful, darling. Kidnappings must agree with you."

Under normal circumstances, Savannah would have reacted to so offensive a comment. But she was feeling unusually light inside, and very indulgent. "A good night's rest will do it every time." Sidestepping Dianne, she gave Susan a hug. "Happy birthday, Sis."

Susan returned the hug. "You, too."

"All set to go?"

"I need another two minutes on my makeup. Dianne distracted me."

Two minutes would be five, and Savannah knew she would be stuck with Dianne during that time. But she said, "Go ahead and finish. I want to give the hospital a call and see how Megan's doing."

Excusing herself, she took off for the den and put through the call. Will answered the phone in Megan's room, his hello a tired one.

"Hi, Will. It's Savannah. How's she doing?"

"Okay."

"Did she sleep last night?"

"Yes."

"Is she feeling any better?"

"I don't know."

"She's still not saying much?"

"That's right."

"And you can't talk freely because she's listening. Has the psychiatrist been in?"

"Several times."

"The detectives?"

"Yes."

"She isn't offering any more than she did before?"

"No." With a breath, he went on more optimistically. "We've been watching television this morning."

"Ah. That's something." It was certainly more than Megan had done the day before. "Do you think she'll talk with me?"

The optimism vanished. "Uh, I don't think so, Savannah. She's not really feeling up to talking on the—wait a second." He put a hand over the phone. For a minute his voice was too muffled for Savannah to make out the words, then he came back. "Hold on."

Savannah held tight to the phone, then her heart gave a lurch.

"Savvy?" It was Megan, sounding pitifully frail, but talking at last.

Savannah wanted to laugh aloud. It was one of those days. "Meg! Oh, Meg, it's good to hear your voice. How are you feeling?"

"I'm sorry, Savvy." The words were little more than a tormented whisper. "God, I'm sorry."

"Shhh. You have nothing to apologize for."

There was a pause, then the same wrenching murmur. "I've made a royal mess of things."

"Are you kidding? You've been the victim of a vicious crime. You have nothing, *nothing* to apologize for."

There was another pause. "You had such high hopes for me."

"I still do. You'll heal, Meggie. You'll work all this out and put it behind you. I know that sounds simplistic, but life goes on. You're a fighter. You've fought things in the past, and you'll fight this, too."

"You don't know."

"No one does. No one knows what you've been through but someone who's been through the same thing. You'll be able to talk with some of those people, honey. There are support groups—"

"No!"

"They'll help."

"They won't. You don't know. You just don't know—" Her voice broke off, swallowed up by a thick silence. Then Savannah heard the first slow, soft sobs.

On the one hand, the sound was wonderful. Up to that point, Megan had been unable to release the anguish she felt. Crying was critical to her recovery. It was also a painful thing to hear.

For the first time that day, Savannah felt a weight on her shoulders. "Ahhh, Meggie," she soothed, wishing she was there, "it's okay. It's okay."

"I just wanted—I wanted—it's your birthday."

Tears came to Savannah's eyes. That Megan remembered the day, after all she'd been through, touched her deeply. "Another birthday. I'm beginning to wish they wouldn't come."

"You should celebrate—not waste time—thinking of me."

"Thinking of you is never a waste of time. You're a very special friend. You always will be."

It was another minute of soft crying before Megan said, "I don't deserve you."

"Nuh-uh. You've got that backwards. I don't deserve *you*." And she meant it. Megan had always had a way of putting things in perspective for Savannah, and it was no different now. "Listen, I'm at Susan's. As soon as she's finished dressing, we're coming by the hospital to—"

"No!"

"Just to say hi?"

"No!"

"But that would make our birthday complete."

"God, no—tell Susan—I love you both—"

"Listen, we're going up to Boston, but we could come by the hospital on the way back—"

"Savannah, it's me," Will interrupted distractedly. More distantly, he said, "Shhh. Okay, sweetheart." Then he came back to Savannah. "I've got to go." He hung up the phone.

Stunned and more than a little concerned, Savannah held

the dead receiver suspended in midair before finally returning it to its cradle.

"I take it she's beginning to come out of it?"

Savannah swung around to find Dianne at the door, looking perfectly settled in, as though she'd been there awhile.

Savannah didn't like Dianne Walker. She was, in her
opinion, the epitome of unconscionable wealth and waste.
Her life was an endless string of social engagements, and
though she lent her name to numerous causes, the only one
she worked actively for was her own beautification. Savannah couldn't call her Susan's friend, because friends didn't
stab friends in the back, which was what Dianne had done
when Susan and Dirk had split.

Why Susan allowed the woman in her house was a mystery to Savannah, but then, admittedly, Savannah was not up
on the latest gossip. She would ask Susan later. In the meanwhile, she had to deal with Dianne and her eavesdropping.

"Megan will be just fine," she said, and prayed it was
true. "She's a strong woman."

"Slightly out of her league, though, don't you think?"

"Excuse me?"

"We both know where she came from. She's had enough
trouble adjusting to our kind of life without something like
this happening."

Any indulgence Savannah had felt earlier was gone.
"*Something like this* would shake any one of us. Forget the
fact of the kidnapping. Have you ever been raped, Dianne?"

Dianne arched an elegant brow. "I've been forced to have
sex when I didn't want to, so yes, I've been raped."

"Ever been raped by two men, repeatedly?"

"I remember an orgy in Puerto Vallarta—"

"I'm not talking about orgies. I'm talking about two men,

total strangers who violently break into your home, take you to some filthy place you've never seen before, and rape you without letting you know when it will end and whether you'll be alive when it does. Have you ever experienced that, Dianne?"

"No, but I'd know how to handle it if it happened. A woman is never powerless where a man is concerned. Even submission can buy her points. And that's what it's about— points. You give me this and I'll give you that."

"We're talking irrational, violent men here."

"Men are men. Each has his weakness. Any man can be bought."

"What a sick view of the world."

One fur-draped shoulder rose and fell in a negligent shrug. "It's a realistic one."

"No. I can guarantee that if you'd been in Megan's shoes, you'd have been as traumatized as she was."

"I doubt that."

Savannah stepped past her on the way to find Susan. "If I were a malicious person, Dianne, I'd wish the experience on you just to see. But I'm not that cruel."

Dianne followed her into the hall. "And that's your weakness, Savannah. You're too good. You don't have enough of the bitch in you."

"Thank God."

"You do fine in your job. You don't have to be a bitch there, just a disciplined technocrat. With the law behind you, you can be firm."

"Suse!" Savannah called from the bottom of the stairs. "Step on it, Suse!"

Dianne looked pensively up the stairs. "Susie's a little too soft, too, but she's doing better. She wasn't demanding enough with Dirk. She let him get away with hell, especially when it came to his secretary. But she's learning. She walked through the party last night like she didn't give a damn about the men there, so of course, that sparked their interest. Even Dirk was looking twice. I don't know why she left so early. She was barely tipsy."

Tight-lipped, Savannah stared at her. "What was Dirk doing with his secretary?" For her efforts at self-control, she earned a droll look from Dianne.

"Must I spell it out? You're not *that* naive, Savannah, are you?"

"How long did it go on?"

"A year or two. When the stupid girl wrote Susan a letter, Susan couldn't ignore it any longer." Dianne eyed her askance. "You knew about the letter, didn't you?"

She hadn't known about the letter, any more than she'd known about the secretary. She had known about Dirk's infidelity, but there had never been a name and face attached. She hurt for Susan, and hurt for herself. She wondered why Susan hadn't told her.

But she wasn't about to give Dianne the satisfaction of knowing she'd dropped a bomb. So she said in a chilly tone, "You can never tell about these things. Even a letter can be more fantasy than not." She looked toward the top of the stairs. "Susan?"

"All set," Susan called, appearing seconds later clipping on an earring. She was fully dressed and made up, and looked stunning.

"Sorry to run out on you this way," Savannah told Dianne a bit airily, "but we're running a little late. We have lunch reservations at two, with a million things to do before then." She turned to Susan. "Want me to drive?"

"No. I'll take the Jag. It needs a good outing." Removing her fur from the closet, she draped it over her arm. "Dianne." She hugged her lightly. "Thanks for dropping by. I'll talk with you soon."

"Sure you won't reconsider for tonight? It'll be fun."

But Susan shook her head. "Can't. I have other plans." The phone rang. "Why don't you walk Dianne out?" she told Savannah as she headed for the den. "I'll get that and meet you out front." She picked up the phone. "Hello?"

"Are you all right?"

Susan shut her eyes. "Sam."

"You were angry before."

Her eyes popped open. "I was in a rush before, and I'm in a rush now. I told you. Savannah and I are going out for the day, and she's always prompt. You should know that. She's out front right now waiting for me."

"Where are you going?"

"Boston."

"Doing anything special?"

In a deliberately high and nasal voice, she said, "All those frivolous little things women like to do."

"You don't have to be snide."

She returned her voice to normal. "Savannah's waiting."

"I'd like to see you tonight."

"I've already answered that, too." She rubbed her damp palm against her silk skirt. "I don't know when we'll be back, and if it's not too late, I've got a party to go to."

"You went to a party last night. Don't you get tired of them?"

"Are you kidding?"

"No, I'm not kidding."

She could hear that he wasn't. His bluntness was one of

the things that made him different. She wasn't quite as bothered by it as she'd been at first. Still, she said, "Well, you should be. I happen to enjoy parties. I have a large group of friends. I enjoy spending time with them."

"Is that before or after you've had a few drinks?"

Her hand tightened on the receiver. She wanted desperately to hang up, but something kept her from it. "Low blow, Sam."

"Only because I care."

She pressed a palm to her chest to ease the sudden tightness she felt there. "Look, I'm all right. It was hard for me being over at Megan's this week, and seeing her the way we found her didn't help. I was overtired when I got home. So I had a few drinks and was sick. I'm sorry you were there to see it."

"I'm not," he said. "You'd been through a lot. You shouldn't have been alone. I was glad to be there. It felt good."

"Not to me. It embarrassed me. It embarrasses me every time I think of it. And every time you call, I think of it Sammy, Savannah's waiting."

"If you'd see me, I'd give you new things to think about."

"Oh, God, here we go."

"I'm serious."

"So am I. That's a feeble line."

"But the thought behind it is sound. I want to see you, Susan."

"No problem. You're good at breaking and entering. Surprise me some time." She hung up, then made a coward's dash for the door to the garage. The phone rang behind her, but she ignored it, and before long the Jaguar's purr drowned it out.

As soon as Savannah got into the car, she told Susan about her talk with Megan. Susan immediately suggested they detour into Providence before heading north. "I know you, Savannah. If we don't make sure she's all right, you'll be thinking about it all day, and I don't want to think about Megan all day. It's depressing."

"Talk about depressing, you should have heard Dianne's theory about the kidnapping. She's convinced that Megan could have handled being raped better than she did."

"Dianne's an imbecile."

"What was she doing at your house?"

"I'm not really sure. She said something about how 'cool' I was last night. She said that Malcolm O'Neill was asking about me after I left. She was probably sniffing around for little tidbits to give him. I'm sure she's trying to impress him herself."

"She's married."

"Since when has that stopped her? If she sets her eye on Malcolm, a wedding band won't put her off. And what better cover than acting as a courier between Malcolm and me?"

"Are you interested in him?"

"Not particularly."

"Then what use do you have for Dianne? It amazes me that you can stand the sight of her, after what she did."

Susan kept her eyes on the road. "She was just sticking up for her brother."

"By publicly denouncing you as co-chair for the Sperry fund-raiser? Not that I ever had any fondness for John Sperry; he would have made a lousy senator. But you'd put in a lot of work on that, and you raised plenty of money. Far more so than Dirk, you had a right to be there, taking pride in what you'd done."

"But you're right. Sperry would have made a lousy senator."

"You didn't think so at the time."

"Maybe I did but couldn't admit it. What you fail to realize, Savvy, is that sometimes people have ulterior motives for doing things. You don't actually believe that the people who organize fund-raisers for charity do it purely out of the goodness of their hearts, do you? They do it for the power it brings. They do it for the publicity, because their names go up in lights alongside that of their cause. They do it for prestige."

"So that's why you went all out organizing a party for John Sperry? You did all that work without even believing in the man?" Savannah's gaze was steady. "I don't buy it."

Susan shot her a dry look. "How about I did it because I had nothing else to do?"

"I think you did it because you happen to be really good at that kind of thing. Do you know that there are people who make careers out of planning functions like that? You have a marketable skill."

"Savannah . . ."

"I know I've said it before, but it's worth repeating."

"I am not going out looking for work."

"We're not talking walking the streets, knocking on doors. We're talking putting out subtle feelers to several large organizations."

"Uh-huh. And what am I going to put on a résumé? I haven't held a paying job in my life."

"You'll put down the nonpaying ones. You've held enough of them."

"Come on, Savannah. I'm named to the boards of institutions for one reason alone—I give money. Anyone with a little smarts knows that the amount of work involved is zip."

"You've planned at least a dozen affairs comparable to the Sperry one. You could get recommendations in a minute."

Susan made a face. "Do I really want to get up at the same time every morning, get dressed up, and go to the same office to do the same thing day after day?"

"It wouldn't be that, and you know it."

"I don't want to work."

"Then that's that," Savannah said a little too shortly, but she let it go. She could only point out the possibilities; it was up to Susan to take them from there. She had learned the hard way that if she pushed too hard, Susan went in the opposite direction. The dynamics between them were complex, but that was one thing that was quite reliable.

Susan tossed her a sidelong glance. "Do we really have reservations for two o'clock?"

"Uh-huh. At Aujourd'hui." She paused. "Do you really have plans for tonight?"

"No. Sam asked me out, but I told him I had a party."

"You could have gone out with Sam."

"I didn't want to be rushed into getting back. Besides, it won't do him any harm to wait."

"Sam isn't good at playing games like that."

"Tough," Susan murmured. Then, unable to resist, she asked, "Who does he usually date?"

"No one special."

"He must go out."

"When he can. His job is demanding. You saw what happened this week—on two hours' notice, he was working for nearly seventy-two hours straight."

"So now he's got the whole weekend off. I can't believe he's going to spend it alone."

Savannah shrugged. "You turned him down."

"Will he rush off and pick up the next best thing in skirts?"

"I don't really know."

Susan looked at her and didn't like what she saw. Savannah seemed perfectly sincere. "If you were to guess, what would you say?"

"I don't really know, Susan. Sammy and I are friends, but I don't keep tabs on what he does."

"Does he pick up secretaries around the office?"

"I've seen him talking with them."

"Do they talk about him afterward?"

"Not to me."

"Does he have a reputation for being hot?"

"Hot?" Savannah found the conversation increasingly amusing. "If you're asking whether he backs secretaries into storage closets and takes them standing up, I doubt it. Sammy has more pride than that."

"What's pride got to do with it? The issue is raw, animal lust."

The words stuck in Savannah's mind, spawning images of Jared's body and the rampant desire they'd shared not so long before. There had been pride in it. Then again, they hadn't made love in a storage closet.

She took an uneven breath. "Sammy strikes me as the kind to savor a woman in the privacy and comfort of his own bed."

"Where does he live?"

"He just bought a new place on the waterfront."

"New places on the waterfront are expensive."

"He's not a pauper."

"Cops don't get paid much."

"He uses his money wisely."

That gave Susan something to consider, and in the silence that ensued, Savannah thought about places on the waterfront, then places in town. Again Jared came to mind. She pictured him in her bed, wondered whether he was still sleeping, wondered whether she should have left a note. She'd debated it at the time. But he'd known that she was leaving, had known where she was going. And, anyway, what would she have said?

More than anything, she wondered when she'd see him again.

"You're looking mellow," Susan observed.

Savannah darted her a startled look, then turned her eyes back to the window. "Must be this birthday, on top of everything."

"Mmm."

"It bothers you, too?"

"I took a good look at my neck the other day. It looks old."

"If so, it's the only place on your body that does. You don't look a day over twenty-six."

"Where'd you get twenty-six?"

"Anything less doesn't have enough class."

Susan smiled. "That's a novel way of looking at it. Good one, Savvy." She took a quick breath. "Why were you late this morning?"

Savannah's heart picked up a beat. She really wanted to

tell the truth. Each time she thought of Jared, she bubbled inside. She wanted to share that.

But she didn't. She knew Susan, knew how Susan felt about Jared's voice, knew how Susan felt about herself as compared to her twin. One part of her wasn't completely sure what Susan would do if Savannah told her about Jared, and she didn't want anything to spoil the day.

Of course, there was still Megan to visit.

Savannah sighed. "I overslept. Everything must have crept up on me."

"You shouldn't have gone into the office yesterday. You deserved a day off."

"No. I'll deserve a day off when I've put away the men who hurt Megan."

"Not *I*, Savvy. *We*. You don't work in a vacuum there. Isn't the investigation out of your hands now?"

"In some respects. But I'll be the one to prosecute, so I want to stay closely involved."

"You shouldn't prosecute. You're too close to the case."

"I'm the best one to do it."

"Won't the defense raise a stink?"

"I'm not a judge. I'm not supposed to be impartial."

"Still, you can be overzealous."

"Not me. I know the rules. I wouldn't do anything to jeopardize the case. But the ones I'm worried about are the guys doing the running around now—the state police and the FBI. Sometimes *they* get overzealous, and if that happens, an important piece of evidence may later be ruled inadmissable. I don't want that to happen."

"So you're keeping your nose in. Have they come up with anything?"

Savannah hadn't spoken with anyone since the afternoon

before, but she was sure she'd have been notified if any leads had come up. "I think," she said, "that they're counting on Megan giving them something."

"Why won't she?"

"She's too upset."

"Maybe her breaking down on the phone with you is a good sign."

"Lord, I hope so. For her sake. She's going to have to get it all out before she can heal. The sooner she starts talking, the better."

When they arrived at the hospital a few minutes later, though, Will told them that Megan hadn't said much after she'd handed him back the phone, and she'd requested a sedative soon after. She wasn't sleeping, just quiet.

"Hi, Meggie," Savannah said softly.

Megan's eyes fluttered, then opened, but they were heavy.

Susan grinned. "We couldn't get going until we'd seen you. Either we're devoted, or we're nuts."

Megan looked from one sister to the other, then closed her eyes and whispered, "You're nuts."

Savannah wished she'd seen sign of a smile, but there'd been none. "How are you feeling?"

"Tired."

"Lots of people coming in to visit?"

She opened her eyes. "Can you stop them, Savvy? Tell them to leave me alone? They keep coming and coming and asking questions. I'm so tired of the questions."

"They're only trying to help. They want to find the men who did this to you."

Turning her head away, Megan closed her eyes again. "They won't find them."

"Not if they don't get some help. Can you tell us any-thing, Meg? There may be something you saw or heard that seems inconsequential to you but may have significance to us. Were they speaking English?"

Without opening her eyes, Megan nodded.

"Did you notice any idiosyncratic speech patterns?"

Megan shook her head.

"Did they sound educated, talk in complete sentences?"

Megan shrugged.

Savannah took a different tack. "Do you have any idea where you were held? Maybe there was some sound, like water or traffic or a banging noise, like machinery?" When there was no response at all, she said, "Did you hear other people talking nearby? That would tell us something."

Susan scowled. "For God's sake, Savannah, Megan's tired of questions. She just said that, now here you go off with a bunch of your own."

"I'm trying to help."

"You're always trying to help, but sometimes the best way to help is to back off."

"But time is important. We've already lost so much."

"If you've already lost so much," Susan said with delib-erate slowness, "it won't hurt to lose a little more." She pat-ted the air with one slim-fingered hand. "Take a deep breath, Savvy. Relax."

"Susan—"

"Shhh," Megan whispered. They both looked around to find that her eyes were open and pleading. "Don't argue."

"We always argue," Susan reminded her gently.

"But don't do it today."

"Why should today be different?"

"It's your birthday. You should be celebrating."

"We'll celebrate when we're done arguing. We're going to Boston."

Savannah leaned closer to Megan and whispered conspiratorially, "If we smuggle in some clothes, will you come with us? You've helped us make it through lots of birthdays. We need you now."

"Not a bad idea," Susan decided. "We could use a buffer. You've always been that."

But Megan was shaking her head.

"Not today?" Savannah asked.

"No."

"Another time?"

Megan shrugged.

"We could go to the island," Savannah suggested. "The three of us, just like we used to do. Those were fun times, weren't they, Meggie?"

"We were young and innocent," Megan said sadly.

"Maybe you two were innocent," Susan interjected, "but not me. I haven't been innocent since I was fifteen, and that was before we ever went to the island together."

"Still, it'd be fun to go back," Savannah said.

"It would."

Expectantly they turned to Megan, but she'd turned her head away. They exchanged a look, then Savannah asked softly, "Can we get you anything in Boston?"

Megan shook her head.

"Are you sure?" Susan asked.

Megan nodded.

Savannah covered her hand, which lay limply on the sheet. "Can I stop in again tomorrow?"

"I'm going home tomorrow," Megan said tonelessly.

"That's great!"

"Good news!"

Megan didn't respond to their enthusiasm.

"Then we'll see you there," Savannah said. She leaned down and kissed Megan's cheek. "Take care, y'hear?"

Susan, too, kissed her. Will walked them to the elevator.

"She responds more to you two than to anyone," he said. "I sometimes wonder why I'm there. I think I make things worse."

He looked nearly as tortured as he had when Megan had been gone. Savannah ached for him. "She's been through an ordeal."

"She's shutting me out."

"It's the nature of the ordeal. She can't face you."

"But I've told her over and over again that I don't care. I've told her that I love her as much—no, more than I did before. She won't listen."

"Just keep saying it. It'll sink in."

"No. She's punishing me. And she's right. It's my fault. If the alarm had been working—"

"No, Will," Savannah said, turning to face him. "You will never know what would or would not have happened if the alarm had been working. It's done. There's no point agonizing over that. Megan loves you. She needs to know that you'll stay by her regardless of what's gone before. She needs to know that you won't be put off by her moods."

"She never used to have moods. She used to be the most even tempered woman in the world."

Susan came forward. "After what she's gone through, she has a right to be moody."

"But she was moody even before the kidnapping. She was worried about—" he waved his hand, "—things. That's what I've done to her."

Savannah took his hand in both of hers. "She loves you, Will. She *loves* you. Whatever has happened, you can work it out. Just stick with it."

Susan looked down at the kid-leather gloves in her hand. "About the business, Will." She looked up. "I know someone who could help." When Will started to shake his head, she hurried on. "I understand the position you're in. Believe me, I now how awful it is to be humiliated in front of people you know. But the man I know works out of New York. I met him through my work with one of the hospitals there, and, if nothing else, he's discreet. Let me call him. He could come down and talk with you, look over the books, go through the mills. He could give you the kind of advice you need, and he won't charge you an arm and a leg for it."

"An arm and a leg is relative."

"Trust me. You'll be able to afford his services."

"How do you know?"

"I know," Susan said with confidence.

Savannah felt that the question of the fee was better deferred. "You could talk with the man, Will. Once Meggie's home and you're both feeling better, you could talk with him and make your own decision."

"This is my family's business. I don't want outside people snooping around."

"If you go bankrupt," Susan pointed out, "you may have no choice. You don't want to go bankrupt, Will. What will come of the family business then?"

Savannah softened the blow. "Just think about it. Okay, Will?"

Though skeptical, he nodded. Savannah and Susan had to be content with that, particularly since the elevator had arrived. With encouraging smiles for Will, they joined the people inside for the trip to the street floor.

Once there, Savannah caught Susan's arm. "A quick phone call. I'll be right back." She hurried to a nearby phone booth, closed the door, and punched out her own number.

The phone rang a full ten times before Jared picked it up.

The sun rose inside Savannah, bringing a smile of relief and pleasure to her face. "I wasn't sure you'd still be there."

"I wasn't sure I should answer. When it rang so many times, I decided that it was either you, in which case I wanted to talk, or someone who wanted you badly, in which case I wanted to know who it was."

"If it hadn't been me, who would you have said *you* were?" she asked, still smiling.

"Your cleaning man."

"But he comes on Thursdays."

"Ah. Well, then, I guess he changed days this week. Where are you?"

"Visiting Megan at the hospital. We're leaving for Boston now." She paused for the tiniest space of time before turning the question back to him. "Where are you?"

"Where do you think?"

She wasn't sure if she dared think, but she couldn't seem to help it. "Still in bed?"

He stretched out a lazy "Ummm. I like your bed. Mind if I stay a little while longer?"

"No. Oh, no. Stay as long as you want."

"What I want," he said in a throaty voice, "is to stay until you get back. Any idea when that'll be?"

"No. We got a late start, and Susan doesn't have any plans for tonight, so I can't really leave her alone—"

"I'll take both of you out."

"You don't need to—"

"Of course I don't need to, but I want to."

"But I really have no idea when we'll be back."

"I'd wait here until whenever."

"Uh, maybe it's not such a good idea."

"You're afraid I'll fall for your sister. That's crazy, Savannah. Do you honestly think that I can look at another woman after what we did this morning? I'm as good as a eunuch."

Eyes downcast, she thought about that for a minute, then said in a very soft voice, "You don't sound like a eunuch. Susan's already in love with your voice. She'll fall for the rest of you if she gets a look."

"I wouldn't parade into a restaurant naked."

"You wouldn't have to."

The compliment rendered him silent for a minute. Then he said, "She's your sister. You can't hide me from her forever."

"I know." She let out a breath. "I feel guilty."

He was quickly contrite. "Don't feel that, babe. It'll wait. I can meet Susan another time. It's just that I wanted to see you."

Savannah smiled again. "Thank you." She took the telephone cord between her thumb and forefinger. "Jared?"

"Hmmm?"

"This morning was nice."

"It was, wasn't it?"

She nodded, then realized that he couldn't see it. "You made my birthday special."

"I'm glad."

"Do you think you'll sleep most of the day?"

"Nah. Maybe for a couple of hours more, but since

you're not coming back here, I'll go over and work on my boat. Can I see you tomorrow?"

"I have to work tomorrow."

"All day?"

"Just about. I have a trial starting on Monday."

"An interesting one?"

"Uh-huh. Insurance fraud via arson." She looked up when Susan tapped on the glass door. "I've got to run." Ducking her head, she brought her fingertips to the bridge of her nose. Short of turning her back, it was the only way she could buy a bit of privacy. "Thanks again for the flowers and the . . . the . . ."

"Birthday bang?" he filled in so innocently that she had to laugh. "My pleasure. Literally."

She was floating on air. "I hope so."

"Believe it." He paused for an instant. "Can I call you at the office tomorrow?"

"The switchboard's closed. There's a private line." She told him the number. "Got it?"

"Got it. Have fun today."

"I already have," she said, smiling softly. "Bye-bye."

Chapter 13

⁓

SUSAN AWOKE LATE SUNDAY morning with a hangover. As hangovers went, it could have been worse, but the headache and its accompanying muzziness were harsh reminders of the party she'd thrown for herself the night before.

Determined to do nothing more strenuous than spend the day in the living room with the newspaper, she managed to shower, pull on a pair of sweatpants and a sweatshirt, and draw her hair into a wide clip behind one ear. Then she stretched out on the sofa.

It was a good fifteen minutes before she realized she didn't have the paper. With some effort, she got up and went to the door—only to open it and find Sam Craig standing on her doorstep.

She was not ready for Sam. Shoving the door closed, she turned back toward the living room. Only after she lowered herself to the sofa and gingerly set down her head did she realize that he had followed her in.

She threw an arm over her eyes. "Sorry, but I don't grant audiences this early in the day."

Sam tossed the Sunday *Journal* onto the coffee table. It hit the glass with a clap that made Susan jump, then moan.

He understood the problem at once. "Ahhh. We've got a hangover. Must have been quite some party."

"It was," she droned. "Lots of fun and laughs."

"And booze."

"Uh-huh."

"How'd you get home?"

"I drove. How else would I get home?"

"You could have had some guy drive you. Maybe he's upstairs right now getting dressed. Was it that kind of night, Susan?"

She rolled to her side, with her back to him, but he simply sat in the space she had unwittingly provided. With a hand on the sofa back and one on its arm, he had her caught. "Was it?"

Susan felt a rush of misery. In its wake, the words spilled out. "No. There was no man. There was no party. I got back here at ten last night and drank all by myself." She shot an angry look over her shoulder at him, then as quickly closed her eyes against the pain in her head. "Are you satisfied?"

"No," he said quietly. "I think I'd rather you'd been with people. At least, then you could say that they were the ones who kept your glass filled."

She put her arm over her eyes. "I didn't use a glass. I drank straight from the bottle."

"Why?"

"Because I didn't feel like using a glass."

"Why were you drinking?"

"Because I wanted to."

"Didn't you enjoy the day with Savannah?"

"Sure."

"But you were unhappy when you got back here."

"Something's wrong with the Jag."

"Come on, Susan." He tugged at her arm, but she kept it firmly in place. "A person doesn't get drunk over a car."

"It's as good a reason as any."

"Only if you want to ignore the reasons that count."

Raising her arm only enough to peer up at him, she said, "Another time, Dr. Freud, I'd love to hear your theory." She dropped the arm back to her eyes. "Right now I'd like silence."

Sam gave it to her for several minutes, during which time he studied the curve of her ear, the line of her jaw, the slope of her neck. Though she was of good height and ample curves, there was something fragile about her, physically and emotionally. It cried out to him. It made him feel compassionate and passionate. He had seen her at her worst, and she still turned him on.

"Sam?" came the voice beneath the arm, sounding wary now. "You're too quiet. What are you thinking?"

"I'm thinking that I'd drink myself to oblivion, too, if I was confined in this mausoleum."

"Mausoleum? This house is worth one-point-three million on the open market."

"Let the open market have it. It's a mausoleum." He stood and reached down for her, hauling her to her feet.

She tried to wrench her arms free. "What do you think you're doing?"

"Getting you out of here." He ushered her into the hall. "This house wasn't made for a single woman. It's got shadows in every damned corner." He took her fur from the closet.

She pulled back. "It's my house. It's quiet." Her eyes sharpened on him in accusation. "And it doesn't manhandle me."

Draping the coat around her shoulders, Sam pulled the lapels tightly together and backed her to the wall. He pushed one of his thighs between hers, but it was the pressure of his hips that pinned her there. "I won't manhandle you, Susan," he said, looking at her mouth. "That wasn't what I had in mind."

"I'm not up to this," she wailed softly.

He met her gaze. "I know. You have a lousy headache. Everything from your neck up feels thick. That's why you're coming with me without a fuss."

Despite her confusion, Susan felt an inkling of interest. "Where to?"

"My place. Once we get there, you can lie down to your heart's content. I won't bother you."

She wasn't sure if she liked the sound of that. "You're going to ignore me?"

"No. I'm going to make you some breakfast, then let you sleep." He plopped a kiss on her cheek, then stepped back. "We'll decide what you want to do when you're feeling better."

At that moment she missed the feel of his weight against her. A bit contrarily, she said, "I always read the paper on Sundays."

"Fine." Retracing his steps, he took the paper from the coffee table, then paused. "The whole thing, or just the society section?"

She glared at him, then took the fur from her shoulders, but before she could get it back into the closet he blocked the way. "What are you doing?"

"I'm staying here. I have a headache and being with you won't help."

"It'll help."

"You get on my nerves."

"That's good, isn't it? If I bored you, we'd be in trouble."

He had a point. Still, there was a limit, especially to what he had in mind. "You do know that this is absurd, Sam, don't you?"

"What is?"

"Us."

"What's *us*? We met on a job, and now I'm giving you a hand when you don't feel well."

"There's more."

"You mean this?" Without a second's warning, he ducked his head and caught her mouth. His lips were firm and intent, fluidly molding hers to his will.

From the start, Susan had objected to his cocky confidence. He always had an answer for everything and a stubborn will of his own.

Just then, she didn't think his will was so bad.

When he released her, she was slightly short of breath. "Yes. That."

"Want another?"

She hadn't quite recovered from the first. So she shook her head. And that hurt.

"Ooooops," Sam said. He spread her coat around her shoulders, this time waiting until she slid her arms into the sleeves. Then, securing the Sunday paper under his arm, he guided her to the front door.

He drove a sporty Mazda that looked to be no more than a year or two old. "You weren't chasing after Will in this the other night."

"I don't use this for work."

"You own two cars?"

Pulling out of the driveway, he shot her a look. "Is that so surprising?"

"Yes. You're a cop. I didn't think cops earned much money."

"With overtime, we do just fine. My lifestyle isn't outrageous. I have money left over for things like cars."

"And condos on the waterfront?"

He shot her another look. "Who told you about that?"

"Savannah."

"What else did she tell you?"

"Not much."

The Mazda's hum was the extent of the noise for the next few minutes. As the familiar sights of Newport passed from view, Susan felt increasingly uneasy. She knew Newport, but Sam Craig and his world were foreign. It seemed important to her that she not make a fool of herself in front of him.

Closing her eyes, she put her head back.

"How do you feel?" he asked.

"Okay."

"Head still hurt?"

"Uh-huh."

"You're not going to throw up all over my car are you?"

She let him wonder for a minute before she said, "The last time I heard that question, I was in a Testarossa being driven by a man who could as easily have redone the interior of the car as he could have bought a new necktie. He just didn't want the mess." She smiled dryly. "You men are all the same."

"That's a sexist statement if I ever heard one."

She shrugged.

"I'd be glad to pull over if you feel sick."

"I don't. And I don't usually get sick. Friday was an aberration."

"You hold your liquor better on Saturday, Sunday, and Monday?"

"Damn it," she muttered and swung her head toward him to argue, only to wince at the sharp pain that shot across her forehead. Reversing direction, she turned as far from him as she could within the confines of the car, burrowed into her coat, and concentrated on willing the pain away.

Nothing further was said during the drive to Providence. She put on a pair of sunglasses, and even then she kept her eyes closed against the day's bright light. She realized that they had reached their destination when Sam stopped the car.

She wasn't sure what to expect. When Savannah had mentioned a condo on the waterfront, she pictured Drew Wyker's place in Manhattan. It was an ultramodern high rise, made of steel and glass.

Sam's place was nothing like that. It was more of a garden apartment, rising only two flights, with glass, but no steel in sight. It was Cape Cod style, with cedar shingles stained gray and sparkling white trim. There looked to be a dozen or so units in the complex.

"New?" Susan asked as Sam guided her to the front door.

"Brand new. I've only been here a few months."

"It has charm."

Opening the door to a small foyer, he led her directly through to the living room. Seeing the bricked walls, the broad expanse of glass, and the cushiony sofa from which one could view the river, she realized there was charm inside the place, too—charm, if very little furniture.

"Like I said," Sam explained when he caught her looking

around, "I've just moved in. I haven't had much time to order things. And I'm not even sure what to order. I'm not a decorator." Taking her coat, he gestured toward the sofa. "Please."

It wasn't so much his use of that word as the look on his face that touched Susan. She could have sworn that he was uncertain of himself. Cocksure Sam Craig was unsure of himself.

It helped.

Slipping onto the sofa, she eased off her sneakers and curled her legs under her. After a minute of sitting straight, she lowered her head to the sofa's arm. Behind her, Sam rummaged in the kitchen, but she didn't have the inclination at that moment to see what he was doing. Nor did she have the inclination to ask for a tour. Her head was still throbbing. Her eyes hurt. Sleep was the easiest, most noble escape.

She awoke some time later to the smell of fresh coffee and the sizzle of bacon. Before she could do more than drop her feet to the floor and sit up, Sam was lowering plates of food to the small area rug that lay between the sofa and the tall window of glass that overlooked the river.

Without a word, he went back to the kitchen, returning this time with a pitcher of orange juice and a stack of dishes, silverware, and glasses. After he arranged everything to his satisfaction, he sat back on his heels.

"Breakfast is served."

Susan was still feeling groggy. "What time is it?"

He glanced at his slim black watch. It was different from the practical one he had worn when he was working, just as the plaid shirt he now wore was a step up from the old, faded sweatshirt. He still didn't look conventional; his shirtsleeves were rolled to the elbow and his shirttails hung out over jeans that, while clean, were torn at the knee. But he had obviously made an effort to dress, and, muzzy as she was, she noticed.

"It's nearly two-thirty," he told her.

She lifted her chin in acknowledgment, relieved to find that the pain in her head had eased. "This must be brunch, then."

"Isn't it a little late for that, too?"

"No," she said and took the plate he offered. It was filled with an assortment of breakfast goodies. "It's Sunday. Anything goes."

"Tell me about Saturday."

"Coffee first."

He poured her a cup. Carefully, she set the plate down beside her on the sofa, took the cup, and held it between her hands. She sipped it slowly, savoring its strength. As the caffeine seeped into her system, the fuzzy feeling faded.

Sitting cross-legged on the floor, Sam alternated between eating and watching her. He could hardly believe that she was in his home, and that she had entered it without a condescending quip. Though he adored the place, she was obviously used to far larger and more elaborate surroundings. He didn't need large, and he didn't want elaborate.

Nevertheless, Susan added class to the place.

"Saturday," he prompted, lest he get carried away with his thoughts. "How was it?"

"Fine." She helped herself to a piece of raisin toast.

"What did you do?"

"Shopped. Had lunch. Went to the exhibit of Dutch landscape painters at the museum. Shopped some more."

"Did you buy anything?"

She gave him a look that answered him quite well—and adorably, he thought. He grinned. "Tell me."

"A handbag, two pairs of shoes, a darling silk dress for spring, and a bunch of stuff that was black, intimate, and sexy."

"Don't stop there."

"That's all I bought."

"What kind of *stuff*?"

She took another bite of toast and shrugged. "Silk stockings, garter belts—you know, Sam, personal stuff."

He could picture it all too well. "When do you wear stuff like that?"

"All the time."

"Are you serious?" he asked. His voice sounded strange, but there was nothing strange about the bulge in his pants. He had been hard a lot lately.

"Of course, I'm serious. I like feeling feminine."

Sam cleared his throat. "What about Savannah? Does she buy silk stockings and garter belts, too?"

Susan stared at him hard. "What's Savannah got to do with this?"

Her vehemence startled him. "Not much. I was just asking."

"I thought there wasn't anything going on between Savannah and you."

"There isn't."

"Then why do you want to know whether she was buying sexy underwear?"

"It was just a thought. Innocent conversation."

"But why do you have thoughts like that about Savannah?"

"I don't. I mean, it was just an extension of what you

were saying. You and Savannah were shopping together. You bought something sexy. I wondered if she did, too."

"Does it matter?"

"Of course not!" He sent a helpless glance skyward. "Christ, Susan, you're making a big deal over nothing. I don't give a good goddamn what Savannah wears under her clothes, but at the time it was the first thing that came to mind. If you want to go on talking about what you wear to feel sexy, be my guest. If I jump you before you make it to your eggs, it won't be my fault."

Susan studied him in silence. Then she said, "You want me?"

"Are you blind, deaf, and dumb?"

Her eyes flashed and she stood so quickly that her plate tottered on the next cushion. "No, I am not blind, deaf, and dumb." Her arms were straight, her hands in fists by her sides. "Don't you ever, *ever* suggest that I'm any one of those things. I may not be as brilliant as my sister Savannah, but I am not stupid." She stormed to the side of the room, coming to an abrupt halt at the window, where she crossed her arms over her chest and stewed.

Sam was quickly at her side. His voice was a little uneven, but gentle. "I didn't mean any harm. It was an expression. I was being facetious. You sat there asking whether I wanted you—do you have any idea how much I do? Do you have any idea what looking at you does to me?" Taking one of her hands, he stroked her fingers open, then put her palm against his fly. It was pure torture. "That's how much I want you." He moved her hand to show her the extent of his arousal. "You. No one else, Susan. Just you."

Susan's anger had faded with the gentleness of his voice, and with his arousal beneath her palm, she was quickly aroused, herself. Unable to resist, she began touching him on her own, measuring his length, exploring his shape and fullness. He strained against her hand, and for a minute she was tempted to unzip his jeans and feel his bare flesh. But she wasn't ready to make love. So she slid both hands under his shirt and up to his chest.

He gave her a long, deep kiss. When it was done, she was nearly as short of breath as he. Still, she stepped back.

"I'm not an easy lay," she announced and returned to the sofa.

"Susan . . ." he warned, still painfully aroused.

"Come have your breakfast, Sam."

"I had breakfast at five o'clock this morning."

"*Five.* What were you doing up at five?" She took in a healthy forkful of scrambled eggs.

"Coming home from work."

"You worked all night?"

"That's right."

"And that," she said, pointing her fork at him, "is why you and I would never work. I drank myself silly last night waiting for you to break into my house. I have certain needs. A man can't fill them if he's never around."

Sam hadn't moved. "I'm around now. That's what this argument's about. You come over here and I'll fill your needs real good."

She put the tines of the fork against her lips and looked at the ceiling. "To paraphrase the great Conway Twitty, I need a man with a slow hand." She turned the fork toward his plate. "Eat, Sam. Then we'll see how slow you can be."

With an agonized moan, Sam did an about-face, hung his head, and wrapped a hand around his neck. "You're a witch."

"Mmm. Great bacon. I always burn mine."

"Why are you being so cruel?"

"I guess I'm still a little hungover."

Lips thinned, he turned around. "You just enjoy giving me a hard time. It gives you a feeling of power."

She shrugged. There was no point in denying it.

Sam returned to the rug, poured himself a glass of juice, and drank the whole thing. Then he set down the glass. "So you had a nice time yesterday. I'm glad."

Susan let her mind wander back to the day before. "It was nice." After another minute, she added, "Interesting. Savannah was in a really good mood."

"Isn't she usually?" he asked, then held up a hand. "Look, you were the one who raised the issue of Savannah, not me. If you don't want to talk about her, fine, but don't say things and then expect that I'll be a good little mummy and stare straight ahead. That's not my way."

She realized that. She also realized that she wanted to hear his opinion. "You have my permission to talk about Savannah, and to answer your question, yes, she's usually in a good mood, but yesterday was different. I can't quite put my finger on it. We stopped at the hospital to see Megan before we left, and I know that she was a little down about that. Then she made a phone call from the hospital, and that seemed to cheer her up. I think she's got a guy on the side she's not telling me about."

"Not me," Sam vowed, raising both hands this time. "Not me. I swear it."

She believed him. "Any idea who it could be?"

Sam shrugged. "Savannah comes into daily contact with lots of men. It could be anyone. Didn't you ask?"

"Sure, I asked. She said the phone call was to the FBI

agent who's heading Megan's case. Has anything happened there?"

"Not that I know of, and I'd know."

"She looked pleased while she was talking with him. Maybe he's the one. When I asked, she laughed and denied it, but then, when we were shopping, she bought the most incredible teddy." She arched a brow. "I'm not knocking Savannah's taste, but it's usually a little more sedate when it comes to lingerie. Sweet, maybe even lacy, but certainly more sedate than that teddy."

Sam grinned. "The teddy was real racy?"

Susan didn't like his enthusiasm. "Why does that please you so?"

His grin vanished. "Why are you so fast to jump to conclusions? I am not interested in Savannah." He palmed his crotch. "There's nothing here. Totally soft."

Susan dropped her eyes to the place he touched. "I wouldn't say there's nothing there," she said, watched and waited for a minute, then added, "or that what's there is totally soft."

Gritting his teeth, Sam asked tightly, "Want it now?"

She shook her head.

"Then ease up, honey. Push me too far, and you'll get it whether you want it or not."

His threat excited her. She supposed it had something to do with the fact that she trusted him. She knew he'd never hurt her. And she suspected that whenever he took her, she'd be ready.

"I'm sorry," she said.

He looked irritably off toward the wall, then dropped his head and shook it slowly. When he looked up again, he wore a sheepish grin. "You are incredible, do you know that?"

"Is incredible good or bad?"

"Only time will tell." He took a deep breath. "Okay. We still haven't figured out why you went home and drank last night."

"I didn't know we were here to find out."

"Indirectly, we are. So. Why did you go home and drink?"

"That's indirect?" When he gave her a warning look, she said, "I told you. I was waiting for you to break in and you didn't come."

"You also said that you suspect Savannah has a new man. Does that bother you?"

"Of course not."

"Are you sure?"

"Sure, I'm sure. Besides, maybe I'm imagining things. Savannah doesn't have time for involvement with a man. She has a career."

"Many women have men *and* careers."

"But do they handle both well?" Susan asked in a knowing way. "It seems that every time I turn around another article's being written about the plight of superwoman. Either she's consumed by guilt that she's depriving her family of something, or she's angry that her husband isn't doing his share, or she's too tired to make love. A person only has one head; she can only wear one hat."

Sam popped a rasher of bacon in his mouth whole and talked around it. "That's an interesting statement."

"It's true."

"On the other hand," he swallowed and spoke more clearly, "if you were to say that she can only wear one hat *at a time*, the statement takes on new meaning. Men have to switch hats. I can't wear my cop's cap twenty-four hours a day."

Staring at his complacent expression, Susan had the sinking feeling that she would lose the argument if she pursued it. So she decided a small detour was in order, particularly since he'd raised an interesting point. "I can't picture you wearing any kind of cap," she said and held out her coffee cup for a refill. "Why do you wear your hair so long?"

He poured the coffee. "I like it this way."

"Wouldn't short hair be easier to care for?"

He shrugged. "I have easy hair. Towel dry, and that's it."

"I'd think your superiors would prefer something more traditional."

"Nope. I don't look like a cop. Makes things better for undercover work."

"Do you do much of that?"

"As much as I can. It's interesting."

"And dangerous."

"Sometimes yes, sometimes no. What's wrong with your car?"

Susan had no idea what her car had to do with the discussion, and her look told him so.

"You said something was wrong with it," he explained patiently, "and I know just the person to fix it. Name's Matty Stavanovich. He has the slickest fingers east of the Mississippi."

"Is he an authorized Jaguar repairman?" she asked archly.

Sam laughed.

"What's so funny? It's a legitimate question."

"But the way you said it. There are times when you forget who you are and where you're from, and you say things that are totally uninhibited. Then there are other times when your breeding takes over. That was one of those times. You sounded like the very proper, very wealthy Newport matron."

Susan wasn't sure if he was making fun of her or not. "There's nothing wrong with breeding. Maybe if you had a little more of it, you'd be better off in the world."

"There are many kinds of breeding, Miss Susan. I've had breeding, just a different kind from you."

"Oh?" She dared him. "Tell me about your breeding."

To her surprise, he did just that. "I grew up in western Pennsylvania in a very Catholic home. My parents were devout. They believed that there were certain ways to live and certain ways to think, and they taught me each of those ways. I lived and breathed them until the day I graduated from high school." He paused. "Wouldn't you say that's breeding?"

Susan's eyes went wide for a minute. "I guess I'd have to. But what happened when you graduated from high school?"

"I left home."

"Left? Just went away?"

"Went to college, actually, but I never went home again. I won a scholarship and got a small loan from an uncle, but otherwise I was on my own. My parents didn't want anything to do with me."

Susan didn't understand. "But why? What had you done that was so awful?"

"I was their only son. I was supposed to be a priest."

"Oh my."

"When I told them that that wasn't what I wanted in life," he made a cutting motion with his hand across his neck, "that was it. I was as good as dead."

Susan was stunned. "How can your parents do that?"

"They were extremists and insulated from the rest of the world. They used their beliefs to commit a multitude of sins."

Though he was sitting and speaking very calmly, the look on his face was anything but. Deep inside, he was hurt. And perhaps angry. Susan knew she would be. She wondered what Thanksgiving dinners were like at the Craig home.

"How is it when you see them now?"

"I don't see them. I told you. In their eyes, I'm dead."

"*Still*?"

"Still."

It sounded so stark, so final, Susan cast about for something to soften the situation. "You said you were their only son. Do you have any sisters?"

"One. But she's their daughter. She won't see me either."

"She won't see you? She's an adult and she just goes along?"

Sam had asked himself the same questions dozens of times. "She's afraid of my dad, I guess. She's seen what he's capable of. She doesn't want to be disowned, and in some respects, I can see her point. She's three years younger than me. When all this first happened, she was in no position to go against Dad's dictum."

"She's a lot older now. She must have some resources of her own. She could call you on the phone, arrange to meet you somewhere."

"Not really. She married a guy from home. From what I hear, he's out of the same mold as Dad. They don't have much money, and they have a baby girl. Time is as tight for her now as money."

"A baby?" That made things even worse. "You have a niece you've never seen?"

Sam clearly did not like the direction the conversation was taking. "Yes, I have a niece I've never seen, and it hurts. I've tried to send her gifts but they were all returned unopened. She's five, not much of a baby anymore, and doing just fine without me." He held up the pitcher of orange juice.

Susan declined the offer. She was having trouble conceiving of going through life totally alone. "You must have other relatives. What about the uncle who loaned you money when you started college?"

"He died four years ago, and there's no one else worth seeing. Don't look so stricken, Susan. I have plenty of friends. And I love my work."

But Susan was trying to imagine what it would be like to sever oneself, or be severed from one's roots. The very thought made her feel wobbly. While her father was far from attentive, she had aunts and uncles and cousins. And she had Savannah. Despite all the times in her life when she had resented that, at the moment it was reassuring.

"Easter's coming up," she said on impulse. "You can celebrate it with me."

Sam got to his feet. "The beauty of my job," he said, producing a grin, "is that I often get to work through things like Christmas and Easter and the Fourth of July." He held out a hand. "Want to take a walk? It's peaceful out on the pier."

Without a second thought, Susan put her hand in his. A short time later, they were sitting side by side on the end of the small wooden dock. Susan was wrapped in her fur, Sam in a pea jacket. For a time they said nothing, but simply listened to the rush of the river. Sam was right. The spot was peaceful.

But Susan couldn't stop thinking about what he had said. Peering at him over her collar, she asked, "Do you really like your work?"

"Yes, I really like my work. That's not to say that I want to do it forever. There are other things out there that interest me, too."

"Like?"

"Law. I'd like to be doing what your sister is."

"So, go to law school."

He tossed a splinter of wood into the wind. "Someday I will."

"Why not now?"

"Because I'm not ready."

"If it's a matter of money—"

"It's not. I'm just not ready. Who knows? Maybe I never will be."

Susan stared at him. "How can you not be ready for something that would better your life?"

"I don't know that it would better my life."

"Of course it would. You'd be a lawyer. You'd have a profession. You'd be earning twice as much money as you are now, and you'd have the potential for earning even more."

"Money isn't everything."

"It sure comes close."

He eyed her head-on. "You've got bundles of the stuff. I don't see that you're so happy with your life."

"I'm happy."

His eyes chided her.

"Okay," she conceded, "so I've been going through a rough spell. But it'll pass."

"Only if you make it pass, Susan. Burying the misery in

a bottle will only make things worse. You have to find out what's wrong with your life and take steps to correct it. Do you miss Dirk that much?"

"I don't miss Dirk at all. I haven't missed him since he left."

"Then you're lonely."

"I'm not lonely. I have plenty of friends waiting to do things whenever I want. I could have gone out last night if I hadn't made the mistake of deciding to wait for you to come." She got to her feet. "That was a *big* mistake." She started back toward Sam's door.

He caught up with her in a second, easily matching her strides. "Why did you wait? I asked you out, and you turned me down. Forget the fact that I was called in to work. Did you think I had so little pride that I'd take the risk of getting shot down twice on the same day?"

"I thought you wanted me," she said with her chin tipped up. "I guess I was wrong."

"I do want you."

"Strange way you have of showing it."

Sam stopped in his tracks, grabbed handfuls of his hair and gave a loud growl of frustration. In the next instant, he captured Susan's hand, surging ahead with her in tow. She tried to pull back, but she might as well have been handcuffed to him. He didn't let up until he'd climbed the steps to the small deck off the kitchen and gone inside. Then he backed her into a corner, no more than a foot from the door. With the weight of his body immobilizing hers, he held her face in his hands and kissed her with every bit of the hunger she'd accused him of lacking.

"Once too often," he muttered into her mouth. "You've goaded me once too often."

She tried to talk back, but he wouldn't allow it. His mouth dominated hers, rendering any sound she tried to make little more than a moan.

Controlling her head with his kiss, he gave free rein to his hands. They slid down her neck, rolled around and over her breasts, and continued downward. With every touch, she burned hotter. She tried to stop him, tried to divert him, to regain a drop of the control she had so totally lost, but he was relentless in his quest. Before she could begin to adjust, his hands were in her sweatpants.

She wrenched her mouth free for a breath. "Sam!"

"Too late!" he caught her chin in one hand and recaptured her mouth at the same time that his fingers found the spot between her legs that was already wet with wanting him.

She moaned again when he stroked her more deeply. It was happening too fast. She had the dreadful fear of his possession being over before she'd been able to enjoy it.

"Wait," she gasped. "Give me a minute."

"Too late," he repeated, and in the echo of his words came the rasp of his zipper.

She tried to capture his wrists, but he was too strong and he moved erratically as he worked himself free of his pants and pushed hers past her knees. When those same knees threatened to give way, she clutched his shoulders. In the next breath, his hands were on the backs of her thighs, spreading her legs and lifting her.

"Sam," she whispered frantically. "*Sam.*" Her back hit the wall with the force of his thrust, and then he was inside, filling her to the limit, and she struggled to catch her breath.

Sam swore softly. His eyes were closed, his face buried in her hair. "Susan," he whispered roughly, "Holy

Mother . . ." He withdrew, then surged back, withdrew and surged back.

With a choked cry, Susan erupted into a powerful climax. She was still in its hold when, stroking her twice more, he came himself. His whole body stiffened. His breath was suspended in his lungs. He let it out slowly in a series of quiet gasps.

For a long time, neither of them moved. Neither spoke. They simply breathed and recovered and tried to figure out ways to repeat what they'd just been through.

Susan had never had as satisfying a climax. She wondered whether it was the novelty of Sam, or the fact that he was so different from the other men she had known, or that he had taken her with a bit of force and a lot of conviction. One thing she had to say for him, he didn't waffle.

Forehead against his shoulder, she smiled.

He felt it. "What?"

"Savannah thought you were the type to want privacy and the comfort of a bed." She shot an amused glance toward the door, mere inches from her arm. "Guess she was wrong." Still smiling, she drew back her head and caught his gaze. "So much for a slow hand."

Beneath a damp forehead, Sam's eyes sparkled. "You want a slow hand? I'll give you a slow hand." Cupping her bottom he held her to him and began to shuffle through the kitchen toward the stairs.

"You're going to trip, Sam."

"No, I'm not."

"Your pants are around your knees."

"So are yours."

"Mine are lower, and I'm not the one trying to walk."

"I can make it."

"On the stairs?"

"Sure."

He tripped on the very first one, swore, and finally managed to set her upright on the third step. Hopping from one foot to the other, he got rid of his sneakers, jeans and briefs, then tore off his pea jacket and whipped his shirt over his head without bothering with the buttons.

Stunned by the sight of him naked, Susan couldn't say a word when he started in on her own sneakers and pants. He tossed her fur aside as haphazardly as he had his coat, and she didn't make a sound. She nearly protested when he tugged her sweatshirt over her head, but only because for that short period of time he was out of sight. With her sweatshirt gone, he unhooked her bra and peeled it back. Then, lowering his head, he began to hungrily devour her breasts.

They made love for the second time on the stairs. While it wasn't as fast as the first time had been, it was nowhere near the slow savoring Susan had wanted. That came the third time, on the king-sized bed that was the sole piece of furniture in Sam's bedroom. By the time they were done, Susan was in such a state of divine exhaustion that she couldn't have raised a glass to her lips if she tried.

Chapter 14

⁓

*T*HAT WAS RANDY TRAVIS, *I'm Jared Snow, and you're in cool country, 95.3 FM, WCIC Providence. Right now it's twelve-forty, that's twenty minutes before one on another Monday night in March. If you're lookin' for the best of the best country sounds, you've come to the right place. Before the clock chimes the hour, I'll be kickin' up a new one from Sawyer Brown, an oldie from Linda Ronstadt, and a duet from Crystal Gayle and Gary Morris that'll get you in the mood for love. So refill that coffee cup, curl up, and listen in to 95.3 FM, WCIC Providence, and me."* His voice went lower and more sandy. *"Put down your pencil, darlin', and take a break. That's the word from Jared Snow in the heart of the night. . . ."*

The music rose to swallow his sexy purr, but its memory lingered for a long time within Savannah, and while it did, she put down her pencil, folded up her legs, and wrapped her arms around her knees. Listening to Jared on the radio was a sweet torture, yet she wouldn't have turned him off for the world. For months he had made her nights a little less dark. Now he made her days brighter, too.

Though she hadn't seen him since she'd left him in her

bed on Saturday morning, they had talked on the phone many times. He knew she was on a trial, and he seemed to understand the demands that brought. So he called her for two minutes here, two minutes there.

She couldn't have told him how much those calls meant to her if she'd tried. She wasn't sure if she understood it herself. To have become so quickly dependent on him was a little frightening.

Even more frightening was the frustration she felt at having to settle for phone calls. She wanted to be with him again, lie with him again. Of course, he worked while she slept, and he slept while she worked. It was not the most convenient arrangement.

With a deep sigh, she unfolded her legs, took up her pencil, and edited several thoughts she had jotted down earlier. The trial had gotten off to a good start that morning, with the jury impaneled by noon and the opening arguments heard that afternoon.

She was lucky that she had worked on Sunday and come prepared.

She wasn't wild about opening arguments. They were tough for a prosecutor. She could give her all, only to have the defense stand up and dramatically refute it. Whereas in the course of a trial there were various tactics she could use to call time-out if she felt the momentum was against her, she was helpless during opening arguments. She had to sit quietly through to the end, when she could finally launch into her case.

Closing arguments were easier, since the prosecution went last. Unless the judge chose to give a particularly long-winded set of instructions to the jury, the prosecutor's words were the freshest in their minds when they began to deliberate. That didn't mean she always won her case, but it did give her a psychological edge.

Any edge she could get would be a help on this case. There were three defendants with, all told, twenty-six counts against them. A large part of her job was going to be making sure that the jury didn't get confused, and in that respect, she had her work cut out for her.

Sucking in a deep breath, she put herself to the task. Over the next hour, she reviewed the testimony of each of Tuesday's witnesses, as she had prepared them in the days and weeks before. When she was satisfied that she'd be able to lead them through direct examination without pause, she tossed down her pencil, turned sideways on the desk chair, draped an arm over its back, and thought of Jared. Instantly, the tension that had held her body in its grip while she worked eased, giving way to a soothing warmth.

She didn't know when she would see him again, but she knew she would. Not that she was looking far down the road. A week, a month, two months—as long as their relationship lasted, she would enjoy it. She wouldn't get caught by great expectations that fell flat.

"It's ten before two," he told her in a low, lazy drawl, *"and I'm glad you're still with me. We're not missin' a thing being inside, since there's no moon in sight. CIC weather calls for cloudy skies lingering through the overnight into morning, then burning off by noon, with temperatures climbing to the upper fifties. Not bad for March. But then, nothing's ever bad here at 95.3 FM, WCIC Providence, where we're serving up a little country in the city all day, every day. Right now, I'm kickin' around with the Oak Ridge Boys. Jared Snow in the heart of the night, stay with me. . . ."*

Savannah's eyes were closed, her expression soft, her

chin tilted up just a tiny bit, as if she were awaiting a kiss. When Jared's voice gave way to four-part harmony, her eyes opened with a start.

Standing abruptly, she packed her briefcase for the morning, hurried into the bedroom, undressed, and climbed into bed. There she lay curled on her side with a pillow hugged close and tried not to think about the ache deep inside her. It was only when Jared came on the air again and assured her that he would be there until six that she managed to relax and fall asleep.

"Don't touch that dial. You're tuned to cool country, 95.3 FM, WCIC Providence. I'm Jared Snow, and it's one-oh-four on a starlit Tuesday night. If you caught the PC game, you're probably celebrating along with the Friars. If you didn't catch the game, you'd better know we made the finals, 'cause it's gonna to be all over the papers come morning." Susan imagined him smiling as he said, *"Good goin', guys."* The smile lingered, but the voice got back to serious seduction. *"Here at CIC Providence, I'm kickin' off five in a row with Anne Murray, who's singin' us all a love song. At 95.3 FM, this is Jared Snow in the heart of the night. Listen and love. . . ."*

Susan sat stock still in the echo of his voice. Too soon Anne Murray took over, but Anne Murray wasn't half as exciting as Jared Snow. The man had come to take on a new identity since Sunday. His voice was as divine as ever, and he still stood for power and prestige, but when she pictured him now, he had the face and body of Sam Craig.

Absently, she jiggled the glass she held. In the past months, the clink of ice cubes had come to be a reassuring sound, and since she had only had two drinks all night and wasn't even high, the reassurance registered.

Sam was working. He'd been on duty since noon on Monday, which meant that she hadn't seen him since he'd dropped her back at Newport a short hour before that. How he could work, she didn't know. They hadn't slept for more than two hours at a stretch on Sunday night, and between stretches there had been a most delightful and exhausting activity.

With a feline grin, she took a sip of her drink and slipped a little lower against the bedpillows.

Sam Craig was a gem. He had done things to her that no man had ever done—and she had done things back that were just as shocking to her. She and Sam fought. They could rile each other at the snap of a finger. But they were red-hot in bed.

Her grin remained as she recalled her thoughts of the week before. Oh yes, the bulge in Sam's jeans lived up to its promise, so much so that she wasn't dumping him so fast. Her relationship with him could never last—he just wasn't in her class—but while it did, she planned to enjoy it. Men with the raw, animal hunger, not to mention the stamina of a Sam Craig didn't come along often.

Poor Savannah, she thought. So innocent. She had no idea what she was missing, and Susan did believe, at last, that Savvy was missing a lot. There had never been anything between Savvy and Sam. She couldn't possibly have been so blasé about him if there had been. Sam was the type to be remembered with a blush and a sigh.

Susan blushed. And sighed. She looked down at the magazine on her lap. While he worked, she was going to decorate his house. He didn't know it yet, of course, but he wouldn't object. He couldn't object. She was experienced at decorating, and she had impeccable taste. It would give her something to do. It would give her an excuse not to have lunch with Julie Devore on Thursday or play cards at Monica Lang's on Friday. And it would put to good use the months of *Architectural Digest* that were gathering dust in the magazine rack in the powder room.

Taking a slow sip of scotch, she studied the issue that lay open on her lap. Sam's place should be clean and modern. She wouldn't crowd it with furniture, or with artwork. Dennis Becker would be the decorator to use for an entree to the best stores in New York. Dennis was a friend. He would help her plan everything out, then she would show Sam the plans. He would be hooked.

Anne Murray segued into Alabama's latest. Sliding even lower in bed, Susan balanced the glass on the magazine on her stomach and folded her hands below it.

Life was looking up.

Megan looked down at her fingernails, then curled her hands into balls so that she couldn't see what remained of nails that had once been finely shaped and polished. In the course of the last two weeks, she had systematically chipped away at the polish, then bitten away at the nails. They looked like she'd clawed her way out of a tomb of dirt and rock, but she couldn't seem to stop. She needed an outlet for the anguish she felt inside.

She needed a manicure. But that was out of the question now. Most everything she had hoped for was out of the question now. Even Will seemed beyond her grasp—not because he wanted it that way, but because she did. She couldn't face him and expect his respect, not after the way she'd bungled things.

He was so good. Too good. His sole fault was in falling in love with a loser.

"That was Ricky Van Shelton with 'Life Turned Her That Way,'" came the slow, deep voice from the radio nearby. *"Jared Snow, here, wrapping up a long Wednesday, opening up a new Thursday with you. It's two twenty-five in the A.M. I'll be playing the coolest of cool country sounds until six, so stay tuned to 95.3 FM, WCIC Providence. We've got greats like Reba McEntire, Willie Nelson, and Glen Campbell on tap, but first let's kick in to the sweet harmony of Naomi and Wynonna, the Judds. This is Jared Snow in the heart of the night. Stay cool. . . . "*

Stay cool. Stay cool. Megan closed her eyes, took a deep breath, and willed herself into Jared Snow's peace. She had missed him, missed these moments of escape. She hadn't wanted to ask for a radio at the hospital, and before that, well, she could have asked until she was blue in the face and it wouldn't have done a bit of good.

They were animals, the two of them. *Animals.*

Deliberately she unclenched her teeth and forced herself to take another deep breath.

She was healing. The bruises on her body had turned a sickly yellow, but at least she wasn't as sore. The hot baths helped. She'd been taking three or four a day since she'd come home. She doubted she'd ever quite feel clean again, but the baths were soothing.

And Will had had the jacuzzi fixed. He was so good.

Slowly she opened her eyes to the ledgers that lay open on the desk before her. As good as Will was, he was still a lousy entrepreneur. She didn't know what to do with the mess of his books now, any more than she had before.

At least then she had had a solution in sight.

The prospects of that looked dim now. She had every intention of going along with the original plan, but she would bet her diamond wedding band that she would end up with nothing.

The bastards.

Especially *him*. She couldn't believe his arrogance. He thought he was so smart, when in fact he was nothing more than a lying, cheating fool. His mistake, she decided, was in underestimating her. Somewhere along the line, he decided that she was a not-so-bright, spineless woman, and in all fairness, perhaps she had given him reason to think that. But he was in for a surprise. She'd show him who had the brains.

Savannah would be pleased.

Jared sat in Savannah's office at four-thirty on Thursday, waiting for her to return from court. He shouldn't have come, he knew. She needed space. But Saturday morning seemed light years away. He had begun to wonder whether he had imagined it. Talking on the phone was too short, too distant. He had to see her.

Sprawled in the chair with his jaw propped on a fist, he stared at the open doorway and willed Savannah to come through. Court ended at four; Janie told him that she was usually back in the office soon after, though she often ran out again after that. He hoped this wasn't one of the days when she did the running before the returning.

By four forty-five, he was sitting straighter in the chair, wondering what in hell he was doing. He had been married to a lady lawyer. He had spent five lousy years waiting for Elise to be there when he needed her. It had been a brutal experience.

What he was feeling at that moment, though, was brutal in a different way. Instead of anger and humiliation, he felt loneliness, frustration, and worry. He figured that either he had become a masochist as he aged, or he was just plain crazy.

Then Savannah came through the door, and it all made sense. The intense concentration on her downcast face, her abrupt halt, and the rise of her eyes to his, the brightening of her features, the dawning smile. He stood but didn't say a word. His Adam's apple felt twice its normal size.

Savannah closed the door behind her and came forward. Softly, she said, "This is the nicest thing that's happened today."

He swallowed hard, and even then his voice sounded thick. "It's been a tough one?"

She nodded. "One of my witnesses flubbed up. I doubt the jury will put much stock in his testimony."

"Is his testimony crucial?"

"Not crucial, but important."

"I'm sorry."

Unable to take anything too seriously when she was feeling suddenly light-hearted, she tossed of a mischievous grin. "It's okay. I'll just make the rest of my case brilliant enough to compensate."

"I'm sure you will," he said without the mischief. "I almost came to watch you in court."

Her grin widened into another smile. "Why didn't you?"

"I don't know. Maybe I thought I'd make you nervous."

"I was already nervous."

"I can't believe that."

She nodded with deliberate slowness. "You couldn't have hurt."

"I was worried I'd stick out like a sore thumb."

Savannah couldn't imagine him doing that. If anything, he'd make everyone else look like sore thumbs. But she got his point. "You don't like attracting attention, do you?"

"No. I'd rather keep a low profile."

"You take big chances every time you walk in here, y'-know," she teased softly.

"Some chances are worth taking." Sliding the straps of her briefcase from her shoulder, he tossed the briefcase to the chair he'd just left. "I think I'd like a hug now." Slipping his arms around her, he held her tightly to him.

Feeling a stunning sense of homecoming, Savannah wrapped her arms around his neck, closed her eyes, and sighed at the relief of it all.

Jared made a low, throaty sound. He tucked her even closer, loving the crush of her body against his. "You smell so good," he whispered into her hair.

"Can't," she whispered back. "Too long a day."

"You do. Of flowers and woman and court."

She breathed a giddy laugh. "Musty?"

"Just a little. With the other two, it's mighty potent."

"So are you."

"Musty?"

"Potent."

With the slightest dip of his knees, he lifted her higher against him. He gave a low groan, his mouth by her ear. "I've missed you."

"Me, too."

"Phone calls don't do it."

"I know."

He swayed from side to side, and while the motion was gentle, there was a fierceness to his grip. "I've tried to stay away, Savannah. I know how busy you are."

"It's been an endless week. I'm glad you came."

Setting her down a bit, he raised his head. For a minute he did nothing more than take in the look on her face. Then he covered her mouth with his.

The knowledge came almost instantaneously. He didn't need to stroke her lips softly or open them wider or fill her mouth with his tongue, though he did all those things because his hunger was so great. The instant he kissed her he knew.

The feeling was there, all of it, the heat, the need, the desire. It was as hot and sweet and desperate as it had been on Saturday morning, and as uncontrollable. From a simple kiss came far-ranging cries. The promise of heaven hovered.

"Is there a lock on that door?" he whispered against her lips. The urgency in his voice was that of his body, and it mirrored hers.

"Yes, but we can't—"

"—do it here?" His mouth was open on her neck. He felt her fingers clutching his hair, and the stinging drove him higher. "Sure we can."

Savannah's insides were buzzing, she wanted him so badly. "But this is my office."

He spoke quickly. "We could use the desk, or the chair, or the rug—the rug—we could use the rug." Cupping her bottom, he ground her hips to his. "The rug—I won't hurt you—you could get on top."

"Jared, my God," she whispered brokenly, then wailed

softly, "I can't. I can't. I have a witness waiting for me in the conference room."

Jared went utterly still for a minute, then groaned. A small voice in the distant corner of his mind told him he had been through this before, but a louder voice was quick to refute it. He had never wanted Elise this way. Never.

"I'm sorry," Savannah said. Her eyes held even a deeper apology, and her hands moved gently in his hair to atone for the discomfort they'd caused. "I'm sorry," she whispered.

He caressed her cheek, brushed his thumb over her lower lip. "When, then?"

"The weekend?"

"I can't wait that long."

"Tomorrow night?"

"Tonight."

It sounded wonderful. "But I have to work. My most important witness takes the stand tomorrow."

"We can make it late."

"But *you* work then."

"We can work around my work. Come to the station as soon as you're free."

"It may not be until ten-thirty or eleven."

"That's okay. Take a cab, and bring an overnight bag with you. I'll drop you at work in the morning."

"Uh, I'll need a little sleep somewhere along the way."

"You can sleep in my bed."

"You have a bed at the station?"

He grinned. "A biggie. I live there. The second and third floors are mine." Putting a finger under her chin, he closed her mouth. "I have to sleep sometimes myself. Where did you think I lived?"

"I don't know—I didn't —you talked about your boat."

"April to November. It's only March."

"Of course."

He chuckled. "Of course." He kissed her again, careful to keep it light this time. When he raised his head, he put his hands safely on her shoulders. "I'll see you tonight, then?"

"I'll try."

"*Try* isn't good enough."

"I'll make it. I just don't know what time."

"That's okay, as long as I know you're coming."

"I'll come."

Dipping his head, Jared touched his lips to hers a final time, but he did it so lightly and with such sweet promise that, without thinking, she opened her mouth for more. He ran the tip of his tongue over her lips, then her teeth, then pulled back.

"I'll be waiting," he said in a husky tone that was more intimate than any he used on the air. Then he left.

For the duration of the afternoon and evening, Savannah held the memory of that intimate tone inside her. She thought of it often, and each time she did, she grew warm. At one point, Arnie even asked if she was feeling all right.

"You look a little—I don't know—flushed."

"I'm fine," she said, adding a new blush to what he'd already seen. She tried to keep her mind on track, particularly after that, but she couldn't get through the evening fast enough.

Unfortunately, when she was on trial, her out-of-court hours had to be used not only for preparing the next day's agenda, but taking care of matters relating to other cases she was handling. It wasn't until eleven-thirty, when she was nearly frantic to get away, that she finally managed to escape.

As Jared had suggested, she took a cab, and it was a good thing. If she'd driven, she'd surely have been stopped for speeding, or running a stop sign, or driving up a curb. She felt impatient and eager, more so than she had ever been for a date in her life.

Not that this was just a date like any other. She had never done what she was doing now.

When she rang the bell at the large Victorian house, Jared answered the door. He wore the same sweater and slacks he'd had on earlier. As clothing went, the outfit was tame. There was nothing tame about the look in his eye.

Without a word, he framed her face with his hands and gave her a long and thorough kiss. That was all it took for the level of desire to soar to where it had been that afternoon. Grabbing her hand, he made for the front stairs. She had to trot to keep up, particularly when he began taking the stairs two at a time, but she didn't mind. She was brimming with the same excitement, the same impatience and need.

He didn't stop at the first landing, but continued on up a second flight of stairs. At the top of that was a single door, opening into a single, large room. In most Victorian homes, it would have been the attic. In this one, it was Jared's suite.

Savannah had neither the time nor the inclination just then to explore it. Having kicked the door shut, Jared was kissing her again, and while he did that, he was taking off whatever of her clothes he could.

She helped him. Only when she was naked did they turn their joint attention to his sweater and slacks—at least, she thought their attention was mutual, but he kept interrupting the task to touch her, to stroke her breasts or brush her nipples or splay his hand on her stomach and lower. And each time he touched her, she lost track of what she was doing.

She had to struggle to focus again when he resumed the task himself.

It seemed forever until he was nude, but that was forgotten the instant their bodies touched. Foreplay was unnecessary. Jared was hard, and Savannah was wet. Neither of them had the presence of mind to do anything but complete the joining they had been thinking about since that afternoon.

Crossing her ankles at the small of his back, Savannah arched into his thrusts. They came hard and fast, seeming to defy the limits of her body with their depth. Spontaneously, she lifted her head and scraped his nipple with her teeth. His reaction was every bit as spontaneous and feral. She cried out, then sucked back the same breath with the stunning force of her release. Seconds later, Jared surged into a breathtaking climax of his own

"Jesus," he breathed between gasps as he sank down on top of her seconds later. "Jeeesus."

Unable to help herself, and as breathless as he, she laughed. "You're incredible!"

"Look who's talking. I open my front door and you attack me."

"*Me*?"

He didn't allow her to argue, but kissed her silent, then rolled over and drew her to his side. For several minutes, neither of them spoke. Slowly, their breathing returned to normal.

Then Jared, who was usually restrained regarding his feelings toward women, blurted out, "I can't believe you're here."

"I'm not quite sure what here is." Lifting her head from his chest, Savannah looked around. The room was done in navy and cream, very sleek, very modern, very masculine. "Nice. I like the skylights."

"Me, too. Not great for sleeping, though. Do you know what it's like to have sun pouring in through the skylights in the middle of what's supposed to be your night?"

She looked at him, caught the twinkle in his eyes. "Poor baby."

"No sympathy?"

She shook her head. "That's what you get for working at night. Why do you do it, anyway?"

"I like it. It's quiet, peaceful. Usually the worst DJs or the newest are stuck with it. I chose it."

Given the fact that, as owner, he could choose any shift he wanted, Savannah had to admit that he wasn't simply making light of a bad situation. "I wish you didn't have it tonight."

"It won't be a problem."

"If you're down there, you can't be up here."

"So you'll come down there."

Levering herself up, she looked at him seriously. "I'm on trial. I may not need much sleep, but I do need some. Especially now."

"You'll get as much as you want. You can stay with me until you get tired, then come back up here. I'll join you at six."

"Just when I'll be getting up. I have to be in the office by seven-thirty tomorrow morning."

Jared didn't particularly like the sound of that, but at least he would be able to watch her dress. Then he frowned and shot a glance at the door. "Where's your bag?"

"I didn't bring one," she said, feeling vaguely foolish. "I came straight from the office." She scowled, wanting to blame Jared but fearing the fault was her own. "I was in such a rush to get over here that I couldn't stop at home."

"Are you sorry?"

"It would have been more convenient if I'd had my things."

That wasn't what worried him. "Are you sorry about the rush—the urgency?"

Savannah didn't have to think about it for long. The scowl vanished, her features softened. "No," she said. She kissed his chest, then did it again because his skin smelled so good. Then she propped her chin on a hand there and met his gaze. "The urgency's a little scary. I've never felt anything like it before. But it feels good. I'm not sorry."

"Good," he said hoarsely. He cleared his throat and tried again. "Good. Because I'm not. And I've never felt it before either, Savannah. You know that, don't you?"

Just as she nodded, the telephone rang. Jared glanced at the nightstand clock. "Shit." Reaching across her, he picked up the phone. "Two minutes," he told Melissa without so much as a hello.

"That's about all you've got," Melissa said. "Unless you want me to cover for you for a little while."

"Don't offer. I'm apt to take you up on it."

"Want me to stay?"

He actually considered it for a minute, then said, "Nah. I'll save it for a time when I'm *truly* desperate." He winked at Savannah. "I'll be down." In the process of hanging up the phone, he rolled on top of her. "Are you coming down with me?"

Savannah crinkled her nose. "Maybe I should wait till Melissa leaves."

He gave her a look that said the ruse was pointless. "She

knows you're here." At Savannah's frown, he added, "No, she doesn't know what we've been doing, and she didn't see you come in, so if you show up wearing my clothes, she won't think twice."

"She won't have to," Savannah muttered.

Lacing his fingers through hers, Jared stretched her arms high over her head. Bearing his upper weight on his elbows, he looked down at her breasts. "I don't care if she knows," he said absently. More attentively, he said, "Your breasts are beautiful." He lowered his head to kiss first one, then the other. Each kiss sent live wires of heat through Savannah, none of which was helped by the stirring press of his loins.

"Jared," she whispered, wanting him again.

"I have to go."

"Go quickly—or don't go at all."

Kissing her lips, he whispered, "I have to go," and rolled off her and to his feet. She had to console herself with the fact that he was aroused, something that even a fig leaf couldn't have hidden just then.

Crossing to a closet, he opened the louver doors and pushed several hangers around until he found what he wanted. He returned to where she was sitting now on the bed and draped a hunter green flannel shirt around her shoulders. "You'll look fetching," he said, but he was quickly searching the room.

Savannah watched while he located and pulled on the navy briefs he'd taken off such a short time before. She watched him go back to the closet, take out a pair of jeans, and step into them. She watched him pull his sweater over his head and jam his feet into his worn deck shoes.

By the time he came to her, she was hugging the shirt tightly around her, wondering what a man with Jared's sex appeal saw in a woman who had bought an extraordinarily sexy teddy and didn't dare put it on.

Setting a fist on either side of her, Jared brought his face close to hers. "Coming down?" he asked in the soft, sandy voice that sent tingles along her spine.

She gave a quick nod. "In a minute." She touched her hair, which was a mess of escaped tendrils around a spindly knot. "I want to fix myself up."

"Don't fix too much. I like you this way."

She made a face in disbelief.

"I like you this way," he insisted, with greater feeling this time. He kissed her gently. "Gotta run. Don't be long."

Still hugging the edges of the shirt together, she smiled and shook her head. He strode to the door and looked back at her a final time before heading downstairs.

It was during that last look when her heart warmed and her senses seemed to reach out that Savannah first suspected she was in love.

Chapter 15

ON FRIDAY MORNING, Sam took Susan and her Jag to see Matty Stavanovich.

"You never did say whether this Matty was an authorized repairman," Susan murmured as Sam helped her from the car. While she didn't want him to laugh at her again, she did want an answer. The Jag was one of her prized possessions. She felt elegant driving it. When she sat behind its wheel, she was on top of the world. Heads turned. She was in command.

She didn't want just anyone fiddling with her car.

Taking her arm, Sam guided her toward the repair shop's office. "Matty's authorized, all right. He also happens to do a damned good job, which is more than I can say for some authorized repairmen."

"Does he work on your car?"

Sam smirked. "The Mazda's a little too plebeian for his skills. He's very selective."

The office was far neater than she had expected it to be. It was also filled with Beethoven's Fifth, playing a little too loud for comfort.

Matty Stavanovich was nowhere in sight. That didn't

seem to bother Sam, who proceeded to walk around the small room, scrutinizing everything in sight.

"Where is he?" Susan demanded above the music. She expected service.

Sam turned a desk calendar toward him, flipped back several pages to scan what had been written there for the preceding few weeks, turned the calendar right again. Then he went to the elaborate stereo setup against the wall and lowered the volume. "Give him a minute. He'll be here."

Susan watched him nonchalantly thumb through a cluster of papers on the desk. "Are you looking for something?"

"Hmmm?"

"You're being very nosy. Either you're looking for something, or you have terrible manners."

He flashed her a broad smile. Then his gaze slipped beyond her. "Here he comes. The man, himself."

Susan turned to confront a man who was several inches shorter than she, several pounds lighter, several years older. While his features were average, his skin was sallow, contrasting sharply with dark hair that was thinning on top. He wore overalls that barely camouflaged his slenderness. As grease monkeys went, he was immaculate.

"Well, hello," he said, eying her with interest. He held out his hand. "I don't believe we've met. My name is Mattias. You are . . . ?"

In an instant, Susan knew she would let him work on her car. He had slender fingers, the fingers of an artist, or a piano player. Between that and Sam's recommendation, she sensed he would have a way with the Jag.

But the Jag was the only thing she would let him touch. She didn't like his voice. And she didn't like his eyes.

Tucking her hands deeply in the pockets of her jacket,

she tossed a helpless glance at Sam, who came to her rescue by leaning in and shaking the hand that had been extended to her.

"This is Mrs. Gardner," he said. "That's her red Jag out front. She's got carburetor problems. I told her that if anyone could fix it, you could."

With a grin that Susan liked as little as his voice and his eyes, Matty brought his free hand up to clap Sam on the shoulder. "Well, well. Sam Craig. How've you been, old friend?"

"Working hard, Matty."

"I'm sure you are," Matty drawled. "I haven't seen you in a while."

"That's right. I've been out on assignment each time you've been brought in. Cranston this time?"

"That's what they say."

"And you're innocent as a babe."

"Naturally."

"Innocent as a babe, and as quick-fingered as ever, eh?"

Matty flexed those fingers and shrugged. "I have to stay in shape, now, don't I?"

Susan knew she was missing something. But she was content to let Sam do the talking. Matty Stavanovich gave her the creeps. The less he looked at her the better.

Sam was walking around the office, studying again— this time the framed certificates on the wall, the piles of papers neatly criss-crossed on top of a file cabinet, an obligatory pinup from the most recent *Sports Illustrated* swimsuit issue, several snapshots. He pointed to one. "From Cancún, I take it?"

"You've done your homework."

"It's right there on your calendar, bold as day. A five-day trip to Cancún. Was it a nice one?"

"By all means," Matty said. "And those were taken at Chichén Itzá. Marvelous Mayan ruins there. I had a private guide. He told me some fascinating things."

"I'm sure." With a final glance at the pictures, Sam moved on to the wall calendar beside the phone. "We'll get you one day," he said softly, almost absently. "You know that, don't you?"

"Not at all," Matty returned pleasantly. "I'm a very careful man. I don't make mistakes."

"Everyone makes mistakes," Sam said as his eye skimmed notations on the calendar. "Somewhere, you'll slip up. Then we'll have you."

Susan was beginning to get the gist of things she didn't want to know. She wondered exactly where Sam had brought her.

"We'll see," Matty hummed at Sam's prediction. He cupped his chin between thumb and forefinger and looked into the distance. "I may want to retire someday, to settle down, let the state foot my bills. Then again," he dropped his hand and said whimsically, "I may decide to go abroad. I've always fancied retirement in Switzerland."

"I'll bet you have," Sam said, less indulgently now.

Sensing the shift in mood, Matty rubbed his hands together. "But that's a long way off, and right now I have a job to do. I'm flattered that you're sending me work." He turned to Susan with smile that again grated on her. "I take it you have a ride home?"

"She does," Sam answered possessively.

Matty nodded. With a smooth, catlike walk, he went behind the desk and took a work-order form from the drawer.

Sam gave him the information he needed, and Susan was happy to let him do it. She was even happier when they left.

"What was going on there?" she asked as soon as they'd hit the fresh air.

"Where?"

"There. What was all that between you and him?"

Sam opened the Mazda's door for her. "Just a little good-natured kidding."

She waited until he slid behind the wheel to confront him. "Good-natured kidding, my foot. Neither one of you was kidding. Is that man an authorized repairman, or is he a crook?"

"Don't worry. He'll fix your car," Sam said, patting her knee.

She batted his hand away. "Is he a crook?"

Sam started the car, pulled away from the curb, then shot her a look. He had the distinct feeling that she wouldn't settle for anything but the truth, so that was what he gave her.

She was livid. "The Cat? You had me leave my car with *the Cat?* How *could* you?" she cried, grabbing for the wheel. "Sam Craig, how *could* you? Turn around. We're going back."

He held the wheel steady despite her efforts to turn it. "I wasn't lying to you, Susan. He happens to be the best one to fix your car."

"I'm not totally ignorant." She gave another tug. "I've read about him. I've even heard Savvy talk about the Cat, but the name Stavanovich never registered. How could you do this to me, Sam?"

"He'll fix your car," Sam insisted.

"But he knows me now," she wailed. "You gave him my

name and my address. Who do you think's going to be next on his hit list?"

"Not you, and that's a promise. You're safer now than you were before. He never preys on customers."

Susan was only mildly mollified, though she did sit back in her seat. "There's more than one way to prey." She screwed up her face. "What a smarmy little man. He's the kind to turn vicious in bed."

"You've had experience with kinds like that?"

"Once," she said with distaste. "That was enough."

Satisfied that her distaste was genuine, Sam glanced her way again. "You don't have to worry about Matty. He's pretty careful with women. They'd be too apt to scream and yell if something went wrong."

"Unless he threatened them into silence."

"A little guy like Matty?"

"He wouldn't have to use physical force. Doing the kind of work he does for the kind of clients he does, he probably picks up all the latest gossip. Do you think he'd be adverse to blackmail?"

"I doubt he'd try it. It's not his style. I'm telling you, Susan, he's got a good thing going as the Cat. He's probably got millions stashed in numbered bank accounts. His strength is his cleverness. One of the reasons he's been so successful is that he works alone. He's not about to go stupid on us at this late date and start playing rough with women. You're safe. Trust me."

He reached over to chuck her chin and left his hand to slide down her neck and under the lapels of her blouse.

"I should trust you?" Susan asked, but her voice had lost its edge. No doubt it had something to do with the long, blunt-tipped fingers that had stolen into her bra.

"About as far as you can throw me. Where do you want to go?"

They'd talked of picking up a VCR for Sam's place, but Sam had to go to work later that day, and Susan wasn't in the mood for shopping.

"My place?" she asked, catching her breath. Sam's finger was brushing her nipple, setting the rest of her on fire.

"You got it," he said and stepped on the gas.

"We have to get moving," Savannah worriedly told the small group gathered in the conference room at five that afternoon. "Time is passing. We're getting flack from the press. I'm getting flack from upstairs. Megan is having trouble getting on with her life. And whoever kidnapped her is having a good laugh." With a quick breath, she turned to Mark Morgan, the FBI agent on the case. "Anything new, Mark?"

"Not much. Nothing's turned up at points of departure, but we don't know what we're looking for. We've sent alerts throughout the country for unlikely-looking persons spending money freely, but that could as easily net half the population of Las Vegas as our men. We're going through files of kidnappings and attempted kidnappings in other states, but kidnappers don't usually do it twice. We're also working through lists of recent escapees from either federal or state penitentiaries. Theoretically, an escapee would be able to put three million to good use. But the kidnapping was carefully planned, so whoever it was would have had to have been around this area for a while beforehand. We're canvasing the area with mug shots. Someone may recognize a face."

Savannah turned her questioning eyes to Peter Sprange, who was with the state police.

"I don't have much more. The hospital tests tell us that we have two men, blood types A positive and O positive. Both have dark hair. That's about it. Mrs. Vandermeer hasn't been able to give us anything. We've checked out every recent parolee in the state, but aside from three, they're all accounted for. We're working on those three, but two have different blood types and the third is an unlikely candidate."

Savannah looked at Sam, who was representing the local police, but he slowly shook his head. "We're looking for a needle in a haystack, and we don't even know which haystack it is. We need Megan's help, Savannah."

Savannah was discouraged. "I know. But I hate to pressure her." She turned to the last person in the room, a counselor trained in rape therapy. "Do we dare push her?"

"I think we do," the woman said, then corrected herself. "I think *you* do. She won't have any part of me. She's totally resisting the idea of therapy, individual or otherwise. But it's been a week since she was let go. While the horror is still very real, it's not as immediate as it was last Friday. You can push, but gently."

Savannah didn't want to push anyone anywhere. She had just completed a full day in court, and although she would be wrapping up her case on Monday, the pressure wouldn't let up until the verdict was announced.

She planned to visit Megan over the weekend, though. And yes, she would push. She intended to solve this case.

Sitting forward in her chair, she went from one person in the room to the next, asking questions, asking each for additional resources to call on during the next week. Then, knowing that there wasn't much more she could do, she thanked them for coming and adjourned the meeting.

Sam stayed after the others had left. "How's the trial going?"

She raised her eyebrows wearily, but said, "Pretty well, actually. There have been one or two glitches, but one or two is nothing. I think we've got a good shot at winning."

"If you hadn't thought that, you'd never have gone to trial."

She smiled crookedly. "True." Then she studied him more closely. He was propped on the edge of the conference table, at ease physically. Still, he looked like a man with something on his mind. "I talked with Susan the other night," she said. "She mentioned she'd seen you."

"Did she?"

"Uh-huh. I got the impression that it was more than just a hello on the street."

"It was," he said in a way that said far more.

Pressing her fingers to her lips, Savannah covered a smile. "You don't look decimated. I take it you came out the winner?"

"I'm not sure either of us won, or lost. In some respects, we're pretty evenly matched."

Savannah tapped her fingers against her lips and said nothing.

Sam faced her head-on. "Okay. What are you thinking?"

One of the nice things about her relationship with Sam was its honesty. Dropping her hands to her lap, she said, "I'm thinking that I love my sister and that you'd be good for her, but that she'll be a handful if you decide to take her on."

"I already have."

His firm response took her by surprise. "Oh. Ah, well then, I guess I should give you a hug and wish you good luck?"

Sam thought of her doing that, thought of telling Susan about it, and found himself right at his reason for seeking out Savannah now. "I want to ask you something," he said. "She's really hung up on you. Do you know that?"

"Hung up?" Savannah didn't like the sound of that. It sounded pathological. "I wouldn't call it hung up."

"Well, she is. She compares herself to you all the time. She gets uptight whenever I mention your name. At the beginning, she was convinced we were having an affair."

"Well, we're not."

"I know that and you know that, but it's taken Susan a while to believe it."

"Does she now?"

"I think so. She still gets nervous when I talk about you. I didn't dare tell her I'd be seeing you today, and God forbid she should walk in that door right now, there'd be all hell to pay."

Savannah grinned. "You're sounding almost henpecked."

"It's not funny, Savannah. She is unbelievably jealous of you. Has it always been that way, or do I bring out the worst in her?"

Savannah's grin faded. "It's not you. The situation may be complicated since we see each other at work. But there's always been a sibling rivalry between Susan and me."

"You're twins." He put two fingers together. "You should be this close."

"We're sisters." She made a wide vee with her fingers. "Sometimes we're this close." Then she relented. "We're close. I shouldn't say we're not. But we do compete with each other."

"I don't see you doing it."

Savannah thought of the feelings of inadequacy that still hit her at times. When she was with Jared, his attentiveness banished them. Still they lingered. "I do it, just in different ways from Susan."

"She thinks you're much smarter than she is."

"That's the myth, I suppose. Who knows how smart Susan is? She's never given herself much of a push. Are you going to give her a push, Sammy?"

"Me? I'm not out to push her anywhere."

"What are you out to do?"

He thought about that for a minute, then said quietly, "Make her happy. Make me happy."

It was sweet how he'd put it, she thought. If he could do what he wanted, she'd be happy for them both. "What about the drinking?" she asked, anxious for his opinion. "Do you think it's a serious problem?"

"I wouldn't call Susan a full-fledged alcoholic, if that's what you mean. Drinking isn't the be-all and end-all of her life. When she's busy, she doesn't think of doing it. It's when she's bored or angry or alone that she hits the bottle."

"You can't be with her all the time."

"No. But maybe I can give her a purpose."

"Like . . ."

He grinned. "Making me happy. What would you say if I tried to domesticate her?"

Slipping her hand under the straps of her briefcase, Savannah stood. "I'd say you were nuts. I thought you weren't out to reform her."

"I'm not. But if she chooses to stay home planning dinner—"

"—and then you don't make it home because you're sent on an emergency assignment, what's she going to do?" She fingered her briefcase before looking back at Sam. "I love you, Sammy. You know that. And I love Susan, and there's nothing I'd like better than to see the two of you together, but if you're serious about it, that's something to be considered. I could cope with the absences because I have my work, but unless Susan has something, what's she going to do?"

"I don't know," he said. "I'll have to find something."

"She'll have to find herself something. There are things she can do, but the effort has to come from her if it's going to work. She hasn't reached the point of wanting to try."

"Then I'll have to get her to that point."

"How're you going to do that?"

"I don't know."

"I've tried. It hasn't worked."

"So *I'll* try."

"And if it still doesn't work?"

"I *don't know*. Why are you so down when it comes to Susan?"

"I'm not down," Savannah said quickly, then meekly asked, "Am I down?"

"You don't think she can pull herself out of the hole she's in."

"Of course, I do—"

"You don't. Honestly."

"Honestly, I do. But you can't do it for her. She has to do it herself."

"And you're not willing to help?" He rose from the table

and faced her. "I sensed it about her drinking. You know what's happening but you won't do a thing to stop it."

"What are you talking about? I've talked with her time and again about the drinking. I've asked her to stop, begged her to stop. I've spied on the condition of her bar. But short of calling her an alcoholic and dragging her off to AA, what can I do? I can't hold her hand twenty-four hours a day."

"Maybe you don't want her to succeed."

"Excuse me?"

"You heard. You admitted that the two of you are in competition with each other. Maybe you're afraid that if she cleans up her act and makes something of her life, she'll come out ahead."

"I don't believe I'm hearing this," Savannah murmured.

"Is it the truth?"

"No, it is *not* the truth. The competition doesn't go that far. It's never reached the point of having a winner or a loser."

"Susan thinks she's the loser."

"Well, there are times when I think *I'm* the loser, so we're even." Bowing her head, she put two fingers to the ache between her eyes. "I don't want this. Not today. It's been a long week." She shifted her fingers to her lips, then slowly looked up. "I do love Susan, Sam, but I'm not her keeper. Say the word and I'll do what I can to help, but I won't run her life for her. I'm too busy running my own."

Sam didn't want to argue any more than she did. "The weekend's here," he said quietly. "You'll get a rest."

With a smile and a skyward glance, she said, "Lord, I hope so."

*   *   *

By ten o'clock, Savannah was sound asleep in Jared's bed. After her talk with Sam, she had met with several of the other lawyers in the division about incidental cases, cleaned things up in her office, gone to aerobics class for the first time that week, then stopped home for an overnight bag.

Jared had taken one look at her face and put her to bed. Curled against him, she had fallen asleep almost instantly. When she woke up, it was to the sound of his voice sifting like warm sand from the speaker on the wall.

"It's two o'clock, and you're taking in a little country in the city at 95.3 FM, WCIC Providence. That was the Bellamy Brothers with 'Santa Fe,' and this is Crowell and Cash. I'm Jared Snow, and I'll be kickin' around with the coolest of cool country sounds until six. In the heart of the night, stay with me. . . ."

Savannah yawned, then grinned and stretched. She liked waking up to Jared's voice. Better still, she liked waking up to his body, but that was a special treat, reserved for special times.

Feeling incredibly revived for the middle of the night, she pushed the blanket back and slipped from the bed. Pausing only to freshen up in the bathroom, she was soon on her way downstairs. A week before, she would have been appalled to think of running around WCIC Providence in Jared's flannel shirt. But she had become familiar enough with the house in the heart of the night to know that Jared would be alone in the sound room.

The headphones were around his neck, and his eyes were downcast, directed at a stack of papers when she entered the office. He didn't see her, so for a minute she simply stood and looked at him through the glass wall.

He was a beautiful man, she thought, though his beauty had come to be tied up in her mind with thoughtfulness, gentleness, and intelligence. She didn't know much about the details of his past. They had spent so little time together that the depth of her feelings shocked her. But she couldn't ignore them. When she thought of him, her heart swelled. So did the nerve endings deep in her belly. And when she looked at him as she was doing now, she felt excitement mixed with the same inner peace she had associated with him from the start.

Glancing up then, he caught sight of her and broke into a brilliant smile. It was all the invitation she needed. Crossing the office, she entered the sound room and closed the door firmly behind her. Then she went to where he sat and slid an arm around his neck.

Hugging her to his side, he turned his face up for a kiss. She gave him one, and at his silent coaxing, a second. He would have liked to go on like that for a while, except that he knew he'd want more pretty quickly. So he left it at two kisses and asked, "How'd you sleep?"

"Just fine."

"I thought you'd be out of it for the night. You were exhausted."

"The week finally got to me, I guess."

"You could have slept longer."

She shook her head. "I woke up to your voice and an empty bed. It was lonely up there. I thought maybe you were lonely down here."

He slid a hand over her back. "I was."

Threading her fingers into his hair, she asked, "How are you fixed for coffee?"

"I made a fresh pot a little while ago. Want some?"

"Mmm, yes." Leaving him, she went back through the office to the kitchen, helped herself to a cup, then returned.

Jared was in the process of fading one song into another. Hesitant to disturb him, she waited at the door until the new song was underway. Then he motioned her to him and drew her onto his lap.

For a minute he just looked her over. He loved the way his shirt ended at midthigh to expose plenty of skin. He loved the way her pony tail bounced when she moved. He loved the traces of sleep in her eyes and the soft pink color on her cheeks. "You look great." Unable to resist, he slid his hand down her leg. "Warm enough?"

"Uh-huh." She took a sip of her coffee. "Jared?"

"Mmm?"

"Why country?" When he tossed a questioning glance back toward the cart rack, she said, "You could have bought any station you wanted. Why this one?"

"It wasn't country when I bought it. It was jazz. And not doing well. My other stations are country. Rhode Island needed a good country station, so here we are."

"When you bought the other stations, were they country?"

"No. One was oldies, the other two, top forty."

"Why did you change them?"

"For the same reason I changed this one. They weren't doing well as they were, and where they were, there was need for a good country sound. Besides, I like country."

That was what she wanted to know. "How come?"

He gave a one-shouldered shrug. "It's good music. Smooth. Relaxing. Fun sometimes, serious other times. The quality of the artists' voices isn't drowned out by lots of other garbage. You don't have to fight to hear the words."

"Do you listen to the words?"

He nodded.

"So do I," she admitted softly. She was a hopeless romantic when it came to music. "The lyrics can be very poignant." She was thinking that they dealt first and foremost with love, but rather than say it, she took another sip of her coffee. "Susan listens. So does Megan."

"How's she doing?"

"Megan? She sounds better on the phone. I'm going over to see her tomorrow." Her voice thinned. "She has to start helping us with this investigation. We have so little else."

"Nothing from the FBI?"

"Nothing. I've never seen a crime so clean. It's incredible. There hasn't been one slip up to give us clues. I can understand that Megan doesn't want to think about the men who hurt her, but if she doesn't think about them, they'll never be caught."

"Do you think she's repressing things without knowing it?"

"I thought that at first. I'm not sure I do anymore. She doesn't seem confused when I ask, just negative. She has to get past that. There must be something she can tell us about those men. Or where she was held. Or what they gave her to eat. If she had McDonald's food every day, we'd know she was held near a McDonald's. Mostly what we need, though, are physical descriptions. If she'd agree to work with a police artist, we might come up with a picture to circulate."

"Won't the men be long gone by now?"

"Probably. But we can track them down. God, I hope Megan gives us something soon."

As she talked, Jared had felt the slow rise of tension in

her body. It was always this way with Savannah and work. She was good at what she did, but she paid a price. It was up to him to counter that price.

Leaving an arm around her, he put on the headset and faded out the last song as he spoke soft and low into the mike. "This is cool country, 95.3 FM, WCIC Providence, and that was Highway 101. It's two twenty-five on the CIC clock, with the temperature holding at a brisk forty-four degrees. Lock your door and settle in. I've got a string of six on the way, kickin' off with the Trio—Dolly Parton, Linda Ronstadt, and Emmylou Harris. This is Jared Snow in the heart of the night, I'll be back. . . ." The music rose as he turned off the mike. Seconds later, he dropped the headphones to the console and looped both arms around Savannah's waist.

"When will the trial be done?" he asked.

"Late next week, I'd guess."

"What will you do then?"

She breathed out a dry laugh. "Catch up on all the work I haven't done since I've been on trial."

He gave her a skeptical look, when she nodded in confirmation of what she'd just said, he asked, "Won't you take a few days off?"

"I don't have the time."

"Make the time." He paused. "DeBarr isn't that much of a slavedriver, is he?"

"No. It's me. I like to be up on things."

"You'll crack at the rate you're pushing yourself."

She shook her head. "It hasn't been so bad this time. You've helped."

He couldn't have asked for a better answer. Still, it wasn't enough. "Let me help more. I'll plan something for next weekend. You'll at least take the weekend off, won't you?"

"Mmm, but I may not be free. I mentioned to Susan that we should get Megan away. My family has a place on Marco Island. The three of us used to go there for vacations right up through the time we graduated from college. Susan and I thought that if we could get Megan there, it would be a good escape for her. She needs something. If my trial ends next week, we may do it next weekend."

Jared felt disappointed in an old, familiar way, and on the tails of disappointment came annoyance. Then he stopped, thought about Savannah, thought about the situation. And he realized that he wasn't being thrown over for a bunch of shallow politicians but for something deeper and more personal, and in that sense, important. He agreed with Savannah that if the trip helped Megan, it would be worth the time.

With the flick of his fingers, he freed her hair from its pony tail and wove a hand through the long tresses. "So when will I have you for the weekend?" he asked.

She felt a flow of warmth inside. "The one after that?"

"I'll be putting the boat in the water then."

"Can I help?"

He gave a slow nod.

"Tell me about it—the boat. How many sails does it have?"

"Three. And an engine. And a modern galley. And a big bed."

"How big?"

"Big enough."

They were grinning at one another. Savannah wasn't aware that the Trio's song had given way to a different sound until Jared cocked his head. She listened. The song was "Slow Dancing."

"Want to?" he asked softly.

With a nod, she set down her coffee cup and slid from his lap, then went easily into his arms as he stood. She had never thought of dancing with Jared, but it was like nothing she had ever experienced. He held one of her hands down by his thigh and slanted his other arm across her back to mold her close. The beat of the music was a quiet pulse. He went with it, but slowly, slowly and with just enough movement to heighten the flex of his body against hers.

Savannah felt surrounded—by his arms, his legs, his heat. His scent was male, warm and heady. Moving her face against his neck, she felt the pulse of his life's blood. It was in sync with the slow, steady sway of his body, which was in sync with the beat of the music—all of which was in sync with her needs and wants. Her world, at that moment, was in perfect harmony.

Feeling utterly content, she tiptoed up and slid her arm more tightly around his neck. It was a beautiful moment, one she wished she could freeze and call back at will. She felt no loneliness, no fear, simply love.

Bidden by an unconscious directive, she dropped her head back and looked up at him. His eyes met hers, the one with a slight cast, both with smoky gray flecks. Lowering his head, he kissed her once, twice, three times.

Their bodies barely moved by the time the third kiss was done, and neither of them noticed when "Slow Dancing" segued to "Sure Feels Good." That was taken for granted.

Teasing her open mouth with the tip of his tongue, Jared worked the buttons of her shirt open one by one.

Savannah held tightly to his shoulders and whispered, "You're working."

"I know. It's okay. We won't do anything."

But he touched her, cupped her bare breasts in his hands, kneaded them, taunted her nipples with short, dabbing strokes. She felt her flesh swell into his. Her hands clenched tightly at the nape of his neck; she began to breathe less evenly.

"Jared."

"It's okay, babe. I'm just touching. Feel good?"

Her head fell back, her eyes closed. "Mmmm."

Backing up a step, he lowered himself to his chair and drew her between his open legs. Before she had sufficient time to prepare for it, he brought her breast to his mouth. She cried out at the wetness, cried out again when he began to suck. While he pushed up her flesh with his hand, his whole mouth manipulated her nipple. The tugging sensation went straight to her womb, making her lean in closer. She wondered whether he had slipped something into her coffee, when he released that first breast, covered its wet center with his thumb, and promptly turned his attention to its mate.

She sank her hands into his hair. The pleasure he gave her was so intense it hurt, but rather than pulling back, she held him closer. His name was an aching sound when she called him this time.

"I love doing this," he whispered against her hot flesh.

"But we can't. Not here. Not now."

One part of Jared knew she was right. The other part knew that he had three more songs before he was needed again, and he couldn't think of a finer way to spend that time. "Just a little more."

She started to protest, but he released the last of the shirt's buttons and pushed the flannel fabric aside. He ran his hands up and down her sides, coaxing her panties lower with each stroke.

Suddenly Savannah didn't want him to stop. Heart pounding, she looped her hands loosely over his shoulders and arched her back. He took her hint, capturing her breast again with his mouth at the same time that his hands found a home.

They were magic. Within minutes, they had her begging for release, but she didn't want the release to be one-sided. Sinking to her knees, she set rushing fingers to work on his belt. Unfastening it, she looked up at him while she unsnapped his jeans, then eased his zipper down.

"This is crazy," she told him.

He shifted to help her work around his erection. "No."

"It is. You're supposed to be working." The zipper was down. Tugging at his briefs, she dropped her eyes to the hard flesh she'd released. He was beautiful there, too, she thought. Tall and straight, strong, velvety. Her thumbs worshipped him for an instant, then, unable to resist, she leaned forward and took him into her mouth.

He had her up so fast that she wasn't quite sure what had happened until she felt herself on his lap being firmly impaled.

She gasped at the fire inside her, then caught her breath and forced herself to slow down. Jared seemed to do the same, with the end result a sweet, simmering rocking against one another, an extension of the dancing they'd done, with their bodies more intimately joined.

The rise was slow and steady, the reward their explosive climaxes. When it was over and they sat, panting, with damp foreheads together, Savannah gave a broken laugh.

"I saw a cartoon in *Cosmopolitan* once. A bare-breasted female DJ sat at her mike, telling her listening audience that she hoped they enjoyed the album she'd just played as much as she had. In the background a man was pulling on his pants." She took in another rough breath and said in delight, "You should be *ashamed* of yourself, Jared Snow. What would the FCC say if they knew what you've just done?"

"No doubt they'd take my license away, and you know what?" he took her face in his hands and turned it to his. "I wouldn't care." He kissed her. "That was worth far more than a broadcasting license any day."

For a minute, Savannah looked at him, slightly overwhelmed by the sensations within her. Then she said in a very soft, heart-bound voice, "There are times like these when I feel so happy I feel guilty."

That wasn't quite what Jared wanted to hear. "Why guilty?"

"Because I have so much. I look at Susan. I look at Megan. I have so much."

"You deserve what you have."

"Maybe I deserve my career. I've worked hard for that. But I don't deserve you. There are times when I'm not quite sure what to do with you."

Jared dropped his gaze to the point below their bellies where they were still joined and said in a husky drawl, "Looks to me like you're doin' fine."

A fleeting smile crossed her face before she grew serious

again. "I don't think I expected to ever meet someone like you."

Jared basked in her adoration. "What am I like?"

Having no idea how to put into words what she was feeling, she simply said, "You're . . . here. You're calm, constant. You're a stabilizing force."

He wanted to believe her, but he wasn't sure he could. "You happen to be one of the most stable women I know."

She eyed him skeptically. "Most stable women don't get the shakes when they're all alone late at night."

"How do you know? You don't see them then. For all you know, they do worse. Besides, getting the shakes has nothing to do with personal stability. It has to do with high-powered people and tension that has no other outlet. Some people let it out as it happens. Some hold it in. That's you. You're totally together at work. The tension comes out in the shakes at night."

Very gently, he started to ease her off him. When she tightened her thighs around his, he said, "My songs run out soon. I'd better be ready." Setting her on her feet, he bent over to retrieve her panties and hand them to her. Standing, he adjusted his pants. Then he drew a second chair close and urged her into it. When they were sitting knee-to-knee with their hands linked, he said, "I don't want you feeling guilty about us."

She didn't want to feel guilty. Lord, she didn't. Locked into his gaze, she wanted to be guilt-free and happy forever after.

Still, she thought of Susan and most urgently of what Sam had said that day, and as inappropriate as the timing seemed, she heard herself say, "When we were growing up, Susan was the one who was big with the guys. She needed that, because I did better in school, and she needed to shine at something. She married Dirk right around the time I was graduating from law school. I've always wondered whether she did it to put herself one step past me. I had my career, she had marriage. Then her marriage fizzled, while my career has continued to grow." She paused, looked down at her hands, seeming so pale against Jared's. "I want Susan to be happy. I really do."

"No one's ever doubted that."

She looked up. "Sam has. He told me so today. He wonders whether I'm deliberately not pushing Susan forward because I don't want the competition. I've never looked at it that way. I've never been conscious of doing anything like that, but maybe it's been a subconscious thing. I just don't know. I've only pushed her as far as I thought wise. Maybe my judgment's been clouded. Sometimes I blame things on work; I tell myself I'm so busy that I can't be constantly looking over her shoulder—but maybe that's an excuse to mask something else."

"You can't read so deeply into everything, Savannah."

"I have to. I want to do what's right."

"You've been doing what's right—"

"But I'm not helping Susan."

"She's an adult. You've said it yourself, and I agree. You can only do so much. She has to take command of her own life."

"But I feel so *bad* for her."

Jared was working hard to understand. He rarely saw his own brother and was just as happy that way, but Savannah clearly was of a different mold in that regard. "Is she truly miserable?"

"You saw the bottle of scotch under her arm. She could

be headed for real trouble if something doesn't give. Thank goodness, Sammy seems to care. He could make the difference. I hope so. I haven't been able to."

Jared touched her cheek. "You can't do everything, Savannah. If you're a big part of Susan's problem, it would make sense that your efforts don't work." He grabbed at a lock of her hair. "When am I going to meet her?"

"Soon."

"When?"

"I don't know."

"You're not still worried that I'll fall for her over you, are you?"

With a sheepish smile, Savannah shook her head. "I don't think so."

"So? I want to meet her, and Sam, and Megan."

"I thought you wanted to keep a low profile."

"I'm not exactly talking about going up the State House steps and shouting my way onto the front page of the *Journal*."

"Word spreads. Between Susan and Megan, the grand society of greater Providence could suddenly know that Jared Snow is a gorgeous hunk of man."

He gave a diffident smile. "Your words. They're biased." When Savannah shook her head, he said simply, "Maybe I'm ready to take the risk."

But Savannah wasn't sure she was. "I think," she said in a smaller voice than before, "that I'd like to keep you to myself a little longer."

"You can have me to yourself. No one can take away what we have here or upstairs or at your place. But I want to know what your life's about. I want to know who else is in it." His voice went deeper. "I want to know what I'm facing."

He said the last with an intensity in his eyes and in his voice that she hadn't expected. Its implications took her breath away.

Chapter 16

THE FOLLOWING WEDNESDAY MORNING, Sam returned to his house after working around the clock. He found Susan in the living room with a man he didn't know. Smiling her pleasure when he appeared at the door, she quickly went to him and slid an arm around his waist.

"I was wondering when you'd be back."

"What's happening?" he asked casually, but there was a wariness in his eyes, which never once left the stranger.

"Come." She took his hand and led him into the room. "This is Dennis Becker. He's been helping me. We've come up with some ideas that you'll love. Dennis, Sam Craig."

The two men shook hands, Sam far more cautiously than Dennis, who burst out with, "It's a pleasure to meet you, Sam. I've worked with Susan, and her father before her, but this job is something quite different. You have a delightful place here. The interaction of light and lines is fantastic. By the time we're done, you'll have something to be proud of."

Slowly Sam turned to Susan. Quietly he asked, "What's this about?"

Susan slid her elbow through his and said proudly, "I'm decorating your home. You told me that you don't have the time or the talent. Well, I have both, and what I don't have, Dennis does. We've put together a whole plan with diagrams, pictures, estimates. Come see."

She tugged on his arm, but he held back. He had spent the last twenty-four hours doing surveillance on two of Rhode Island's heaviest drug dealers. One of their customers had OD'd practically before his eyes. He had blown his cover trying to get the man to the hospital before he died.

The last thing he wanted to see at that moment was a decorating plan.

Brushing his fingers over his upper lip, he bought himself a minute to search for moderately tactful words. "Uh, Susan, do you think we could make it another time?"

"But Dennis is here now."

"Another time?" he repeated.

"But we have all the plans here. All you have to do is point to what you like, and we'll go ahead with the order. It takes a minimum of three months for delivery on most of these things."

Aware of a growing annoyance, Sam worked to keep his voice low and even. "I don't think this is the right time."

But Susan was enthusiastic enough not to heed his warning. "This is the *perfect* time. Dennis is in from New York. We've both put a lot of thought into this, and we're ready to act."

"You should have clued me in."

"And ruined the surprise?" Leaving his side, she bent over the sofa and raised a multicolored drawing of his living room furnished to the hilt. "Is this gorgeous or what?"

Sam was quickly realizing that bad timing wasn't the only problem. If Dennis had come from New York with elaborate drawings, no less, there were already expenses to be paid. Though Susan hadn't yet asked for a cent, Sam wondered whether, left to her own devices, she'd spend him broke.

Suddenly the most basic differences between them reared up and hit him between the eyes. Unable to face that after what he had just been through, he said, "I'm exhausted. I'm going to bed." Turning on his heel, he left the room.

Slightly bewildered, Susan looked from where he'd vanished to Dennis and back. "Give us a minute," she said and ran in pursuit of Sam. She caught him on the stairs and followed him up, hissing, "Sam, *Dennis* is here."

Without breaking his stride, Sam went right on into the bedroom. He tossed his jacket to the bed. "Fine. You visit with him."

"He's not here to visit. He's here to do business."

"Whose business?" He whipped his sweatshirt over his head and came out looking a little more rumpled, but no softer. "Not mine. I didn't invite him, and I sure didn't hire him."

"No one hired him. He's doing me a favor by being here. He doesn't get any money until you agree to the plans."

Sam tossed the sweatshirt on top of the jacket. "And how much does he get then? A flat ten thousand for his services?"

"Five thousand, plus expenses and a commission on the furniture. As decorators go, he's not bad."

Sam sputtered out a laugh. "'As decorators go, he's not bad.'" Susan, I don't have an extra five thou for Dennis, and even aside from Dennis, the estimate you've got is probably three times my budget." He kicked off his sneakers. "You forget who you're dealing with." Sitting on the bed, he went to work on his socks.

"If money is the problem, I'll help you out."

"No way."

"Why not?"

His eyes bored into her. "Because I don't do things like that. If I buy a condominium, it's because I can afford it. If I decorate it, I'll do it in a way I can hack. I'm not a charity case. Until you came along, I thought I was doing real well financially. I don't want you telling me that what I earn isn't enough. I pay my own way, Susan. I'm no gigolo."

She was taken aback, but only for a minute. "I thought you wanted a nice place."

"I already have a nice place," he said, tossing one sock aside, "and I resent that little man downstairs—or you— suggesting that it isn't adequate as it is. I like this place. I never said I was in a rush to decorate it, and I never gave you permission to do it. I never gave you permission to do anything." Tossing the second sock aside, he stood.

"I thought we were beyond that."

"Beyond what? Talking? Discussing things? Asking the other's opinion?" He was working himself into a royal snit, letting off the frustration that had built through a tense and sleepless night. "What kind of relationship is this, anyway?"

"That's a good question," Susan said. Everything inside her suddenly hurt. Her pain came out as indignance. "Apparently I overestimated it."

"Damn right, you did. We've know each other for little more than two weeks, yet you assume I'll lie down and let you walk all over me. Let me tell you something, sweet-heart," he jabbed his bare chest with his thumb, "no woman does that to me. I'm the man in my house. I make the decisions."

Susan was stunned. "I don't believe I'm hearing this," she murmured, then raised her voice. "You're a fraud, Sam

Craig! You have long hair and sing a liberal song, but it's a front. You're a cop, as traditional as they come. Your woman is good for two things, food and sex. You're little better than a Neanderthal."

Hands on his hips, he glared at her. Wearing nothing but a low-slung pair of jeans and a disgruntled expression, he did look primitive. "Maybe, but that's the way it is. I've lived alone for a long time and I don't like people waltzing in and taking over. This is my house. Got that? And another thing—I don't like coming home from work grubby and tired to find you dripping in silk, playing footsies with a guy I don't know."

Susan mirrored his angry stance, planting her own hands on her hips. "Maybe you don't like coming home from work to find me, period."

Running his fingers through his hair, he looked away. "I'm tired. I don't need this shit."

Having long since forgotten the importance of keeping her voice down, Susan cried, "There wouldn't have been *any* shit if you'd been a little cooperative. But you couldn't do that, could you? You take delight in making a fool of me. You always have." She drew herself up straight. "Well, I don't need *that* shit. I don't know why I bother with you at all."

"Because," he said in a sarcastic drawl, "you like where I take you in bed. Face it, sweetheart. That's the crux of the appeal."

"You're crude."

He barked out a laugh. "Crude? Me? Look who's talking."

"I'm not crude."

"Want some quotes?"

She didn't, and she was too upset to want much of anything but a speedy escape. "I thought we could find a comfortable meeting ground, but that's impossible. You're a lost cause, Sam. You have no class. None at all." With her hair flying, she whirled around and left while she still had the last word.

On Wednesday afternoon, Savannah delivered her final argument to the jury. The judge's charge was brief and to the point, and by three o'clock the jury was sent off to deliberate. Savannah retired to her office to await their return, but by nine o'clock, they were sequestered for the night. With no hope of a verdict then, Savannah stopped home for the mail before going to Jared's. After sleeping the night away in his bed, she awoke feeling on edge.

"Is it always this way?" he asked, having been replaced by the morning DJ in time to wake Savannah. Now he stood by the side of the bed, while she sat at the edge, leaning against him as he stroked her back.

It was a divine way to wake up, Savannah knew. She only wished she could enjoy it fully. But she was tense. "When a trial goes longer than three or four days, there's more at stake. It's hard when the jury's out."

"Any idea how long they'll be?"

She shook her head against his stomach, then wrapped her arms around his waist. "Could be two hours or two days. I don't want to begin to think about any longer than that."

Fortunately, she didn't have to. The jury came back shortly after noon that day with guilty verdicts on nineteen of the twenty-six counts. It was a definite victory for Savannah and the state, and in its wake came multiple interviews with the media and a meeting with Paul. As she'd gotten in the habit of doing, Savannah took her assistants, in this case Arnie and Katherine, out for a celebratory dinner to thank them for their help on the case, but the celebration wasn't a lingering one. Savannah wanted to go home. She wasn't feeling well.

Jared called her at her townhouse at nine. He already knew the verdict; she'd left him a message earlier, and he'd followed the news reports, but he hadn't spoken with her since morning. "You must be thrilled."

"Uh-huh."

It was a minute before he said anything. Then, "You don't sound it."

"I'm so tired."

"Are you shaking?"

"I'm too tired for that. I'm just lying down."

That didn't sound like the Savannah he'd come to know. If she wasn't asleep, she was awake and doing something. He felt a glimmer of concern. "Are you feeling okay?"

"Sure."

"Are you sure?"

"I'm sure."

"Can I come over?"

"Uh-uh. I'd be lousy company."

"I'm not asking for a barrel of laughs. I'll read while you rest."

"No. I think I'd rather be alone. Just to come down a little. Okay?"

"Sure," he said, but the minute he hung up the phone, he knew that it wasn't. Savannah didn't sound right to him. If something was bothering her, he wanted to know what it was. He wanted to know what "coming down a little" meant.

She was used to being alone. He wanted her to get unused to it.

Without risking another refusal, he drove to her townhouse, then had to wait too long for comfort after he'd rung the bell. Finally, she answered the door.

Her face was bare of makeup, her hair tumbling past her shoulders. Her long robe was wrapped tightly round her and sashed at the waist, and her bare feet looked fragile. In fact, she looked fragile all over, he realized. Yes, she looked tired. More, she looked washed out.

"I was worried," he said to explain his presence, and stepped inside before she could protest.

Not that she would have done that. Deep down inside, she was glad he'd come. She'd told him not to, still he was there, which pointed to things like concern and affection. It also pointed to strength. He had countermanded her request. Few men she had known recently would have done that.

More than anything, though, she was glad not to be alone.

Quietly, she returned to the living room sofa and lay down, curling her legs beneath the robe. He hunkered down before her.

"Aren't you feeling well?"

"I'm okay."

He touched her cheek. It was cool, as was her hand, which he enveloped in his. "Congratulations on the case. You should be proud of yourself. I'm proud of you."

She gave a weak smile and whispered, "Thanks."

"You came across beautifully on the news. Beautiful, and beautifully."

Again she gave him a weak smile, but it didn't last long. In the instant before she closed her eyes, he could have sworn he saw a well of sadness in them. Lightly, he stroked her hair.

"Is there a letdown at the end of a trial?"

"Sometimes," she said without opening her eyes. "You've been living and breathing the trial for days, suddenly it's gone."

"Is that what you're feeling now?"

It was a minute before she answered. "No. I'm relieved it's over. It's been a tough one. I've had a lot else on my mind."

"Like Megan?"

"And you."

"Mmmm. I like the way that sounds. Now if I could get a little smile to go with it." She gave him a little smile. "That was puny. Try again."

Her smile was fuller this time, if a bit helpless. She opened her eyes to look up at him. He was so sweet. So gentle. Lord, she loved him.

Her smile faded. Unconsciously, she drew her legs up a little tighter.

Jared was attuned to her every move. "You're not feeling well. Is it your stomach?"

"I'm okay."

He persisted. "Is it your stomach?"

"I have cramps."

"From something you ate?"

She shook her head and closed her eyes again. "I got my period this afternoon."

Of all the possibilities, that had been furthest from his mind. But now he relived the conversation they'd had right after they'd made love for the very first time. She had been more than prepared to have his baby. They had argued about the merits of single parenthood. He had told her he wanted to be involved.

But there wasn't any baby. He felt a sudden and unexpected twinge of sadness. "Ahhhh, Savannah," he whispered. "I'm sorry."

"It's okay. Just cramps."

"It's more than that."

She looked up at him, startled to see his expression. "It's probably just as well," she said, trying to sound nonchalant but failing miserably. "I have a life, you have a life, we barely know each other."

"I love you."

Her eyes widened a fraction. Seconds later, she gave a quick shake of her head. "You don't know me well enough."

It didn't make sense any more to Jared than it did to her, still he felt it, and it was worth repeating. "I do love you."

Her heart was thudding. "But I'm wrong for you. I have a career, like Elise. I can't give you what you want."

"You would have given me a baby. That's part of what I want."

She thought about the baby that wasn't, closed her eyes, and murmured, "I don't know why I've thought so much about it lately. I'm not that old. I could have babies for the next ten years." While that was true, it didn't make her feel better. She burrowed more deeply into the cushions.

Jared lightly stroked the underside of her jaw. "Can I get you anything? Aspirin? Tea?"

She shook her head.

"It could happen next month, or the next," he told her softly. "I don't have any intention of using birth control."

"Maybe we should. Maybe there's a message in this. Maybe I'm not meant to be pregnant right now."

"There's no message. But it's only been two weeks. Some couples work at it for years." When she didn't respond to that, he put a hand on her stomach and moved it in a light, circular motion. "Can I hold you?"

"You are."

"Hold you in my arms."

She shrugged.

He wasn't quite sure what it meant, but it hadn't been a no, and he needed to hold her. Slipping his arms under her as he came to his feet, he turned, sat down, and settled her so that she was resting against him with her knees comfortably bent.

"Okay?"

She nodded, but she felt weepy. It wasn't just her period. It was all the different things that had happened in the past two weeks—Megan, Jared, the trial, turning thirty-one. She usually looked at the bright side of things, but she was too drained to do that just then.

"Why don't you skip work tomorrow?" Jared asked. His mouth was pressed against her forehead, his voice a light rasp. "The rest would do you good."

"I have too much catching up to do."

"But you're not feeling well."

"I'll be better by morning."

He wanted to argue, but who was he to know about the intimate workings of her body? "Are you definitely going to Marco Island on Saturday?"

"If Susan can make the arrangements. I'll rest there." She whispered a snort. "Good timing. You and I couldn't do much with me this way."

"Shows how much you know," Jared drawled, drawing her eyes to his. His voice was low, just sandy enough to underscore his thoughts. "I could pleasure you. There are ways other than intercourse. And you could pleasure me. You've already shown me how. But that's not the only reason I want to be with you. There's more to us than sex."

"I know."

"Do you?"

She nodded.

"I'd want you with me this weekend, whether we make love or not."

She felt worse than ever. "I have to go with Susan and Megan."

"I understand," he said, trying hard to.

"If I could have chosen any other time, I would have, but Megan needs it now, and Susan does, too. She and Sam had a fight. I think she'd like to be gone right now."

"It's okay," he said, but he was jealous as hell. "There's lots I can do."

"With my trial just over, it's a perfect weekend for me to go. We'll leave late tomorrow and be back late Sunday."

"I'm used to being alone."

"Don't *say* that," she wailed. "I feel so bad."

So did he. He didn't want Savannah going to Florida with Susan and Megan. He wanted her to himself. Holding her close, he spoke against the top of her head. "I'm not being fair. I know it's important for you to go. I'll miss you. That's all."

"I'll miss you, too," she whispered and buried her face against his chest. Somewhere in the back of her mind, a bell rang, but she was too wrapped up in Jared's warmth to pay it heed until he mentioned it himself.

"Are you expecting someone?"

Puzzled, she looked up and shook her head.

"That was your doorbell." Sure enough, it rang again. He glanced at his watch. "It's ten-fifteen. Any idea who it could be?"

Again she shook her head, whereupon the bell rang a third time, then a fourth, fifth, and sixth in rapid succession.

"Someone's angry," he decided. Shifting Savannah, he slipped out from under her. When she started to rise, he pressed her back down. "Let me."

For a woman of wealth, Savannah was not pampered. She didn't usually sit still long enough for that. But she sat still now. Given the tender state of her insides, she appreciated not having to move.

Jared recognized Susan the instant he opened the door. Though he had only glimpsed her once before, she wasn't the kind of woman a man forgot. For one thing, her thick, auburn hair was too striking. For another, she was statuesque and in that, unusual. And while she wasn't holding a bottle of scotch this time, he could tell she had done so not long before. The scent was faint, but distinct.

The insistent ringing of the doorbell had aptly conveyed her annoyance. It was evident in her expression when he opened the door, although it almost comically vanished as soon as she saw him.

"Oh my." She glanced at the townhouse to her left, then her right. "Am I at the wrong one?"

"No," Jared said and stood back. "Come on in."

But Susan didn't move. She stared at him with dawning awareness, her frown returned. "You're Savannah's delivery boy." She leaned forward and called, "Savannah?" but her eyes never left Jared.

On the living room sofa, Savannah was immobilized by a momentary panic. She had known that sooner or later Susan would have had to find out about Jared, but she had counted on later. She didn't want that confrontation now. Under the best of circumstances, she couldn't hold a candle to Susan in appearance, and this was far from the best of circumstances.

But there was no avoiding the meeting. She simply had to decide how best to handle it. Her first impulse was to join Jared at the door, but that required too much effort. Instead she drew herself higher on the sofa and called, "Come on in, Suse."

Tearing her gaze from Jared, Susan swept past him. She was frowning when she stopped before Savannah. "What's wrong?"

"Exhaustion. Cramps."

"Cramps." Susan sighed in dismay. "Cramps. You've done it again, haven't you? Here we are, all set to go off for a weekend of sun and surf, and you've got your period. This happens every time."

Savannah was thinking that it shouldn't have happened this time, though not for the reason Susan thought. She glanced at Jared, who had followed Susan into the room and was standing to the side with a hand in his pocket. "Unfortunately, I had no say in the matter," she told Susan. "Is everything okay? I didn't expect you."

"Obviously," Susan drawled. Her gaze bounced from her sister to Jared and back. "What's he delivering this time?"

"A little consolation," Savannah said on impulse.

"Consolation? Since when do you need consolation? You won your case. That must please you. Another victory for the legal eagle."

Jared wasn't sure he liked her tone of voice. It gave him the same unsettling feeling his brother did. But she wasn't his brother, she was Savannah's sister. He trusted that Savannah knew best how to handle her.

"It was a victory for the people of this state," Savannah said quietly. "I'm just glad its over."

"So who's he?" Susan asked, tossing her head toward Jared.

"He's a friend. Susan, Jared."

Susan gave him a slow once-over. "Not bad for a friend." She eyed his leather jacket. "I didn't think it was from Kmart." Slipping out of her fur, she tossed it over the free end of the sofa and sank into a nearby chair. "Is he joining us?"

Savannah had fully expected Susan to make an instant play for Jared, but that wasn't happening. And Jared, while he studied Susan in a curious kind of way, looked far from enamored. That gave Savannah a bit of courage.

"The question," she amended, "is whether you're joining us. What's up?"

"You know what's up," Susan muttered, glowering. "Sam Craig is a bastard. Do you know what he had the gall to do? After I went to the trouble of taking pictures of his place, sending them by courier to Dennis Becker, spending hours on the phone with Dennis telling him what I had in mind, and arranging for him to fly in, Sam wouldn't even give us the time of day. If that's an example of the kind of gratitude your friends show, I'm not sure I want to meet this one." She tossed her head in Jared's general direction.

Savannah sent Jared an indulgent glance before facing Susan again. "You were going to decorate Sam's place?"

"Yes, I was. That's *was*. Past tense. I have no intention of doing another thing for Sam Craig. I have no intention of *seeing* him again." Abruptly, she sat forward. "He's a throwback, do you know that? He's a throwback to the Stone Age. So you think he's a modern man? Think again. Old-fashioned as they come."

"Sam?" Savannah asked in some surprise.

"Yes, Sam. He makes all the decisions. No give and take. A regular dictatorship. He's the king of the castle, period. Have you ever heard anything so backward?" Before Savannah could answer, Susan turned on Jared. "Are you the dictator type, too, or have the times actually sunk into that pea-brain of yours? Pea-brains," she repeated, turning back to Savannah. "That's what men have, and if we don't watch out, we'll be in trouble. Look what happened to the dinosaurs. Their tiny pea-brains couldn't cope with change, so they died off. If we sit back and let men rule the world, that may well be our fate." With a certain finality, she sank back in her chair.

There was total silence. Then Savannah took a breath and said, "Well. That's an interesting theory."

"There's merit to it. Men are far inferior to women. Just look at what they're doing to the world. People are dying in Central America and Northern Ireland and the Middle East, and it's not women who are doing the killing." She threw a hand up in disgust. "Why I waste my time on them is beyond me. They're not worth it. Not for a minute."

"I don't know," Savannah mused. "Seems to me there are a few things they can give us that we can't give ourselves."

Susan was surprised, not by the suggestion itself, but by Savannah's making it. Savannah wasn't a sexual being. She was an intellectual one. Traditionally, she'd have been the one to talk about the ills of the world, with Susan tossing in the sexual innuendo. It seemed that the tables were momentarily turned.

Susan's excuse was her anger at Sam. She wondered what Savannah's was. Studying her curiously, she asked, "Are you okay?"

"I'm fine."

Then it had to be Jared. More curious now, Susan turned to him. "How do you know Savannah?"

"We met through her work," he answered. He had both hands in the back pockets of his jeans and was standing, almost lazily, with his weight on one hip.

"Are you a lawyer, too?" she asked, and went on before he could answer. "You don't look like the men Savannah usually brings home."

"I don't bring scads of men home," Savannah protested.

Susan whispered, "Don't tell him that. Keep him guessing." She faced Jared. "Lawyer?"

"Nope."

"Politician?" she asked, but she doubted that. He looked just a little too comfortable in his jeans and sweater to be the type to spend hours on end in a suit.

"Nope."

There was something familiar about him, but she couldn't decide what it was. An awful thought struck. "Oh God, you're not another cop, are you?" She rose from her seat. "Because if you are," she ranted, stalking to the side of the room, "you can tell Sam Craig everything I said." She whirled around. "You guys spend your days and nights playing cops and robbers, and you go so far undercover that people rarely see the real you. But I saw the real Sam, and he's no knight in shining armor. He's a louse." She turned suddenly cautious eyes on Savannah. "Have you seen him?"

Savannah was beginning to think Susan was truly smitten. "Not since last week. When did you two fight?"

"Yesterday."

"He hasn't called since then?"

"Are you kidding?" Susan drawled sarcastically. "Macho man isn't about to stoop to apologizing. I'm sure that as far as he's concerned, he's totally in the right."

"And as far as you're concerned, *you're* totally in the right."

"Of course."

"I guess that's that, then," Savannah said.

"Exactly." Chin held high, Susan returned to her chair. She sat down, crossed her legs with an elegant flourish, and laced her fingers together on her lap. She looked as though she planned to sit for a while.

Had Susan been anyone but Savannah's sister, Jared would have picked up the silver-fox fur and held it in a blunt invitation for her to leave. He couldn't quite believe that she was sitting there so complacently, totally unaware of interrupting anything. Then he remembered some of the things Savannah had said, and it occurred to him that, quite possibly, Susan didn't realize there was anything to interrupt.

He intended to correct that.

Crossing to the sofa, he hunkered down as he had before, framed Savannah's body with his arms and said in a near whisper, "Want that aspirin now?"

She shook her head, smiled, and whispered back, "I'm okay."

"Maybe you should go to bed."

"In a little while. You have to go to work soon, don't you?"

He nodded. "I want to know you're okay before I leave."

"I'm fine," she assured him. Her smile was soft and gentle, while her eyes devoured his face. "But I'm glad you came." When he leaned forward, she kissed him.

Susan stared. She had taken Savannah at her word, that she and Jared were friends. Apparently, that was only half the story. As improbable as it seemed that Savannah, the brain, was romantically involved with as sexy a man as Jared, Susan couldn't find any other explanation for their low, intimate tones and that kiss.

And the kiss went on. What Jared had intended to be short and sweet became an expression of love, and love couldn't be rushed.

As for Savannah, she momentarily forgot Susan was there.

Susan cleared her throat. "Savannah?"

Jared was the one to hear and reluctantly end the kiss. "Yes?" he answered.

"I was calling Savannah."

Savannah blinked. "Uh-huh?"

"Am I interrupting something?"

"Uh . . ." She looked dazedly at Jared.

"Yes, you're interrupting something," he said. His voice was a bit more hoarse than it had been. "But I have to leave, anyway."

Again Susan felt a twinge of recognition that was just beyond her grasp. "Where are you going?"

"Work. I'm on from twelve to six."

"On?" she echoed, but even as she said the word, she had the awful feeling that she understood. The voice. It was the voice. Smooth, but low and gravelly. Seductive. Compelling.

"Jared? Jared what?"

"Snow," he said. "I do a radio show—"

"I know," Susan interrupted, then was quickly silent. Her eyes were wide on him as he rose to his full height. He was spectacular looking, she thought, but she had figured he would be, with a voice like his. She could easily believe every one of the rumors she'd heard about him. In person, he exuded the same confidence she had heard night after night in his voice.

She should have seen it sooner, but she'd been preoccupied with Sam. She supposed she still was, because she felt no inclination to come on to Jared, which was quite rare for her. She wondered whether Sam had ruined her for other men. If so, that was another bone of contention between them.

But Jared Snow. Jared Snow and Savannah? She couldn't believe it. "You two are seeing each other?" she asked, though it was clear that they were.

Savannah nodded. And in that instant, Susan felt a flash of anger. Savannah had her career. She didn't need a man like Jared Snow on top of it. It wasn't fair that she should have everything.

But Susan wasn't about to make a fool of herself in front of Jared. She was enough of a social animal to be gracious, regardless of what she was feeling inside.

So she smiled. "That's wonderful, but you should have told me, Savvy. How long has it been?"

"Not long," Savannah said. She could see that Susan's back was straight against the cushions of the chair and knew exactly what Susan was doing and feeling. "We met soon after the kidnapping."

Susan turned her smile on Jared. "I listen to your show all the time."

"I'm glad."

"You make it, you know. I'm not half as tempted to listen during the day. You add something." Abruptly, she sat forward and stood. "But I'm interrupting you." She had her coat in her hand in a flash and was turning it over her shoulder as she headed toward the door.

Worried, Savannah did get up then. "Wait. It's okay—"

"No, no," Susan insisted. "I was only gong to complain about Sam, and you have better things to do with your time."

"Don't go," Jared said. He was thinking along Savannah's lines, realizing that Susan would be better off with someone than alone. "I'm leaving anyway. Stay and visit with Savannah."

But Susan wanted to leave and leave quickly. She was having trouble pulling off the show she thought she'd be able to pull off with ease. She wanted to go home, maybe yell and scream for a while, most certainly have a drink, and she couldn't do any of those things at Savannah's. "Uh-uh. I have to run. Nice meeting you, Jared," she tossed over her shoulder as she opened the door. "Savvy, I'll talk with you tomorrow."

"Can I drop you home?" Jared asked.

That brought Susan to a standstill on the front step. She gave him a challenging look. "I live in Newport. You'd never make it there and back in time for your show. Besides, my car is here. But thanks. It was a nice gesture."

Savannah slipped in front of Jared. "What will you do at home?"

"What do most people do late at night?"

"Stay here. You could go home in the morning."

But Susan wanted out. "Talk with you later," she said as she went down the steps.

"What time's our plane?" Savannah called. She was half worried that Susan was upset enough to back out of the trip.

To her relief, Susan called back, "Six-thirty." Then she slid into the Jaguar, started the engine, and flew down the street.

Chapter 17

⌒

Susan had chartered a small plane to fly them to Marco Island. It was wonderfully convenient, though there were moments when Savannah wished they'd been on a crowded commercial flight. With only three of them in the cabin, well behind the pilot and copilot, the silence was awkward. It didn't bode well for a relaxing weekend.

Susan was angry. She felt betrayed, hurt, jealous—so much so that she couldn't begin to analyze all that churned inside her. She had considered canceling the weekend, but spending Saturday and Sunday with Savannah and Megan, as depressing as it promised to be, was less odious than spending a lonely weekend partying in Newport. Still, she barely looked at Savannah, and when she did, her eyes were sharp. She talked some with Megan, and gave brief answers to anything Savannah asked, but for the most part, she kept to herself. More out of defiance than thirst, she held a drink in her hand the entire time.

Megan was nearly as quiet as Susan. Sitting by the window, she spent most of the trip staring out at the clouds, wishing she were back in the cocoon of her house in Providence. She didn't want to see people, or have people see her.

She was convinced that the entire world knew about the kidnapping and would be staring. Yet she had agreed to come of her own accord. For one thing, Will needed a break. He'd been frantic with worry; she wanted to show him that she was on the mend. For another, she had fond memories of times in Florida with Savannah and Susan; she'd been helplessly lured by that spirit. And finally, she knew that she couldn't hide forever. She had something important to do when she got back. She had to be strong.

It was hard, though. She could talk with Susan or Savannah, but only briefly and on the most mundane of topics. Inevitably a phrase or word or expression would trigger something inside her, and she'd remember what she'd done and then she would be swamped with guilt. She prayed things would improve as the weekend passed.

Savannah, too, kept her hopes high. The house on Marco Island was large and open. The pool was lovely, the private beach warm, clean, and quiet. And then there was the Florida sun. Savannah was convinced that given several hours of that, their moods would mellow and their tongues would loosen. They badly needed to talk as they used to, heart to heart, all three of them.

Of course, when they arrived at the villa it was nearly ten at night, which ruled out the therapeutic effects of pool, beach, or sun. They were enthusiastically greeted by the Stockleys, the English couple who tended the house. Husband and wife kept up a running conversation through a light snack, after which both Megan and Susan pleaded exhaustion. Savannah sat for a while on the back veranda overlooking the ocean, wishing she were back with Jared, then feeling guilty for wishing it. She could hardly believe that he loved her, and she didn't quite know what to do about it.

When she thought of him, she felt alternately exhilarated and terrified. Neither emotion was appropriate for the weekend. She had her work cut out for her.

Megan was the first to awaken the next morning, but she lay in bed for an hour, half hoping that the others would be basking in the sun by the time she went down. They weren't. Savannah was on the patio, reading the morning paper, savoring the fresh strawberries and cream that Mrs. Stockley had set out. She looked up and smiled broadly when Megan joined her.

"Just in time. If you'd been much later, I might well have eaten them all." She pushed the silver serving bowl toward Megan and dipped her head toward a chair. "Sit. Eat. They're delicious."

Megan sat and helped herself to a few strawberries. "Is Susan up?"

"No." With studied ease, Savannah looked at the paper while Megan began to eat. After several minutes, she glanced up. "How was your sleep?"

"Not bad." Megan gave a small, self-conscious grin. "I missed listening to the radio. At least he's not on tonight, so there won't be anything to miss."

Jared. Savannah's heart knocked against her ribs for a minute before stilling. Megan was going to have to know about Jared, too, but this wasn't the time. "Would you like to see the paper?"

Megan shook her head. "The paper can be just as depressing as real life."

"Real life doesn't have to be depressing." When Megan rolled her eyes, Savannah asked, "How's everything with Will?"

"Just fine."

Savannah nearly left it at that. But something goaded her on. After another minute or two of silence, she said gently, "He told me things were tight financially. I suggested he hire a financial adviser. The right person could help."

Megan didn't answer at first, and when she did, her eyes were averted. "I've told him that, too, but he's resisted the idea. He's a proud man."

"Which can be a strength or a weakness."

"Mmm." She lowered her eyes then and concentrated on her strawberries. At the same time, Mrs. Stockley emerged to pour hot coffee and take orders for eggs. When Megan declined the offer, the portly woman wasn't pleased.

"You've lost weight, Megan. Beautiful as ever, but skinny. Now, I know what you're thinking," she said with a raised finger. "You're thinking that I'm jealous because I wish I was thin, and you may be right. But still, I've only got you for two days and in that time I see it as my responsibility to feed you right. Therefore, what will you have? One, two, or three eggs? Soft-boiled, poached, scrambled, or fried?"

Megan couldn't help but smile. "Some things never change," she told Savannah, then said to Mrs. Stockley, "One egg, easy over."

"Two eggs, easy over, with a croissant," Mrs. Stockley said as though repeating the order, and then turned to Savannah. "Your regular?"

Savannah grimaced. Her regular was two eggs scrambled with cheese, and a pecan roll. "I haven't had that since the last time I was here." She sucked in her stomach and looked from Mrs. Stockley to Megan. "Do I dare?"

"You dare," Mrs. Stockley said and vanished before Savannah could argue.

Moments later, Susan swept onto the patio. While Savannah was wrapped in a muted sarong and Megan wore a long toweling robe, Susan was more dramatic in a flowing white caftan. It was a perfect foil for her toenails, which were painted scarlet, and her red hair, which was a wild tumble of curls made even wilder by the warmth of the southern air.

Apprehensive, but determined not to show it, Savannah offered a casual, "Hi, Suse."

Susan looked annoyed. "So bright and chipper." Softening, she asked Megan, "How're you doing, hon?"

"Not bad." Megan gazed out toward the gulf. "It's a gorgeous day."

Ignoring Susan's snub, Savannah followed Megan's gaze. She'd always loved the view from the patio, particularly when the sun was high in a clear blue sky, as it was now. Its rays danced between the fronds of tall palm trees to sprinkle the surface of the kidney-shaped pool with fairy dust. Beyond the pool was a sandy beach, and beyond that, the waves. She remembered likening Jared's coloring to blue sky over a sandy beach. The thought warmed her.

"Should we stay by the pool," she asked, knowing that Susan preferred that to the sand, "or go to the beach?"

"The beach," Megan answered without pause. "I've always loved the sound of the waves. It put me to sleep last night. I needed it."

Susan was lounging indolently in her chair. She had her long fingernails steepled against one another and her lips pursed. "What we needed," she said in a slow, not entirely pleasant tone, "was Jared Snow to croon to us. You listen to him, don't you, Meggie?"

"All the time."

"Have you ever wondered who he really is? Or what he looks like? Or who he dates?"

Megan didn't answer, because Susan was suddenly staring at Savannah. Savannah opened her hand against the edge of the glass table. "Not now, Suse."

"Why not?"

"Because we're here, and he's there."

"And you want to keep your secret a little while longer? You must have died when I went to your house on Thursday night. Why in the hell did you let him open your door?"

"He opened the door because I wasn't feeling well, and, besides, it's not such a great secret that I'm seeing him."

"So why didn't you tell me?"

"Because there was never a good time."

"Never a good time—I don't *believe* you. We spent our birthday together, the entire day, and don't tell me that you weren't with him then, because I'm not dumb. There was the matter of that phone call, with those dreamy little smiles. And that teddy. He was the reason you bought it, and if that wasn't a good time to tell me about him, I don't know what would have been." She barely paused for a breath. "There were dozens of times that day when you could have said something, and there've been dozens of times since. I'm your sister, for God's sake! That man isn't just anybody, but you didn't see fit to clue me in that you even knew him, much less were having an affair with him. How do you think I felt ringing your bell and finding him there?"

"Angry," Savannah said. "But you have no right to be angry, Susan. Maybe hurt, or disappointed—"

"Angry!"

But Savannah wasn't yielding. "No. I should have told

you sooner, I was wrong about that, but I felt I had valid reasons for not doing it."

"Valid reasons, my foot!"

"There *were*."

Megan shouted, "Whoa!" Startled, Savannah and Susan swung their heads her way as she asked, "What's going on? Who is Savvy involved with?"

"Jared Snow!" Susan cried before Savannah could say the name herself. "She's having an affair with Jared Snow."

Megan's eyes widened. "Jared Snow?"

"Your Jared Snow. My Jared Snow. All of Rhode Island's Jared Snow, only he isn't really ours." She glared at her sister. "He's Savannah's."

Megan was having no part of Susan's fury. Her eyes remained wide and, however briefly, she escaped the pall that had hung over her since the kidnapping. "Really, Savvy?"

The brief question, asked in a hushed, but excited tone was justification in itself for Savannah's having pushed for the weekend. Often before, Megan had been a buffer between Savannah and Susan, stepping in when their arguments approached the absurd. There had been times when Savannah had resented it. She could have kissed Megan now, though. "Really," she acknowledged with a smile.

"What's he like?" Megan whispered. "Handsome?"

Still smiling, Savannah nodded.

"Tall? Well built?"

Savannah nodded at each.

"On the radio, he seems totally at peace with himself and the world. Is he in real life?"

That took more than a nod. "His life has had ups and downs, but right now he's pretty content with what he's doing."

"What about his voice? Does he always talk that way? Lord, do I love the way he talks. I swear, I could listen to that lazy drawl all night—"

"For God's sake, Megan," Susan cried. "Stop drooling. You're married."

Megan replied with a strength that was reminiscent of her old self. "Of course I'm married. I'm not saying that I want to have an affair with him, just that I'm intrigued. I love Will," she told Savannah. "I'm no threat to you."

"I know that," Savannah said gently.

"So tell me more about him. What color are his eyes?"

"Blue."

Megan sucked in a breath. "And hair?"

"Sandy. Blond, brown, maybe a little silver."

"How old is he?"

"Old enough to know better," Susan injected archly.

Savannah frowned at her. "What do you mean?"

"He should know that you're married to your job."

"I'm not—"

"How much time do you have to give a man? Seriously, Savannah, can you be both a lawyer and a wife?"

For the first time, Savannah grew defensive. "No one mentioned my being a wife."

"Then, woman. Lover. What kind of man will stand for the kinds of hours you keep?"

"You're incredible!" Savannah cried. "The other night you were accusing Sam of being old-fashioned. Look who's talking. Nowadays women *do* do both, and their men respect them for it." She prayed she'd said it with conviction, because she wasn't sure it was true.

"Which raises a whole lot of other questions," Megan put in a loud enough voice to capture both sisters' attention.

"How did you meet? When do you see him? That has to be a real problem, since he works all night."

"I'd like to hear the answer to that one, too," Susan announced, tipping her head to a haughty angle. "Normal lovers spend their nights together. You two can't do that."

Savannah took a deep, calming breath. This part of Susan's challenge she didn't mind, particularly since it channeled the discussion away from the issue of how she and Jared had met. She didn't want to go into that in front of Megan, particularly when Megan seemed to have forgotten the kidnapping for the moment.

"It takes a little imagination," she said with a dry grin.

"Do you stay at his place?" Megan asked.

"Sometimes."

"Where does he live?" Susan asked.

That one gave Savannah a twinge of discomfort. But she couldn't think of a way to duck the question without arousing even more curiosity. "He owns the big Victorian that houses the radio station. He lives on the second and third floors."

Megan loved that. "So you sleep in his bed while he's on the air. Do you have *any idea* how many women in Rhode Island would go nuts if they knew that?"

Savannah shrugged. "They must guess that he has someone."

"No, no," Megan said, "that's not the fantasy. The fantasy is that he's talking to me," she tapped her fingertips to her chest, "and only me. I don't think about his woman."

Susan snorted. "I saw a cartoon once in *Cosmopolitan*. There was this lady DJ who was sitting nude at the mike while her lover pulled on his pants." Savannah had put her coffee cup to her lips and was hiding behind it, but Susan's focus was on Megan. "She was telling her listening audience that she hoped they'd enjoyed the album she'd just played as much as she had." She looked at Savannah. "Is that what you do?"

Savannah would have choked if she'd actually been drinking the coffee. Spared that, she took refuge in indignation, firmly setting down the cup and frowning at her sister. "That's a really personal question, Suse, and inappropriate."

"It's not inappropriate at all. It's exactly what this discussion's about."

"Do I ask you what you do in bed? Did I ever ask where or how often you and Dirk made love?"

Susan's head was tipped at that same slightly haughty angle. "No, but you could have. Dirk and I made love wherever the mood took us, usually four or five times a week. We tried positions you've probably never even heard of. There was one that we used in the car one night—"

Hands over her ears, Savannah interrupted her. "I don't want to hear this."

But Susan was on a roll. Making Savannah squirm gave her perverse pleasure. "Maybe you'd rather hear about what I do with Sam. He's a beautiful animal, Savannah. Has the rhythm and the moves. I've never seen a man with such sweet glory between his legs—"

It was Megan who quietly interrupted her. "Don't, Susan."

"Don't what?"

"Cheapen something that should be private and beautiful. If you enjoy Sam, that's great. But don't tell us the intimate details."

Susan hadn't expected criticism from that quarter. "You wanted intimate details about Jared Snow."

"Details, but not intimate. I don't want to know the really private things. It's embarrassing."

Susan looked from one face to the other in disbelief. "What's the matter with you two? We used to sit around discussing things like this all the time. All of a sudden, you've both gone prudish on me."

"Some things are sacred," Megan said and focused unseeingly on the beach. She was thinking about Will, thinking about how beautiful loving used to be between them and how she couldn't even undress in front of him now. The bruises were fading, but their memory remained. When she thought of Will entering her body, she thought of those other, brutal invasions.

It didn't take a genius to interpret the stricken look on her face. Susan went very quiet, while Savannah put her hand on Megan's. "It'll get better," she said softly. "It will."

Megan averted her eyes, then nodded, and Mrs. Stockley chose that moment to return with breakfast, giving them a diversion. Only when the older woman had returned to the kitchen with Susan's order did Savannah speak.

"I'm sorry if I've offended either of you for not having mentioned Jared sooner. Maybe I should have, but I thought I was doing the best thing."

Having vented her anger, and having been sobered by Megan's look, Susan was calming down. It still irked her that Savannah hadn't seen fit to tell her about Jared. Mostly it irked her that Savannah, who had so much else, should have Jared at all. But the fact was that having seen the man in person, Susan wasn't interested in him. Sure, he was handsome and had stud proportions. But those proportions didn't set off any sparks inside her. Certainly not in the way Sam's did, damn his Neanderthal hide.

"Is it a big thing—your relationship with him?" she asked Savannah, cautious but curious.

"I'm not sure," Savannah answered, then realized that if, as it seemed, Susan was setting enmity aside, she owed her more than equivocation. "Yes," she corrected, "it's a big thing. But I don't know where it will lead. You're right. I have a career. If he wants a woman to be waiting at home with a gourmet dinner each night, he's got the wrong one."

"He wouldn't want that," Megan said. "Not Jared Snow."

"How would you know?" Susan asked, but teasingly.

"I just know." Megan looked at Savannah. "Then again, better not listen to me. I seem to be striking out a lot lately."

"Oh, hush," Savannah scolded. "Eat your breakfast." She was greatly relieved when Megan did just that, because she didn't want anything to reverse the ease in tension that had miraculously emerged in the wake of Susan's attack. There would be time to talk more later. For now, it was enough that the ice had been broken.

They spent what was left of the morning and most of the afternoon lounging by the pool, alternately bathing in the sun and reading in the shade. Though they didn't talk much, there was a sense of quiet camaraderie sweetened by memories of such times past when they had been vacationing from school or simply escaping for several days of enjoying idleness and each other. Now, as then, they didn't stray from the house, not even to eat out. Mrs. Stockley was as good a cook as any chef and far more willing.

After dinner that night, they settled into Adirondack chairs on the back veranda. The night air was warm, redolent with the scent of lush greenery and the sea. Moon shadows played over the pool, but the real romance lay in the play of light on the waves.

They sat in varied poses—Savannah with one knee crossed over the other, Megan with her legs bent and her heels tucked against her bottom, Susan with her feet propped up on the wood railing before her. Each sipped from a slender glass of Amaretto.

For a time, they were lost in silent musings. Then Susan, who hadn't had more to drink than a glass of wine with dinner and now the liqueur, sighed and said, "How complicated life becomes as we get older. I think back to the times we used to come here. Our greatest worry was who to date. Things were so simple. We were so young."

Savannah turned her head against the wide wooden slats of the chair and said, "You make us sound ancient."

"Sometimes I feel it. Sometimes I think that the best years of my life are behind me. Look at my hands." She held them up, graceful in the dim light from the house. "I see lines that weren't there a year ago, and I know that they won't go away. The body doesn't lie."

Savannah gave a soft laugh. "You're gorgeous, Susan. I can't believe you're worried about a few lines on your hands. You're not getting older; you're getting better."

"No, no. I'm getting older. I'm getting older, Retin-A and all."

"You got lots of sun today," Megan reminded her.

"But I like looking tanned."

"Then you'll have to live with the wrinkles," Savannah said.

Susan shot her a look. "You got color today, too. Aren't you worried about your skin?"

"No. There are too many other things to worry about."

"You don't think about aging?"

"Oh, I think about it. When I'm forty, I'll think about it more, and when I'm fifty, I'll think about it even more. Right now, I'm more concerned with maturing than aging."

Megan had always been intrigued by Savannah's semantic distinctions. "What's the difference?" she asked.

"Maturing implies positive growth. It represents all the good parts of aging."

But Susan couldn't see any. "Aging, maturing, getting older—one's as bad as the next. I'm getting older. That's all. I'm getting older, and what do I have to show for it?"

Savannah had to bite her tongue. She'd given Susan the solution to that problem time and time again, and wasn't sure she wanted to argue about it now.

Megan wasn't as hesitant. "You have things to show for it."

"Like what?"

"Financial security."

"I had that the day I was born."

Which was one of the things Megan had always envied. But there were others. "You have lots of friends. You have positions on the boards of three different organizations—or is it four?"

"Five, but what is that worth? Really. I go to meetings several times a year. That's it."

"You could do more, if you wanted," Savannah said before she could stop herself.

"Ah, yes. I could work. Well, that's just fine for you to suggest. Your life is geared toward slavery. Mine isn't." In search of an ally, she turned to Megan. "Do you want to work?"

"I do work," she answered. "I do the bookkeeping for the

business." She looked from one surprised face to the next. "Math was always my strong point. I'm a natural for the job."

"But to do the bookkeeping for all that?" Susan said.

"It's not so much."

Savannah joined in. "I knew you did personal bills, but I hadn't realized you did the rest."

"Someone had to. Will couldn't. He draws a blank when it comes to ledgers."

"Aren't the accounts done by computer?" Savannah asked.

Megan shook her head. "Will doesn't like computers."

"It's all done by *hand*?" Susan asked. "Mistake, Meggie. Make him get a computer."

Even in the dim light, Megan's look was eloquent. Will wasn't in the position to spend money on computers, any more than he was in the position to hire a financial adviser.

"At least," Savannah said, "that explains the mess on the desk in your upstairs office. There were papers all over." Her voice was soft, teasing. "Remember when we tripled senior year? Your things were totally scattered. You knew just where everything was and could always find whatever you wanted, but don't ask me how. Neat you weren't."

"I'm not much better now," Megan confessed dryly. "I try. I do try. The cleaning men only come once a week, and things get messy in between. But I hate cleaning. Hate cleaning." She gave the words individual emphasis. "I'm sure it's because my mother was a fanatic about it. She always said that just because we didn't have the money that some people had, that didn't mean we couldn't live in as clean a house. So she made me clean everything in sight. As soon as I left the house, I rebelled."

She grew suddenly quiet and looked down at her hands. "During the time she lived with Will and me, we had a maid. I'm glad she isn't around to see the mess I've made."

Savannah was thinking of how immaculate the bedroom had been that night, and she would have pointed it out had she not known Megan was talking about a deeper mess. "You had nothing to do with Will's financial problems."

Megan said nothing.

"Savvy's right," Susan said. "You can't blame yourself for that."

"Will would have been better off if he'd married someone like either of you. I've brought nothing to this marriage."

"Will *adores* you," Savannah argued. "He was a bachelor for years, a lonely man. You've brought him happiness."

"I've brought him grief."

"No, *happiness*." Taking a breath, she broached what she knew was on Megan's mind. "What happened the other week wasn't your fault any more than it was Will's. It just happened. It was an ugly, hurtful thing, but you can put it behind you, Meggie. You can."

Megan was very quiet for a minute before murmuring, "I don't think so."

"Sure, you can. Once we catch the men who did it, they'll be put away for life. Any little thing you can remember would help us find them."

Megan didn't answer, but seemed to withdraw into a world of her own. She took a sip of the liqueur in her glass, sat back in her chair, and stared off toward the horizon. Clearly, she didn't want to think about the men who'd kidnapped and raped her, and Savannah could understand that.

Savannah could also see that pushing her just then would do no good.

So she tamped down the sense of urgency she felt when she thought of all the leads she didn't have, and scowled. "How did we get off on this, anyway?"

"We were talking about cleaning house, which I hate too," Susan said, "and before that about working, and I don't care what either of you say, I don't want the pressure of a job. Studies have found that women are having more and more heart and high blood pressure problems, and it's because there are more of us—more of *you*— in the work force than there were ten or twenty years ago. Woman wasn't meant to scurry around from seven in the morning until ten at night wearing a sedate little business suit."

Savannah had never pictured her sister wearing sedate little business suits. "Seven in the morning until ten at night? What kind of job are you thinking of?"

"The kind that will deliver prestige, power, and respect," Susan said without pause.

Savannah nodded. "I see." She took a breath and echoed, "The job has to deliver prestige, power, and respect."

"If it's going to be worth the effort."

"No halfway possibilities?"

"What'd be the point of that?"

"The point is doing something that's interesting and, therefore, rewarding."

"That's an idealistic viewpoint if ever there was one. Realistically, that's not why people work. People work for the money, which I don't need, and the power, which I do."

"Why do you need power?"

"Because that's the basis for respect. I want people to look at me and know that I'm a somebody."

"You *are* a somebody. You don't need power."

"So why should I work?"

Savannah pressed the glass she held to her forehead. "I think we're back at square one."

"You're right. The whole issue of work drives me nuts, but it always comes up. Times have changed. Things were much simpler when we were younger." Her voice softened. "Don't you ever think back, Savvy? Your life is hectic. Don't you ever pine for simpler times, when you had less responsibility?"

Savannah thought about it for a minute. "Not really. There's a plus side to having responsibility."

"I might have figured she'd say that," Susan told Megan, who was sitting quietly, not revealing the direction of her thoughts.

"But I'm serious," Savannah insisted. "Along with responsibility comes control. I like having that control."

"Ah ha! So you want power, too."

"Not power. Control."

That brought Megan from her silence. "What's the difference?"

Savannah took a minute to pick the right words. "This is my own distinction, mind you, but as I see it, power has a negative connotation. It has to do with manipulating either people or events. Control, on the other hand, implies a greater say in what you do with your life. I can't always determine the outcome of things at work; I don't have that power. But I can determine the route I take to get to an outcome. I like being able to do that."

"You're very lucky," Megan murmured.

Savannah turned to her. "Hmm?"

"To be in control that way. To be in command of yourself and your life. To be so *together*."

Savannah thought of the times she'd sat in her wing-backed chair and shook from the inside out. "I'm not as together as you think. I have my moments."

"Like when?" Susan asked, mildly challenging.

Savannah was more than willing to meet that challenge. She had nothing to hide. "When I'm very tense about something. When I'm terrified that what I'm doing is wrong or not enough."

"You don't do things wrong," Megan said.

"Sure, I do. I make mistakes."

"Like when?" Susan repeated, a little crossly this time.

"There have been times when I've undertried or overtried cases. There have been times when I've miscalculated the reaction of the judge or the jury to a particular tactic. I could cite you specific cases, but you'd be bored and I'd be embarrassed."

Susan would have pushed for those cases if it hadn't seemed childish. "The press is totally in the dark. They love you."

Savannah shrugged. "We have people in the office who work at fostering that love."

Susan had assumed that was the case, still the outcome was envious. "Do you think Paul will run for governor?"

"Eventually."

"Will you run to fill his place?"

"No."

"Why not?"

"Because I don't want *that* much responsibility."

"I was under the impression," Susan said, "that Paul puts in less hours than you and the others."

"He does. But he's the one who takes the flak when something goes wrong. The buck stops with him. I'm not sure I want that. And I *know* I don't want to have to campaign every two years. Even now, it's tough. My job is dependent on Paul being reelected, so every two years I sweat a little."

"The alternative is private practice."

"That's right," Savannah said.

Megan perked up. "You're thinking of making the move? But you love what you're doing."

"I'm not saying that I'm making the move. But it is an alternative if I ever reach the point of needing greater stability. I'd also have greater control over my time if I were in private practice. The sheer volume of cases that crosses my desk can be overwhelming. In private practice, I could control that."

"Control," Susan mused and said to Megan, "We should each have a little of that control." To Savannah she said, "This is the first I've heard you talk about private practice. If I didn't know better, I'd say that Jared Snow had something to do with it."

Savannah was quick to deny it. "Jared? He hasn't mentioned a thing—"

"That's not what I meant. I meant that if you're thinking about having more control over your time, it might be because you're thinking marriage—"

"I'm not—"

"And if you're thinking of marriage at this point in your life, the likely candidate would be Jared Snow."

"No. I'm not getting married so fast. I'd have a baby before I'd get married."

"A baby?" Susan breathed. "Are you serious?"

Savannah was a minute in answering. "Would that be so terrible?"

"You don't have time for a baby, any more than you have time for a man."

"I can make time for what I want. Any of us can do that. It's called taking your life in your own hands."

"But a baby," Susan went on, still slightly stunned by the suggestion. "Do you have any idea how much time and effort that takes?"

"People have been doing it for years," Savannah said lightly.

"But why marriage over a baby?" Megan joined the conversation to ask, sounding vulnerable enough to remind the others how much she had wanted a baby herself.

Savannah was momentarily chastised for her lightness. She took another moment to think about the question. "I'm not sure," she finally said. She looked at her hands. "I just think I could handle a baby better than a husband. A husband is a human being with fully developed needs and wants. A baby's needs and wants can be shaped to fit its mother's lifestyle."

"Are you kidding?" Susan asked. "A baby is totally dependent. If you want to talk responsibility, a baby is about the biggest one you could get."

"You don't want one?"

"No."

"Never?" Megan asked quietly.

For the first time, Susan wavered. "How can I say never? I have no idea what the future holds. But right now the last thing I can think about is having a kid."

"Are you thinking about Sam?" Savannah asked.

Susan sent her a sharp look. "I'm trying not to. He's an

imbecile. I don't care if he is the best lover in the world, he's still an imbecile."

"Will you see him when you get back?" Megan asked.

"No."

Savannah couldn't believe that. "You had an argument. Every couple has arguments."

"Sam and I have some very basic differences."

"I should hope so."

"You know what I mean."

Savannah did. She was also convinced that Susan felt more for Sam Craig than she'd felt for a man in a long time. Yes, the argument had hurt her pride, but the hurt went deeper. "You can work out your differences."

"I don't know. We're really a poor match."

"How so?"

"His job, his house, his bankroll—need I go on?"

"Those are all secondary to the way you two work as people. Personally," Savannah told her, "I think you'd be good for each other. Sammy is a wonderfully warm and compassionate person."

Susan snorted. "You didn't see him the other day."

"He was very good to me," Megan said, drawing both Susan's and Savannah's eyes her way. "He made me feel safe. I believed everything he said."

"Oh, he's honest," Susan conceded, but more gently. "He means what he says. Not that I always *like* what he says."

"Would you rather he tell you only what you want to hear?" Savannah asked. "You've known too many men like that. I'd think you'd welcome the honesty."

"Maybe I would if I had something more to offer."

"What do you mean?"

"Hell, Savvy, Sam can't respect me. He can respect you.

You're smart and accomplished. But what do I represent to him? A spoiled brat."

"He's fascinated by you. He sees great potential."

"What about me as I am?"

"That's what fascinates him. I think he likes the fact that you haven't 'arrived.' He'd be intimidated if you had a career."

"He should be intimidated because I have money, but he isn't. He couldn't care less about that."

"Sam is Sam."

"Uh-huh, and where does that leave me?"

"Where do you want to be left?"

"I don't know!" Susan cried and went silent.

For a time, none of them spoke. Then Savannah said in a pensive voice, "I do think life is about potentials. You say my expectations are too high, Suse, and maybe they are. But I want to be everything I can be. So I push myself. Sometimes I make it, sometimes I don't. But if I don't push, I'll never know. I don't want to be an old lady thinking of what might have been."

Her words lingered in the night air for a long, long time. When the silence was broken again, it was on a lighter note, which was what they all needed just then.

By Sunday morning, the pace of the island had fully infiltrated Savannah's system. She didn't even try to read, but lay quietly on the beach listening to the rhythmic rush of the waves. When she moved, it was at half-speed and, even then, she moved reluctantly.

Megan and Susan seemed lost in a similar state. It was just like it used to be.

"This is heaven," Susan murmured, barely moving her mouth as she lay utterly still on a lounge chair in the sun.

Feeling warm and relaxed, Megan hummed her agreement.

Savannah was feeling decidedly irresponsible. "Why is it that the more we rest, the more we want to?"

"It's the sun," Megan answered, moving her mouth no more than the others. "It's a sedative."

"That's not the sun," Susan said. "That's old age."

"Speak for yourself," Savannah told her.

"I don't care what it is," Megan decided. "I'll take it."

Such was the general consensus of opinion. But time was passing, and Monday approached. Savannah didn't want to return to work without having gotten some information from Megan. Still, she was torn. Megan was relaxed on the island. To start prodding would jeopardize that relaxation. So Savannah put it off for as long as she could, though she feared that if she waited until they were back in Providence, Megan might retreat inside herself again.

It actually started on the plane ride home. Megan got a distant look, and maintained a troubled silence. At that point, Savannah figured she had nothing to lose. Taking advantage of the fact that Susan had dozed off, she slipped into the seat beside Megan.

"How're you doing?" she asked softly.

Megan continued to stare at the pitch black of the sky. "The weekend was too short."

"You must be looking forward to seeing Will."

She was, but not unequivocally. She wished she were coming home under different circumstances. "Susan's right. Life has become very complicated." Her eyes filled with tears and her chin trembled. "Oh, Savvy," she whispered, "what am I going to do?"

Savannah grasped her arm firmly. "You're going to go back home and take control of your life."

"Fine for you to say. You're the master of control. It's your forte. I've been trying to get it all my life, but I keep coming up short. How do you do it? How do you manage to make everything work?"

"I don't. I have problems just like everyone else."

"But you end up on top."

"That depends on how you define *on top*. I look at you and see how close you and Will are. I've missed that, Meggie. I've missed the loving. I have a super job, but when the job's done, what's left? Not much more than the silence of an empty room."

"You have Jared now."

"But for how long? How long can I keep him?"

Megan was surprised by Savannah's doubt. "As long as you want."

"I don't know about that."

"You'll keep him."

Savannah shrugged.

"Where's your optimism?" Megan asked.

"Giving way to realism, I guess. I'm trained as a lawyer; I've never had much experience holding a man. So what's down the road for me? More empty rooms? If that's what you call being on top, you're crazy. But look at you. You have Will. Do you have any idea how sick with worry he was when you were gone? He worships you, Meg. In that sense, *you're* the one on top."

Megan brushed the corner of her eye with the side of her thumb. "He's a good man."

"Yes, he is. So you're going back to Providence. You and Will are going to do what's necessary to put the business back on its feet." She paused for a fast breath. "And you're going to work with me to find the men who hurt you. You need that, so you can put the kidnapping behind you, and I need it, but I can't do anything without your help. You're the one in control."

The pleading look on Megan's face was a precursor to silence.

"Don't clam up on me, Meggie. I need your help."

But Megan had already turned her eyes back to the window.

"*Please*," Savannah whispered. "Anything, Meggie. I know how painful it must be to think about, but I need you to do that. For me?" When Megan said nothing, she pushed. "For *you*. Do it for you. So many times you've said you wanted to be in command of your life. *Do it*. This is your chance."

Savannah's words sunk in, but it wasn't until the following morning that Megan acted.

Chapter 18

⁓

MEGAN MADE THE CALL from a phone booth on the outskirts of town. Her palms were damp; her stomach felt tied in knots. But she forced herself to punch out the number and sound fully in command.

The voice that answered the phone wasn't the one she wanted. "I'd like to speak to your boss," she demanded.

"Hold on," she was told seconds before the phone clattered onto a hard surface. Amid strains of Mahler, she heard a distant shout, and the ensuing wait seemed interminable. When she heard voices again, her stomach twisted so sharply she actually feared she'd throw up. But she breathed in through her nose and steadied herself.

"Hello?" came the male voice she knew she would detest until the day she died.

Slowly, distinctly, and icily, she said, "I want my money."

"Excuse me?"

"My money. As planned."

"Who is this?"

"You know exactly who it is and exactly what you're supposed to do. I'll be in tomorrow. You'll put two and a half million in my trunk."

"I'm sorry," he said in a syrupy tone that stuck to the fine hairs on the back of her neck. "You must have the wrong number."

"I don't think so. I'll be in tomorrow for my money."

"Then you'll be in for a disappointment."

"You don't have it?"

There was a pause, then a patiently light, "Money? I don't have anyone's money. I don't know what you're talking about. Who *is* this?"

Megan wasn't surprised by his denial. She expected it, just as she expected the fury she still felt. She had lived with it for days.

"You don't have my money?" she asked, her voice trembling with anger.

"No, I don't have your money," came the answer.

Clenching her jaw so hard that it hurt, Megan hung up the phone before she said something rash. Her breathing was shallow. Her entire body was tight. Fearing a breakdown, she remained there for another minute with her eyes closed, praying for strength. She knew he would welch on the deal. She had known it from the first time he touched her, and nothing he had done afterward had hinted otherwise. Still, she'd had to ask, just to know for sure. With certainty came an odd wave of power. It was, indeed, her turn to take command.

Returning to her car, she headed home.

Two hours later, shortly before noon, Megan entered Savannah's office. Will was with her, wearing the fury on his face that she felt inside. On the outside, though, she was subdued and pale. At Will's urging, once the door to the office had been closed, she said in an ominously quiet voice, "The man you want is Matty Stavanovich. He was the one who kidnapped me."

Savannah was sure she had heard wrong. "Matty Stavanovich?"

Slowly and with genuine distaste, Megan nodded.

"That can't be," Savannah murmured, sagging back against her desk. "Matty's a cat burglar. He's never gone in for kidnapping, much less rape."

"It was him."

"Are you sure?"

"Megan wouldn't lie about something like that," Will said curtly.

Still, Savannah looked at Megan in bewilderment. "Are you *sure*?"

The look on Megan's face answered the question even before she said in a tense monotone, "Two months ago, I took my car in for new brakes. I had to take it back a month later because the brakes didn't feel right. One of the pads was defective. At least, that's what he said when he replaced it." She caught in a sudden breath. "At the time, I thought he was a disgusting man. I couldn't get out of there fast enough. I swear, I had a premonition."

Savannah put a hand to her heart, which was thudding wildly. After a minute, she reached for the phone. "Let me get some of our people in here." She placed an emergency call to Sam, then to Mark Morgan at the local FBI office. After leaving a message for Paul, who was at a meeting, she drew up a chair close to Megan's. "Tell me again. Are you absolutely sure it was Matty?"

"Yes."

"You recognized him because of the work he did on your car?"

"Yes."

Savannah took a shaky breath. She had always known they would get the Cat one day, but never in a million years had she dreamed it would be on a kidnapping rap.

Will touched Megan's shoulder. "Tell Savannah about the other man."

Megan wrapped her arms around her stomach. "Stavanovich called him Pal, nothing but that. I'd never seen him before. He was bigger, more physical." She stopped short.

"Go on," Savannah urged gently.

"He raped me first."

Savannah wanted to wrap her arms around her own stomach, but she knew this was not the place or the time to indulge her own feelings. So she put a gentle hand on Megan's arm and said softly, "Matty Stavanovich has been out there for the last two weeks, carrying on business as usual. Sam took Susan to his place last week; she left the Jaguar for him to fix." She paused for a bewildered second before asking, "Why didn't you tell us sooner?"

Megan swallowed hard. "I couldn't. He threatened me with even worse things than he'd already done, and he threatened to hurt Will."

"But you're telling me now."

With another swallow, Megan rose from her chair. She crossed the room and stared unseeingly out the window. "I can't live with his threats hanging over my head. I thought about it all last night and then again this morning. I drove around and around thinking about it. I liked being in Florida because I felt safe there. But it's not my home, and I can't spend my life running." She turned to face Savannah. "You were right when you said that I had a chance to take control of things. I want that control. I want my life back. I want Matty Stavanovich punished."

Savannah was watching her, wide-eyed, still having trouble believing that the Cat had suddenly changed his style. "Are you sure, Meggie? Before the others get here, are you absolutely sure that Matty was the one?"

"For God's sake, Savannah!" Will exclaimed.

Megan stiffened. "You don't believe me."

"I do, but it's a serious charge and there are a world of emotions involved. I want you to be certain that you're pointing a finger at the right man."

"I am."

"Matty?"

"Yes." She tightened her arms around her waist, and, though she was even paler than before, she forced herself to go on. "You can check his blood type with the tests they ran at the hospital. And you can check his body. He has a birthmark shaped like a light bulb just under his right nipple, and he's not circumcised."

Savannah let out a helpless moan.

Will swore, crossed the floor, and took Megan in his arms. Despite the rigidity of her body, he held her tightly, pressing her head to his chest in a futile attempt to shield her from thoughts that were repulsive to them both.

Just then, Sam arrived. Savannah met him at the door and, keeping her voice low, filled him in on the turn of events. She was barely done when Mark Morgan joined them. Both men questioned Megan gently. It was an unpleasant necessity. Though tense and upset, Megan stood firm in her conviction that Stavanovich had been her abductor.

The wheels of justice began to roll. Within hours, Megan had identified mug shots, blood types had been matched up, a search and arrest warrant was issued. At five o'clock that afternoon, the Cat was taken into custody.

Savannah didn't get home until well after nine that night, and when she did, it was to find Jared waiting in her living room. She had never been so glad to see anyone in her life.

Taking one look at her, he folded her in his arms and held her while she trembled. In time, her body began to relax. Only then did he speak.

"You shouldn't have to go through this, babe. It's not right, so much tension."

"It's part of the job," she said quietly, then looked up at him. "Besides, this time there's excitement, too," and it was there in her eyes. "We got him, Jared. We may not have nailed him for burglary, but if we can get a conviction for what he did to Megan, he'll spend the rest of his life behind bars."

Jared had caught the evening news, but that had only given him the bare outlines of the case. "Isn't it a little bizarre—the Cat doing something like this?"

"I thought so. I honestly didn't believe Megan at first. But she was insistent, and Megan's never been an overly imaginative person. She's down to earth. She's always had an eye for details. Matty's blood type was right. She identified things on his body that she couldn't have possibly known unless she'd seen him naked." She paused, looking at Jared all the while, then said in a low voice, "I know what you're thinking. Sam was thinking it, too. So was Mark. You're thinking that maybe Megan had an affair with Matty totally independent of the kidnapping. You're thinking that if it went awry, she could pin this on him out of revenge, but none of that's possible. Megan loves Will. There's no way she'd have an affair with Matty or any other man. Besides, she was kidnapped. Money was demanded and delivered. And she was brutalized. We have concrete proof of that."

"How about the second man who was involved? Have you found him?"

"Matty claims total innocence, so he's not about to talk of a second man. Megan gave us a detailed description of him, though. The police are working on it."

Tempted by her upturned face, Jared lowered his head and kissed her. It had nothing to do with what she was saying, but he had felt the urge, and she didn't protest. Her mouth molded to his with the sweetness he'd come to expect.

Taking her to his side, he headed for the kitchen. "Why did Megan take so long to come forward?"

Savannah took comfort from his nearness to discuss things that might well have set her to shaking again. "Trauma. Fear. That's how it works. But she's angry now, too, and that's given her a strength she didn't have before. Still, we've assigned a police detail to watch her until we get the second man."

"Have you found any of the money?"

"No. And I doubt we will. Just as we've never been able to recover the money Matty made on his burglaries. We find the goods from time to time, but I'm sure the money's been safely stashed." Her fingers tightened on a handful of sweater at his waist. "The man is incredible, Jared. He pulled a burglary the night after the kidnapping and tossed it in as a red herring. He had a standard alibi to offer when he was questioned. He always has an alibi. This time it was a trip to Mexico, and it covered five days, starting one before the kidnapping."

"The police are checking it out?"

"You bet. He had travel brochures and plane tickets and hotel receipts to show, but he's done that before. It's his typical MO. He's always gone, *always*, when one of these brilliant burglaries takes place. No doubt he sends someone in his place while he hangs around here to do his thing. In the past our resources have been limited, so we've only been able to go so far in our investigation. This time, the FBI's working right along with local and state police. Unless we get a positive ID from someone like a flight attendant or hotel clerk, Matty will be in big trouble. Megan's testimony will hang him."

Jared could feel her anger. "You want that."

"Yes, I want it. Life in prison is too lenient for someone who did what he did to Megan." Hearing her own vehemence, she let out a breath and said meekly, "I take that back. The death penalty gives me the willies. I'll settle for life in prison."

Jared shot her a half-grin. "You're a tough one."

She returned the half-grin a bit dryly. "Don't you know it."

He kissed the tip of her nose this time. "What'll it be? Coffee, tea, or me?"

"Tea now. You later."

"I work later."

"So?"

He grinned and went for the tea. Savannah watched him, thinking how comfortable he was in her home, how natural it felt to have him there. And how good it was not to be alone. Because on nights like this, when she couldn't easily put aside the events of the day, she liked having someone to talk with. She had never fully realized what she had been missing before. Talking to Jared gave her an outlet for her tension.

"Savannah?" His back was to her.

"Mmm?"

"What about music? Did Megan say anything about his listening to CIC?"

Savannah didn't answer at first. He had to turn to catch her headshake. "I asked her about that when we were questioning her about where she was held. Apparently, Matty played music constantly. Not country, though. Classical."

"Classical." Jared was relieved. "Then he wasn't inspired by the station."

She shook her head.

"His wording of the ransom note was pure coincidence?"

"Either that, or another red herring."

"Incredible," he murmured, turning back to his work, and Savannah knew just what he meant. Had it not been for the ransom note, they would never have met. It was a sobering thought which kept them preoccupied until Savannah's tea was ready.

"Can you imagine," she said, "the gall of the man walking around this town like nothing's happened? Most kidnappers would take the money and run. Not Matty. He was too clever for that."

"Why do you think he did it?" Jared asked as he put her cup on the tiled countertop.

Savannah wasn't sure about that, and it bothered her. "Greed, maybe, but I'd have thought he had plenty of money in Switzerland already. Maybe he had sexual motives, though Meg said the other one started the rape." She gave the ghost of a shudder and wrapped her hands around the teacup for warmth. "I'm guessing it was an exercise for Matty. He'd already done his burglary thing and he knew he could stump us with that. He wanted to see how much more he could get away with. Maybe he wanted to *show us* how much more he could get away with." She threw back her head. "Well, his days of getting away with things are over."

Jared stirred instant coffee into a cup of boiling water. "I take it he's locked up for the night?"

"You bet. Given the charge, we asked for high bail and got it. Matty didn't dare come up with it, or we'd have wondered where he got the money. So he's safely stashed. He'll be arraigned in the morning. If all goes well, I'll take the case before the grand jury next week, then he'll be indicted and formally charged. With any luck, we'll be on trial within ninety days. The sooner this is over for Megan, the better."

"And for you," Jared added as he studied her features. There in her home at the end of a long work day, she looked far more delicate than she did at other times. "It'll be a strain. Would you consider letting someone else try the case?"

"Absolutely not. I have the know-how and the drive. I want to do it."

He reached across the counter to touch her cheek. "I know you do, but is it wise?"

"I'm trying this case, Jared," she said determinedly. "I'm trying it, and I'll win. Men like Matty can't be allowed to get away with what they do. There are laws to protect us from the Stavanoviches of the world, and if I can't enforce those laws, what good am I?"

"You can only do our best. You can't guarantee a conviction."

"I know that," she said and sank onto a stool. Her voice went quieter. "I know that. I also know that if we'd been able to get the Cat on a burglary charge, he wouldn't have been free to hurt Megan like he did."

Jared didn't like what he was hearing. "You don't actually blame yourself, do you?"

"Not personally. As you've told me any number of times, I'm only one member of the law enforcement community. We all failed Megan, but I'm the one who has a chance to right that wrong."

"You're making it your own personal cause."

"No. I'm prosecuting a case that has to be prosecuted."

"But you're taking it all on your own shoulders. Don't do that, babe. The law takes strange twists. Stavanovich could be acquitted on some technicality that has nothing to do with you or the way you try your case. Don't set yourself up for a fall."

Savannah looked at him with bewilderment. "You sound like my sister. She says I do that all the time, but she's wrong. If I approach this case with a mind to win, I'll win."

Jared wished he could believe that, but he was a realist. He'd had his share of exposure to criminal law and knew the twists a case could take. He'd seen Elise give everything she had to a case and then, through no fault of her own, lose. It hadn't happened often, but it had happened, and he remembered the anguish. He didn't want Savannah to have to suffer that. She was much more vulnerable. Then again, maybe it was just that he cared much more for her than he had for Elise.

He took her face in his hands. "I love you," he whispered against her lips. "I missed you last weekend."

Savannah closed her eyes and breathed in his scent. "I missed you, too."

"One phone call wasn't enough."

"I know. But I had trouble getting off by myself to make even that one call. The others were always around."

He kissed her cheek, then her chin. "You've got pretty color on your face." His mouth slid down her neck. "How far does it go?"

"How far does what go?" she whispered, burying her fingers in the heather of his hair.

"Your tan." He was unbuttoning her blouse, nuzzling his way to her breasts. "Mmm. Toasty here. You went topless?"

Savannah felt weak. He could do that to her so easily. She held more tightly to his hair. "It was a private beach."

"Mmmm. Not bad." He had unhooked her bra and kissed first one breast, then the other. "Did you go bottomless, too?" he asked against her swelling flesh.

"No."

He went still. "I don't believe you."

"I swear it."

He looked up and, in a raspy voice, said, "Show me."

"I can't."

He stood. "Why not?"

"I'm drinking tea."

"What's drinking tea got to do with it?" he asked. Slipping his arms around her, he raised her just enough so that he could bunch her skirt up with his fingers. When he returned her to the stool, her slim skirt was around her waist and he was sliding a small triangle of silk over her legs.

She cried his name in a whisper, but he was kneeling

again, looking at what he'd laid bare. "You're right," he said in a low, lazy drawl. "You wore a bottom. Not a very big one, though." He touched the pale line that circled her hips.

"It was a bikini," she managed to say, though how she didn't know. Her insides were humming. Her mouth was dry, she was sure because every bit of moisture in her body had rushed to that special spot between her legs.

He slid his thumbs back and forth over the skin that had been hidden from the sun, then lower, through the nest of tight, chestnut curls at the apex of her thighs. Savannah gasped softly, but she didn't protest when he drew her forward on the stool, then put his mouth where his thumbs had been.

His kiss was deep and wet, and while his tongue loved her, his hands stroked her thighs, holding them ever wider until her moment of release came. She was still in the throes of orgasm when he opened his jeans and entered her, and when he climaxed soon after, she was right with him.

Just as she was with him when, some time after that, they left for the station.

They were made for each other, Jared knew. It didn't make sense to him at times, particularly when he thought about her career, but when he thought about who and what she was inside, he had no doubts.

She was his.

Susan was bored. Then again, maybe she wasn't bored so much as unsettled. She had heard about the Cat's arrest and had wanted to be with Megan, but Megan was with Will, and Savannah was still at work, or had been until eight o'clock, when Susan had stopped trying her number.

Desperate to get out of the house, she'd agreed to play bridge at Felicia's, but she hadn't played well at all. Her mind was elsewhere. By eleven, she had had more than enough.

"Are you sure you're okay?" Felicia asked as Susan put on her coat.

"Just tired," Susan said with a smile. She gave Felicia a hug. "Thanks for having me over." She called into the other room, "Take care, you two," then slipped out the door.

The fresh air brought immediate relief. Still, as she began the drive home, she felt uncomfortable and restless. She was filled with an energy that had nowhere to go.

For that reason, she was willing to believe she had been speeding when the lights of a cruiser suddenly filled her rearview mirror. Not that she was concerned; speeding tickets were easy to fix. But being caught was an embarrassment.

Pulling over to the side of the road, she rolled down her window and waited, contemplating the best approach to take. Indignance would do no good, nor would anger; she'd tried them before and failed. She could act surprised, even appalled that she'd been speeding. Or perplexed that she'd been stopped. That sometimes worked. As did seduction, but she wasn't in the mood to be the seductress.

All the contemplation in the world, though, couldn't have prepared her for the man who approached with a prowl in his walk, wearing faded jeans and a pea jacket. Too late, she realized that the cruiser wasn't a cruiser at all, but a worn sedan with a blinker that had already been put back inside.

One look at Sam and she thought she'd cry. She couldn't make out his expression. She knew her own had to be stricken. Straightening her head, she stared at her steering wheel and remained quiet.

Sam braced his hands on the open window, leaned down, and asked cautiously, "How are you, Susan?"

She kept her voice neutral. "Okay. Was I speeding?"

"What do you think?"

"I don't know." She waited for him to say something. When he didn't, she darted him a quick glance. It was a mistake. He was too close. Her heart beat more erratically than before.

Looking back at the steering wheel, she said, "I wasn't paying attention."

"Why not?"

She was silent for a minute, then answered him with a shrug.

"What were you doing back at that house?" he asked.

She glanced at him. "How did you know where I was?"

"I saw your car."

"But why are you here? This isn't your jurisdiction."

"When you weren't home, I started cruising around."

"Looking for a Jaguar?" She laughed, but it was forced, and feeble, at that. "You must have had a time. They're a dime a dozen around here."

"Only one has your plates."

For the second time in as many minutes, Susan wanted to cry. She didn't understand that, which made her angry. "What do you want, Sam? If I was speeding, ticket me. Otherwise, let me leave. It's late, and I'm tired."

"You sound sober."

She rounded on him. "I am sober. I was playing cards with some friends. Believe it or not, we don't always drink ourselves into a stupor."

"Did you win?"

"No. I lost. I played a lousy game. Are you happy?"

Sam wasn't happy. He hadn't been happy since Susan had stormed out of his home the Wednesday before. Straightening, he took a step back and said in a very quiet voice, "Get out of the car."

"What for?" she snapped. Being near him, but not near enough, pained her. She didn't think she could take much more.

"Get out of the car."

"Are you charging me with something?"

"No, I'm simply asking you to get out of the car."

"And if I don't, what will you do? Charge me with violating an order of a police officer? For God's sake, Sam, can't you do better than that?" She reached for the ignition. "It's late. I'm going home."

Suddenly a long arm crossed in front of her. Her hand was imprisoned and removed from the keys, which were as quickly removed from the ignition. The next thing she knew, her door was opened, Sam had taken her arm and all but lifted her out. Seconds later, she stood against the car, imprisoned by his flanking arms.

"Please, Sam," she whispered. "Let me go."

"We have to talk."

She gave a small shake of her head. "I think everything was said last week."

"And you're satisfied with that?"

"Aren't you?"

"Not for a minute. Not for a minute since you left have I been satisfied."

Squeezing her eyes shut, she wailed softly, "Oh God, don't do this to me."

"Do what?" Sam demanded.

Her eyes opened with a snap and she focused sharply on his face. "Talk of satisfaction in that tone. Bring it down to its lowest form. Make it physical. Because it was more than that, Sam. Always. I'm a living, feeling person, not a sex object. If you think that my sole purpose in life is to satisfy your urges—"

Sam's look was just as sharp. "I *never* thought that. For Christ's sake, what do you take me for?" His lips thinned, and he dropped his arms to his sides. "Stupid question, Craig. She told you what she takes you for. She takes you for a dumb cop. A Neanderthal, without a touch of class."

The words haunted Susan, particularly as they came from Sam's mouth. She had hurt him—which was precisely what she'd intended at the time, only now the hurt boomeranged. "I don't take you for that," she rushed out.

"You said it."

"I was angry. You'd just told me that I only appealed to you in bed."

"Nuh-uh. I never said that. I said that I only appealed to *you* in bed."

"But that's not true."

"That's what I felt. You made me feel it, coming in the way you did, trying to change everything about my life."

"I didn't do that. I didn't want to change everything. All I wanted to do was to decorate your house. I mean, what else could I do? I'm not good for much else. I'm not a great cook or a great cleaner, not that you need either of those things since you do them fine by yourself. I don't have a career for you to respect like Savannah—"

Sam cut her off. "Don't bring her into this, Susan. This is between you and me. Savannah's irrelevant."

"Okay, but still, what do I know? I know how to plan fund-raisers. Does that impress you? Of course not. I know how to arrange flowers, but you're not a flower person. And I know how to decorate. I was trying to be useful. That was the only thing I could think to do. So I thought wrong."

"You sure did. You made me feel like a bush-league nothing. It's bad enough that you're loaded. I'm not. Never have been, never will be. I can't begin to measure up to the other men you know when it comes to assets. I can't give you anything you don't already have—"

"I've never *asked* you for anything—"

"That's not the point. It's a matter of pride, Susan. Don't you see? I'm proud of what I have. I'm proud of what I've done with my life. You suggested it wasn't good enough—"

"I didn't!" she cried and reached for his arms. "Listen to me. You were the one who said I said it wasn't good enough. I love your place. It has more warmth to it, even without a stitch of furnishing, than my house does. But you mentioned decorating, so I thought I'd do it. I guess I got carried away. I thought you'd be pleased. I wanted that." Then she realized something else, and with the realization came a return of the vulnerability she had been feeling so much lately. Releasing his arms, she tucked her hands in her pockets and said quietly, "I wanted to please you, just . . . wanted to please you."

Looking at her, seeing the rawness of her expression, hearing the naked need in her tone, Sam couldn't doubt her. "Why, Susan?" he asked softly. "Why would you want to do that?"

He had no way of knowing that his own expression was as raw or his tone as naked. But Susan saw and heard, and the urge to cry that had hit her earlier brought tears to her eyes now. "I don't know," she whispered. Taking her hands from her pockets, she closed her fingers around the lapels of his jacket and clung to the wool. "I don't know. You're so different from other men I've known. I can't stop thinking about you."

He touched her chin with no more than his thumb and forefinger. "The feeling's mutual." When a tear trickled from the corner of her eye, he blotted it up. "I want to see you again."

Susan wanted that more than anything in the world, but the problems that had driven them apart remained. "We fight so much. I don't know if I can go on like that with you. It hurts, Sam."

"It hurts me, too, but it hurts more to be without you. Can't we try it again? Can't we approach the thing differently this time?"

"Like how?" she asked cautiously.

He thought for a minute, searching for the words to express what he meant without offending her. "Maybe it was too physical before. For both of us." He hurried on. "We're great together in bed, but we let that be the starting and stopping point of our relationship. It was a high. We fell back on it, especially when we were feeling insecure about so many other things."

"You've never felt insecure."

"Of course I have. That's what I've been trying to tell you. I feel insecure a lot when I'm with you. It's a new feeling, and I'm not sure how to handle it, but I have to do something, because it's there. You're special, Susan. Classy. Don't you think I want to please you, too?"

"You do," she whispered.

"Not as much as I'd like. You said I was traditional, and

I never thought of myself that way, but when it comes to you, I guess I am. Possessive. Protective. Give you a few drinks, and you need a protector. Stone sober, you're pretty self-sufficient."

"Shows how much you know," Susan murmured but said no more because there was something else she needed just then. Slipping her arms inside his coat and around his waist, she leaned against him for the warmth that had been so missing from her life.

Making a small sound deep in his throat, Sam crushed her close. He didn't try to kiss her. He just needed to hold her. He needed to know that they'd have another chance. "Ahhh, sweetheart," he breathed into her hair. "You feel so good."

"I always did."

"Not like this. This is special." He hugged her tightly for another minute, then took her face in his hands, turned it up, and spoke with exquisite gentleness. "You teach me a lot. You may not believe that, but it's true. You teach me things about myself. Like being old-fashioned. I am, I suppose. And that's not the best way to be in this day and age."

"Then again," Susan argued, able to do so because he'd made the admission first, "it's not such an awful thing. There are times when a woman wants to feel protected."

"Do I do that for you?"

She nodded. "Besides that, you think. You say what you feel."

"You don't always like what I say."

"It's not what you say that bothers me, as much as the way you say it. When you yelled at me last week—"

"I didn't yell. You were the one who yelled."

"Well, it *felt* like you were yelling. I felt like I'd been slapped in the face. I really wanted to help, Sam. It wasn't a question of walking all over you. I thought you'd be happy. *That* was what I wanted."

Sam had no comeback, because his mind was grappling with the sudden realization that of all the women he had known, none had ever said that to him. That Susan, who had so much and was by some measures spoiled, should be the one to say she wanted him happy—and to say it with such sincerity—affected him deeply.

Unable to speak, he lowered his head and kissed her, but it wasn't the kind of fevered kiss they'd so often shared before. It was a kiss from the heart, deep and filled with soul.

Susan, who'd never received a kiss like it, was stunned. It pulled at something deep inside her, sparking thoughts of once upon a time and forever after. But before she could begin to grapple with those thoughts, the approach of a third car intruded.

Still holding her face in his hands, Sam looked around, then watched in disbelief when a full-fledged police cruiser drew to a halt. The officer riding shotgun rolled down his window.

"Any problem here, folks?"

"No, sir," Sam drawled.

"How about moving along, then?"

"Yes, sir." But he didn't budge.

The officer waited for a minute, then looked at Susan. "Is this man giving you trouble?"

"He's been giving me trouble since the day I met him," Susan replied sweetly, "but I think things are under control. Thank you."

"Why don't you both move on, then."

"We will," she said and smiled up at Sam.

"Now," the officer prompted.

Sam returned Susan's smile and, brushing his thumbs over her cheeks, said in a low voice, "Your place is closer."

"Yours is nicer."

"All that way in two cars?"

"Follow me while I drop off the Jag, then we'll go together."

"I like the sound of that. I want you close."

"I like the sound of *that*."

"Uh, excuse me," came the police officer's voice, less patient this time. "This is a public street. I doubt the good folks of Newport would appreciate prolonged tête-à-têtes at this hour."

Sam had an inkling that something was coming when Susan drew herself straighter, but he wasn't quick enough to catch her when she slid around him and approached the cruiser.

"Officer, I *am* the good folks of Newport, and quite frankly, I resent your interference."

"Susan," Sam murmured as he put an arm around her from behind, "let's just do as the good officer says." He began drawing her back toward the Jag.

"You don't have to take this from him," she argued. "You're a lieutenant."

Sam gave the officer an apologetic grin. "She's a spirited one," he said, and guided Susan into the car. As soon as he closed the door, the police officer started to roll off.

"He's a cop, you turkey!" Susan shouted through the open window. "He's one of you—"

Sam silenced her with a sound kiss. By the time he let her up for air, she had an arm draped around his neck. In her eyes he could see subtle accusation for what he had done, but the accusation faded quickly, fallen prey to the deeper feelings that had been released before the cruiser had arrived.

"I'll be right behind you," he said softly.

She nodded.

"Drive slowly."

She nodded again.

Unable to resist, he kissed her again, then returned to his car.

Chapter 19

SAVANNAH SPENT THE WEEKEND with Jared on his boat. She had to laugh when she thought of how casually he had called his small yacht a boat. Built of fiberglass with interior trimmings of ash, its amenities included a galley as modern as Savannah's kitchen, a washer and dryer, a king-size bed, and a luxurious bath.

Jared had had the craft put in the water on Friday, but there was plenty of cleaning and polishing to do before he was satisfied with its condition. Working alongside him, Savannah enjoyed every minute.

Not that they worked the entire time. They talked a lot, slept a lot, and loved a lot. She had never been happier.

On Sunday evening, she told him so. It had been a beautiful day, mild and fragrant as was the best of early April on the Rhode Island coast, and though the air had begun to chill with the setting of the sun, an inner glow kept them warm. They were below deck, facing each other from opposite corners of a sofa with their legs snugly entwined, sipping from glasses of the wine Jared had uncorked for the occasion.

"This has been great," she said with the kind of soft smile that never failed to make his heart turn over.

His chuckle was like the wine, light and dry. "Then you're a glutton for punishment. I've made you work all weekend."

"No, no. It's been great. A vacation, even more so than last weekend in Florida. There's something truly therapeutic about what we've done."

He nudged her bottom with his bare foot, which was tucked there for warmth. "You hate cleaning."

"But this was different. I've loved it. Really I have." When he arched a skeptical brow, she insisted, "Really. I'd do this any time with you."

Jared's heart turned over again. But then, it had been turning over practically since the first time he'd seen Savannah. In some respects, she'd turned over his whole life, certainly his outlook on the future.

"Marry me, Savannah."

She caught her breath.

"I love you," he said, and his voice was as low and deep and intense as she'd ever heard it. "You haven't said the words, but I think you feel them, and I can't risk letting that go. Let's get married."

Savannah didn't know what to say. Somewhere in the back of her mind she had wanted him to ask, then feared that he would. Confused, she whispered his name on a broken breath.

"Is that a yes, or a no?" he asked.

"I don't know. I don't know what to say."

"Do you love me?"

She hesitated for just a minute, not because she didn't know the answer, but because saying it aloud implied a commitment. But that time had come. "Yes," she said, then with greater feeling, "Yes."

Setting his wine glass on the carpet, he leaned forward, took her under the arms, and brought her forward to straddle his hips. He locked his hands at the small of her back. "Say it."

Savannah smiled. "I love you."

"Again."

"I love you," she said, and the smile became a grin, because it seemed so absurd that she hadn't said the words sooner.

So she sat there grinning, loving his face with its rough-hewn features, its faintly squared chin with a ghost of a dimple, its eyes of pale blue with gray flecks, the one with its slight cast. She loved the sandy hair that tumbled across his forehead, brushed the tops of his ears, hit his collar in back. She loved the way his shirt was open to midchest, laying bare a faint sprinkle of tawny hair, and the way he sat eye to eye with her, though she was on his lap.

"I do," she whispered. Looping her hands, wine glass and all, around his neck, she came forward for a kiss.

"Then marry me," he said when the kiss was done.

She pressed her temple to his. "For a man who was burned once before, you're in a big rush."

"There's no comparison between this and that."

"We're both lawyers."

"You're as different from Elise as night from day."

"I have a demanding career. I won't always be here, and when I am here, my mind may be there."

"I don't care whether your mind's here or there," he returned, "as long as you're wearing my ring. You're right; I've been burned once, and because of that I should be wary of ties that bind. But I'm not. *Because* I've been burned once, I know what I want, and you're it. I can live with your career. It's part of who you are. Say you'll marry me."

"I want to," she whispered, and one part of her did. That part wanted Jared bound to her so that he couldn't escape, so that no other woman could have him, so that all those who listened to him night after night would know he was taken. On the flip side, though, the thought of ties like that scared her. "Marriage is rough."

"All good things are."

"But I've seen it fall apart so often. Where I come from, marital rifts are more common than bliss."

"You're parents were happy."

"Uh-huh, and my mother died nearly twenty years ago. Who knows what would have happened if she had lived?"

Jared was taken off-guard by the thought. "Do you really wonder about that?"

"Once in a great while it crosses my mind. People are always telling me to be realistic, and the fact is that my dad is a difficult man. Maybe he would have been different if Mom had lived. Then again, maybe Mom would have had enough at some point." She paused, desperately wishing she could make Jared understand. "So many of the people I know are on their second or third tries. I don't think I could bear it if something happened to us."

"Something's *already* happened to us," Jared said, looking as frustrated as he sounded. Under his breath, he mumbled, "I don't believe this," then more loudly, "You're saying that since we love each other so much, we don't dare risk marriage. That doesn't make sense! If we love each other so much, marriage isn't a risk."

With a breath, he then dared to voice the idea he'd clung to of late. "You need me, Savannah. You're as independent a woman as I've ever met; you have financial security, a career, a home. But you need me. I saw it in your eyes that first time we met, and I've seen it lots of times since. It's just a flicker sometimes, but it's there, an intense loneliness, almost desperation. You need a soul mate, and I'm it."

Savannah couldn't argue with anything he'd said. Nor did it surprise her that he'd analyzed the situation so well. He was that kind of man. Still, his solution frightened her.

Sliding a hand down his shirt front, she grasped a button. "We could live together for a while, just to make sure this is what we want."

"I don't have to make sure. I already know."

The warmth of his body penetrated his shirt to soothe the backs of her fingers. "That's what you say now, but you may feel differently after a month or two."

Slowly he shook his head. "The only way I'd feel differently would be to love you more." His hands rose on her back. "I love you, Savannah."

"You say that—"

"I *mean* it. I know all about your career and how demanding it is. I've lived with it for the past few weeks, but it hasn't mattered. We've made time to be together, and we've done it without any severe hardship on either of our parts. Am I right?"

She couldn't deny it. "But that's different from year after year of seeking warmth from a woman who is forever engrossed in depositions and affidavits and bills of particulars."

Jared let a moment of silence pass. "You talk of wanting a baby. How can the woman you've described possibly make a good mother?"

"She can. I can. I'd do things differently if I had a baby. I've already told you how."

"Then having a baby means more to you than having me?"

"No!"

"That's how it sounds."

"No. I don't mean it that way. It's just . . . just . . ."

"What?" he asked more gently. "Tell me. I have to know."

With a quick breath, she blurted out. "You frighten me. You're so perfect."

"I'm not—"

"To me, you are. I always thought that if I married it would be to someone a little older and sedate, someone who was successful enough to indulge me in my career. You— you're successful and dynamic and gorgeous. You should be with someone like Susan, someone who can devote her whole life to you."

"No offense to your sister, but I don't want that kind of woman. I'd feel smothered, and bored."

"But you have needs and wants. I want to satisfy them, but I don't know if I can. I don't want to disappoint you, Jared. I'm scared that I would."

Jared looked off to the side. "This really boggles my mind. You talk like I'm some kind of god and like you'd have to be a goddess to fill my needs." His eyes went to hers. "I'm not a god, Savannah. I'm human. I have faults like everyone else. It takes two to make a marriage work or not work, and I've already blown it once before. So obviously I'm not such a joy to live with."

"She didn't love you like I do."

Savannah blew his mind with that remark. It was another

minute before he could speak, and then his voice was more hoarse. "I know you, Savannah. I know you're a lawyer, and I know what time demands that puts on you. I want you in spite of all that, maybe because of it. You're an interesting woman. Your life is never static. I'm not asking that you be a traditional wife. I don't want a traditional wife." He made a face. "Hell, what kind of traditional wife is going to put up with her man working all night? Or living on a boat? Not that I'm planning to live here forever, but for now it's fine. It wouldn't be fine for a woman who's around all day. She'd go stir crazy."

Thrusting a handful of fingers through his hair, which fell right back down on his brow, he glanced toward the far end of the salon. Frustration was written all over his face. "How can I make you understand? You have an idea of what I want and need that's not what I want and need at all." He looked back at her. "You're convinced you'd make a lousy wife, but that doesn't make sense. Take this weekend. If we'd been married this weekend, I wouldn't have expected any more or less from you. So why shouldn't we be married?"

She tugged at his button. "That goes the other way, too. If this weekend was perfect, why should we change a thing?"

"Because I want bonds. I want to know you're mine. See, I'm not perfect. I'm insecure."

"You are not."

"When it comes to you, I am." With finality, he said, "I want us married."

Leaning forward, Savannah pressed her face to his neck. He smelled so good. Even now, especially now, after a full day's work, he was man through and through. "Oh, Jared."

His arms went around her. "What is it you want?"

"A little time. A little time to get used to us. It's still so new. If you think you're feeling insecure, I'm feeling ten times more so."

"You shouldn't."

"But I do. For me, marriage was always something way out there in the great beyond. I never dwelled on it. Maybe I purposely avoided thinking about it, because I'm not sure I'd do it well, and if I can't do that, maybe I don't want to try. I'd have certain expectations of myself if I were married, far more so than if we were living together."

"That's crazy."

"Maybe, but it's so. I've never spent much time picturing myself as a wife. I've pictured myself a mother more, but even then, we're talking dreams."

"So dream about us."

"Lately that's all I do."

Framing her face with his hands, he said in a tone that was raw and pleading, "I love you. Why won't you believe me? You're so positive about everything else in life. Why not about us?"

"Because," she said with her heart in her throat, "you mean so much to me. When the optimist in me runs free, I imagine all sorts of beautiful things—us, kids, health, and happiness. Then I get nervous and I begin to think that one person can't have it all. I have a successful career. I'm not sure I can do justice to more."

"You *can*. You can have it *all*."

She wanted to believe him. He spoke with such confidence that she almost did. Still there were fears that gnawed and nagged. In an attempt to ward off those chilly fingers of doubt, she hugged him closer.

"Agh!" he cried and went suddenly straight. He twisted

an arm to his back and brought his hand out wet. "Uh . . . babe?"

It was a minute before Savannah realized what she'd done. Eyes wide, she looked at the empty wine glass she held at his shoulder, then at Jared. In a small voice, she said, "I forgot it was there."

His look said, "You sure did," as he began unbuttoning his shirt. "So," he tried to sound casual without feeling it at all, "you want to put the wedding off just a little?"

She nodded.

"A month or two?"

She shrugged.

"But you will marry me?"

"If you still want it."

"I'll want it." He peeled the shirt off first one arm, then the next. "What if you get pregnant?"

"I'm not getting pregnant so fast."

He tossed the shirt aside. "We're not doing anything to prevent it."

Captivated by his chest, she spoke distractedly. "But it's not happening."

"Maybe it will this month."

"No." She spread both hands over his ribs, letting her thumbs meet at the faint, central line of hair. "It won't happen for a little while."

Jared was intrigued by her certainty. "Why not?"

"Because," she said, taking a breath, "the next few months are going to be ugly. I don't want our baby to be tainted by that."

"Our baby." Jared grinned. "Sounds nice." In the next instant, though, the grin vanished. "Will I be competing with Stavanovich for your attention?"

"Not competing—"

"You can't let him dominate your life, Savannah."

"He won't—"

"He'd *better* not."

She couldn't help but grin. "Or what? What'll you do to poor Matty?"

"I won't do a damn thing to poor Matty. It's poor you I'll do things to." He leaned forward, all the way forward until Savannah's back hit the sofa cushions. "If necessary," he loomed over her, "I'll keep you right here on this boat, naked and hot," a more husky drawl, "just beggin' for it."

"You could do it," she whispered, sliding her hands up his chest, "and without much effort. It doesn't take much to get me hot when I'm around you."

"What about naked?" he asked. The gray flecks in his eyes had darkened.

At the slight pressure of her hand, he backed off her. She stood and began to undress, slipping off first her jeans, then her shirt, then her panties and bra. Her movements weren't purposefully seductive, yet the effect on Jared couldn't have been greater if she had done a bona fide strip tease. His face was flushed and his chest felt suddenly tight.

She looped her arms around his neck. "I'm naked."

"I know," he said in a raspy murmur. While he cupped her breast and sucked her nipple far into his mouth, his free hand set the rest of her on fire. When his fingers finally wound up high between her legs, he whispered, "You're hot."

"And begging," she breathed in a broken whisper. Her hands went to the snap of his jeans. "Please, Jared, hurry." She lost patience with his zipper and, instead, began to stroke his swollen flesh through the denim.

With a soft curse, he struggled out of the jeans. Then he stood, brought her tight against him and moaned. "God, do I love you."

"Then help me," she whispered without restraint. She wasn't sure why, but she had no patience at all. She needed him inside, and she needed it now. Backing her up a step until the backs of her knees touched the large, square coffee table, he lowered her to its surface and slowly, sensuously, stretched out over her. Linking his fingers with hers by her head, he watched her face as he entered her.

She was beautiful all the time, he thought, but especially at the moment of his penetration. Her face was always the same, with elements of surprise and delight, yet always different, depending on what they'd been doing or discussing beforehand. This time, mixed with a canvas of love was relief, and even in spite of the relief, she was raising her thighs higher on his, opening herself to a deeper possession.

Jared would have possessed her soul if she had let him, but he had to be satisfied with her body and her heart. Some time later, when he lay damp and spent between her thighs, he thought of that possession and realized how tenuous it was.

"You'll be mine," he whispered into the tangled cloud of chestnut hair that cushioned his face.

"I am yours," she whispered back.

"Forever and ever, amen?"

"I want that."

"Then marry me."

"Soon."

"Now."

"Soon."

Taking her with him, he rolled off the table and onto the rug with a thud.

"Jared!" she cried, on top now. "Good God, what are you trying to do?"

"Knock some sense into you."

"I have all the sense I need." She shaped her hand to his jaw, which hadn't been shaved in a day and was pleasantly rough. "I just need time. That's all. A little time to feel totally sure I'm the right one for you."

He came back with, "What about my being the right one for you?"

She wanted to say that he was, that if she ever married, it would be to him. But she knew that would only spark a renewed why-wait attack, and she had had enough of the argument for a day.

So she grinned and said, "Right? Right may have nothing to do with it. Face it, bud. You're stuck with me awhile. I'm not goin' nowhere until I hear more about the Grumpslaw."

Jared hadn't thought about the Grumpslaw since the morning he'd talked Savannah to sleep, and he had no intention of thinking about the Grumpslaw now. So if that was what she needed to set her free, he mused with some satisfaction, she was in for a long imprisonment.

Imprisonment was a major topic of discussion the following Friday night when Savannah and Jared joined Susan and Sam for dinner at an inn in Wakefield.

"The question is where to hold him," Sam was explaining to Susan as they finished their salads. "The man's like grease. He could slide through our fingers and be gone just like the stuff he's stolen over the years. So we need maximum security, but the facilities are all mobbed, which doesn't bode well for keeping a close eye on him."

"Not to mention the havoc he'd play with an overpacked prison population if given the chance," Savannah added.

Susan wasn't sure if she believed that. "I'd have thought it would be the other way around. Matty's a runt. I'd picture him being kicked around—" She caught herself. "I almost said mercilessly, except that he doesn't deserve any mercy. It'd serve him right to be raped. He's an animal."

"But clever, very clever," Sam said. "He's been in prison before and no one touched a hair on his head. He can manipulate people when he has to, and they don't even know he's done it."

Savannah had read the reports, too. She knew everything there was to know about Matty Stavanovich, but whether she recognized the *real* Stavanovich was impossible to tell. He was a master of deceit. "We've got him, though. The grand jury didn't have much of a problem returning the indictment." She had appeared before the grand jury on Wednesday. Stavanovich had been formally charged on Thursday, and bail had been revoked. He was being temporarily held in a federal facility pending a decision on placement. "If necessary, we'll keep him where he is and push for a speedy trial, which would suit me just fine."

Jared recalled the incredible amount of work, not to mention the pressure that accompanied the kind of trial Savannah faced. He'd lived through more than one trial like it with Elise. For those days and weeks, he'd been shut out of her life. He knew that Savannah would never do that, still he felt uncomfortable about the burden she would carry. "You talked about three months," he said. "Will that give you enough time to prepare your case?"

"It should."

He turned to Sam. "Any leads on the Cat's accomplice?"

Sam wished there were. He and Hank had been but two of many assigned to the case, and neither the state police nor the FBI, both of which had greater resources than the local police, had had any luck. "He's probably left the area, but we'll keep after him. He can only run so far. The drawing the artist came up with after working with Megan has been circulated through departments all over the country. Something may turn up, either on him or on a second accomplice."

"Second?"

Savannah explained. "Someone went to Mexico. It couldn't have been Matty, since he was here raping Megan—"

Susan interrupted. "For God's sake, Savvy, do you have to be so blunt?"

"She was raped," Savannah said quietly.

"Okay, but don't repeat it time and again."

"You were the one who mentioned rape before."

"I was referring to the Cat, and he deserves it. Meggie didn't."

"I know that."

Sam leaned close to Susan. He knew that Savannah's words had hit her the wrong way. She was extremely sensitive when it came to Savannah. Though this dinner had originally been Susan's idea, she'd entertained second thoughts once the invitation had been extended and accepted. Those second thoughts had been cause for more than one neat scotch.

Despite all Sam had said and done to assure her, Susan was convinced that he would see her beside Savannah and decide he had chosen the wrong twin after all. Not that Savannah was available. Still, Susan worried.

Unnecessarily, as far as Sam was concerned.

Opening his hand on her thigh beneath the cover of the white linen tablecloth, he asked softly, "Want us to talk about something else?"

But Susan was determined to handle it. It upset her to think of Megan and what she had been through, but if Savannah could do it, so could she. Besides, this was Sam's work. She didn't want him to think he couldn't talk shop when she was around.

She held up a hand in apology to Savannah. "Sorry. Go on. You were talking about Mexico."

Savannah looked at Sam, who hitched his chin back at her. So, in a quiet voice, she continued. "Matty claims he was in Mexico during both the kidnapping and the Cranston heist. He has all kinds of paperwork to prove it. Obviously someone went in his place. Whoever it was may not have even known what he was doing."

Jared found that hard to buy. "I can't believe that someone would spend a week, or five days, or whatever, signing someone else's name without knowing what he was doing."

"Oh, he knew what he was doing," Savannah corrected, "he just didn't know why. Matty's the type to come up with an explanation that a patsy would find perfectly logical."

Susan thought of the day she and Sam had left the Jaguar with Matty. "I saw plenty of mechanics around his shop. Would he have sent one of them?"

Sam shook his head. "We've checked. They're all clean, but we expected that. Matty wouldn't do anything so obvious. He probably used someone from somewhere else entirely."

"Like where?"

"Your guess is as good as mine. He's been all over the country, Matty has. We wouldn't know where to begin."

"So what do you do?"

"We track down every clerk who processed his receipts and pray that one of them will take a look at Matty's picture and swear that he wasn't the one who signed the bill. We can also take those receipts to a handwriting expert who'll tell us whether or not Matty was the one who signed. He very conveniently kept the receipts for us, but they're carbons. We want the originals for a more valid analysis. We're working on getting them now."

"Any sign of the money yet?" Jared asked.

Sam shook his head.

"Or Megan's gun? Or her watch?" Susan asked.

"The guy covers his tracks," Sam acknowledged begrudgingly. "We won't find those things. We won't even find any clothes with tiny glass splinters that could be matched up to the French door he broke. He dumped everything."

"Do you know where he held her?" Jared asked.

"Nope. Megan didn't see a thing. She was in a laundry bag coming and going. She said the drive was endless, at least an hour, she thought. Given the terror she must have been feeling, I'm sure it seemed longer than it actually was. It was probably closer to half an hour, but even then there's a lot of territory to cover. Half an hour could have taken them into either Massachusetts or Connecticut."

Jared had been closely following the televised news reports on the case. "Stavanovich's face has been all over the place. What are the chances of someone coming forward—maybe one of his unsuspecting dupes?"

"Not great," Savannah said. "Let's face it. The friends of men like Matty don't sing in the boys' choir. Like Sam says, he's clever. I'd put money on the fact that whoever he used has good reason to keep his or her mouth shut, and even better reason to fear him."

"He's a disgusting man," Susan muttered simply because she needed the outlet.

No one argued.

But Jared was lost in thought. He had originally been intrigued by Matty the Cat, and now he was intrigued by Matty the kidnapper. "He planned it all out. It's incredible. He mapped out every little detail of the crime, even planned a second crime, the robbery, to coordinate with it, and he had an alibi for both. How much you want to bet that he used cars he was servicing to transport Megan from one place to another."

Savannah and Sam looked at each other.

"Possible," she mused.

"Probable," he decided.

But Jared wasn't done. "And the fact that he never robbed clients of his, yet he chose to kidnap a client. He deliberately broke the mold." He sat back in his seat, leaving a hand on his fork, pushing a sliver of onion around his otherwise empty salad bowl. "And then there's the issue of the ransom note. He's a classical music buff, yet he chose wording for the note to suggest he listened to country. He thought of everything."

"Maybe not," Savannah cautioned. "There are still a couple of things that don't make sense."

He abandoned the fork. "Like?"

"Like the alarm system. How did he know it wasn't working? I want to find that out."

"The tour guide," Susan murmured.

The other three stared at her.

"Tour guide?" Savannah echoed blankly.

"When we were in Matty's office that time, Sam was looking at the pictures on his wall. They were taken in Mexico, in Chichén Itzá. Matty said he'd hired a private guide to see the ruins there." With a hint of smugness, her gaze moved slowly from one face to the next. "I've been to Cancún, and to Chichén Itzá. The trip takes somewhere around two hours each way. Allowing for another hour, minimum, at the ruins, Matty and his guide would have been together for five hours at the least." Her eyes held Sam's. "Unless Matty's private guide was an idiot, he'd be the one to say yea or nay to a picture of Matty."

Sam studied her for a minute, then arched a pleased eyebrow. "Not bad. Not bad at all."

Jared thought it was brilliant. "Could be what you need," he told Savannah, who was grinning.

"I'd *love* it. It would be the kind of slip up that would drive the Cat nuts." She looked at Sam.

"I'll put someone to work on it first thing in the morning."

Susan beamed. "There. Now that we've solved your case, Savvy, we can eat." Tipping her head, she crooked a finger at the busboy. "We're ready for our main course. If you'd be so good as to pass that message along . . ."

Jared and Savannah returned to Providence just in time for Jared to change into jeans and go on the air. Savannah sat with him in the sound booth for a while. She was comfortable there now, knew when she could talk and when she

couldn't. While the music played, they talked quietly—
about Susan and Sam, about the difficulty Savannah was
having with one of the other lawyers in the division, about
the office building in Honolulu that Jared had just sold and
the high rise he was buying in Seattle.

At times they simply listened to the music. Watching
Jared during those times, Savannah grew convinced that he
was a true romantic. He felt the words. The subtle changes
in his features suggested that he could put himself into a
song as easily as she could, and that knowledge only enhanced her feelings for him. He was a sensitive man. His
manner toward her proved it. She loved him deeply for that.

It was nearly two in the morning when he woke her up.
She was sitting on the floor and had fallen asleep against his
leg. Fearing that she would end up cramped and sore if she
stayed that way much longer, he sent her upstairs to bed.

At two-thirty the first call came. A light went off on the
telephone console signaling his private line. Having just
started a new song, he reached for the receiver.

"Hello?"

At first there was silence.

"Hello?" he said again.

A woman's voice came on then, quiet, almost timid.
"Jared?"

He didn't recognize the voice, which puzzled him. The
list of people with access to that number was short. "Speaking."

Again there was silence. Had the call come in on any one
of the station's other lines, he would have been tempted to
hang up. But this was his private line, so he waited.

Finally, the same quiet, hesitant voice came again. "I just
wanted to thank you. You've given me strength."

Jared searched his brain for a flicker of familiarity but found none. "I'm glad." Gently he asked, "Who is this?"

"I've been listening for almost as long as you've been in town. The nights are so long. If you hadn't been here . . ."

Still gently but more puzzled than ever, he asked, "Who is this?"

There was a long pause, then a small click.

Replacing the receiver, Jared put both elbows on the table before him and his chin in his hands. Several things about the call bothered him, first and foremost that it had been on his private line. Besides that, he had been disturbed by the woman's near-whisper. There had been a tightness to it. He wondered why.

When it came time to move into the next song, he brought the mike close. "You're listening to 95.3 WCIC Providence," he said in a low, lyrically husky drawl. "That was George Strait, and this is Jared Snow, keepin' you company through the darkest hours of the day. The graveyard shift they call it; I can understand why. It can be long and lonely when you're sittin' by yourself. So listen in. I'll play you the best I've got, a little country in the city at WCIC Providence, kickin' off a string of six with Earl Thomas Conley. Jared Snow, here, in the heart of the night, think bright so I'll know you're there. . . ."

He wasn't sure what he wanted to say, but hoped he said it anyway. Knowing he could do no more, he returned to the contracts he had been reading before the call had come in.

Earl Thomas Conley segued to the Eagles, who segued to Juice Newton, who segued to the Desert Rose Band. Then the button on the telephone console lit up again.

He had an odd premonition as he reached for the phone, even hesitated a minute, wondering whether he should just let it ring. But that would be harder than answering. "Hello?"

"I'm sorry I hung up," the woman said softly, quickly. "I shouldn't be calling, but I have to talk to someone, and the rest of the world is asleep."

Jared didn't pretend not to connect this call with the last. "How did you get my number?"

"By accident," she said in the same fragile but hurried way. "No, that's wrong. I meant to get it. It wasn't hard. With a little ingenuity, most things aren't hard to get. It's knowing what to do with them that's hard."

"You knew what to do with my number," Jared reminded her.

"But I lost my nerve and hung up."

"And now you've called back." He didn't want to ask her name lest she hang up again. She was clearly upset about something. He felt an odd responsibility to draw her out. "Do you live here in Providence?"

She paused, letting a moment pass before asking, "Are you really as calm in real life as you sound on the air?"

"This is real life. What you hear is what you get."

"I wish I could get it," she said wistfully, and more slowly now. She'd apparently realized that she wouldn't lose her nerve, which, Jared assumed, was why she'd been rushing out her words. "I could use a little of that peace."

"Have things been rough for you lately?"

"Lately? God, yes. But it's not only lately. Things have been rough all my life."

"Want to tell me about it?" Jared surprised himself by asking. He wondered what he was letting himself in for, but wouldn't have taken back the question. He wanted to know who she was and where she'd gotten his number. For that, he was going to have to establish rapport with her.

She hesitated for a long time before saying, "I can't."

"And you won't tell me your name?" When she said nothing, he asked, "What will you tell me?"

She hesitated again, then sounding confused, even distracted, asked, "Have you ever been in a situation where you planned something out and thought you had everything right, and then things backfired?"

Jared though of his marriage to Elise. "I've had that happen."

There was a minute's pause, then a surprised, "You have?"

"Yes. Is that what's happened to you?"

She answered his question with another. "How did you handle yours?"

"I took a good look at where I was vis-à-vis where I wanted to be. In my case, I'd been mistaken about that goal. Before I could do anything, I had to decide where I was going."

"Did you?" She made a noise. "That was a dumb question. Of course, you did. You're there now."

"Almost," Jared said, thinking of Savannah.

"Almost? Do you think you'll make it all the way?"

"I don't know. I think so, but there aren't many sure bets in life."

"I know," she said sadly. "I used to think there were. I was wrong."

"Are you married?" She didn't answer. "How old are you?" At times she sounded eighteen, at other times fifty. She vacillated between the vulnerability of youth and the disillusionment of middle age.

She wasn't telling her age, either. So he took a different tack.

"Things can't be as bad as you think. Maybe it's the night. Problems always look worse when you're tired. Have you slept?" It was nearly three in the morning. His system was used to it; his schedule accommodated it. But he was in the minority.

"I slept a little."

"Why don't you try for a little more?"

"I want to, but when I lie down and close my eyes, I start thinking about everything that's gone wrong, and I realize that things could get worse, and I don't know what to do!"

The fine thread of desperation that Jared had heard in her voice seemed to swell with her cry. "Shhhh," he soothed. "You'll work things out."

"I can't."

"Sure, you can."

"You don't understand. I've done some awful things!"

Jared was beginning to feel like a confessor, and he was increasingly uncomfortable with the role. This was no random prank caller, but a woman with serious problems. Unfortunately, he was neither a priest nor a psychiatrist. He wasn't sure quite how to handle her.

"I wish I knew your name," he murmured half to himself, but she heard.

"It doesn't matter," she said, suddenly more subdued. "Just talk to me."

"What should I say?"

"Tell me to stay calm. Tell me to keep my wits. Tell me that panicking won't do any good."

"It won't."

"I know. But what will? Nothing's gone as I planned. I'm scared."

Jared didn't doubt it for a minute, but he felt helpless. "I want to help, but I can't do that unless you tell me more. I need to know who you are."

His plea was met by silence.

"Or *where* you are."

Silence still.

"Are you at home?" he paused. "At a friend's?"

Nothing.

"Then tell me more about your problem. I'm probably not the person you should be speaking with. If you give me a better idea of what's wrong, I'll direct you to someone who *can* help."

"You don't understand," she said defeatedly.

"I'm trying to. *Help* me."

His plea seemed to echo over the line. The silence that replaced it was final.

"You've hung up again, haven't you?" he murmured into the phone. When there was no answer, he replaced the receiver.

He didn't budge until it was time to identify the station again, and as soon as he'd done that, he went back to thinking about the call. He had to decide whether to do anything about it, and, if so, what. More immediately, he had to decide what to say if she called again.

But the remainder of the night passed uneventfully, and when he joined Savannah in bed shortly after six, it wasn't a mystery woman's call that was on his mind. It was Georgia, as always.

Chapter 20

Susan had always liked the month of May. She thought of it as a time of emergence, a time when things were fresh and new, when the worn, tired face of winter yielded to spring's rebirth. Most immediately, that meant putting furs and wools and downs into storage and coming out in the open with the brightest and best of the coutures' new look.

At least, that was what spring had meant to her in the past. This year was different. Though her wardrobe was as smashing as ever, she found little excitement in showing it off.

Sam was forever on her mind.

When they were together, life was positively beautiful. At those times, she didn't need expensive new clothes to give her a kick. She dressed more casually than she ever had, sometimes preferring a slacks outfit that she'd bought two years before, or a soft pair of jeans and a sexy silk blouse. Other than the planning that went hand in hand with wanting to turn him on, she rarely thought of clothes when she was with him. Nor did she think of alcohol. He kept her busy. They talked about everything, they read and they shopped for the few pieces of furniture he decided to buy. They grilled dinners on the deck and they made love.

Then he went to work and everything changed. Those were the times when she returned to Newport. Bored and lonely without him, she was looking to fill her time. But she was increasingly impatient with those of her crowd whom she saw, and increasingly disinterested, all of which brought her thoughts right back to Sam.

She felt in limbo, suspended between two very different worlds. Much as she loved Sam, she didn't know where their relationship was going. Any way she looked at it, they were from opposite sides of the track. While she liked having money and the things it could buy, Sam refused to take a cent from her. She wasn't sure she could moderate herself to fit his standard of living.

Yet thought of a future in Newport, with more of the same for the rest of her life, depressed her.

She wanted to talk with Savannah, but between Jared and work, Savannah was preoccupied. And anyway, Savannah was on her black list. She had everything—a job, a love, the kind of attention that Susan craved. Perhaps it was just as well Savannah was busy.

The only other person who'd met Sam and might understand her dilemma was Megan. Each time Susan called, though, Megan had other plans, and while she sensed that such plans were fictitious, she couldn't push the issue. Megan was worried about the upcoming trial. By comparison, Susan's problems seemed petty.

So she was left without an outlet. Frustrated that Sam wasn't with her, wanting to escape the uncertainty of their relationship, even wanting to defy him in her way, she drank. She usually did it in Newport, where she'd have more time to sleep it off before he found her, but there were times when she settled into Sam's new leather easy chair with a bowl of ice, a glass, and a bottle of Chivas Regal.

That was just what she did on a night in the middle of May when Sam went undercover to get information on a call-girl ring that was allegedly putting more than one Brown coed through school. Susan didn't like the case. She didn't like the idea that Sam would be mixing with coeds any more than she liked the idea that the suspected mastermind of the ring was a local politician with reputed ties to the mob. Most of all, though, she didn't like the fact that she was alone.

She wasn't drunk, just slightly dazed, when the phone rang. It was barely ten. Somewhere through the mist in her brain came the thought that it might be Sam. She nearly got up. Then she realized that if her words were slurred, he'd know just what she was doing and be disappointed in her. It was one thing to defy him, another to disappoint him. She didn't want to do the latter. Besides, her legs were too heavy to move.

Propping the glass on her lips, she waited through the second, third, and fourth rings until the answering machine went on, then smiled lazily at the sound of her own sexy voice.

"Hi. You've reached the right number at the wrong time. If you'd care to leave your name and number, the good lieutenant will get back to you as soon as he can. Ciao."

The beep sounded. Seconds later, a gravelly voice said, "This is Captain Divine from the Butler Police Department. We have an emergency situation here. I have to talk with Sam Craig as soon as possible." He gave the number, then hung up.

Susan stayed where she was. Captain Divine. Cute. Some yo-yo was having a good time.

She started to tip the glass to her lips, then righted it. Leaning forward carefully to compensate for any lessening of her coordination, she set it on the floor by the bottle. Then she sank back in the chair and thought about the call.

It was probably a joke. Captain Divine had to be a comic strip character.

Still, for a comic strip character, he'd sounded grim. And where was Butler?

Pushing herself from the chair, she maneuvered her way to the answering machine, pressed the replay button, and listened to the message again. There was a strange feel to the call. She wasn't sure whether, in her predrunkenness, she was imagining it, or whether it was simply strong enough to penetrate that same semidrunkenness.

Fumbling for the nearby pad and pencil, she listened to the call again. This time she jotted down the number the man had given. There was an area code, but it wasn't one she recognized, not that she was up for recognizing much. And as for Butler, it didn't ring any bells at all.

Much as she wanted to put the message aside, return to the large, leather easy chair and finish her drink, she couldn't. Something inside told her that the call wasn't a prank.

Grasping the telephone, she contemplated putting through a call to Sam. She couldn't reach him directly, she knew, but she could relay a message through the department. Even they might have trouble; when Sam went undercover, there was often no way to reach him until he resurfaced. She assumed that if it were a dire emergency, contact could be made. Somehow. If it were a dire emergency.

The problem was that she didn't know what kind of an emergency the grim Captain Divine had in mind.

That could be remedied, she decided. But first, she had to be able to think more clearly. To that end, she ran the water in the sink until it was steaming hot, dumped two generous spoonfuls of instant coffee into a cup, filled the cup with the water, and drank it down. While she was waiting for the caffeine to take hold, she went out to the deck and let the chilly night air do its share. Within ten minutes, she felt that while she wasn't as sharp as she might have been, she could safely carry on a conversation without embarrassing either herself or Sam.

Returning to the phone, she punched out the number on the pad. Indeed, it got her though to the Butler Police Department, but to an Officer Sackett.

"Captain Divine, please," she said. "I'm calling on behalf of Sam Craig." She was immediately put through to the man who had called nearly twenty minutes before. "My name is Susan Gardner," she told him. "I'm a close friend of Lieutenant Craig's. Your message came through, but Sam is on duty. I don't know exactly when he'll be able to return your call. If there's a real emergency, I could try to have someone from the department contact him."

"I think you should do that," the man responded. He sounded as grim as he had before, and this time, Susan couldn't blame her muzziness. She was growing more sober by the minute.

"Can I ask what this is about?"

"There's been an accident. Several members of Mr. Craig's family were involved."

"Oh, no," Susan breathed. Her heart was beginning to pound. "If you're calling Sam, it must be bad."

"I think he should get out here as soon as possible."

Susan didn't ask where here was. Sam's family lived in western Pennsylvania; she assumed Butler was in that area. "I'll call the department," she said. "Sam will call you as soon as we reach him."

"I'll be here."

Susan pressed the button to disconnect the call, then quickly punched out the number of the Providence police. Once she relayed the message to the officer who answered the phone, she could do nothing but sit and wait for Sam to call.

The waiting was hard. She tried to imagine where Sam was and what he was doing, but that made her nervous. Then she tried to imagine what kind of accident had befallen his family, which members were involved, and what condition they were in, but that was worse.

By the time an hour had elapsed, she'd realized two things. The first was that she wasn't sure she wanted to be involved with a police officer if it meant waiting, wondering, and worrying while she was totally out of touch. The second was that she wasn't sure she could *avoid* involvement with one, since the level of fear she felt on his behalf was directly related to the depth of her love.

When the phone finally rang, she jumped, then snatched up the receiver. "Sam?"

"This had better be good," he warned.

"Thank God they could reach you," she breathed. "A Captain Divine called from the Butler Police Department. There's been an accident, Sam. He said it involved your family. I don't know the details, but he left a number. He said you should call him as soon as you could."

Sam was silent for a minute before quietly asking for the number.

She gave it to him. "Will you let me know what's happened?"

"Let me see first," he said in that same quiet voice. "Thanks, sweetheart."

Susan replaced the receiver, swallowed hard, then headed back toward the large leather chair. Her eye fell on the Chivas, and she was sorely tempted to reverse the effects of the caffeine and fresh air by taking a healthy dose of the stuff. Except that she didn't feel she could drink a thing. Her stomach was tied in a knot of worry.

But the worry wasn't all. She'd been fumbling through her relationship with Sam, wishing she had more to offer. This was her chance. If he needed her, she wanted to be sober.

Scooping up the bottle of scotch, the glass, and what remained of the bowl of ice from the floor, she put them away, then sank into the sofa to await word from Sam. It came thirty minutes later, but not in the phone call she'd expected. Sam, himself, walked through the front door.

One look at him told her the news was bad. His face was pale, his eyes confused. His shoulders sagged, as though suddenly burdened with an awesome weight.

Taking his hand, Susan held it in both of hers while her eyes asked the question she couldn't quite voice.

"There was an automobile accident," he told her. "My parents were in the car with my sister, Lynn, and her husband. My mother is the only one alive." Susan gasped. "The other three were killed outright. I have to go." Closing his hand around hers, he drew her with him toward the stairs.

"Will she be all right?"

"I don't know. She's in critical condition."

"Oh, Sam," Susan whispered, "I'm so sorry."

He didn't say anything, but he clung to her hand until he'd reached the bedroom, where he dropped it to take a duffel from the closet. "I'm driving straight through," he said as he went to the dresser. "With waits and transfers, it'd take just as long to fly."

Wanting only to help, Susan said, "I'll charter you a plane. I have a friend who's in the business." Then she realized what she'd said. "Forget that. I'll drive with you." She went for her own overnight bag.

Sam went on with his packing. "You don't have to do that."

"I want to do it. If I'm along, one of us can drive while the other sleeps."

"I don't think I'll be doing much sleeping."

"Still, you shouldn't be alone."

"I'm used to it."

"Not at a time like this." She took a skirt, then a pair of pumps from the closet, infinitely grateful that she had a fair supply of clothes there. Sam would never have considered her going if they had to stop in Newport first. "Besides, I'd rather be with you than stay here."

She was pressing the skirt into her bag when Sam put a hand on her arm. "This won't be fun," he cautioned. "I'm going to have to arrange three funerals. At least."

Tears came to her eyes. "That's why I should be there," she said. Wrapping her arms around his neck, she gave him a quick hug. "I love you, Sam. I want to be with you."

For an instant, arms trembling, he completed the embrace and held her tightly. Then he released her and returned to his packing. After another minute and without looking up, he said in a low voice, "Could you phone your friend? If he can get someone to fly us there, it would save hours."

Susan didn't have to be asked twice. With a single phone call, she'd arranged for the flight. They'd be going in a private plane, one that was smaller and less luxurious than that in which she, Savannah, and Megan had flown to Florida, but she didn't mind, and she was sure Sam wouldn't. She didn't think he'd see his surroundings at all. His mind was in Butler.

The flight was an uneasy one. The plane had to plow its way through rain clouds that thickened the night. But they landed safely, and an unmarked police car was waiting to drive them directly to the hospital, where a doctor apprised Sam of his mother's condition.

She was in the intensive care unit. Having suffered multiple fractures, the most severe to her skull, she was unconscious. The prognosis was bleak.

Walking down the hall with Sam toward the ICU, Susan could feel his anguish radiating through the fingers that held hers so tightly. She was close enough to him to know what he was feeling far more than fear for his mother's life. He hadn't seen the woman in fifteen years. At that moment, he was deeply regretting the separation.

Susan paused at the door to the glass-enclosed unit. When Sam glanced quickly at her, she whispered, "You go in. She doesn't know me."

But he tugged on her hand. His eyes were wide, pleading in the way of a man not accustomed to pleading.

Susan didn't hesitate any longer. She'd made a decision

back in Providence, when she'd put away the scotch, that she wanted to be there for Sam. He needed her now.

Janet Craig looked pale and fragile against the pristine white sheets. A small woman, she'd reached her midfifties with a minimum of wear. Only the finest of lines, sprinkled at the corners of her eyes and mouth, marred the softness of her skin. Her hair was the same natural brown shade as Sam's.

While Susan saw all that, Sam only saw the bandages that swept diagonally around her head, the tube that was taped to her mouth, the machines by her bed, the needles that forged entry to her veins. She was his mother. He knew what she was supposed to look like, and it wasn't this.

"Mom," he whispered. Dropping Susan's hand, he bent over the still figure on the bed. "Mom?" He cleared his throat and forced himself to speak louder. "Mom? It's Sam."

His voice cracked at his name. Afraid she would cry, Susan pressed a fist to her mouth. Her throat was so tight that she doubted she'd have been able to say a word. But Sam either had greater strength than she, greater determination, or both.

"I'm here, Mom. Just got in a little while ago. The doctors are taking really good care of you. You'll be fine. Just fine." He paused. "Can you hear me, Mom?"

His mother showed no sign of awareness.

Sam wore a look of raw fear when he glanced up at Susan, but there was little she could say to ease his grief. The doctor hadn't left much room for hope.

With the lightest of hands, Sam touched his mother's cheek. His fingers trembled on her hair, then on her arm. Taking care around the intravenous needle, he slipped his fingers through hers.

"When I was little," he murmured, moving his thumb over her pale skin, "she used to hold my hand. I always thought it was because she was afraid I'd run off and get lost, and she probably was, but I liked it when she did it. She wasn't an openly loving person, but when she held my hand I felt safe. Loved."

He leaned close again. "I'm here, Mom. I'm going to take care of you. Just open your eyes and look at me. Know I'm here."

Susan pressed her fist harder against her mouth.

"It's Sam. Can you hear me, Mom? It's Sam." He held his breath, watching in vain for a response that didn't come. After an interminable minute, he let that breath escape. "I'm going to see Dad now." his voice broke again, but he forced himself on. "I'll be back, Mom. You work on getting better for me. Okay?"

Tears were pooling on his lower lids when he turned to face Susan. He took her hand again, then, as though knowing that he needed more, drew her close and held her tight. His voice was a ragged whisper by her ear. "It shouldn't have happened this way. Not this way."

Susan didn't know whether he was talking about the accident or his reunion with his family. Neither should have happened that way, she knew. "Don't give up hope," she whispered. "Modern medicine can do wonders."

"They think she's already brain-dead."

"Wait till they know it. Don't assume the worst until then."

Dragging in ragged breath, Sam straightened. He glanced back at his mother, called, "I'll be back, Mom," then took Susan's hand again and led her out to the hall, where he looked down at her. "Do you want to go somewhere to wait?"

Susan knew where he was going. He had to identify the bodies of his father, sister, and brother-in-law. It promised to be a heartrending task. He was giving her an out.

But she shook her head. "I'd rather stay with you."

"You don't have to. I'm okay."

"I want to."

"Are you sure?"

She nodded.

He didn't smile; she doubted he was capable of it just then. But the way he held her hand, keeping her close by his side as they walked toward the elevator, told her that he appreciated what she was doing, and as long as that was the case, she knew she'd do whatever she could to ease his pain, even if it meant increasing her own.

The elevator opened. They entered it and began the short trip to hell.

Fifteen minutes later, the same elevator returned them to the ICU floor. They were both paler and more drawn. Heads down, they started down the dim corridor toward Janet Craig's room, only to stop at the sound of Sam's name and look up.

A policewoman stood by the nurse's station holding the hand of a tousle-haired little girl who looked to be no more than five. The child was wearing a light jacket and sneakers over flannel pajamas. Her eyes were large and frightened.

For a minute, Sam didn't breathe. Then he whispered, "My God. Oh my God." Slowly, he approached the little girl. Though his voice had risen above a whisper, it was hoarse. "Courtney?" He reached out to touch her face, but she shrank back against her custodian.

"She was with a sitter," the policewoman explained softly. "It's better that she be with family."

Bewildered, Sam looked from the woman to the child and back. "Where's John's family?" He'd thought for sure that his brother-in-law had parents or siblings in the area.

But the policewoman silently shook her head.

The look Sam sent Susan verged on panic. She was feeling a little of it herself. If Sam's mother died, Sam would inherit a daughter. He didn't know what to do with a child. Neither did she.

Someone had to do something, though. The policewoman couldn't stand there forever holding the child's hand, and the child was obviously scared.

Trying to recall what people had said to her when she was six and had been separated from her mother and Savannah in Saks, Susan came forward and squatted before the little girl. "Courtney's a beautiful name," she said gently. "Do you have a middle one?"

The child nodded.

Susan waited. When the name wasn't forthcoming, she said, "I bet it's Jane."

The child shook her head.

"Alice?" Susan asked.

Another headshake.

Susan tried again. "Dawn?"

"It's Marie," Sam told her without taking his eyes from his niece.

Susan gave him a quick glance of thanks, then turned back to Courtney. "He knows that because he's your uncle. His name's Sam. Samuel John Craig."

"I don't know him," the child said in a small, high voice.

"That's because he lives way off in Rhode Island. But he's your mommy's brother."

"Where is my mommy? She was supposed to bring me a Kit Kat, but it wasn't there when I woke up."

Susan shot a helpless glance in Sam's direction. At her silent bidding, he, too, hunkered down. "It's still the middle of the night," he said. "Are you tired?"

The child shook her head. Her eyes were wary, her tiny lips pressed together as though she might cry.

Susan didn't want that to happen. Nor did she want another question about Courtney's mom. Eventually the answer would have to come, but now wasn't the time. Instinct told her that it was critical to establish rapport with the child.

So she exclaimed softly, "Oh my, what's this?" The tip of something promising was peeking from the child's jacket pocket. Very carefully pulling on a furry white ear, she extricated a small stuffed bunny.

"That's Peter," Courtney told her.

"Peter Rabbit?" Susan cradled the miniature creature in her hand. "He's adorable!"

"The Easter bunny brought him. They're cousins."

"Peter and the Easter Bunny? You must be very special for the Easter bunny to give you one of his cousins."

One shoulder moved in a half-pint shrug, while she pinched in the corner of her mouth.

Sam spoke then. "Do you have any cousins of your own? Any people cousins?" He was having trouble grasping the fact that he might be the child's only living relative.

Courtney went silent again and shook her head.

Susan knew what Sam was getting at. In an attempt to help, she said, "You must have had quite some Easter to get a bunny like this. Did your grandma make dinner?"

"Mommy did," the little girl told her.

"Were your grandma and grandpa there?"

Courtney nodded.

"Who else was there?"

"Just my daddy."

"Any aunts and uncles?"

Courtney shook her head, then said in that small, high voice, "I don't have any of those. Betsy Winters says I can have some of hers. She hates them."

Sam remembered all the times he'd tried to send things to his niece, and he felt a sudden urge to take the child in his arms. But she'd made it clear that he frightened her, so, instead, he said, "You have an uncle now, Courtney. I'll take good care of you."

"I want my mommy."

"Are you hungry? Would you like something to eat?"

"I want my mommy."

"How about a Kit Kat? I'll bet we could find one somewhere in a machine."

"I don't want *your* Kit Kat," she said. Her chin was beginning to tremble. "I want my mommy's."

Susan's heart was breaking, not only for the child but for Sam. He was doing his best to put the little girl at ease, but he hadn't had much practice with children. And even if he'd been an expert, he wasn't at his best. The family he hadn't seen for fifteen years, but had held in his heart far longer than that, had suddenly been torn from him. He was in mild shock.

Susan shot a beseechful glance at the policewoman, thinking that maybe she'd know something brilliant to say. But the woman was younger than Susan, wore no wedding band, and had "I'm only the courier" stamped on her face. Even as Susan looked at her, she glanced at her watch.

Courtney continued to stare at Sam. "Is he a boy or a girl?" she asked no one in particular.

Grateful for the diversion, Susan answered. "Sam? He's a boy."

"But he's got long hair. Only girls have long hair."

"Boys do sometimes. Sam's is only long in back. I kinda like it."

"I don't. I don't like him. I don't want him for my uncle."

The policewoman did speak then, showing more insight than Susan would have credited her with moments before. "I think you're being used as a scapegoat, Mr. Craig."

Sam could understand that. It didn't make things any easier for him, though. Nor did thinking how much better things would have been if the child had known him. That was water over the dam.

But something had to be done. Marshaling his thoughts, Sam reached into the back pocket of his jeans and pulled out his badge and identification. "My name's Sam," he told Courtney, "just like Susan said. I'm a detective with the police department." He offered the leather folder that held the badge and ID to the child. "Want to hold it?"

Courtney was still looking wary, but she did raise one small hand to take the folder.

"I don't wear a uniform," Sam went on, "because that scares people off sometimes. I try to look like just anybody on the street." As he said it, he realized that wouldn't make any sense to the child. If she'd never seen a man with long hair, she wasn't going to believe that he looked like just anybody on the street, and he wasn't about to tell her about rapists, pushers, and pimps. "Do you really think my hair's too long?"

Courtney nodded.

"I could cut it if that would make you feel better."

She moved her head and shoulder in a way that said she didn't know whether that would make her feel better or not.

"Maybe you'll think about it and let me know," he said.

Without giving an answer, Courtney looked at Susan. "I have to go to the bathroom."

Susan swallowed, then stood. "Okay." She slid her damp palms down the sides of her jeans and held out her hand.

Courtney looked up at the policewoman, who said, "You go ahead. I'll bet Susan's even better at pajama snaps than I am." She held her hand, to which Courtney still clung, out to Susan.

"I'm *great* at pajama snaps," Susan said as she took the child's hand. Knowing that the policewoman would be gone before she returned, she mouthed a quick "Thank you," then turned to Sam, who had risen also. "Why don't you go down the hall?" she suggested softly, cocking her head in the direction of his mother's room. "Courtney and I will take our time. We'll go exploring. Maybe we'll even find some hot chocolate and doughnuts." She gave the child's hand a playful tug. "How does that sound?"

Courtney made the same I-don't-know gesture with her head and shoulder, but the neutrality of the response didn't bother Susan at all. She was feeling an odd sense of control. And she was helping Sam.

He knew it and was grateful. After fifteen long years, he wanted to spend some time with his mother. There were things he wanted to say to her, whether she heard him or not, before she died.

Seeking a bit of Susan's warmth, he curved his hand around the back of her neck. His eyes showed the thanks that he couldn't put into either a smile or words. He did manage a small smile for Courtney because he knew how much she needed it. Then, with a knot in his throat, he watched the two of them head off down the hall.

His mother died late that afternoon. He'd been with her through most of the day and was holding her hand when her heart finally stilled. Aware of what had to be done, he forced himself through the business of arranging for the funerals. He spent a sad hour walking through the house he'd grown up in, then joined Susan and Courtney at his sister's house, less than a mile away.

Late Thursday night, Susan reached Savannah at Jared's. "I didn't want you to worry," she said after she'd explained where she was and why, but that was only one of the reasons she'd called. She felt as though her own life had taken a drastic turn. She needed Savannah's levelheadedness and encouragement.

"I feel so bad for Sam. He's crushed."

Savannah, who loved Sam in her own platonic way, grieved for him, too. "How's he handling it?"

"He hasn't broken down and torn at his clothes, if that's what you mean, but he's in awful pain. It's there in his eyes. Who wouldn't be? He's just lost both of his parents and his only sibling. And he's become the father of a child who's as upset as he is."

"Does the little girl know the truth?"

"Sam told her tonight. He figured he had to, but I'm wondering whether it would have been better to have a priest do it. Courtney's decided that Sam's the bad guy in all this. She doesn't like him very much, which doesn't bode well, considering that she's going to be living with him for the next thirteen years."

"Then he'll be bringing her back to Providence?"

"There's no one else at all. He has some distant cousins; there are some on his brother-in-law's side. But none of them know Courtney. None are even close enough to know what's happened. And even if one of them offered to take her, I doubt Sam would let her go. And he shouldn't. She's his sister's child."

Twirling the telephone cord around her fingers, Susan spoke in a loud, desperate whisper. "What am I going to do, Savvy? I'm not ready to be a mother. I have enough trouble wondering whether I can be what Sam wants, and now all of a sudden this little girl comes along. She's adorable. I really like her, and she's taken to me more than she has to Sam, for what it's worth. But she's a *child*, Savvy. She's little more than a *baby*. I'm *lousy* with kids. What am I going to do?"

"First off," Savannah said, "you're going to stay calm. You won't be any good to anyone unless you do."

"You don't understand," Susan went on in that same frantic half-whisper. "She has to be taken *care* of. I'm talking the most basic needs. While Sam was at the hospital this morning, Courtney and I came back here. I had to help her get dressed. I had to make her lunch. I had to figure out something to do to keep her busy. She needs help taking a bath and brushing her teeth and combing her hair. And that's just the tip of the iceberg. Sam may not be thinking about it yet; he's still trying to deal with the shock of the deaths. But I'm thinking about it. Courtney needs a room to sleep in. She needs clothes. She has to be enrolled in school. She has to be looked after while Sam's at work, and you know what his schedule's like."

She paused to take a breath. "I mean, talk about putting pressure on a relationship. I'm not sure where I stand with Sam. He's never mentioned marriage. I'm his lover. That's it. His lover. So what happens to that, now that he's an instant father? What am I *doing*?"

Savannah used the silence that followed as a buffer between emotion and reason. "What you're doing," she said slowly and gently, "is helping Sam cope with an incredibly frightening situation."

"I'm scared to death myself. How can I possibly help him?"

"You did it today. You took care of Courtney. You might not know what to do with a child, but you managed today. She survived, didn't she?"

"Barely."

"Barely is better than not at all. The poor child must be feeling lost and lonely."

"So am I. Sam's sound asleep. We were up all last night, and today's been a nightmare. But he sleeps while I sit here and worry." She moaned, then muttered, "God, I need a drink."

"That's the *last* thing you need. You have to be able to think straight."

"I'm not sure that'll help. I'm telling you, Savvy, I'm in over my head."

"You are not. You can handle anything you set your mind to."

"*You're* the one who can do that. Not me."

"Yes, you. You have an incredible opportunity here. You love Sam, don't you?"

"If I didn't, I'd have been long gone by now."

"So if you love him, you'll make things work."

"You're not *hearing* me, Savannah. I don't know *how* to make things work."

"You'll learn. You'll take one day at a time. You'll feel your way along."

"Yeah. Right along the ground in the dirt. And I'm apt to bring Sam and Courtney right down there with me."

"You can *do* it, Susan. I'm telling you. You can *do* it!"

"I'm glad someone believes in me."

"Sam does. Otherwise, he'd never had brought you along. He needs your help. And don't you see? This is your chance to show him that you can do what needs to be done. It's your chance to show *yourself* that you're perfectly capable of being what Sam wants." She hesitated, then spoke more softly. "I'm envious of you. You can really have it all."

Of the many words Savannah had said that night, those were the ones that lingered longest with Susan.

Chapter 21

MEGAN HAD ADMIRED SAVANNAH from the very first of their academy days. While Susan was the more gregarious, perhaps the more exciting of the two, Savannah had been the one with the level head on her shoulders. She was the one the others sought out when things got rough, and Megan had done her share of the seeking.

Technically, Megan was bright, and she knew it. What she didn't always know was how to channel that intelligence along the most productive lines. Savannah, on the other hand, was a master of the overview. She could stand back and analyze a situation, then suggest the best course of action.

Megan had consciously studied Savannah's approach. She firmly believed that if she could master it, she'd have the world in the palm of her hands, and for a while, it looked as though she'd done it. She graduated from the academy near the top of her class, went through college with similar ranking, and landed a plum of a job as the mathematical consultant to an electronics conglomerate headquartered in Boston. While she had no intention of working her life away, her job gave her exposure to some of the most successful entrepreneurs in the Northeast.

She hadn't made the most of that situation. Though she was a math whiz, she was far less sure of herself socially. She'd been intimidated by some of the men she'd met, turned off by others. When, totally out of the professional context, she met gentle, unimposing William Vandermeer, she readily fell in love.

For several years, she was unabashedly happy. She didn't work, and she didn't miss it. Then the business began to flounder. She helped Will out where she could, but the downward spiral continued. When things got so bad that Will was taking pills to sleep and she spent half the night worrying herself sick, she took a leaf from Savannah's book, analyzed the situation, and came up with the one solution that seemed to hold hope of returning things to where they'd been.

It would have worked had it not been for Matty Stavanovich.

Now Matty was in prison awaiting trial, and Megan felt a measure of satisfaction in that. She was furious whenever she thought of him, and when she wasn't furious, she was afraid. She'd covered her tracks; she was sure of it. But she didn't trust Stavanovich. She'd done that once. She wasn't making the same mistake twice.

Between fear, anger, and a guilt that never left her for long, she wasn't good for much of anything but wandering aimlessly through the house. She didn't want to go out, didn't want to be seen. Everyone in town knew what had happened. She couldn't bear the thought of their stares. So she stayed within the protective walls of her house and agonized.

Stand back. Look at things from a distance. That was what Savannah always said, and Megan tried to do it, but she'd never had to face anything like this before.

Take it step by step, day by day. Savannah always said that, too, and while Megan was a little more successful there, she still found it hard.

For one thing, she couldn't talk with Will as she used to. He treated her with kid gloves, and she let him. At times she wished he'd get angry, so that she could blurt out the truth. After all, what she'd done, she'd done for love. But he never raised his voice to her, and she couldn't make herself tell him. He was overtaxed as it was, since the business was in worse shape than ever.

For another thing, the rest of the world seemed to be merrily making its way through May and into June. Friends of theirs were busy opening summer homes on Nantucket or in Bar Harbor. Others were in the final stages of planning trips that Megan would have given anything to take, if only to get her out of Rhode Island and away from the mess of her life.

Even Susan was on the move. Understandably, her time was in short supply, but since she was spending so much more of it at Sam's place in Providence, she saw Megan often. Usually she had Courtney with her, and though she talked on the sly of being a lousy mother, Megan couldn't see any sign of that. More often than not, Susan sent home the woman Sam had insisted she hire and took care of the child herself. She clearly loved the little girl, clearly loved Sam. Megan was sure they would marry one day.

Savannah, too, visited often, but her visits were as much business as pleasure, since she brought the latest news on the case against Matty. Most often, that news concerned one pretrial motion or another that had been filed, argued, won, or lost. At other times, the news was more pithy.

There was the day when Savannah told Megan that a witness had been found who saw a Mercedes leave Matty's shop at midnight on the night of the kidnapping. And the day when she told Megan that of four Mercedeses in Matty's shop at the time, one of the owners, who'd left her car for the week while she'd been in Palm Beach, claimed that the odometer read ten miles less when she picked it up than when she'd left it, which suggested tampering. Then, of course, there was the day when Savannah triumphantly announced that Matty's alibi had been broken. Susan's hunch had been right; the Mexican guide who'd spent the better part of a day shuttling a Matty Stavanovich from one ruin to another was vehement that the man he'd driven around was not the same as the one in the picture shown him by the police.

Still, Megan's testimony was the key to the case. That meant Savannah's reviewing it with her again and again and again. Once would have been too much for Megan; the repetition nearly drove her wild. But it served its purpose. With each run through of the questions that either Savannah or the defense attorney might ask, Megan grew more sure of her script. Indeed, there were times when she began to imagine that her testimony was the whole truth and nothing but.

It was the other times that got to her, though, the times when fear took over. Those were the times when, in the dark of night, she picked up the phone and called Jared.

He was wonderful. He no longer asked her name, but he recognized her voice and was incredibly gentle. Yes, he coaxed her to tell him what was wrong. She'd have been disappointed if he hadn't. He wanted to help, but unless she told him the truth, he couldn't do that.

She couldn't tell him, of course. She couldn't incriminate herself that way. She supposed she gave little hints from time to time, but she couldn't imagine that he'd put two and two together, and even if he did, he wouldn't betray her. Their late-night talks were private and special. If he didn't feel that, she reasoned, he wouldn't answer the phone.

She was infinitely grateful that he did. She doubted he understood how much comfort he brought her, though on more than one occasion she'd tried to tell him. He was always calm and together. If the sound of his voice on the radio was soothing, the sound of his voice on the phone was even more so. She called more often as the trial approached, needing more frequent assurance that things would work out.

Savannah, too, grew more keyed up as the trial approached. She showed no signs of nervousness at the office, where she juggled her full load of cases with the same competence as always, but she was having trouble eating, and sleep came only in two- to three-hour shifts.

That was why, at four in the morning, she was in the office within sight of Jared when one of the calls from Megan came through. She'd been sitting at the desk, making notes on a yellow legal pad when the telephone rang. She looked up in time to see Jared lift the receiver.

For a minute, looking at him, she forgot about the call. He was a beautiful man; she'd thought it the first time she'd seen him, and she thought it even more now. Though she knew his body nearly as well as she did her own, there were times like this when, in a flash of fresh awareness, she had to stop and catch her breath. Wearing denim cutoffs, he seemed all tawny, hair-spattered legs. His T-shirt hugged his chest and shoulders; his arms were every bit as well formed and masculine as his legs. And his hair, the hair she loved to touch, fell as casually as ever over his brow.

Swiveling around in his chair to use the control table as a backrest, he cradled the phone to his ear, bringing her thoughts back to the call he'd received. He didn't look at all surprised by it. From time to time he frowned, but there was a gentleness to his expression that aroused Savannah's curiosity.

"Who is it?" she mouthed.

He held up a finger to say he'd answer her shortly, which she took to mean that it wasn't a simple matter of mouthing a name. He didn't talk for long, no more than five or six minutes, but as soon as he'd hung up the phone, he put on the headphones and went on the air to announce the time, the weather, and the songs he was playing. When he'd finished doing that, he set the headphones on the console and went to the door of the booth. Opening it wide, he leaned against the doorjamb.

Savannah's eyes asked the question she'd mouthed earlier, and for a minute Jared stood there looking puzzled. Then he shrugged.

"I don't know who it was," he said. "I've been getting the calls on and off for a while now."

"You talked. You looked like you knew."

"In one sense I do. It's the same caller each time."

Savannah shot a glance at the clock on the wall. "At four in the morning?"

"Sometimes earlier, sometimes later. She varies the day and the time."

"She?"

Pushing off from the doorjamb, Jared strolled over to where Savannah sat. "Not to worry." He slipped his fingers into her hair and exerted just enough pressure to tip her head back. "You're my only girl." He planted a firm kiss on her lips.

"But she calls you in the middle of the night while I'm asleep," Savannah teased in the last breath of the kiss. Less teasingly, she asked, "What does she say?"

"Not much." He sat on the edge of the desk, took her hand, and wove his fingers through hers. "She says that talking with me calms her. She never stays on long, and she apologizes for taking my time. But she's upset about something, something that's very wrong in her life. She won't tell me what it is."

"How often does she call?"

"Once a week, maybe a little less." He thought about that, then corrected himself. "It's been more lately. That was the second call in a week."

Savannah found the idea of a nameless woman's fixation a little frightening. "I thought you didn't take calls like that."

"I don't. But she calls on my private line. I remember when she did it the first time, I let the conversation go on because I wanted to find out how she got that number."

"Did you?"

"No. And I still don't know. The only people who have that number are people who have good cause to have it. I can't believe one of them is passing it around. And it's not like she dialed it by accident. She said my name right off the bat."

"Scary," Savannah said. "She could be a little nuts."

"We're all a little nuts. She doesn't sound unusually so, just troubled."

"Maybe you shouldn't take the calls."

"You're not jealous?" he chided.

"No," she said, and she wasn't. "But the more you talk, the more involved you get. If she had problems, she should see a professional. She may seem only a little nuts now, but what if she gets worse?"

Jared hadn't thought about that. "I feel sorry for her. She's a sad character. And the calls are harmless. Not once has she said anything threatening or suggestive. Sexual innuendo is the farthest thing from her mind."

Savannah tried to imagine the conversations they might have had. "Have you been able to learn anything about her?"

Taking a deep breath, he pressed her hand flat on his bare thigh. He never tired of the feel of Savannah's skin on his. "She evades personal questions, but little things have come out."

"Like?"

"Like she's married."

"That's good," Savannah said in quick relief. "Then again, maybe not. What kind of married woman calls another man in the middle of the night? What's her husband doing though all his?"

"Sleeping, I guess. I've never heard any voices in the background. I picture her being alone in whatever room she's in."

"Do you have any idea of her age?"

"Sounds like she could be anywhere between twenty-five and forty. If I had to pin it down, I'd say in her early thirties."

"And you don't know what her problem is?"

"She talks about thinking things out and then messing up. She compares being rich to being poor. I get the impression that she started out poor and has had a taste of rich, but is about to lose it."

"Then money is the core of her troubles."

"In some ways. In other ways, she's more upset about deception. She talks about that a lot. She seems to feel that she's lied to the people she loves, and she's having trouble dealing with it."

"Do you have any idea where she lives?"

"She won't say. If the calls become troublesome, I'd have the phone company put a tap on the line."

"Maybe you ought to do that anyway."

But Jared didn't want to just yet. He felt an odd sense of loyalty to the woman. She asked so little, just an ear and a few words of encouragement. Turning her in seemed like a betrayal.

Savannah sensed his reluctance. "If she's calling more often, it could be because things are getting worse for her. Maybe she really needs help."

"I keep pushing that. I have names to give her—psychiatrist, social worker, bank loan officer, priest—but she isn't buying."

"Maybe you ought to call the psychiatrist anyway."

"And do what? He can't sit here waiting for her call. She can't be forced into treatment."

"Does she sound high on drugs or anything?"

"No. Just scared."

"You should call the psychiatrist."

But Jared couldn't do that. "I'll wait. Just for a little while."

"Doesn't she make you nervous?"

"No. I told you. She's harmless." He squeezed her hand. "Really, babe."

Savannah eyed him dryly. "If she's so harmless, how come you didn't tell me about her?"

There was no mystery to it. "Because you've always been sleeping when she's called before, and by the time I get upstairs I have other things on my mind." They both knew what those other things were. "Besides, you've been busy lately. This is nothing, Savannah. Really." Tightening his fingers around hers, he drew her up and held her between his thighs. In a softer, more sandy voice, he said, "How do you feel?"

"Pretty good."

"You should be tired."

She shrugged, but there was a look in her eye that said she knew what he was thinking.

"Are you?" he asked softly.

"I don't know."

"When were you due?"

"Last week."

"You're not usually late."

"I know," she said, then slipped her arms around his neck and hugged him. "I'm afraid to hope."

He ran tender hands over her back. She was wearing a soft, white nightgown that flowed to her ankles and gave her a delicate look and feel. "You said it wouldn't happen till after the trial."

"I was close. The trial starts in two weeks."

"You should see a doctor."

"Too early."

"Then do a test at home."

"I'd rather wait. My body will let me know if it's true, and there's nothing I can do differently in the meanwhile."

He held her back. "You can take it easy."

"No. I have to prepare for this trial."

"What if you push yourself too much and something happens?"

"Then it wasn't meant to be."

"But you want the baby?"

She smiled. "Uh-huh."

"And me? Do you want me?"

"Wanting you was never the issue."

"I don't mean sex."

"Neither do I. The issue wasn't whether I wanted you, but whether you wanted me."

Locking his hands at the back of her waist, Jared was quick to protest. "I never had the slightest doubt—"

"Maybe I said that wrong," she interrupted. "The issue was my *believing* that you want me."

"How can you question it?"

"You know how. We've been through it before."

"But time has passed. Do I seem unhappy living with you?"

She thought about it for a minute, then shook her head.

"Right," he said. "I've lived just fine with your schedule. And with you. You give me everything I want and need."

"But I'm a walking—"

"—law brief. You've said that before. But I seem to remember three times in the last six weeks when you played hostess to, all told, nearly two dozen of my business associates."

"I didn't play hostess. Other people did the work."

"So you didn't do the cooking yourself. No career

woman has time for that. But you made the arrangements—twice at restaurants, once with a caterer on the boat."

"Susan told me what to do."

"But you did it, and don't tell me it wasn't a whole lot of work, because I know it was. Food, flowers, tables and chairs, background music—you coordinated everything. And then you stood there by my side, looking absolutely gorgeous, so calm and collected that no one could believe you'd put in a full day at the office." He caught his breath, but nothing could stop the flow of warmth in his eyes. "Do you have any idea how proud I was of you?"

Savannah felt the warmth of that pride as a glowing ember deep inside her. "You've told me," she said humbly.

"And I'll tell you again. And again. You played hostess, and you did it with flair. Face it, lawyer lady, you're not quite as limited as you thought." He took a deep, slow breath. "So, do you believe that I want you?"

She hesitated for just a minute. "I'm getting there. I have doubts sometimes. But you're still hanging around." She shot a look at her surroundings and amended that to, "*I'm* still hanging around."

"Only because I have to work. Otherwise I'd be at your place. Or on the boat. But I don't like the idea of your being there while I'm here working. This way I can run upstairs and check on you."

"Against FCC regulations," she reminded him with a crooked grin.

"Ahhh," he teased, "such a stickler for legalities."

"I always was. Susan called me a goody-two-shoes. I played by the book, while she broke every rule."

"Goody-two-shoes?"

She nodded. Too late, she realized that she'd set herself up.

"If you play by the book," Jared advised in a dead-serious drawl, "then we have to get married. We're in love. We're living together. And you may be pregnant."

"Later."

"Pregnant?"

"Married. We'll get married later."

"Why wait?"

"Because I can't think straight with this trial coming up."

"So? I love you anyway."

"This trial is really important to me, Jared."

"I can understand why. But just think. If we get married now, one part of your life will be completely settled. You'll be able to focus your concentration that much more."

"Could work the other way around," she reminded him. "I could be that much more distracted."

"I won't distract you."

"You do. All the time. Take now. Since I couldn't sleep, I was going to do some work. So here you are." She glanced toward the sound room. "Aren't you supposed to be in there getting ready to fade something or other in or out?"

"In a minute." Lowering his head, he kissed her gently, then deepened the kiss until she'd begun to melt against him. Only then did he warn, "I won't let you go. I'll keep after you until you give in. We're going to be married, Savannah. Count on it."

Later, thinking back on those words, he had to commend himself for his confidence. Because the fact was that he could tell her whatever he wanted, but the decision was hers. When it came to determining the future direction of their relationship, she was the one in the driver's seat.

*   *   *

Savannah felt in control as the trial approached. Her exhibits were ready. Her witnesses were ready. She spent the Fourth of July weekend with Jared on the boat preparing her opening argument, until she had it planned to her satisfaction, presentation and all.

The trial was to start on Wednesday. On Tuesday night, she had a minor attack of the shakes. Jared was working. She was upstairs, and her first thought was to run down to him. Then she stopped, turned up the radio, and let the balm of his voice wash over her.

Her mind wandered where it would, free-associating. Not surprisingly, her free associations centered on Jared. What surprised her was the speed with which her body calmed. It wasn't that she was any less nervous about the trial, or any less determined to win a conviction. But for the first time, approaching a trial, she saw the trial in a broader context. Other things had come to mean as much to her as the law. She'd achieved a certain perspective. Her life had filled out.

All of Wednesday and the first of Thursday were spent picking a jury. Shortly after eleven that second morning, Savannah gave her opening argument. She spoke for fifty minutes, outlining the contents of her case. The talk during the lunch break was unanimous in commending the power of her statement. When court reconvened, she was feeling as confident as she ever had.

That confidence was shattered over the course of the next thirty minutes. In an argument delivered with flair, the Cat's attorney, a surprisingly straight lawyer named Walter Woodward, stunned not only Savannah, but every other lawyer, media representative, and spectator in the room by claiming that the mastermind of the kidnapping had been none other than the supposed victim, Megan Vandermeer.

Savannah listened in disbelief, and for several minutes after he was done, her rage was such that she was nearly paralyzed inside. On the outside, though, she was the image of self-control. That self-control was critical. While a case was to be tried on its facts, the jury had eyes. The jury saw everything. Just as it would see that Stavanovich was being represented by a lawyer as clean-cut and dignified as Megan's husband, so it would see that Savannah was confident enough in her case not to be affected by the bizarre claims of the defense.

Once past that moment of immobility, her mind shot into gear and sped onward. The first thing she did prior to opening her case was to approach the bench and request that the jury be sequestered. Her argument was that the media would have a field day with the defense's claims, and that sequestering was the only way to ensure an unbiased jury. Woodward fought it. Even the judge was reluctant; sequestering a jury involved considerable work and taxpayer expense. But he didn't want a conviction overturned on appeal any more than Savannah did. So he agreed. The jury was polled. Only one member, a woman with children in day-care, found being sequestered a hardship. That juror was excused and one of the four alternates was named in her place.

Savannah opened her case then, calling Will as her first witness in an attempt to establish that a kidnapping had indeed taken place. Question by question, she led him through that day in March, from the time when he'd discovered his wife missing to the meeting he'd had with Paul, Anthony, and herself. She put the ransom note into evidence, deliberately making eye contact with each of the jurors as she walked the note past for their inspection. Throughout her questioning of Will, she stressed the shock he had experienced and the anguish he'd felt.

Cross-examining him, Woodward emphasized the failing of the family business and the stress both Vandermeers had been under. Will held up well under his questioning. He strongly refuted Woodward's subtle suggestions that Megan was dissatisfied with him and his inability to support her in style. When court recessed for the day, Savannah felt that her case had held firm.

Megan had spent the day in Savannah's office. Her reaction upon learning of the defense argument was much the same as Savannah's had been. She went utterly still, momentarily stunned, before erupting into a fury.

"That bastard!" she spat. Her eyes were wide, her nostrils flaring with each labored breath she took. "That *bastard!*"

"The jury will think so, too," Savannah said in an attempt to calm her. "You'll see. By the time we've put our case before them, they'll be livid that Stavanovich should even *hint* that you were involved."

Savannah took her prediction a step further when, several hours later, she met Jared for dinner at a small Italian restaurant that had become a favorite of theirs. "It's another version of the old line that the woman who's raped incited it. You watch," she said angrily. "He'll claim she asked for that rape. Despite the medical testimony showing how battered and bruised she was, he'll claim she invited it."

Jared considered that possibility. "He's taking a big chance. Your jury is seven females to five males."

"Thank goodness. I'll have to count on those women being as incensed as I am. Can you believe it, Jared? Can you believe he'd say that? Megan has never, *never* committed a crime. She's as honest as the day is long. Do you think she'd truly be capable of planning and carrying out her own kidnapping?"

Jared wished he could answer, but the fact was that he didn't know Megan. She was the one person close to Savannah whom he hadn't yet met, much less spent time with. Savannah regretted it, he knew; she apologized often. But Megan had refused to leave the house for anything remotely social, and when Savannah suggested bringing Jared around, she seemed so uncomfortable that Savannah chickened out. Time enough when the trial was done, she reasoned.

Jared had been satisfied with that until now. Since he'd heard Woodward's opening argument that afternoon, weird things had been running through his mind. Time and again he pushed them away. Still they returned, pesty little germs of doubt that wouldn't leave him alone.

He debated discussing them with Savannah, but at that moment her anger was intense. It had abated somewhat by the time they'd finished dinner, but by then she was looking so tired that he was reluctant to reopen the wound. So he kept his doubts to himself, brought her home, and put her to bed, then went to work.

First thing Friday morning, Savannah called Sam to the stand. An experienced witness and, therefore relatively easy to lead through direct examination, he testified not only to what he'd found when he'd arrived at the Vandermeer house on the day of the kidnapping, but to the work he and Hank had done there that afternoon and on succeeding days. Savannah introduced into evidence the tape of the kidnapper calling to arrange the drop. Sam also described Will's emotional state. The defense objected to this line of questioning but was overruled. The overall effect of his testimony, as summed up more than once by Savannah, was that a legitimate act of violence had been committed.

Woodward asked one or two token questions, then sat down.

The agent from the insurance company, whom Savannah called to the stand next, corroborated what Sam had said. Savannah made a point of drawing out, then repeating the fact that Will had bought the policy soon after he'd married Megan, and that such policies weren't unusual among the wealthy.

Woodward had no questions for the agent.

Following the lunch break, Savannah called the Warwick police officer who had been in the first cruiser to arrive at the telephone booth in which Megan had been dumped. He described her condition, described her reactions to the arrival of her husband, described Sam's taking her off in his car.

Savannah had time to get in the first of the medical testimony before court recessed for the day. Since the jury was sequestered, the judge called for a Saturday session, which suited Savannah's purposes just fine. She felt the momentum was hers and was just as happy not to break it.

It took all of Saturday for her to get through the medical witnesses. There was a doctor to testify to Megan's physical condition when she'd been brought to the hospital, both a rape counselor and a psychiatrist to testify to her emotional state. Knowing that the medical testimony was critical given the defense's chosen approach, Savannah took her time and spared no detail. Indeed, the picture painted was so brutal that she was grateful Megan wasn't in the courtroom to hear it. She had a hard enough time with it herself.

As always, though, no one knew that but Jared, who trundled her off at the end of the day for an evening sail and a night on the boat. Gradually, her pallor became less pronounced. She ate a solid breakfast on Sunday, slept for another few hours, then went ashore to spend time with Megan, whose testimony was forthcoming.

Between direct and cross-examination, Megan was on the witness stand for two solid days. She was a sterling witness, poised and quiet, just nervous enough, just angry enough, just tearful enough. Not once did she waver from her story, even when Woodward went after her, and go after her he did.

"During the last six months, you had occasion to bring your car to the defendant's shop, did you not?"

"I did."

"How many times?"

"Twice."

"For what purpose?"

"There was a problem with my brakes. It was supposed to have been fixed the first time. Since it wasn't, I had to take it back."

"Was it fixed then?"

"Yes."

"So you didn't have to return a third time?"

"No."

Woodward straightened his shoulders and looked at the jurors. "That first time you brought your car in—when was that?"

She'd already said it twice, but she said it again. "In January."

"Is it not true that at that time you were acutely aware of your husband's financial problems?"

"I was aware of those problems long before then."

"And you'd tried to help, but nothing was working?"

"I was only doing the books. I didn't expect to be able to turn the business around."

"Who did you expect to do that?"

"I had faith that Will would. I still do."

"But last January, whatever he was doing wasn't working, was it?"

Telling herself to stay calm, Megan took a breath. "No."

"Last January, you were aware that something had to be done or the business would go under, isn't that true?"

"Will and I had both been aware of that for a long time."

"Please answer the question, Mrs. Vandermeer—"

"Objection," Savannah called. "The witness has already answered the question. Defense counsel is playing with words."

"A yes or no is all I want," Woodward said firmly.

"Sustained," the judge decided.

Woodward rephrased his question. "Is it not true, Mrs. Vandermeer, that at the time you brought your car to be serviced by the defendant you were aware of the precarious state of your husband's business?"

Megan didn't see how she could get around that one, so she said with as much dignity as she could, "Yes, that's true."

"Were you aware of the insurance policy your husband had taken out to cover ransom demands in a kidnapping?"

"Yes. He told me about it soon after we were married."

"Since you worked with the books, you knew that three million dollars would be a comfortable boost for the business, did you not?"

"No."

"No?" He drew his head back, as though mildly stung. "Three million dollars is a lot of money. Didn't it cross your mind that it could come in handy?"

"I'm not a businesswoman. I have no idea how much money the business needs to put it back on its feet."

"Wouldn't you have *guessed* that three million might do it?"

"I never thought about it."

"Think about it now. Doesn't three million sound tempting—"

"Objection," Savannah called. "The question is irrelevant."

"Sustained," the judge said.

Woodward went smoothly on. "Had you ever heard of Matty Stavanovich before that January day when you brought your car into his shop?"

"Yes."

"In what context?"

"He'd worked on the cars of several of my friends."

"Had you ever heard of him in any other context?"

"Yes."

"And what context was that?"

"There were articles in the paper linking him to burglaries that have been committed in different areas of the state."

Woodward gave a solemn nod. "Did you think he was a thief?"

"He was never brought to trial."

"But did you think he might be guilty?"

"If I had, I wouldn't have brought my car to him."

Turning his back on the witness stand, Woodward walked leisurely toward where Stavanovich sat at the defense table. Just shy of it, he pivoted to face her again, raising his voice to cover the added distance. "Is it not true, Mrs. Vandermeer, that, knowing the stories that had been widely circulated about the defendant, you figured he'd be a perfect patsy?"

"No," Megan said.

"After you left your car with him that first time, didn't the wheels in your mind start turning? Didn't it occur to you that Stavanovich might be just the guy you needed?"

Megan stared at him with a look of disgust on her face.

"Did it not occur to you, Mrs. Vandermeer, that your own tracks would be covered if you let a suspected crook take the fall?"

"No."

"Didn't the convenience of it strike you? You could pass money and messages back and forth simply by bringing your car in for servicing. Didn't that cross your mind?"

"No."

Woodward paused, straightened, put one hand in his trouser pocket and came slowly closer. "Refresh our memory, Mrs. Vandermeer. How long have you been married?"

"Six years."

"Six years. And how old are you now?"

"Thirty-one."

"That would have made you twenty-five when you were married?"

"That's right," Megan said. She felt a sense of foreboding in the pit of her stomach. Savannah had warned her what to expect; still, it was hard.

"Very few women nowadays reach the age of twenty-five without having taken a lover or two. Or three or four or more. Was that the case with you?"

"Objection!" Savannah called. "The question is irrelevant."

"Not so," Woodward told the judge. "I'm trying to determine something about the character of this witness."

"Her sexual history has nothing to do with this case," Savannah argued, though she was neither surprised nor worried when the judge simply told Woodward to rephrase his question.

"Was William Vandermeer your first lover?"

"No."

"Then you had had others."

"One."

Blatantly skeptical, Woodward stared at her. "Only one lover up to the age of twenty-five?"

"That's right," Megan said. She was never more grateful for Savannah's coaching than at that minute. Without it, she'd have been totally unsure of what to say. With it, she spoke in a quiet, confident voice. "We were together for three years during college. He went home to graduate school in San Francisco. I stayed east."

Woodward milled that over. "Have you been faithful to your husband?"

"Yes."

"You haven't taken any lovers since you've been married?"

"No. I love my husband."

"I'm not talking about love. I'm talking about sex. Have you ever taken a lover?"

"No."

"Have you ever wanted to take a lover?"

"No."

"Your eye hasn't ever wandered, even the slightest bit?"

"No."

He let the space of several breaths pass undisturbed, then

scratched the side of his head and said, "Frankly, I find that hard to believe. You're an attractive woman. You run in circles that allow for a certain amount of freedom—"

"Objection!"

"Sustained."

"You see free sex all around you—"

"Objection!"

"Sustained."

"—and you've never been tempted?"

"No," Megan said.

"Not by some of the brawny young men Matty employs?"

"No."

"Not even when you wanted Matty Stavanovich to do your bidding?"

"No!"

"Look at him, Mrs. Vandermeer." Woodward turned toward his client. "Do you think he's an attractive man?"

Matty was wearing a crisp white shirt, a striped tie, navy blazer, and gray slacks. As he'd been doing since the start of the trial, he was sitting straight in his chair, looking appropriately concerned.

Megan's lip curled. "No."

"Not even the tiniest bit?"

"No!"

Woodward shrugged. "I suppose you wouldn't have to find him attractive. If you wanted something from him badly enough—"

"Objection!"

"Sustained."

"No further questions, your honor."

*   *   *

Matty Stavanovich was the sole defense witness. Guided through his story by Woodward's questions, he claimed that Megan Vandermeer had approached him about the kidnapping during her second visit to the shop. She had it all planned out, he said, from the ransom note, which she made herself, to the point of entry into her home, to the day and time of both the staged abduction and the exchange of the money. Under the plan, Matty was to hold the three million until she contacted him, at which point she would bring her car in for servicing, and her share would be placed in its trunk. He claimed he'd done that, and that his share, $250,000, had been deposited in small amounts in banks in each of six states strewn around the country.

As for the rape, Matty claimed that his accomplice had been the one to use force. He had, himself, never once manhandled Megan. He admitted that he'd had intercourse with her, but swore that it had been a pleasurable experience for them both.

Savannah began her cross-examination that afternoon. Her major objective was to prove Stavanovich a liar. To that end, she produced his past criminal record and questioned him on it at length. Then she asked him about each of the burglaries that had taken place in the state since he had arrived. Though Woodward vigorously objected to each reference and the judge sustained each one, Savannah made her point.

She questioned Matty about the alibi he'd originally given the police. "It was intricately thought out. You had airline tickets, hotel and tour receipts, even photographs. Not that I'd have expected less from a man who has successfully pulled off so many burglaries—"

"Objection," Woodward called.

"Sustained."

"You're a clever man, Mr. Stavanovich. You pride yourself on the brilliance of your thefts—"

"Objection!"

Savannah walked back to the prosecutor's table to lift up a file folder. "I'm quoting from the report of the court psychiatrist who evaluated the defendant before his 1981 conviction in California. Shall I enter this into evidence?"

"Not necessary, Ms. Smith. The objection is overruled. Continue."

Savannah dropped the folder on the table and returned to Matty. "Is it fair to say, Mr. Stavanovich, that you are a careful man?"

Matty considered that for a minute. "Yes. I'd say that."

"Is it, therefore, fair to say that you would never have agreed to collaborate with Mrs. Vandermeer unless you felt that her plan was sound?"

Matty tipped up his head a fraction. "Yes."

"Yet you took elaborate steps to create an alibi. Was that to cover the burglary you staged in Cranston the night after the kidnapping?"

"Objection!"

"Sustained."

"Why," Savannah went on undaunted, "was it necessary for you to concoct such an elaborate alibi if the plan you'd worked out with Mrs. Vandermeer was so sound?"

"Because women can be flighty," Matty answered without pause. "I wanted to cover myself just in case."

"You wanted to cover yourself. Yourself. What about her? What was her alibi?"

"I don't know. That was her problem."

"You didn't check it out? A brilliant thief like you didn't

check it out? Or," she said more loudly, "were you only concerned with yourself because Mrs. Vandermeer was, in fact, nothing more than a victim? Isn't this simply one long cock-and-bull story you've come up with to save your hide?"

"No, it is not."

"You're a very clever man, Mr. Stavanovich. A master. Not many people could come up with a story like yours, particularly after the supposed mastermind of the scheme winds up brutally raped. Was that in the original plan?"

"I've already said that my accomplice was the violent one."

"Your accomplice. Where is this accomplice?"

"I don't know."

"You didn't want him to verify your story?"

"He would have done that."

"But you couldn't find him."

"That's right."

"Because he knew he was in big trouble well beyond the rape—"

"Objection."

Savannah moved on. "Strange, this accomplice business. You always work alone, Mr. Stavanovich. If, as you claim, Mrs. Vandermeer was willing, why did you need an accomplice?"

"It was simply a convenience—"

"For when Mrs. Vandermeer was tied hand and foot to the bed," Savannah finished with a look of distaste for the jury to see. "But I do agree with you. A kidnapping takes two men—"

"Objection," Woodward called. "The prosecutor's opinion has no place in the cross-examination of this witness."

The judge agreed. "Sustained," he said.

Savannah moved on. She went through every inch of his story, questioning it, throwing doubt where she could. By the time she'd finished with him on Thursday morning, she was repulsed by his smugness and offended by his arrogance. She could only hope that the jury was as turned off as she.

After Matty's appearance on the stand, the defense rested its case. Woodward delivered his closing argument shortly after lunch. It was relatively brief as closing arguments went and involved a simple recapping of the facts as Woodward saw them. His client, he concluded, had spoken in his own defense and, as sworn, was guilty neither of kidnapping nor of rape. Clearly, he claimed, the state had failed to prove its case beyond a reasonable doubt.

Savannah spoke for two hours, delivering one of the most impassioned arguments of her career. When she was done, the judge briefly charged the jury, then sent them off to deliberate.

The hours of deliberation were always difficult for the parties involved. For Savannah, this time, it was pure hell.

Chapter 22

⌒

THE JURY DELIBERATED until shortly after ten. During that time, Savannah remained in her office. Jared was with her. Her assistants wandered in and out, as did Anthony Alt, whose ascerbic comments only added to the stress. Paul called from time to time. Megan was at home with Will.

When it became clear that there would be no decision that night, Savannah and Jared left for his house. Neither of them said much during the drive, and when they arrived, they went upstairs to the living room and took possession of separate chairs.

Slipping out of her shoes, Savannah folded her legs in front of her and pressed her face to her knees. After several minutes, she looked up to find Jared's watchful eyes on her. Her own were tormented.

"Have I made a mistake?" she whispered.

Jared didn't answer at first. He was going through a torment of his own, wondering just how honest he should be. The seeds of doubt that had plagued him since the defense first aired its claims had grown until he was sure that Megan had been the one calling him for emotional support in the heart of the night. He hadn't been positive until the start of her testimony, when he'd easily recognized the voice. He added to that the fact that she could have gotten his private number when Savannah had called him from Marco Island. And the fact that she'd been skittish when, at the end of that day in court, they'd finally been introduced. And the fact that he hadn't received a call since the start of the trial.

It all fit together like a puzzle, and it gave him the uneasy feeling that Megan did have something to hide.

More than once, he'd opened his mouth to tell Savannah. But she'd been embroiled in the trying of her case, and, for what it was worth, the case was strong. Moreover, Megan staunchly proclaimed her innocence. Now that the work was done, though, and the immediate tension of performance had passed, Savannah looked as torn as he felt.

He had to know what she was thinking when she wondered whether she'd made a mistake. "In what sense, babe?" he returned softly.

"Is she innocent?"

"Do you have doubts?"

The look in her eyes said she was weighing her words on the knowledge that once spoken, they would be irretrievable. But the doubts were too strong. "There are some things about this case that have bothered me from the start. I couldn't find an explanation for them, so I ignored them, because they were really small things. All the larger things made sense." She paused, frowned, blurted out, "If I buy into the Cat's defense, those small things fall right into place."

"What things do you mean?"

"The alarm system, for starters. It was broken. Stavanovich is an expert at disengaging alarms, yet he made no attempt to do it at Megan's. The alarm system hadn't been touched. Like he already knew it was broken. But there was no way he could have known that for sure—unless Megan told him."

She hugged her legs tighter. "Then there's the way it was done so cleanly. Sammy and Hank went through that library with a fine-tooth comb and couldn't find a thing. That doesn't usually happen. Usually there's a hair or a thread, *something* to link the perpetrator to the crime, especially if the victim puts up a fight. Megan did that, but was it a staged one? The Mercedes they used tested clean in the lab, too. There should have been microscopic pieces of the laundry bag she was supposedly stuffed in. But there weren't."

"And the business of the ransom note," she said with a new breath. "Megan could have made it. In a minute. She had all the materials right there at her fingertips, including supermarket bags. She had *plenty* of those. The house was loaded with food. I mean, when I went there after the kidnapping, I found three bags of coffee beans. Three bags of coffee beans. Don't ask me why she needed three bags of beans, or why she had so much other food in the refrigerator. Unless she was planning to be gone for a while.

"Same thing with neatness. Megan was always a slob. The office upstairs where she'd been working on the books had papers strewn around, typically Megan. Not the rest of the house. It was neat as a pin. Again, like she was planning to be away. She knew that Will liked things neat; she always felt guilty that she wasn't a better housekeeper. Maybe she cleaned things up to make up to him for what she was doing."

"Do you think she did it on her own?" Jared asked.

"I don't want to think she did it at all!" Savannah cried, then lowered her voice. "But I doubt Will could have been involved. I saw him through a good part of the time Megan was gone. He couldn't possibly have faked that anguish. Of course," she said facetiously, "if I was wrong about Megan, I could be wrong about him."

Her eyes grew beseechful. "Do you think I was wrong, Jared? Do you think I got so wrapped up in punishing the man who raped Megan that I overlooked things I should have seen?"

Lately Jared had spent a lot of time contemplating questions like that. "I think you acted on the facts as you saw them."

"But were they wrong?"

He came forward in his seat and let his hands fall limply between his knees. "She was raped. Do you have any doubt about that?"

"None at all," Savannah said. "Even if she did plan the kidnapping, she didn't plan the rape, and I don't give a flying shit about what Stavanovich says, she wouldn't willingly let him touch her." She dropped her voice and muttered, "Kinky sex, hah. The only way Megan would let that piece of scum near her would be if he tied her hand and foot, which we know he did. She would never, *never* be unfaithful to Will. She loves him too much."

Her voice trailed off. After a minute's silence, she said quietly, "That would have been the reason for doing it. She loved him. She wanted him to have enough money to get the business back on its feet. She wouldn't have stolen the money for herself, but she might have stolen it for Will. If she stole it at all." Releasing her legs, she sat back in the chair with a tired sigh. "There's still no sign of the money. We've found the two hundred and fifty thousand that Matty told us about, but the rest? Nothing. We've checked every possible outlet, and we can't find a cent. Now, does that make sense, if the woman staged her own kidnapping for the sake of recovering money to pour into her husband's business?"

It didn't make sense to Jared, but then, he feared some would think his judgment as warped as Savannah's. After all, he wasn't going to tell her about the phone calls. He wouldn't add to her doubt. It wouldn't serve any practical purpose. Megan Vandermeer had been cruelly raped. On that fact alone, Matty Stavanovich deserved to be convicted.

He was. Late Friday afternoon, the jury returned with verdicts of guilty for both kidnapping and rape. Sentencing was set for two weeks later.

At Anthony Alt's urging, Paul faced the press with Savannah. Given the doubts she'd had, and those she continued to have, she relished the support. Somehow she could tell herself that if Paul DeBarr, the next governor of Rhode Island, was sticking up for her, she'd done something right.

Matty Stavanovich was sentenced to twenty years for each offense, to be served concurrently. While there was some talk around town that Savannah should have fought for an even tougher sentence, she ignored it. She was comfortable with the knowledge that Matty would serve the same amount of time he would have if he'd been convicted of rape alone.

*   *   *

Within two weeks of the sentencing, Megan called Savannah to say that Will had sold the business, that they were putting the house on the market and leaving Providence.

It was the first time they had talked since the sentencing. Savannah was having trouble reconciling the fact that, very probably, Megan had used her. The closeness they had once shared seemed tainted by truths unspoken and trust betrayed. It was the sad ending of a dear friendship, and Savannah, who was feeling more susceptible to her emotions than usual, wasn't sure how to say goodbye.

That was why, on the Sunday after Megan's call, when Sam, Susan, and Courtney were spending the afternoon with Savannah and Jared on the boat, Savannah suggested that Susan and she take a few minutes out for a quick visit with Megan. Since the men weren't about to be left behind, and Courtney certainly couldn't be left alone, the five of them piled into the Pathfinder.

The house that had been in the Vandermeer family for years looked old and tired, since Will no longer made even token attempts at upkeep. Left without hope of a facelift, it seemed to sag more than ever.

Inside, the rooms were strewn with packed cartons. What furniture hadn't been sold was covered with padding. The walls were a checkerboard of squares where pictures that had hung for years hung no more.

Will was on the phone. Diplomatically, Jared and Sam took Courtney out to explore the backyard, leaving Savannah and Susan inside, on the carpeted steps with Megan.

Wearing jeans and shirts, the three of them looked as they might have looked, sitting together, chatting, ten years before. Their faces were more mature and somber, though, and the chatter was more a quiet, sad talk.

"Where will you go?" Savannah asked.

Megan gave an awkward shrug. "We'll be leaving for Saint Croix tomorrow. The Websters have loaned us their villa for as long as we want it. Will has been in touch with some people about buying into a textile business in North Carolina. If it pans out, we'll be moving to Winston-Salem."

"Winston-Salem, North Carolina," Susan drawled. "Sounds good enough."

Megan looked down at her hands, which were sandwiched between her thighs. "I can't stay here. Rhode Island is too small. I'd never escape—" she lifted a shoulder, "—everything." Her shoulder returned to normal, but she didn't take her eyes from her hands. "Between the sale of the house and the business, we'll have a nice kitty. We can start over somewhere where they won't look at us and stare."

Savannah couldn't help but think that if what she suspected were true, an odd kind of justice had been served. Megan was being punished. She'd suffered through the rape, through the ordeal of the trial, through endless days and nights of private agony. She and Will had a long road ahead of them, particularly given Will's track record as an entrepreneur. If he'd failed once, he could fail again. Savannah prayed he would either go into something with partners who knew what they were doing, or hire a business manager.

"Will you be working?" she asked.

Megan nodded. "With Will. We're in this together." She paused. "I love him. I don't care where we live or what we do." A flicker of pain crossed her features. "Unfortunately, he cares. He has more pride than I do. Selling the business has been one of the hardest things he's had to do." She manufactured a small smile. "But he's trying. He's looking forward to doing something different, and if he can find something that makes him happy, I will be, too. That's all I've ever wanted," she said in an even softer voice, but there was an intensity to the look she gave Savannah. "All I've ever wanted is to be a helpmate to Will."

The words, the look, and the tone spoke simultaneously of justification and apology. Then Megan forced a small laugh. "Pretty old-fashioned, huh? I must be a gross disappointment to you two."

"Disappointment?" Susan asked. "Because you care about pleasing the man you love?"

"Because that's about *all* I care about. You both have other interests. You always have. You've always lived the kind of lives I wanted to live, only I never made it. I've been obsessed with the basics. When I was a kid, it was survival. As an adult, it still is, only survival now means salvaging my marriage. It's taken a battering. There's been so much pressure. . . ." Her words trailed off in a moment of pain.

"None of us escapes those basics," Savannah mused, realizing it as she spoke. "It may seem like we do. It may seem like our lives are fuller or more exciting than yours, but the bottom line is always the same."

"Men," Susan said.

Savannah shot her a look. "I'm serious."

"So am I. We thought we were hot shots, didn't we? We thought we were the cat's meow, modern women taking the world by storm. You were the lawyer. I was the femme fatale." She forced a dry smile. "It's pretty empty, isn't it?"

"Oh yes," Savannah said.

"But you have Jared," Megan told her, then turned to Susan, "and you have Sam."

"For now. Having Courtney has thrown in a new twist."

"But you adore her."

"So does Sam. She's finally warmed up to him, which means that my role as buffer is over. Now there are dozens of decisions to be made concerning her future. Some we agree on, some we don't. But that's not the twist. The twist is that Sam has to want me independently of Courtney."

"He does," Savannah said. She'd had enough frank discussions with Sam to know it was true. She also knew that though her sister still drank on occasion, she hadn't been drunk in months, which wasn't to say the problem was solved, simply that it was temporarily eased. Knowing that Sam cared, and how much he cared, was a comfort to Savannah. "Sam loves you."

"He says it."

"It's true."

"There are times when I wonder. But I'm trying to make a go of this. I'm working real hard at it. It's not easy."

"No relationship is," Savannah said. "But do you want it to work?"

"Yes," Susan answered, then went on with conviction, "Sam Craig may never earn a million, but he makes me feel like a somebody. I don't remember any man ever making me feel that way before. Yes, I want him." She paused. "Like you want Jared?"

Without answering the question, Savannah said, "I wish I could give him more."

"He doesn't want more. Hasn't he told you that?"

"Many times. Still, I wish I could give him more."

"Has he mentioned marriage?" Megan asked.

"Oh yes."

Susan scowled. "And you're putting him off because you don't think you can give him enough? Savannah, are you nuts? The man loves what you *are*, not what you're not. He isn't asking for superwoman; she wasn't the one he fell in love with. And if you're going to say that you wished you looked like me, save your breath. First thing in the morning, I look just as lousy as either of you."

Savannah grunted, but softly, and didn't speak.

"Sad, isn't it?" Megan said at last.

"What?"

"That we judge ourselves in relation to each other. Why do we do that? We always have, and it's a little sick when you think about it. You two may be twins, but you're still individuals, and I don't even have the same blood as you. So why can't we accept ourselves for what we are?"

"I don't know," Savannah said. She sensed that some of the competitiveness between Susan and her could be traced to their father's constant comparisons, but not all. They were adults. They should have wised up.

Susan frowned. She'd just realized that what she'd told Savannah moments earlier about looks could easily be turned around to apply to brains. She supposed that just because Savannah had decided to become a lawyer didn't mean that she was any smarter, particularly since she was being so dumb about Jared. The question remained as to whether Susan was being any smarter about Sam.

"I'll miss you two," Megan murmured. There was something furtive about the way she said it, almost as though she didn't think she had the right to claim a shared past.

Savannah thought about that past. They'd been friends for half their lives, and the friendship had been good. Regardless of present truths or untruths, that friendship deserved more than a cursory dismissal. "We'll keep in touch."

But the look on Megan's face said that might not happen.

"We will," Susan vowed. "We'll compare our gray hairs, our liver spots, our sagging bottoms."

Megan's eyes were moist, but she rolled them anyway and grinned feebly at Savannah. "She's all yours."

"I'm not sure I want her."

"I do," Sam said, coming up from behind. He seized Susan in a playful stranglehold that clamped her head to his side. "We're hungry. I thought we were going out for something to eat."

Susan made a grotesque choking sound. The instant his arm loosened, she called him a name.

"Come join us," Savannah said to Megan. "Just for a little while?"

But Megan shook her head.

"For old times' sake?" Susan asked.

Megan gave a visible swallow. "I'd better not," she said brokenly. "This is hard enough——" Her throat jammed.

Throwing an arm around her, Savannah hugged her hard. "Take care, Meggie," she whispered, then stepped back to give Susan a turn.

"Be happy," Susan whispered, as choked up as Megan. Turning away, she let Sam take her hand and lead her to the door, where Courtney waited.

Jared approached then, and Megan eyed him nervously. Coming up close, he took her hand and said so that only she could hear, "Sometimes we do all the wrong things for all the right reasons. We can be our own worst enemies. It takes a while to get over that."

"I know," she whispered.

"Try, Megan. You've been given another chance. Make it work. I know you can." He took her in his arms and held her for a minute. "We'll be rooting for you." Then he set her back, kissed her lightly on the forehead, and joined Savannah.

Savannah spent hours thinking about her and Susan's last visit with Megan, about what the three of them had said. So much of it made sense. She didn't understand why she hadn't seen it before.

She tried to imagine what her life would have been like if she'd never had Susan or Megan as points of reference. Certainly less rich. Flatter. More one-dimensional. Susan was her sister, Megan her friend. She'd taken their best points and tried to match them, making her a more complex person than she might have otherwise been. Through contrast and comparison, they'd pushed her toward realizing her potential.

At least, that was the optimist's view. But it was the one Savannah clung to, and largely because of it, she agreed to stop at Megan and Will's after work on Tuesday to pick up the keys for the realtor. The movers had left. Megan and Will were racing to catch their plane to Saint Croix. The keys were tucked in the tray of the planter outside the front door.

Savannah found them without any problem. Instead of pocketing them and heading home, though, she turned toward the house, looked at the door for a minute, then slowly unlocked it and let herself in.

The front foyer was warm, fallen prey to the August heat that had poured over the toiling movers. While the large hall inside was cooler, it was a chamber of echoes for her slightest step.

For a long time, Savannah stood motionless in the hall,

feeling the emptiness of the place, listening to its silence. Then, almost idly, she wandered into the living room. She thought of the generations of Vandermeers who had lived within its walls—Will's grandparents and parents, Will, and Megan, who was never quite a Vandermeer, yet perhaps more dedicated to the Vandermeers than any of the others.

That was why she'd done it. If she'd done it. *Had* she done it? The living room floor creaked as Savannah crossed it, drawn irresistibly toward the library. It was as empty as the rest of the house. Shadows fell over the shelves where books had once been, cast there by the evening sun that slanted in through the French doors. She had expected to have an eerie feeling about the room. Instead, she felt nostalgia.

The library, more so than any other room in the house, was a nerve center. Business had been transacted there, family matters discussed, social affairs planned. With the dismantling of this room, an era had passed.

An era had passed. It was time to move on.

Will and Megan had sold the business and were selling the house. An era had passed. They were moving on.

Susan had turned her back on the idle rich in favor of being a policeman's wife and mother to a five-year-old daughter. An era had passed. She'd moved on.

And an era had passed for Savannah, too, she realized. The long nights of being alone, of working herself to the bone to mask the void that gnawed at her from within, were behind her. Ahead was a richer life.

A new lightness settled over her as she stood in the empty library. She thought of Jared, then of the baby she carried, and a private smile softened her lips. She wanted them, both of them, more than she had believed possible.

Maybe that was what being thirty-one was all about. Maybe it was about putting things in perspective, setting priorities, closing a chapter in one's life, and opening a new one. She was ready. It was time.

And with that realization came one more. Looking at the French door that had been shattered one Monday night in March, she realized that she didn't want to know whether Megan Vandermeer had planned her own kidnapping. Knowing wouldn't change a thing. Megan wouldn't be brought to trial; without the money, there was no case, and Megan clearly didn't have the money. So maybe the Cat had double-crossed her, and if that was so, it was poetic justice. Besides, Megan had her own conscience to live with, which was a sentence far greater than one any judge might mete out.

As for Savannah's conscience, the only thing weighing on it was that she hadn't shared her new insights with Jared. Turning on her heel, she set off to remedy that situation.

"It's twelve-oh-four," came the deep, sandy voice that Rhode Island knew and loved, *"that's four minutes after twelve on a breezy September Monday. You're tuned to 95.3 FM, WCIC Providence, where the country sounds are always cool. I hope your Labor Day weekend was as sweet as mine. This morning's* Journal *was right; I got married. But that doesn't mean I won't be here as always, bringing you a little country in the city from twelve to six. I've got a super string of stars to kick off the month, including the likes of Ronnie Milsap, Reba McEntire, and Kenny Rogers. Right now I'm wantin' to hear Randy Travis say, 'Forever and*

Ever, Amen.'" His voice grew deeper. *"This is Jared Snow in the heart of the night, and that's a vow. . . ."*

"That was Sawyer Brown, and this is Jared Snow comin' to you through the driving snow on a stormy February Wednesday." The voice was deep and familiar, but it had a special lilt that couldn't quite be denied. *"It's twenty-seven degrees out there, but you don't want to stray from the fire unless you've got good cause. I did. My son was born four hours ago. He and his mom are tucked safe and warm at the hospital, listenin' in, like you. So don't touch that dial. It's set for cool country, 95.3 FM, WCIC Providence. On a special night, I'll be bringin' you special songs, kickin' off with the Gatlin Brothers and 'Love of a Lifetime.'"* He paused for a split second, and when he went on, his voice was more hoarse. *"Jared Snow, here, in the heart of the night, believe it. . . ."*

"You've been tuned to 95.3 FM, WCIC Providence, and Jared Snow. It's a promising Saturday in May, five fifty-six in the A.M. At the stroke of six, I'll be on my way, but I'm leavin' you in good hands. Noel Lappan is kickin' on right after the news, and starting Monday night, Christopher Nix will be easin' you through the heart of the night. I'll miss you all. I've had a good three years here at CIC, but my baby's gettin' bigger and my wife's indulged me far too long. I don't mean to say we'll always be sleepin' through the heart of the night. Sometimes we'll be listening like you, sometimes we'll be remembering how we met, sometimes we'll be lovin' the night away, and if that ain't inducement enough to start

working days," he drawled, *"I don't know what is."* He paused, then said more quietly, seriously, emotionally, *"So I'm goin' home, and all the way I'll have 'Georgia on My Mind.' This is Jared Snow with the rising sun, God-speed. . . ."*

VISIT US ONLINE AT

WWW.HACHETTEBOOKGROUP.COM

FEATURES:

**OPENBOOK BROWSE AND
SEARCH EXCERPTS**

•

AUDIOBOOK EXCERPTS AND PODCASTS

•

AUTHOR ARTICLES AND INTERVIEWS

•

**BESTSELLER AND PUBLISHING
GROUP NEWS**

•

SIGN UP FOR E-NEWSLETTERS

•

**AUTHOR APPEARANCES AND TOUR
INFORMATION**

•

SOCIAL MEDIA FEEDS AND WIDGETS

•

DOWNLOAD FREE APPS

Bookmark Hachette Book Group
@ www.HachetteBookGroup.com